DEATH IN VENICE
AND SEVEN OTHER STORIES

TRIANGLE CLASSICS

ILLUMINATING THE GAY AND LESBIAN EXPERIENCE

A Boy's Own Story
The Beautiful Room Is Empty
by Edmund White

Death in Venice and Seven Other Stories
by Thomas Mann

Giovanni's Room
by James Baldwin

Rubyfruit Jungle
by Rita Mae Brown

Zami/Sister Outsider/Undersong
by Audre Lorde

DEATH IN VENICE

AND SEVEN OTHER STORIES

THOMAS MANN

TRANSLATED FROM THE GERMAN
BY H. T. LOWE-PORTER

BOOK-OF-THE-MONTH CLUB
NEW YORK

These translations of "Death in Venice," "Tristan," and "Tonio Kröger" were originally published in the collection *Death in Venice* in 1930. "Mario and the Magician" was originally published by Alfred A. Knopf, Inc., in 1931. All the other translations were originally published in *Stories of Three Decades*, published by Alfred A. Knopf, Inc., in 1936. The eight stories here were originally published as a collection by Vintage Books, Inc., in 1954. This edition was specially created for Book-of-the-Month Club in 1993.

Printed in the United States of America

CONTENTS

DEATH IN VENICE
AND SEVEN OTHER STORIES

DEATH IN VENICE

Gustave Aschenbach—or von Aschenbach, as he had been known officially since his fiftieth birthday—had set out alone from his house in Prince Regent Street, Munich, for an extended walk. It was a spring afternoon in that year of grace 19—, when Europe sat upon the anxious seat beneath a menace that hung over its head for months. Aschenbach had sought the open soon after tea. He was overwrought by a morning of hard, nerve-taxing work, work which had not ceased to exact his uttermost in the way of sustained concentration, conscientiousness, and tact; and after the noon meal found himself powerless to check the onward sweep of the productive mechanism within him, that *motus animi continuus* in which, according to Cicero, eloquence resides. He had sought but not found relaxation in sleep—though the wear and tear upon his system had come to make a daily nap more and more imperative—and now undertook a walk, in the hope that air and exercise might send him back refreshed to a good evening's work.

May had begun, and after weeks of cold and wet a mock summer had set in. The English Gardens, though in tenderest leaf, felt as sultry as in August and were full of vehicles and pedestrians near the city. But towards Aumeister the paths were solitary and still, and Aschenbach strolled thither, stopping awhile to watch the lively crowds in the restaurant garden with its fringe of carriages and cabs. Thence he took his homeward way outside the park and across the sunset fields. By the time he reached the North Cemetery, however, he felt tired, and a storm was brewing above Föhring; so he waited at the stopping-place for a tram to carry him back to the city.

He found the neighbourhood quite empty. Not a wagon in sight, either on the paved Ungererstrasse, with its gleaming tramlines stretching off towards Schwabing, nor on the Föhring Highway. Nothing stirred behind the hedge in the stone-mason's yard, where crosses, monuments, and commemorative tablets made a supernumerary and untenanted graveyard opposite the real one. The mortuary chapel, a structure in Byzantine style, stood facing it, silent in the gleam of the ebbing day. Its façade was adorned with Greek crosses and tinted hieratic designs, and displayed a symmetrically arranged selection of scriptural texts in gilded letters, all of them with a bearing upon the future life, such as: "They are entering into the House of the Lord" and "May the Light Everlasting shine upon them." Aschenbach beguiled some minutes of his waiting with reading these formulas and letting his mind's eye lose itself in their mystical meaning. He was brought back to reality by the sight of a man standing in the portico, above the two apocalyptic beasts that guarded the staircase, and something not quite usual in this man's appearance gave his thoughts a fresh turn.

Whether he had come out of the hall through the bronze doors or mounted unnoticed from outside, it was impossible to tell. Aschenbach casually inclined to the first idea. He was of medium height, thin, beardless, and strikingly snub-nosed; he belonged to the red-haired type and possessed its milky, freckled skin. He was obviously not Bavarian; and the broad, straight-brimmed straw hat he had on even made him look distinctly exotic. True, he had the indigenous rucksack buckled on his back, wore a belted suit of yellowish woollen stuff, apparently frieze, and carried a grey mackintosh cape across his left forearm, which was propped against his waist. In his right hand, slantwise to the ground, he held an iron-shod stick, and braced himself against its crook, with his legs crossed. His chin was up, so that the Adam's apple looked very bald in the lean neck rising from the loose shirt; and he stood there sharply peering up into space out of colourless, red-lashed eyes, while two pronounced perpendicular furrows showed on his forehead in curious contrast to his little turned-up nose. Perhaps his heightened and heightening position helped out the impression Aschenbach received. At any rate, standing there as though at survey, the man had a bold and domineering, even a ruthless air, and his lips completed the picture by seeming to curl back, either by reason of some deformity or else because he grimaced, being blinded by the sun in his face; they laid bare the long, white, glistening teeth to the gums.

Aschenbach's gaze, though unawares, had very likely been inquisitive and tactless; for he became suddenly conscious that the stranger was returning it, and indeed so directly, with such hostility, such plain intent to force the withdrawal of the other's eyes, that Aschenbach felt an unpleasant twinge and, turning his back, began to walk along the hedge, hastily resolving to give the man no further heed. He had forgotten him the next minute. Yet whether the pilgrim air the stranger wore kindled his fantasy or whether some other physical or psychical influence came in play, he could not tell; but he felt the most surprising consciousness of a widening of inward barriers, a kind of vaulting unrest, a youthfully ardent thirst for distant scenes—a feeling so lively and so new, or at least so long ago outgrown and forgot, that he stood there rooted to the spot, his eyes on the ground and his hands clasped behind him, exploring these sentiments of his, their bearing and scope.

True, what he felt was no more than a longing to travel; yet coming upon him with such suddenness and passion as to resemble a seizure, almost a hallucination. Desire projected itself visually: his fancy, not quite yet lulled since morning, imaged the marvels and terrors of the manifold earth. He saw. He beheld a landscape, a tropical marshland, beneath a reeking sky, steaming, monstrous, rank—a kind of primeval wilderness-world of islands, morasses, and alluvial channels. Hairy palm-trunks rose near and far out of lush brakes of fern, out of bottoms of crass vegetation, fat, swollen, thick with incredible bloom. There were trees, mis-shapen as a dream, that dropped their naked roots straight through the air into the ground or into water that was stagnant and shadowy and glassy-green, where mammoth milk-white blossoms floated, and strange high-shouldered birds with curious bills stood gazing sidewise without sound or stir. Among the knotted joints of a bamboo thicket the eyes of a crouching tiger gleamed—and he felt his heart throb with terror, yet with a longing inexplicable. Then the vision vanished. Aschenbach, shaking his head, took up his march once more along the hedge of the stone-mason's yard.

He had, at least ever since he commanded means to get about the world at will, regarded travel as a necessary evil, to be endured now and again willy-nilly for the sake of one's health. Too busy with the tasks imposed upon him by his own ego and the European soul, too laden with the care and duty to create, too preoccupied to be an amateur of the gay outer world, he had been content to know as much of the earth's surface as he could without stirring far outside his own sphere—had, indeed, never even been tempted to leave Europe. Now more than ever, since his life was on the wane, since he could no longer brush aside as fanciful his artist fear of not having done, of not being finished before the works ran down, he had confined himself to close range, had hardly stepped outside the charming city which he had made his home and the rude country house he had built in the mountains, whither he went to spend the rainy summers.

And so the new impulse which thus late and suddenly swept over him was speedily made to conform to the pattern of self-discipline he had followed from his youth up. He had meant to bring his work, for which he lived, to a certain point before leaving for the country, and the thought of a leisurely ramble across the globe, which should take him away from his desk for months, was too fantastic and upsetting to be seriously entertained. Yet the source of the unexpected contagion was known to him only too well. This yearning for new and distant scenes, this craving for freedom, release, forgetfulness—they were, he admitted to himself, an impulse towards flight, flight from the spot which was the daily theatre of a rigid, cold, and passionate service. That service he loved, had even almost come to love the enervating daily struggle between a proud, tenacious, well-tried will and this growing fatigue, which no one must suspect, nor the finished product betray by any faintest sign that his inspiration could ever flag or miss fire. On the other hand, it seemed the part of common sense not to span the bow too far, not to suppress summarily a need that so unequivocally asserted itself. He thought of his work, and the place where yesterday and again today he had been forced to lay it down, since it would not yield either to patient effort, or a swift *coup de main.* Again and again he had tried to break or untie the knot—only to retire at last from the attack with a shiver of repugnance. Yet the difficulty was actually not a great one; what sapped his strength was distaste for the task, betrayed by a fastidiousness he could no longer satisfy. In his youth, indeed, the nature and inmost essence of the literary gift had been, to him, this very scrupulosity; for it he had bridled and tempered his sensibilities, knowing full well that feeling is prone to be content with easy gains and blithe half-perfection. So now, perhaps, feeling, thus tyrannized, avenged itself by leaving him, refusing from now on to carry and wing his art and taking away with it all the ecstasy he had known in form and expression. Not that he was doing bad work. So much, at least, the years had brought him, that at any moment he might feel tranquilly assured of mastery. But he got no joy of it—not though a nation paid it homage. To him it seemed his work had ceased to be marked by that fiery play of fancy which is the product of joy, and more, and more potently, than any intrinsic content, forms in turn the joy of the receiving world. He dreaded the summer in the country, alone with the maid who prepared his food and the man who served him; dreaded to see the familiar mountain peaks and walls that would shut him up again with his heavy discontent. What he needed was a break, an interim existence, a means of passing time, other air and a new stock of blood, to make the summer tolerable and productive. Good, then, he would go a journey. Not far—not all the way to the tigers. A night in a *wagon-lit,* three or four weeks of lotus-eating at some one of the gay world's playgrounds in the lovely south. . . .

So ran his thoughts, while the clang of the electric tram drew nearer down the Ungererstrasse; and as he mounted the platform he decided to devote the evening to a study of maps and railway guides. Once in, he bethought him to look back after the man in the straw hat, the companion of this brief interval which had after all been so fruitful. But he was not in his former place, nor in the tram itself, nor yet at the next stop; in short, his whereabouts remained a mystery.

Gustave Aschenbach was born at L—, a country town in the province of Silesia. He was the son of an upper official in the judicature, and his forbears had all been officers, judges, departmental functionaries—men who lived their strict, decent, sparing lives in the service of king and state. Only once before had a livelier mentality—in the quality of a clergyman—turned up among them; but swifter, more perceptive blood had in the generation before the poet's flowed into the stock from the mother's side, she being the daughter of a Bohemian musical conductor. It was from her he had the foreign traits that betrayed themselves in his appearance. The union of dry, conscientious officialdom and ardent, obscure impulse, produced an artist—and this particular artist: author of the lucid and vigorous prose epic on the life of Frederick the Great; careful, tireless weaver of the richly patterned tapestry entitled *Maia,* a novel that gathers up the threads of many human destinies in the warp of a single idea; creator of that powerful narrative *The Abject,* which taught a whole grateful generation that a man can still be capable of moral resolution even after he has plumbed the depths of knowledge; and lastly—to complete the tale of works of his mature period—the writer of that impassioned discourse on the theme of Mind and Art whose ordered force and antithetic eloquence led serious critics to rank it with Schiller's *Simple and Sentimental Poetry.*

Aschenbach's whole soul, from the very beginning, was bent on fame—and thus, while not precisely precocious, yet thanks to the unmistakable trenchancy of his personal accent he was early ripe and ready for a career. Almost before he was out of high school he had a name. Ten years later he had learned to sit at his desk and sustain and live up to his growing reputation, to write gracious and pregnant phrases in letters that must needs be brief, for many claims press upon the solid and successful man. At forty, worn down by the strains and stresses of his actual task, he had to deal with a daily post heavy with tributes from his own and foreign countries.

Remote on one hand from the banal, on the other from the eccentric, his genius was calculated to win at once the adhesion of the general public and the admiration, both sympathetic and stimulating, of the connoisseur. From childhood up he was pushed on every side to achievement, and achievement of no ordinary kind; and so his young days never knew the sweet idleness and blithe *laissez aller* that belong to youth. A nice observer once said of him in company—it was at this time when he fell ill in Vienna in his thirty-fifth year: "You see, Aschenbach has always lived like this"—here the speaker closed the fingers of his left hand to a fist—"never like this"—and he let his open hand hang relaxed from the back of his chair. It was apt. And this attitude was the more morally valiant in that Aschenbach was not by nature robust—he was only called to the constant tension of his career, not actually born to it.

By medical advice he had been kept from school and educated at home. He had grown up solitary, without comradeship; yet had early been driven to see that he belonged to those whose talent is not so much out of the common as is the physical basis on which talent relies for its fulfilment. It is a seed that gives early of its fruit, whose powers seldom reach a ripe old age. But his favourite motto was "Hold fast"; indeed, in his novel on the life of Frederick the Great he envisaged nothing else than the apotheosis of the old hero's word of command, *"Durchhalten,"* which seemed to him the epitome of fortitude under suffering. Besides, he deeply desired to live to a good old age, for it was his conviction that only the artist to whom it has been granted to be fruitful on all stages of our human scene can be truly great, or universal, or worthy of honour.

Bearing the burden of his genius, then, upon such slender

shoulders and resolved to go so far, he had the more need of discipline—and discipline, fortunately, was his native inheritance from the father's side. At forty, at fifty, he was still living as he had commenced to live in the years when others are prone to waste and revel, dream high thoughts and postpone fulfilment. He began his day with a cold shower over chest and back; then, setting a pair of tall wax candles in silver holders at the head of his manuscript, he sacrificed to art, in two or three hours of almost religious fervour, the powers he had assembled in sleep. Outsiders might be pardoned for believing that his *Maia* world and the epic amplitude revealed by the life of Frederick were a manifestation of great power working under high pressure, that they came forth, as it were, all in one breath. It was the more triumph for his morale; for the truth was that they were heaped up to greatness in layer after layer, in long days of work, out of hundreds and hundreds of single inspirations; they owed their excellence, both of mass and detail, to one thing and one alone; that their creator could hold out for years under the strain of the same piece of work, with an endurance and a tenacity of purpose like that which had conquered his native province of Silesia, devoting to actual composition none but his best and freshest hours.

For an intellectual product of any value to exert an immediate influence which shall also be deep and lasting, it must rest on an inner harmony, yes, an affinity, between the personal destiny of its author and that of his contemporaries in general. Men do not know why they award fame to one work of art rather than another. Without being in the faintest connoisseurs, they think to justify the warmth of their commendations by discovering it in a hundred virtues, whereas the real ground of their applause is inexplicable—it is sympathy. Aschenbach had once given direct expression—though in an unobtrusive place—to the idea that almost everything conspicuously great is great in despite: has come into being in defiance of affliction and pain; poverty, destitution, bodily weakness, vice, passion, and a thousand other obstructions. And that was more than observation—it was the fruit of experience, it was precisely the formula of his life and fame, it was the key to his work. What wonder, then, if it was also the fixed character, the outward gesture, of his most individual figures?

The new type of hero favoured by Aschenbach, and recurring many times in his works, had early been analysed by a shrewd critic: "The conception of an intellectual and virginal manliness, which clenches its teeth and stands in modest defiance of the swords and spears that pierce its side." That was beautiful, it was *spirituel,* it was exact, despite the suggestion of too great passivity it held. Forbearance in the fact of fate, beauty constant under torture, are not merely passive. They are a positive achievement, an explicit triumph; and the figure of Sebastian is the most beautiful symbol, if not of art as a whole, yet certainly of the art we speak of here. Within that world of Aschenbach's creation were exhibited many phases of this theme: there was the aristocratic self-command that is eaten out within and for as long as it can conceals its biologic decline from the eyes of the world; the sere and ugly outside, hiding the embers of smouldering fire—and having power to fan them to so pure a flame as to challenge supremacy in the domain of beauty itself; the pallid languors of the flesh, contrasted with the fiery ardours of the spirit within, which can fling a whole proud people down at the foot of the Cross, at the feet of its own sheer self-abnegation; the gracious bearing preserved in the stern, stark service of form; the unreal, precarious existence of the born intrigant with its swiftly enervating alternation of schemes and desires—all these human fates and many more of their like one read in Aschenbach's pages, and reading them might doubt the existence of any other kind of heroism than the heroism born of weakness. And, after all, what kind could be truer to the spirit of the times? Gustave Aschenbach was the poet-spokesman of all those who labour at the edge of exhaustion; of the overburdened, of those who are already worn out but still hold themselves upright; of all our modern moralizers of accomplishment, with stunted growth and scanty resources, who yet contrive by skilful husbanding and prodigious spasms of will to produce, at least for a while, the effect of greatness. There are many such, they are the heroes of the age. And in Aschenbach's pages they saw themselves; he justified, he exalted them, he sang their praise—and they, they were grateful, they heralded his fame.

He had been young and crude with the times and by them badly counselled. He had taken false steps, blundered, exposed himself, offended in speech and writing against fact and good sense. But he had attained to honour, and honour, he used to say, is the natural goal towards which every considerable talent presses with whip and spur. Yes, one might put it that his whole career had been one conscious and overweening ascent to honour, which left in the rear all the misgivings or self-derogation which might have hampered him.

What pleases the public is lively and vivid delineation which makes no demands on the intellect; but passionate and absolutist youth can only be enthralled by a problem. And Aschenbach was as absolute, as problematist, as any youth of them all. He had done homage to intellect, had overworked the soil of knowledge and ground up her seed-corn; had turned his back on the "mysteries," called genius itself in question, held up art to scorn—yes, even while his faithful following revelled in the characters he created, he, the young artist, was taking away the breath of the twenty-year-olds with his cynic utterances on the nature of art and the artist life.

But it seems that a noble and active mind blunts itself against nothing so quickly as the sharp and bitter irritant of knowledge. And certain it is that the youth's constancy of purpose, no matter how painfully conscientious, was shallow beside the mature resolution of the master of his craft, who made a right-about-face, turned his back on the realm of knowledge, and passed it by with averted face, lest it lame his will or power of action, paralyse his feelings or his passions, deprive any of these of their conviction or utility. How else interpret the oft-cited story of *The Abject* than as a rebuke to the excess of a psychology-ridden age, embodied in the delineation of the weak and silly fool who manages to lead fate by the nose; driving his wife, out of sheer innate pusillanimity, into the arms of a beardless youth, and making this disaster an excuse for trifling away the rest of his life?

With rage the author here rejects the rejected, casts out the outcast—and the measure of his fury is the measure of his condemnation of all moral shilly-shallying. Explicitly he renounces sympathy with the abyss, explicitly he refutes the flabby humanitarianism of the phrase: "*Tout comprendre c'est tout pardonner.*" What was here unfolding, or rather was already in full bloom, was the "miracle of regained detachment," which a little later became the theme of one of the author's dialogues, dwelt upon not without a certain oracular emphasis. Strange sequence of thought! Was it perhaps an intellectual consequence of this rebirth, this new austerity, that from now on his style showed an almost exaggerated sense of beauty, a lofty purity, symmetry, and simplicity, which gave his productions a stamp of the classic, of conscious and deliberate mastery? And yet: this moral fibre, surviving the hampering and disintegrating effect of knowledge, does it not result in its turn in a dangerous simplification, in a tendency to equate the world and the human soul, and thus to strengthen the hold of the evil, the forbidden, and the ethically impossible? And has not form two aspects? Is it not moral and immoral at once: moral in so far as it is the expression and result of discipline, immoral—yes, actually hostile to morality—in that of its very essence it is indifferent to good and evil, and deliberately concerned to make the moral world stoop beneath its proud and undivided sceptre?

Be that as it may. Development is destiny; and why should a career attended by the applause and adulation of the masses necessarily take the same course as one which does not share the glamour and the obligations of fame? Only the incorrigible bohemian smiles or scoffs when a man of transcendent gifts outgrows his carefree prentice stage, recognizes his own worth and forces the world to recognize it too and pay it homage, though he puts on a courtly bearing to hide his bitter struggles and his loneliness. Again, the play of a developing talent must give its possessor joy, if of a wilful, defiant kind. With time, an official note, something almost expository, crept into Gustave Aschenbach's method. His later style gave up the old sheer audacities, the fresh and subtle nuances—it became fixed and exemplary, conservative, formal, even formulated. Like Louis XIV—or as tradition has it of him—Aschenbach, as he went on in years, banished from his style every common word. It was at this time that the school authorities adopted selections from his works into their text-books. And he found it only fitting—and had no thought but to accept—when a German prince signalized his accession to the throne by conferring upon the poet-author of the life of Frederick the Great on his fiftieth birthday the letters-patent of nobility.

He had roved about for a few years, trying this place and that as a place of residence, before choosing, as he soon did, the city of Munich for his permanent home. And there he lived, enjoying among his fellow-citizens the honour which is in rare cases the reward of intellectual eminence. He married young, the daughter of a university family; but after a brief term of wedded happiness, his wife had died. A daughter, already married, remained to him. A son he never had.

Gustave von Aschenbach was somewhat below middle height, dark and smooth-shaven, with a head that looked rather too large for his almost delicate figure. He wore his hair brushed back; it was thin at the parting, bushy and grey on the temples, framing a lofty, rugged, knotty brow—if one may so characterize it. The nose-piece of his rimless gold spectacles cut into the base of his thick, aristocratically hooked nose. The mouth was large, often lax, often suddenly narrow and tense; the cheeks lean and furrowed, the pronounced chin slightly cleft. The vicissitudes of fate, it seemed, must have passed over this head for he held it, plaintively, rather on one side; yet it was art, not the stern discipline of an active career, that had taken over the office of modelling these features. Behind this brow were born the flashing thrust and parry of the dialogue between Frederick and Voltaire on the theme of war; these eyes, weary and sunken, gazing through their glasses, had beheld the blood-stained inferno of the hospitals in the Seven Years' War. Yes, personally speaking too, art heightens life. She gives deeper joy, she consumes more swiftly. She engraves adventures of the spirit and the mind in the faces of her votaries; let them lead outwardly a life of the most cloistered calm, she will in the end produce in them a fastidiousness, an over-refinement, a nervous fever and exhaustion, such as a career of extravagant passions and pleasures can hardly show.

Eager though he was to be off, Aschenbach was kept in Munich by affairs both literary and practical for some two week after that walk of his. But at length he ordered his country home put ready against his return within the next few days, and on a day between the middle and the end of May took the evening train for Trieste, where he stopped only twenty-four hours, embarking for Pola the next morning but one.

What he sought was a fresh scene, without associations, which should yet be not too out-of-the-way; and accordingly he chose an island in the Adriatic, not far off the Istrian coast. It had been well known for some years, for its splendidly rugged cliff formations on the side next the open sea, and its population, clad in a bright flutter of rags and speaking an outlandish tongue. But there was rain and heavy air; the society at the hotel was provincial Austrian, and limited; besides, it annoyed him not to be able to get at the sea—he missed the close and soothing contact which only a gentle sandy slope affords. He could not feel this was the place he sought; an inner impulse made him wretched, urging him on he knew not whither; he racked his brains, he looked up boats, then all at once his goal stood plain before his eyes. But of course! When one wanted to arrive overnight at the incomparable, the fabulous, the like-nothing-else-in-the-world, where was it one went? Why, obviously; he had intended to go there, what ever was he doing here? A blunder. He made all haste to correct it, announcing his departure at once. Ten days after his arrival on the island a swift motorboat bore him and his luggage in the misty dawning back across the water to the naval station, where he landed only to pass over the landing-stage and on to the wet decks of a ship lying there with steam up for the passage to Venice.

It was an ancient hulk belonging to an Italian line, obsolete, dingy, grimed with soot. A dirty hunchbacked sailor, smirkingly polite, conducted him at once belowship to a cavernous, lamplit cabin. There behind a table sat a man with a beard like a goat's; he had his hat on the back of his head, a cigar-stump in the corner of his mouth; he reminded Aschenbach of an old-fashioned circus-director. This person put the usual questions and wrote out a ticket to Venice, which he issued to the traveller with many commercial flourishes.

"A ticket for Venice," repeated he, stretching out his arm to dip the pen into the thick ink in a tilted inkstand. "One first-class to Venice! Here you are, *signore mio.*" He made some scrawls on the paper, strewed bluish sand on it out of a box, thereafter letting the sand run off into an earthen vessel, folded the paper with bony yellow fingers, and wrote on the outside. "An excellent choice," he rattled on. "Ah, Venice! What a glorious city! Irresistibly attractive to the cultured man for her past history as well as her present charm." His copious gesturings and empty phrases gave the odd impression that he feared the traveller might alter his mind. He changed Aschenbach's note, laying the money on the spotted tablecover with the glibness of a croupier. "A pleasant visit to you, signore," he said, with a melodramatic bow. "Delighted to serve you." Then he beckoned and called out: "Next" as though a stream of passengers stood waiting to be served, though in point of fact there was not one. Aschenbach returned to the upper deck.

He leaned an arm on the railing and looked at the idlers lounging along the quay to watch the boat go out. Then he turned his attention to his fellow-passengers. Those of the second class, both men and women, were squatted on their bundles of luggage on the forward deck. The first cabin consisted of a group of lively youths, clerks from Pola, evidently, who had made up a pleasure excursion to Italy and were not a little thrilled at the prospect, bustling about and laughing with satisfaction at the stir they made. They leaned over the railings and shouted, with a glib command of epithet, derisory remarks at such of their fellow-clerks as they saw going to business along the quay; and these in turn shook their sticks and shouted as good back again. One of the party, in a dandified buff suit, a rakish panama with a coloured scarf, and a red cravat, was loudest of the loud: he outcrowded all the rest. Aschenbach's eye dwelt on him, and he was shocked to see that the apparent youth was no youth at all. He was an old man, beyond a doubt, with wrinkles and crow's-feet round eyes and mouth; the dull carmine of the cheeks was rouge, the brown hair a wig. His neck was shrunken and sinewy, his turned-up moustaches and small imperial were dyed, and the unbroken double row of yellow teeth he showed when he laughed were but too obviously a cheapish false set. He wore a seal ring on each forefinger, but the hands were those of an old man. Aschenbach was moved to shudder as he watched the creature and his association with the rest of the group. Could they not see he was old, that he had no right to wear the clothes they wore or pretend to be one of them? But they were used to him, it seemed; they suffered him among them, they paid back his jokes in kind and the playful pokes in the ribs he gave them. How could they? Aschenbach put his hand to his brow, he covered his eyes, for he had slept little, and they smarted. He felt not quite canny, as though the world were suffering a dreamlike distortion of perspective which he might arrest by shutting it all out for a few minutes and then looking at it afresh. But instead he felt a floating sensation, and opened his eyes with unreasoning alarm to find that the ship's dark sluggish bulk was slowly leaving the jetty. Inch by inch, with the to-and-fro motion of her machinery, the strip of iridescent dirty water widened, the boat manœuvred clumsily and turned her bow to the open sea. Aschenbach moved over to the starboard side, where the hunchbacked sailor had set up a deck-chair for him, and a steward in a greasy dress-coat asked for orders.

The sky was grey, the wind humid. Harbour and island dropped behind, all sight of land soon vanished in mist. Flakes of sodden, clammy soot fell upon the still undried deck. Before the boat was an hour out a canvas had to be spread as a shelter from the rain.

Wrapped in his cloak, a book in his lap, our traveller rested; the hours slipped by unawares. It stopped raining, the canvas was taken down. The horizon was visible right round; beneath the sombre dome of the sky stretched the vast plain of empty sea. But immeasurable unarticulated space weakens our power to measure time as well: the time-sense falters and grows dim. Strange, shadowy figures passed and repassed—the elderly coxcomb, the goat-bearded man from the bowels of the ship—with vague gesturings and mutterings through the traveller's mind as he lay. He fell asleep.

At midday he was summoned to luncheon in a corridor-like saloon with the sleeping-cabins giving off it. He ate at the head of the long table; the party of clerks, including the old man, sat with the jolly captain at the other end, where they had been carousing since ten o'clock. The meal was wretched, and soon done. Aschenbach was driven to seek the open and look at the sky—perhaps it would lighten presently above Venice.

He had not dreamed it could be otherwise, for the city had ever given him a brilliant welcome. But sky and sea remained leaden, with spurts of fine, mistlike rain; he reconciled himself to the idea of seeing a different Venice from that he had always approached on the landward side. He stood by the foremast, his gaze on the distance, alert for the first glimpse of the coast. And he thought of the melancholy and susceptible poet who had once seen the towers and turrets of his dreams rise out of these waves; repeated the rhythms born of his awe, his mingled emotions of joy and suffering—and easily susceptible to a prescience already shaped within him, he asked his own sober, weary heart if a new enthusiasm, a new preoccupation, some late adventure of the feelings could still be in store for the idle traveller.

The flat coast showed on the right, the sea was soon populous with fishing-boats. The Lido appeared and was left behind as the ship glided at half speed through the narrow harbour of the same name, coming to a full stop on the lagoon in sight of garish, badly built houses. Here it waited for the boat bringing the sanitary inspector.

An hour passed. One had arrived—and yet not. There was no conceivable haste—yet one felt harried. The youths from Pola were on deck, drawn hither by the martial sound of horns coming across the water from the direction of the Public Gardens. They had drunk a good deal of Asti and were moved to shout and hurrah at the drilling *bersaglieri*. But the young-old man was a truly repulsive sight in the condition to which his company with youth had brought him. He could not carry his wine like them: he was pitiably drunk. He swayed as he stood—watery-eyed, a cigarette between his shaking fingers, keeping upright with difficulty. He could not have taken a step without falling and knew better than to stir, but his spirits were deplorably high. He buttonholed anyone who came within reach, he stuttered, he giggled, he leered, he fatuously shook his beringed old forefinger; his tongue kept seeking the corner of his mouth in a suggestive motion ugly to behold. Aschenbach's brow darkened as he looked, and there came over him once more a dazed sense, as though things about him were just slightly losing their ordinary perspective, beginning to show a distortion that might merge into the grotesque. He was prevented from dwelling on the feeling, for now the machinery began to thud again, and the ship took up its passage through the Canale di San Marco which had been interrupted so near the goal.

He saw it once more, that landing-place that takes the breath away, that amazing group of incredible structures the Republic set up to meet the awe-struck eye of the approaching seafarer: the airy splendour of the palace and Bridge of Sighs, the columns of lion and saint on the shore, the glory of the projecting flank of the fairy temple, the vista of gateway and clock. Looking, he thought that to come to Venice by the station is like entering a palace by the back door. No one should approach, save by the high seas as he was doing now, this most improbable of cities.

The engines stopped. Gondolas pressed alongside, the landing-stairs were let down, customs officials came on board and did their office, people began to go ashore. Aschenbach ordered a gondola. He meant to take up his abode by the sea and needed to be conveyed with his luggage to the landing-stage of the little steamers that ply between the city and the Lido. They called down his order to the surface of the water where the gondoliers were quarrelling in dialect. Then came another delay while his trunk was worried down the ladder-like stairs. Thus he was forced to endure the importunities of the ghastly young-old man, whose drunken state obscurely urged him to pay the stranger the honour of a formal farewell. "We wish you a very pleasant sojourn," he babbled, bowing and scraping. "Pray keep us in mind. *Au revoir, excusez et bon jour, votre Excellence.*" He drooled, he blinked, he licked the corner of his mouth, the little imperial bristled on his elderly chin. He put the tips of two fingers to his mouth and said thickly: "Give her our love, will you, the p-pretty little dear"—here his upper plate came away and fell down on the lower one. . . . Aschenbach escaped. "Little sweety-sweety-sweetheart" he heard behind him, gurgled and stuttered, as he climbed down the rope stair into the boat.

Is there anyone but must repress a secret thrill, on arriving in Venice for the first time—or returning thither after long absence—and stepping into a Venetian gondola? That singular conveyance, come down unchanged from ballad times, black as nothing else on earth except a coffin—what pictures it calls up of lawless, silent adventures in the plashing night; or even more, what visions of death itself, the bier and solemn rites and last soundless voyage! And has anyone remarked that the seat in such a bark, the arm-chair lacquered in coffin-black and dully black-upholstered, is the softest, most luxurious, most relaxing seat in the world? Aschenbach realized it when he had let himself down at the gondolier's feet, opposite his luggage, which lay neatly composed on the vessel's beak. The rowers still gestured fiercely; he heard their harsh, incoherent tones. But the strange stillness of the water-city seemed to take up their voices gently, to disembody and scatter them over the sea. It was warm here in the harbour. The lukewarm air of the sirocco breathed upon him, he leaned back among his cushions and gave himself to the yielding element, closing his eyes for very pleasure in an indolence as unaccustomed as sweet. "The trip will be short," he thought, and wished it might last forever. They gently swayed away from the boat with its bustle and clamour of voices.

It grew still and stiller all about. No sound but the splash of the oars, the hollow slap of the wave against the steep, black, halbert-shaped beak of the vessel, and one sound more—a muttering by fits and starts, expressed as it were by the motion of his arms, from the lips of the gondolier. He was talking to himself, between his teeth. Aschenbach glanced up and saw with surprise that the lagoon was widening, his vessel was headed for the open sea. Evidently it would not do to give himself up to sweet *far niente;* he must see his wishes carried out.

"You are to take me to the steamboat landing, you know," he said, half turning round towards it. The muttering stopped. There was no reply.

"Take me to the steamboat landing," he repeated, and this time turned quite round and looked up into the face of the gondolier as he stood there on his little elevated deck, high against the pale grey sky. The man had an unpleasing, even brutish face, and wore blue clothes like a sailor's, with a yellow sash; a shapeless straw hat with the braid torn at the brim perched rakishly on his head. His facial structure, as well as the curling blond moustache under the short snub nose, showed him to be of non-Italian stock. Physically rather undersized, so that one would not have expected him to be very muscular, he pulled vigorously at the oar, putting all his body-weight behind each stroke. Now and then the effort he made curled back his lips and bared his white teeth to the gums. He spoke in a decided, almost curt voice, looking out to sea over his fare's head: "The signore is going to the Lido."

Aschenbach answered: "Yes, I am. But I only took the gondola to cross over to San Marco. I am using the *vaporetto* from there."

"But the signore cannot use the *vaporetto.*"

"And why not?"

"Because the *vaporetto* does not take luggage."

It was true. Aschenbach remembered it. He made no answer.

But the man's gruff, overbearing manner, so unlike the usual courtesy of his countrymen towards the stranger, was intolerable. Aschenbach spoke again: "That is my own affair. I may want to give my luggage in deposit. You will turn round."

No answer. The oar splashed, the wave struck dull against the prow. And the muttering began anew, the gondolier talked to himself, between his teeth.

What should the traveller do? Alone on the water with this tongue-tied, obstinate, uncanny man, he saw no way of enforcing his will. And if only he did not excite himself, how pleasantly he might rest! Had he not wished the voyage might last forever? The wisest thing—and how much the pleasantest!—was to let matters take their own course. A spell of indolence was upon him; it came from the chair he sat in—this low, black-upholstered arm-chair, so gently rocked at the hands of the despotic boatman in his rear. The thought passed dreamily through Aschenbach's brain that perhaps he had fallen into the clutches of a criminal; it had not power to rouse him into action. More annoying was the simpler explanation: that the man was only trying to extort money. A sense of duty, a recollection, as it were, that this ought to be prevented, made him collect himself to say:

"How much do you ask for the trip?"

And the gondolier, going out over his head, replied: "The signore will pay."

There was an established reply to this; Aschenbach made it, mechanically:

"I will pay nothing whatever if you do not take me where I want to go."

"The signore wants to go to the Lido."

"But not with you."

"I am a good rower, signore. I will row you well."

"So much is true," thought Aschenbach, and again he relaxed. "That is true, you row me well. Even if you mean to rob me, even if you hit me in the back with your oar and send me down to the kingdom of Hades, even then you will have rowed me well."

But nothing of the sort happened. Instead, they fell in with company: a boat came alongside and waylaid them, full of men and women singing to guitar and mandolin. They rowed persistently bow for bow with the gondola and filled the silence that had rested on the waters with their lyric love of gain. Aschenbach tossed money into the hat they held out. The music stopped at once, they rowed away. And once more the gondolier's mutter became audible as he talked to himself in fits and snatches.

Thus they rowed on, rocked by the wash of a steamer returning citywards. At the landing two municipal officials were walking up and down with their hands behind their backs and their faces turned towards the lagoon. Aschenbach was helped on shore by the old man with a boat-hook who is the permanent feature of every landing-stage in Venice; and having no small change to pay the boatman, crossed over into the hotel opposite. His wants were supplied in the lobby; but when he came back his possessions were already on a hand-car on the quay, and gondola and gondolier were gone.

"He ran away, signore," said the old boatman. "A bad lot, a man without a licence. He is the only gondolier without one. The others telephoned over, and he knew we were on the lookout, so he made off."

Aschenbach shrugged.

"The signore has had a ride for nothing," said the old man, and held out his hat. Aschenbach dropped some coins. He directed that his luggage be taken to the Hôtel des Bains and followed the hand-car through the avenue, that white-blossoming avenue with taverns, booths, and pensions on either side it, which runs across the island diagonally to the beach.

He entered the hotel from the garden terrace at the back and passed through the vestibule and hall into the office. His arrival was expected, and he was served with courtesy and dispatch. The manager, a small, soft, dapper man with a black moustache and a caressing way with him, wearing a French frock-coat, himself took him up in the lift and showed him his room. It was a pleasant chamber, furnished in cherry-wood, with lofty windows looking out to sea. It was decorated with strong-scented flowers. Aschenbach, as soon as he was alone, and while they brought in his trunk and bags and disposed them in the room, went up to one of the windows and stood looking out upon the beach in its afternoon emptiness, and at the sunless sea, now full and sending long, low waves with rhythmic beat upon the sand.

A solitary, unused to speaking of what he sees and feels, has mental experiences which are at once more intense and less articulate than those of a gregarious man. They are sluggish, yet more wayward, and never without a melancholy tinge. Sights and impressions which others brush aside with a glance, a light comment, a smile, occupy him more than their due; they sink silently in, they take on meaning, they become experience, emotion, adventure. Solitude gives birth to the original in us, to beauty unfamiliar and perilous—to poetry. But also, it gives birth to the opposite: to the perverse, the illicit, the absurd. Thus the traveller's mind still dwelt with disquiet on the episodes of his journey hither: on the horrible old fop with his drivel about a mistress, on the outlaw boatman and his lost tip. They did not offend his reason, they hardly afforded food for thought; yet they seemed by their very nature fundamentally strange, and thereby vaguely disquieting. Yet here was the sea; even in the midst of such thoughts he saluted it with his eyes, exulting that Venice was near and accessible. At length he turned round, disposed his personal belongings and made certain arrangements with the chambermaid for his comfort, washed up, and was conveyed to the ground floor by the green-uniformed Swiss who ran the lift.

He took tea on the terrace facing the sea and afterwards went down and walked some distance along the shore promenade in the direction of Hôtel Excelsior. When he came back it seemed to be time to change for dinner. He did so, slowly and methodically as his way was, for he was accustomed to work while he dressed; but even so found himself a little early when he entered the hall, where a large number of guests had collected—strangers to each other and affecting mutual indifference, yet united in expectancy of the meal. He picked up a paper, sat down in a leather arm-chair, and took stock of the company, which compared most favourably with that he had just left.

This was a broad and tolerant atmosphere, of wide horizons. Subdued voices were speaking most of the principal European tongues. That uniform of civilization, the conventional evening dress, gave outward conformity to the varied types. There were long, dry Americans, large-familied Russians, English ladies, German children with French *bonnes*. The Slavic element predominated, it seemed. In Aschenbach's neighbourhood Polish was being spoken.

Round a wicker table next him was gathered a group of young folk in charge of a governess or companion—three young girls, perhaps fifteen to seventeen years old, and a long-haired boy of about fourteen. Aschenbach noticed with astonishment the lad's perfect beauty. His face recalled the noblest moment of Greek sculpture—pale, with a sweet reserve, with clustering honey-coloured ringlets, the brow and nose descending in one line, the winning mouth, the expression of pure and godlike serenity. Yet with all this chaste perfection of form it was of such unique personal charm that the observer thought he had never seen, either in nature or art, anything so utterly happy and consummate. What struck him further was the strange contrast the group afforded, a difference in educational method, so to speak, shown in the way the brother and sisters were clothed and treated. The girls, the eldest of whom was practically grown up, were dressed with an almost disfiguring austerity. All three wore half-length slate-coloured frocks of cloister-line plainness, arbitrarily unbecoming in cut, with white turn-over collars as their only adornment. Every grace of outline was wilfully suppressed; their hair lay smoothly plastered to their heads, giving them a vacant expression, like a nun's. All this could only be by the mother's orders; but there was no trace of the same pedagogic severity in the case of the boy. Tenderness and softness, it was plain, conditioned his existence. No scissors had been put to the lovely hair that (like the Spinnario's) curled about his brows, above his ears, longer still in the neck. He wore an English sailor suit, with quilted sleeves that narrowed round the delicate wrists of his long and slender though still childish hands. And this suit, with its breast-knot, lacings, and embroideries, lent the slight figure something "rich and strange," a spoilt, exquisite air. The observer saw him in half profile, with one foot in its black patent leather advanced, one elbow resting on the arm of his basket-chair, the cheek nestled into the closed hand in a pose of easy grace, quite unlike the stiff subservient mien which was evidently habitual to his sisters. Was he delicate? His facial tint was ivory-white against the golden darkness of his clustering locks. Or was he simply a pampered darling, the object of a self-willed and partial love? Aschenbach inclined to think the latter. For in almost every artist nature is inborn a wanton and treacherous proneness to side with the beauty that breaks hearts, to single out aristocratic pretensions and pay them homage.

A waiter announced, in English, that dinner was served. Gradually the company dispersed through the glass doors into the dining-room. Late-comers entered from the vestibule or the lifts. Inside, dinner was being served; but the young Poles still sat and waited about their wicker table. Aschenbach felt comfortable in his deep arm-chair, he enjoyed the beauty before his eyes, he waited with them.

The governess, a short, stout, red-faced person, at length gave the signal. With lifted brows she pushed back her chair and made a bow to the tall woman, dressed in palest grey, who now entered the hall. This lady's abundant jewels were pearls, her manner was cool and measured; the fashion of her gown and the arrangement of her lightly powdered hair had the simplicity prescribed in certain circles whose piety and aristocracy are equally marked. She might have been, in Germany, the wife of some high official. But there was something faintly fabulous, after all, in her appearance, though lent it solely by the pearls she wore: they were well-nigh priceless, and consisted of earrings and a three-stranded necklace, very long, with gems the size of cherries.

The brother and sisters had risen briskly. They bowed over their mother's hand to kiss it, she turning away from them, with a slight smile on her face, which was carefully preserved but rather sharp-nosed and worn. She addressed a few words in French to the governess, then moved towards the glass door. The children followed, the girls in order of age, then the governess, and last the boy. He chanced to turn before he crossed the threshold, and as there was no one else in the room, his strange, twilit grey eyes met Aschenbach's, as our traveller sat there with the paper on his knee, absorbed in looking after the group.

There was nothing singular, of course, in what he had seen. They had not gone in to dinner before their mother, they had waited, given her a respectful salute, and but observed the right and proper forms on entering the room. Yet they had done all this so expressly, with such self-respecting dignity, discipline, and sense of duty that Aschenbach was impressed. He lingered still a few minutes, then he, too, went into the dining-room, where he was shown a table far off the Polish family, as he noted at once, with a stirring of regret.

Tired, yet mentally alert, he beguiled the long, tedious meal with abstract, even with transcendent matters: pondered the mysterious harmony that must come to subsist between the individual human being and the universal law, in order that human beauty may result; passed on to general problems of form and art, and came at length to the conclusion that what seemed to him fresh and happy thoughts were like the flattering inventions of a dream, which the waking sense proves worthless and insubstantial. He spent the evening in the park, that was sweet with the odours of evening—sitting, smoking, wandering about; went to bed betimes, and passed the night in deep, unbroken sleep, visited, however, by varied and lively dreams.

The weather next day was no more promising. A land breeze blew. Beneath a colourless, overcast sky the sea lay sluggish, and as it were shrunken, so far withdrawn as to leave bare several rows of long sand-banks. The horizon looked close and prosaic. When Aschenbach opened his window he thought he smelt the stagnant odour of the lagoons.

He felt suddenly out of sorts and already began to think of leaving. Once, years before, after weeks of bright spring weather, this wind had found him out; it had been so bad as to force him to flee from the city like a fugitive. And now it seemed beginning again—the same feverish distaste, the pressure on his temples, the heavy eyelids. It would be a nuisance to change again; but if the wind did not turn, this was no place for him. To be on the safe side, he did not entirely unpack. At nine o'clock he went down to the buffet, which lay between the hall and the dining-room and served as breakfast-room.

A solemn stillness reigned here, such as it is the ambition of all large hotels to achieve. The waiters moved on noiseless feet. A rattling of tea-things, a whispered word—and no other sounds. In a corner diagonally to the door, two tables off his own, Aschenbach saw the Polish girls with their governess. They sat there very straight, in their stiff blue linen frocks with little turn-over collars and cuffs, their ash-blond hair newly brushed flat, their eyelids red from sleep; and handed each other the marmalade. They had nearly finished their meal. The boy was not there.

Aschenbach smiled. "Aha, little Phæax," he thought. "It seems you are privileged to sleep yourself out." With sudden gaiety he quoted:

"Oft veränderten Schmuck und warme Bäder und Ruhe."

He took a leisurely breakfast. The porter came up with his braided cap in his hand, to deliver some letters that had been sent on. Aschenbach lighted a cigarette and opened a few letters and thus was still seated to witness the arrival of the sluggard.

He entered through the glass doors and passed diagonally across the room to his sisters at their table. He walked with extraordinary grace—the carriage of the body, the action of the knee, the way he set down his foot in its white shoe—it was all so light, it was at once dainty and proud, it wore an added charm in the childish shyness which made him twice turn his head as he crossed the room, made him give a quick glance and then drop his eyes. He took his seat, with a smile and a murmured word in his soft and blurry tongue; and Aschenbach, sitting so that he could see him in profile, was astonished anew, yes, startled, at the godlike beauty of the human being. The lad had on a light sailor suit of blue and white striped cotton, with a red silk breast-knot and a simple white standing collar round the neck—a not very elegant effect—yet above this collar the head was poised like a flower, in incomparable loveliness. It was the head of Eros, with the yellowish bloom of Parian marble, with fine serious brows, and dusky clustering ringlets standing out in soft plenteousness over temples and ears.

"Good, oh, very good indeed!" thought Aschenbach, assuming the patronizing air of the connoisseur to hide, as artists will, their ravishment over a masterpiece. "Yes," he went on to himself, "if it were not that sea and beach were waiting for me, I should sit here as long as you do." But he went out on that, passing through the hall, beneath the watchful eye of the functionaries, down the steps and directly across the board walk to the section of the beach reserved for the guests of the hotel. The bathing-master, a barefoot old man in linen trousers and sailor blouse, with a straw hat, showed him the cabin that had been rented for him, and Aschenbach had him set up table and chair on the sandy platform before it. Then he dragged the reclining-chair through the pale yellow sand, closer to the sea, sat down, and composed himself.

He delighted, as always in the scene on the beach, the sight of sophisticated society giving itself over to a simple life at the edge of the element. The shallow grey sea was already gay with children wading, with swimmers, with figures in bright colours lying on the sand-banks with arms behind their heads. Some were rowing in little keelless boats painted red and blue, and laughing when they capsized. A long row of *capanne* ran down the beach, with platforms, where people sat as on verandas, and there was social life, with bustle and with indolent repose; visits were paid, amid much chatter, punctilious morning toilettes hobnobbed with comfortable and privileged dishabille. On the hard wet sand close to the sea figures in white bath-robes or loose wrappings in garish colours strolled up and down. A mammoth sand-hill had been built up on Aschenbach's right, the work of children, who had stuck it full of tiny flags. Vendors of sea-shells, fruits, and cakes knelt beside their wares spread out on the sand. A row of cabins on the left stood obliquely to the others and to the sea, thus forming the boundary of the enclosure on this side; and on the little veranda in front of one of these a Russian family was encamped; bearded men with strong white teeth, ripe, indolent women, a Fräulein from the Baltic provinces, who sat at an easel painting the sea and tearing her hair in despair; two ugly but good-natured children and an old maidservant in a head-cloth, with the caressing, servile manner of the born dependent. There they sat together in grateful enjoyment of their blessings: constantly shouting at their romping children, who paid not the slightest heed; making jokes in broken Italian to the funny old man who sold them sweetmeats, kissing each other on the cheeks—no jot concerned that their domesticity was overlooked.

"I'll stop," thought Aschenbach. "Where could it be better than here?" With his hands clasped in his lap he let his eyes swim in the wideness of the sea, his gaze lose focus, blur, and grow vague in the misty immensity of space. His love of the ocean had profound sources: the hard-worked artist's longing for rest, his yearning to seek refuge from the thronging manifold shapes of his fancy in the bosom of the simple and vast; and another yearning, opposed to his art and perhaps for that very reason a lure, for the unorganized, the immeasurable, the eternal—in short, for nothingness. He whose preoccupation is with excellence longs fervently to find rest in perfection; and is not nothingness a form of perfection? As he sat there dreaming thus, deep, deep into the void, suddenly the margin line of the shore was cut by a human form. He gathered up his gaze and withdrew it from the illimitable, and lo, it was the lovely boy who crossed his vision coming from the left along the sand. He was barefoot, ready for wading, the slender legs uncovered above the knee, and moved slowly, yet with such a proud, light tread as to make it seem he had never worn shoes. He looked towards the diagonal row of cabins; and the sight of the Russian family, leading their lives there in joyous simplicity, distorted his features in a spasm of angry disgust. His brow darkened, his lips curled, one corner of the mouth was drawn down in a harsh line that marred the curve of the cheek, his frown was so heavy that the eyes seemed to sink in as they uttered beneath the black and vicious language of hate. He looked down, looked threateningly back once more; then giving it up with a violent and contemptuous shoulder-shrug, he left his enemies in the rear.

A feeling of delicacy, a qualm, almost like a sense of shame, made Aschenbach turn away as though he had not seen, he felt unwilling to take advantage of having been, by chance, privy to this passionate reaction. But he was in truth both moved and exhilarated—that is to say, he was delighted. This childish exhibition of fanaticism, directed against the good-naturedest simplicity in the world—it gave to the godlike and inexpressive the final human touch. The figure of the half-grown lad, a masterpiece from nature's own hand, had been significant enough when it gratified the eye alone; and now it evoked sympathy as well—the little episode had set it off, lent it a dignity in the onlooker's eyes that was beyond its years.

Aschenbach listened with still averted head to the boy's voice announcing his coming to his companions at the sand-heap. The voice was clear, though a little weak, but they answered, shouting his name—or his nickname—again and again. Aschenbach was not without curiosity to learn it, but could make out nothing more exact than two musical syllables, something like Adgio—or, oftener still, Adjiu, with a long-drawn-out *u* at the end. He liked the melodious sound, and found it fitting; said it over to himself a few times and turned back with satisfaction to his papers.

Holding his travelling-pad on his knees, he took his fountain-pen and began to answer various items of his correspondence. But presently he felt it too great a pity to turn his back, and the eyes of his mind, for the sake of mere commonplace correspondence, to this scene which was, after all, the most rewarding one he knew. He put aside his papers and swung round to the sea; in no long time, beguiled by the voices of the children at play, he had turned his head and sat resting it against the chair-back, while he gave himself up to contemplating the activities of the exquisite Adgio.

His eye found him out at once, the red breast-knot was unmistakable. With some nine or ten companions, boys and girls of his own age and younger, he was busy putting in place an old plank to serve as a bridge across the ditches between the sand-piles. He directed the work by shouting and motioning with his head, and they were all chattering in many tongues—French, Polish, and even some of the Balkan languages. But his was the name oftenest on their lips, he was plainly sought after, wooed, admired. One lad in particular, a Pole like himself, with a name that sounded something like Jaschiu, a sturdy lad with brilliantined black hair, in a belted linen suit, was his particular liegeman and friend. Operations at the sand-pile being ended for the time, the two walked away along the beach, with their arms round each other's waists, and once the lad Jaschiu gave Adgio a kiss.

Aschenbach felt like shaking a finger at him. "But you, Critobulus," he thought with a smile, "you I advise to take a year's leave. That long, at least, you will need for complete recovery." A vendor came by with strawberries, and Aschenbach made his second breakfast of the great luscious, dead-ripe fruit. It had grown very warm, although the sun had not availed to pierce the heavy layer of mist. His mind felt relaxed, his senses revelled in this vast and soothing communion with the silence of the sea. The grave and serious man found sufficient occupation in speculating what name it could be that sounded like Adgio. And with the help of a few Polish memories he at length fixed on Tadzio, a shortened form of Thaddeus, which sounded, when called, like Tadziu or Adziu.

Tadzio was bathing. Aschenbach had lost sight of him for a moment, then descried him far out in the water, which was shallow a very long way—saw his head, and his arm striking out like an oar. But his watchful family were already on the alert; the mother and governess called from the veranda in front of their bathing-cabin, until the lad's name, with its softened consonants and long-drawn *u*-sound, seemed to possess the beach like a rallying-cry; the cadence had something sweet and wild: "Tadziu! Tadziu!" He turned and ran back against the water, churning the waves to a foam, his head flung high. The sight of this living figure, virginally pure and austere, with dripping locks, beautiful as a tender young god, emerging from the depths of sea and sky, outrunning the element—it conjured up mythologies, it was like a primeval legend, handed down from the beginning of time, of the birth of form, of the origin of the gods. With closed lids Aschenbach listened to this poesy hymning itself silently within him, and anon he thought it was good to be here and that he would stop awhile.

Afterwards Tadzio lay on the sand and rested from his bathe, wrapped in his white sheet, which he wore drawn underneath the right shoulder, so that his head was cradled on his bare right arm. And even when Aschenbach read, without looking up, he was conscious that the lad was there; that it would cost him but the slightest turn of the head to have the rewarding vision once more in his purview. Indeed, it was almost as though he sat there to guard the youth's repose; occupied, of course, with his own affairs, yet alive to the presence of that noble human creature close at hand. And his heart was stirred, it felt a father's kindness: such an emotion as the possessor of beauty can inspire in one who has offered himself up in spirit to create beauty.

At midday he left the beach, returned to the hotel, and was carried up in the lift to his room. There he lingered a little time before the glass and looked at his own grey hair, his keen and weary face. And he thought of his fame, and how people gazed respectfully at him in the streets, on account of his unerring gift of words and their power to charm. He called up all the worldly successes his genius had reaped, all he could remember, even his patent of nobility. Then went to luncheon down in the dining-room, sat at his little table and ate. Afterwards he mounted again in the lift, and a group of young folk, Tadzio among them, pressed with him into the little compartment. It was the first time Aschenbach had seen him close at hand, not merely in perspective, and could see and take account of the details of his humanity. Someone spoke to the lad, and he, answering, with indescribably lovely smile, stepped out again, as they had come to the first floor, backwards, with his eyes cast down. "Beauty makes people self-conscious," Aschenbach thought, and considered within himself imperatively why this should be. He had noted, further, that Tadzio's teeth were imperfect, rather jagged and bluish, without a healthy glaze, and of that peculiar brittle transparency which the teeth of chlorotic people often show. "He is delicate, he is sickly," Aschenbach thought. "He will most likely not live to grow old." He did not try to account for the pleasure the idea gave him.

In the afternoon he spent two hours in his room, then took the *vaporetto* to Venice, across the foul-smelling lagoon. He got out at San Marco, had his tea in the Piazza, and then, as his custom was, took a walk through the streets. But this walk of his brought about nothing less than a revolution in his mood and an entire change in all his plans.

There was a hateful sultriness in the narrow streets. The air was so heavy that all the manifold smells wafted out of houses, shops, and cook-shops—smells of oil, perfumery, and so forth—hung low, like exhalations, not dissipating. Cigarette smoke seemed to stand in the air, it drifted so slowly away. Today the crowd in these narrow lanes oppressed the stroller instead of diverting him. The longer he walked, the more was he in tortures under that state, which is the product of the sea air and the sirocco and which excites and enervates at once. He perspired painfully. His eyes rebelled, his chest was heavy, he felt feverish, the blood throbbed in his temples. He fled from the huddled, narrow streets of the commercial city, crossed many bridges, and came into the poor quarter of Venice. Beggars waylaid him, the canals sickened him with their evil exhalations. He reached a quiet square, one of those that exist at the city's heart, forsaken of God and man; there he rested awhile on the margin of a fountain, wiped his brow, and admitted to himself that he must be gone.

For the second time, and now quite definitely, the city proved that in certain weathers it could be directly inimical to his health. Nothing but sheer unreasoning obstinacy would linger on, hoping for an unprophesiable change in the wind. A quick decision was in place. He could not go home at this stage, neither summer nor winter quarters would be ready. But Venice had not a monopoly of sea and shore: there were other spots where these were to be had without the evil concomitants of lagoon and fever-breeding vapours. He remembered a little bathing-place not far from Trieste of which he had had a good report. Why not go thither? At once, of course, in order that this second change might be worth the making. He resolved, he rose to his feet and sought the nearest gondola-landing, where he took a boat and was conveyed to San Marco through the gloomy windings of many canals, beneath balconies of delicate marble traceries flanked by carven lions; round slippery corners of wall, past melancholy façades with ancient business shields reflected in the rocking water. It was not too easy to arrive at his destination, for his gondolier, being in league with various lace-makers and glass-blowers, did his best to persuade his fare to pause, look, and be tempted to buy. Thus the charm of this bizarre passage through the heart of Venice, even while it played upon his spirit, yet was sensibly cooled by the predatory commercial spirit of the fallen queen of the seas.

Once back in his hotel, he announced at the office, even before dinner, that circumstances unforeseen obliged him to leave early next morning. The management expressed its regret, it changed his money and receipted his bill. He dined, and spent the lukewarm evening in a rocking-chair on the rear terrace, reading the newspapers. Before he went to bed, he made his luggage ready against the morning.

His sleep was not of the best, for the prospect of another journey made him restless. When he opened his window next morning, the sky was still overcast, but the air seemed fresher—and there and then his rue began. Had he not given notice too soon? Had he not let himself be swayed by a slight and momentary indisposition? If he had only been patient, not lost heart so quickly, tried to adapt himself to the climate, or even waited for a change in the weather before deciding! Then, instead of the hurry and flurry of departure, he would have before him now a morning like yesterday's on the beach. Too late! He must go on wanting what he had wanted yesterday. He dressed and at eight o'clock went down to breakfast.

When he entered the breakfast-room it was empty. Guests came in while he sat waiting for his order to be filled. As he sipped his tea he saw the Polish girls enter with their governess, chaste and morning-fresh, with sleep-reddened eyelids. They crossed the room and sat down at their table in the window. Behind them came the porter, cap in hand, to announce that it was time for him to go. The car was waiting to convey him and other travellers to the Hôtel Excelsior, whence they would go by motor-boat through the company's private canal to the station. Time pressed. But Aschenbach found it did nothing of the sort. There still lacked more than an hour of train-time. He felt irritated at the hotel habit of getting the guests out of the house earlier than necessary; and requested the porter to let him breakfast in peace. The man hesitated and withdrew, only to come back again five minutes later. The car could wait no longer. Good, then it might go, and take his trunk with it, Aschenbach answered with some heat. He would use the public conveyance, in his own time; he begged them to leave the choice of it to him. The functionary bowed. Aschenbach, pleased to be rid of him, made a leisurely meal, and even had a newspaper of the waiter. When at length he rose, the time was grown very short. And it so happened that at that moment Tadzio came through the glass doors into the room.

To reach his own table he crossed the traveller's path, and modestly cast down his eyes before the grey-haired man of the lofty brows—only to lift them again in that sweet way he had and direct his full soft gaze upon Aschenbach's face. Then he was past. "For the last time, Tadzio," thought the elder man. "It was all too brief!" Quite unusually for him, he shaped a farewell with his lips, he actually uttered it, and added: "May God bless you!" Then he went out, distributed tips, exchanged farewells with the mild little manager in the frock-coat, and, followed by the porter with his hand-luggage, left the hotel. On foot as he had come, he passed through the white-blossoming avenue, diagonally across the island to the boat-landing. He went on board at once—but the tale of his journey across the lagoon was a tale of woe, a passage through the very valley of regrets.

It was the well-known route: through the lagoon, past San Marco, up the Grand Canal. Aschenbach sat on the circular bench in the bows, with his elbow on the railing, one hand shading his eyes. They passed the Public Gardens, once more the princely charm of the Piazzetta rose up before him and then dropped behind, next came the great row of palaces, the canal curved, and the splendid marble arches of the Rialto came in sight. The traveller gazed—and his bosom was torn. The atmosphere of the city, the faintly rotten scent of swamp and sea, which had driven him to leave—in what deep, tender, almost painful draughts he breathed it in! How was it he had not known, had not thought, how much his heart was set upon it all! What this morning had been slight regret, some little doubt of his own wisdom, turned now to grief, to actual wretchedness, a mental agony so sharp that it repeatedly brought tears to his eyes, while he questioned himself how he could have foreseen it. The hardest part, the part that more than once it seemed he could not bear, was the thought that he should never more see Venice again. Since now for the second time the place had made him ill, since for the second time he had had to flee for his life, he must henceforth regard it as a forbidden spot, to be forever shunned; senseless to try it again, after he had proved himself unfit. Yes, if he fled it now, he felt that wounded pride must prevent his return to this spot where twice he had made actual bodily surrender. And this conflict between inclination and capacity all at once assumed, in this middle-aged man's mind, immense weight and importance; the physical defeat seemed a shameful thing, to be avoided at whatever cost; and he stood amazed at the ease with which on the day before he had yielded to it.

Meanwhile the steamer neared the station landing; his anguish of irresolution amounted almost to panic. To leave seemed to the sufferer impossible, to remain not less so. Torn thus between two alternatives, he entered the station. It was very late, he had not a moment to lose. Time pressed, it scourged him onward. He hastened to buy his ticket and looked round in the crowd to find the hotel porter. The man appeared and said that the trunk had already gone off. "Gone already?" "Yes, it has gone to Como." "To Como?" A hasty exchange of words—angry questions from Aschenbach, and puzzled replies from the porter—at length made it clear that the trunk had been put with the wrong luggage even before leaving the hotel, and in company with other trunks was now well on its way in precisely the wrong direction.

Aschenbach found it hard to wear the right expression as he heard this news. A reckless joy, a deep incredible mirthfulness shook him almost as with a spasm. The porter dashed off after the lost trunk, returning very soon, of course, to announce that his efforts were unavailing. Aschenbach said he would not travel without his luggage; that he would go back and wait at the Hôtel des Bains until it turned up. Was the company's motor-boat still outside? The man said yes, it was at the door. With his native eloquence he prevailed upon the ticket-agent to take back the ticket already purchased; he swore that he would wire, that no pains should be spared, that the trunk would be restored in the twinkling of an eye. And the unbelievable thing came to pass: the traveller, twenty minutes after he had reached the station, found himself once more on the Grand Canal on his way back to the Lido.

What a strange adventure indeed, this right-about face of destiny—incredible, humiliating, whimsical as any dream! To be passing again, within the hour, these scenes from which in profoundest grief he had but now taken leave forever! The little swift-moving vessel, a furrow of foam at its prow, tacking with droll agility between steamboats and gondolas, went like a shot to its goal; and he, its sole passenger, sat hiding the panic and thrills of a truant schoolboy beneath a mask of forced resignation. His breast still heaved from time to time with a burst of laughter over the contretemps. Things could not, he told himself, have fallen out more luckily. There would be the necessary explanations, a few astonished faces—then all would be well once more, a mischance prevented, a grievous error set right;

and all he had thought to have left forever was his own once more, his for as long as he liked. . . . And did the boat's swift motion deceive him, or was the wind now coming from the sea?

The waves struck against the tiled sides of the narrow canal. At Hôtel Excelsior the automobile omnibus awaited the returned traveller and bore him along by the crisping waves back to the Hôtel des Bains. The little mustachioed manager in the frock-coat came down the steps to greet him.

In dulcet tones he deplored the mistake, said how painful it was to the management and himself; applauded Aschenbach's resolve to stop on until the errant trunk came back; his former room, alas, was already taken, but another as good awaited his approval. *"Pas de chance, monsieur,"* said the Swiss lift-porter, with a smile as he conveyed him upstairs. And the fugitive was soon quartered in another room which in situation and furnishings almost precisely resembled the first.

He laid out the contents of his hand-bag in their wonted places; then, tired out, dazed by the whirl of the extraordinary forenoon, subsided into the arm-chair by the open window. The sea wore a pale-green cast, the air felt thinner and purer, the beach with its cabins and boats had more colour, notwithstanding the sky was still grey. Aschenbach, his hands folded in his lap, looked out. He felt rejoiced to be back, yet displeased with his vacillating moods, his ignorance of his own real desires. Thus for nearly an hour he sat, dreaming, resting, barely thinking. At midday he saw Tadzio, in his striped sailor suit with red breast-knot, coming up from the sea, across the barrier and along the board walk to the hotel. Aschenbach recognized him, even at this height, knew it was he before he actually saw him, had it in mind to say to himself: "Well, Tadzio, so here you are again too!" But the casual greeting died away before it reached his lips, slain by the truth in his heart. He felt the rapture of his blood, the poignant pleasure, and realized that it was for Tadzio's sake the leavetaking had been so hard.

He sat quite still, unseen at his high post, and looked within himself. His features were lively, he lifted his brows; a smile, alert, inquiring, vivid, widened the mouth. Then he raised his head, and with both hands, hanging limp over the chair-arms, he described a slow motion, palms outward, a lifting and turning movement, as though to indicate a wide embrace. It was a gesture of welcome, a calm and deliberate acceptance of what might come.

Now daily the naked god with cheeks aflame drove his four fire-breathing steeds through heaven's spaces; and with him streamed the strong east wind that fluttered his yellow locks. A sheen, like white satin, lay over all the idly rolling sea's expanse. The sand was burning hot. Awnings of rust-coloured canvas were spanned before the bathing-huts, under the ether's quivering silver-blue; one spent the morning hours within the small, sharp square of shadow they purveyed. But evening too was rarely lovely: balsamic with the breath of flowers and shrubs from the near-by park, while overhead the constellations circled in their spheres, and the murmuring of the night-girted sea swelled softly up and whispered to the soul. Such nights as these contained the joyful promise of a sunlit morrow, brim-full of sweetly ordered idleness, studded thick with countless precious possibilities.

The guest detained here by so happy a mischance was far from finding the return of his luggage a ground for setting out anew. For two days he had suffered slight inconvenience and had to dine in the large salon in his travelling-clothes. Then the lost trunk was set down in his room, and he hastened to unpack, filling presses and drawers with his possessions. He meant to stay on—and on; he rejoiced in the prospect of wearing a silk suit for the hot morning hours on the beach and appearing in acceptable evening dress at dinner.

He was quick to fall in with the pleasing monotony of this manner of life, readily enchanted by its mild soft brilliance and ease. And what a spot it is, indeed!—uniting the charms of a luxurious bathing-resort by a southern sea with the immediate nearness of a unique and marvellous city. Aschenbach was not pleasure-loving. Always, wherever and whenever it was the order of the day to be merry, to refrain from labour and make glad the heart, he would soon be conscious of the imperative summons—and especially was this so in his youth—back to the high fatigues, the sacred and fasting service that consumed his days. This spot and this alone had power to beguile him, to relax his resolution, to make him glad. At times—of a forenoon perhaps, as he lay in the shadow of his awning, gazing out dreamily over the blue of the southern sea, or in the mildness of the night, beneath the wide starry sky, ensconced among the cushions of the gondola that bore him Lidowards after an evening on the Piazza, while the gay lights faded and the melting music of the serenades died away on his ear—he would think of his mountain home, the theatre of his summer labours. There clouds hung low and trailed through the garden, violent storms extinguished the lights of the house at night, and the ravens he fed swung in the tops of the fir trees. And he would feel transported to Elysium, to the ends of the earth, to a spot most carefree for the sons of men, where no snow is, and no winter, no storms or downpours of rain; where Oceanus sends a mild and cooling breath, and days flow on in blissful idleness, without effort or struggle, entirely dedicated to the sun and the feasts of the sun.

Aschenbach saw the boy Tadzio almost constantly. The narrow confines of their world of hotel and beach, the daily round followed by all alike, brought him in close, almost uninterrupted touch with the beautiful lad. He encountered him everywhere—in the salons of the hotel, on the cooling rides to the city and back, among the splendours of the Piazza, and besides all this in many another going and coming as chance vouchsafed. But it was the regular morning hours on the beach which gave him his happiest opportunity to study and admire the lovely apparition. Yes, this immediate happiness, this daily recurring boon at the hand of circumstance, this it was that filled him with content, with joy in life, enriched his stay, and lingered out the row of sunny days that fell into place so pleasantly one behind the other.

He rose early—as early as though he had a panting press of work—and was among the first on the beach, when the sun was still benign and the sea lay dazzling white in its morning slumber. He gave the watchman a friendly good-morning and chatted with the barefoot, white-haired old man who prepared his place, spread the awning, trundled out the chair and table onto the little platform. Then he settled down; he had three or four hours before the sun reached its height and the fearful climax of its power; three or four hours while the sea went deeper and deeper blue; three or four hours in which to watch Tadzio.

He would see him come up, on the left, along the margin of the sea; or from behind, between the cabins; or, with a start of joyful surprise, would discover that he himself was late, and Tadzio already down, in the blue and white bathing-suit that was now his only wear on the beach; there and engrossed in his usual activities in the sand, beneath the sun. It was a sweetly idle, trifling, fitful life, of play and rest, of strolling, wading, digging, fishing, swimming, lying on the sand. Often the women sitting on the platform would call out to him in their high voices: "Tadziu! Tadziu!" and he would come running and waving his arms, eager to tell them what he had done, show them what he had found, what caught—shells, seahorses, jellyfish, and sidewards-running crabs. Aschenbach understood not a word he said; it might be the sheerest commonplace, in his ear it became mingled harmonies. Thus the lad's foreign birth raised his speech to music; a wanton sun showered splendour on him, and the noble distances of the sea formed the background which set off his figure.

Soon the observer knew every line and pose of this form that limned itself so freely against sea and sky; its every loveliness, though conned by heart, yet thrilled him each day afresh; his admiration knew no bounds, the delight of his eye was unending. Once the lad was summoned to speak to a guest who was waiting for his mother at their cabin. He ran up, ran dripping wet out of the sea, tossing his curls, and put out his hand, standing with his weight on one leg, resting the other foot on the toes; as he stood there in a posture of suspense the turn of his body was enchanting, while his features wore a look half shamefaced, half conscious of the duty breeding laid upon him to please. Or he would lie at full length, with his bath-robe around him, one slender young arm resting on the sand, his chin in the hollow of his hand; the lad they called Jaschiu squatting beside him, paying him court. There could be nothing lovelier on earth than the smile and look with which the playmate thus singled out rewarded his humble friend and vassal. Again, he might be at the water's edge, alone, removed from his family, quite close to Aschenbach; standing erect, his hands clasped at the back of his neck, rocking slowly on the balls of his feet, daydreaming away into blue space, while little waves ran up and bathed his toes. The ringlets of honey-coloured hair clung to his temples and neck, the fine down along the upper vertebræ was yellow in the sunlight; the thin envelope of flesh covering the torso betrayed the delicate outlines of the ribs and the symmetry of the breast-structure. His armpits were still as smooth as a statue's, smooth the glistening hollows behind the knees, where the blue network of veins suggested that the body was formed of some stuff more transparent than mere flesh. What discipline, what precision of thought were expressed by the tense youthful perfection of this form! And yet the pure, strong will which had laboured in darkness and succeeded in bringing this godlike work of art to the light of day—was it not known and familiar to him, the artist? Was not the same force at work in himself when he strove in cold fury to liberate from the marble mass of language the slender forms of his art which he saw with the eye of his mind and would body forth to men as the mirror and image of spiritual beauty?

Mirror and image! His eyes took in the proud bearing of that figure there at the blue water's edge; with an outburst of rapture he told himself that what he saw was beauty's very essence; form as divine thought, the single and pure perfection which resides in the mind, of which an image and likeness, rare and holy, was here raised up for adoration. This was very frenzy—and without a scruple, nay, eagerly, the aging artist bade it come. His mind was in travail, his whole mental background in a state of flux. Memory flung up in him the primitive thoughts which are youth's inheritance, but which with him had remained latent, never leaping up into a blaze. Has it not been written that the sun beguiles our attention from things of the intellect to fix it on things of the sense? The sun, they say, dazzles; so bewitching reason and memory that the soul for very pleasure forgets its actual state, to cling with doting on the loveliest of all the objects she shines on. Yes, and then it is only through the medium of some corporeal being that it can raise itself again to contemplation of higher things. Amor, in sooth, is like the mathematician who in order to give children a knowledge of pure form must do so in the language of pictures; so, too, the god, in order to make visible the spirit, avails himself of the forms and colours of human youth, gilding it with all imaginable beauty that it may serve memory as a tool, the very sight of which then sets us afire with pain and longing.

Such were the devotee's thoughts, such the power of his emotions. And the sea, so bright with glancing sunbeams, wove in his mind a spell and summoned up a lovely picture: there was the ancient plane-tree outside the walls of Athens, a hallowed, shady spot, fragrant with willow-blossom and adorned with images and votive offerings in honour of the nymphs and Achelous. Clear ran the smooth-pebbled stream at the foot of the spreading tree. Crickets were fiddling. But on the gentle grassy slope, where one could lie yet hold the head erect, and shelter from the scorching heat, two men reclined, an elder with a younger, ugliness paired with beauty and wisdom with grace. Here Socrates held forth to youthful Phædrus upon the nature of virtue and desire, wooing him with insinuating wit and charming turns of phrase. He told him of the shuddering and unwonted heat that come upon him whose heart is open, when his eye beholds an image of eternal beauty; spoke of the impious and corrupt, who cannot conceive beauty though they see its image, and are incapable of awe; and of the fear and reverence felt by the noble soul when he beholds a godlike face or a form which is a good image of beauty: how as he gazes he worships the beautiful one and scarcely dares to look upon him, but would offer sacrifice as to an idol or a god, did he not fear to be thought stark mad. "For beauty, my Phædrus, beauty alone, is lovely and visible at once. For, mark you, it is the sole aspect of the spiritual which we can perceive through our senses, or bear so to perceive. Else what should become of us, if the divine, if reason and virtue and truth, were to speak to us through the senses? Should we not perish and be consumed by love, as Semele aforetime was by Zeus? So beauty, then, is the beauty-lover's way to the spirit—but only the way, only the means, my little Phædrus." . . . And then, sly arch-lover that he was, he said the subtlest thing of all: that the lover was nearer the divine than the beloved; for the god was in the one but not in the other—perhaps the tenderest, most mocking thought that ever was thought, and source of all the guile and secret bliss the lover knows.

Thought that can merge wholly into feeling, feeling that can merge wholly into thought—these are the artist's highest joy. And our solitary felt in himself at this moment power to command and wield a thought that thrilled with emotion, an emotion as precise and concentrated as thought: namely, that nature herself shivers with ecstasy when the mind bows down in homage before beauty. He felt a sudden desire to write. Eros, indeed, we are told, loves idleness, and for idle hours alone was he created. But in this crisis the violence of our sufferer's seizure was directed almost wholly towards production, its occasion almost a matter of indifference. News had reached him on his travels that a certain problem had been raised, the intellectual world challenged for its opinion on a great and burning question of art and taste. By nature and experience the theme was his own; and he could not resist the temptation to set it off in the glistering foil of his words. He would write, and moreover he would write in Tadzio's presence. This lad should be in a sense his model, his style should follow the lines of this figure that seemed to him divine; he would snatch up this beauty into the realms of the mind, as once the eagle bore the Trojan shepherd aloft. Never had the pride of the word been so sweet to him, never had he known so well that Eros is in the word, as in those perilous and precious hours when he sat at his rude table, within the shade of his awning, his idol full in his view and the music of his voice in his ears, and fashioned his little essay after the model Tadzio's beauty set: that page and a half of choicest prose, so chaste, so lofty, so poignant with feeling, which would shortly be the wonder and admiration of the multitude. Verily it is well for the world that it sees only the beauty of the completed work and not its origins nor the conditions whence it sprang; since knowledge of the artist's inspiration might often but confuse and alarm and so prevent the full effect of its excellence. Strange hours, indeed, these were, and strangely unnerving the labour that filled them! Strangely fruitful intercourse this, between one body and another mind! When Aschenbach put aside his work and left the beach he felt exhausted, he felt broken—conscience reproached him, as it were after a debauch.

Next morning on leaving the hotel he stood at the top of the stairs leading down from the terrace and saw Tadzio in front of him on his way to the beach. The lad had just reached the gate in the railings, and he was alone. Aschenbach felt, quite simply, a wish to overtake him, to address him and have the pleasure of his reply and answering look; to put upon a blithe and friendly footing his relation with this being who all unconsciously had so greatly heightened and quickened his emotions. The lovely youth moved at a loitering pace—he might easily be overtaken; and Aschenbach hastened his own step. He reached him on the board walk that ran behind the bathing-cabins, and all but put out his hand to lay it on shoulder or head, while his lips parted to utter a friendly salutation in French. But—perhaps from the swift pace of his last few steps—he found his heart throbbing unpleasantly fast, while his breath came in such quick pants that he could only have gasped had he tried to speak. He hesitated, sought after self-control, was suddenly panic-stricken lest the boy notice him hanging there behind him and look round. Then he gave up, abandoned his plan, and passed him with bent head and hurried step.

"Too late! Too late!" he thought as he went by. But was it too late? This step he had delayed to take might so easily have put everything in a lighter key, have led to a sane recovery from his folly. But the truth may have been that the aging man did not want to be cured, that his illusion was far too dear to him. Who shall unriddle the puzzle of the artist nature? Who understands that mingling of discipline and licence in which it stands so deeply rooted? For not to be able to want sobriety is licentious folly. Aschenbach was no longer disposed to self-analysis. He had no taste for it; his self-esteem, the attitude of mind proper to his years, his maturity and single-mindedness, disinclined him to look within himself and decide whether it was constraint or puerile sensuality that had prevented him from carrying out his project. He felt confused, he was afraid someone, if only the watchman, might have been observing his behaviour and final surrender—very much he feared being ridiculous. And all the time he was laughing at himself for his serio-comic seizure. "Quite crestfallen," he thought. "I was like the gamecock that lets his wings droop in the battle. That must be the Love-God himself, that makes us hang our heads at sight of beauty and weighs our proud spirits low as the ground." Thus he played with the idea—he embroidered upon it, and was too arrogant to admit fear of an emotion.

The term he had set for his holiday passed by unheeded; he had no thought of going home. Ample funds had been sent him. His sole concern was that the Polish family might leave, and a chance question put to the hotel barber elicited the information that they had come only very shortly before himself. The sun browned his face and hands, the invigorating salty air heightened his emotional energies. Heretofore he had been wont to give out at once, in some new effort, the powers accumulated by sleep or food or outdoor air; but now the strength that flowed in upon him with each day of sun and sea and idleness he let go up in one extravagant gush of emotional intoxication.

His sleep was fitful; the priceless, equable days were divided one from the next by brief nights filled with happy unrest. He went, indeed, early to bed, for at nine o'clock, with the departure of Tadzio from the scene, the day was over for him. But in the faint greyness of the morning a tender pang would go through him as his heart was minded of its adventure; he could no longer bear his pillow and, rising, would wrap himself against the early chill and sit down by the window to await the sunrise. Awe of the miracle filled his soul new-risen from its sleep. Heaven, earth, and its waters yet lay enfolded in the ghostly, glassy pallor of dawn; one paling star still swam in the shadowy vast. But there came a breath, a winged word from far and inaccessible abodes, that Eros was rising from the side of her spouse; and there was that first sweet reddening of the farthest strip of sea and sky that manifests creation to man's sense. She neared, the goddess, ravisher of youth, who stole away Cleitos and Cephalus and, defying all the envious Olympians, tasted beautiful Orion's love. At the world's edge began a strewing of roses, a shining and a blooming ineffably pure; baby cloudlets hung illumined, like attendant amoretti, in the blue and blushful haze; purple effulgence fell upon the sea, that seemed to heave it forward on its welling waves; from horizon to zenith went great quivering thrusts like golden lances, the gleam became a glare; without a sound, with godlike violence, glow and glare and rolling flames streamed upwards, and with flying hoof-beats the steeds of the sun-god mounted the sky. The lonely watcher sat, the splendour of the god shone on him, he closed his eyes and let the glory kiss his lids. Forgotten feelings, precious pangs of his youth, quenched long since by the stern service that had been his life and now returned so strangely metamorphosed—he recognized them with a puzzled, wondering smile. He mused, he dreamed, his lips slowly shaped a name; still smiling, his face turned seawards and his hands lying folded in his lap, he fell asleep once more as he sat.

But that day, which began so fierily and festally, was not like other days; it was transmuted and gilded with mythical significance. For whence could come the breath, so mild and meaningful, like a whisper from higher spheres, that played about temple and ear? Troops of small feathery white clouds ranged over the sky, like grazing herds of the gods. A stronger wind arose, and Poseidon's horses ran up, arching their manes, among them too the steers of him with the purpled locks, who lowered their horns and bellowed as they came on; while like prancing goats the waves on the farther strand leaped among the craggy rocks. It was a world possessed, peopled by Pan, that closed round the spell-bound man, and his doting heart conceived the most delicate fancies. When the sun was going down behind Venice, he would sometimes sit on a bench in the park and watch Tadzio, white-clad, with gay-coloured sash, at play there on the rolled gravel with his ball; and at such times it was not Tadzio whom he saw, but Hyacinthus, doomed to die because two gods were rivals for his love. Ah, yes, he tasted the envious pangs that Zephyr knew when his rival, bow and cithara, oracle and all forgot, played with the beauteous youth; he watched the discus, guided by torturing jealousy, strike the beloved head; paled as he received the broken body in his arms, and saw the flower spring up, watered by that sweet blood and signed forevermore with his lament.

There can be no relation more strange, more critical, than that between two beings who know each other only with their eyes, who meet daily, yes, even hourly, eye each other with a fixed regard, and yet by some whim or freak of convention feel constrained to act like strangers. Uneasiness rules between them, unslaked curiosity, a hysterical desire to give rein to their suppressed impulse to recognize and address each other; even, actually, a sort of strained but mutual regard. For one human being instinctively feels respect and love for another human being so long as he does not know him well enough to judge him; and that he does not, the craving he feels is evidence.

Some sort of relation and acquaintanceship was perforce set up between Aschenbach and the youthful Tadzio; it was with a thrill of joy the older man perceived that the lad was not entirely unresponsive to all the tender notice lavished on him. For instance, what should move the lovely youth, nowadays when he descended to the beach, always to avoid the board walk behind the bathing-huts and saunter along the sand, passing Aschenbach's tent in front, sometimes so unnecessarily close as almost to graze his table or chair? Could the power of an emotion so beyond his own so draw, so fascinate its innocent object? Daily Aschenbach would wait for Tadzio. Then sometimes, on his approach, he would pretend to be preoccupied and let the charmer pass unregarded by. But sometimes he looked up, and their glances met; when that happened both were profoundly serious.

The elder's dignified and cultured mien let nothing appear of his inward state; but in Tadzio's eyes a question lay—he faltered in his step, gazed on the ground, then up again with that ineffably sweet look he had; and when he was past, something in his bearing seemed to say that only good breeding hindered him from turning round.

But once, one evening, it fell out differently. The Polish brother and sisters, with their governess, had missed the evening meal, and Aschenbach had noted the fact with concern. He was restive over their absence, and after dinner walked up and down in front of the hotel, in evening dress and a straw hat; when suddenly he saw the nunlike sisters with their companion appear in the light of the arc-lamps, and four paces behind them Tadzio. Evidently they came from the steamer-landing, having dined for some reason in Venice. It had been chilly on the lagoon, for Tadzio wore a dark-blue reefer-jecket with gilt buttons, and a cap to match. Sun and sea air could not burn his skin, it was the same creamy marble hue as at first—though he did look a little pale, either from the cold or in the bluish moonlight of the arc-lamps. The shapely brows were so delicately drawn, the eyes so deeply dark—lovelier he was than words could say, and as often the thought visited Aschenbach, and brought its own pang, that language could but extol, not reproduce, the beauties of the sense.

The sight of that dear form was unexpected, it had appeared unhoped-for, without giving him time to compose his features. Joy, surprise, and admiration might have painted themselves quite openly upon his face—and just at this second it happened that Tadzio smiled. Smiled at Aschenbach, unabashed and friendly, a speaking, winning, captivating smile, with slowly parting lips. With such a smile it might be that Narcissus bent over the mirroring pool a smile profound, infatuated, lingering, as he put out his arms to the reflection of his own beauty; the lips just slightly pursed, perhaps half-realizing his own folly in trying to kiss the cold lips of his shadow—with a mingling of coquetry and curiosity and a faint unease, enthralling and enthralled.

Aschenbach received that smile and turned away with it as though entrusted with a fatal gift. So shaken was he that he had to flee from the lighted terrace and front gardens and seek out with hurried steps the darkness of the park at the rear. Reproaches strangely mixed of tenderness and remonstrance burst from him: "How dare you smile like that! No one is allowed to smile like that!" He flung himself on a bench, his composure gone to the winds, and breathed in the nocturnal fragrance of the garden. He leaned back, with hanging arms, quivering from head to foot, and quite unmanned he whispered the hackneyed phrase of love and longing—impossible in these circumstances, absurd, abject, ridiculous enough, yet sacred too, and not unworthy of honour even here: "I love you!"

In the fourth week of his stay on the Lido, Gustave von Aschenbach made certain singular observations touching the world about him. He noticed, in the first place, that though the season was approaching its height, yet the number of guests declined and, in particular, that the German tongue had suffered a rout, being scarcely or never heard in the land. At table and on the beach he caught nothing but foreign words. One day at the barber's—where he was now a frequent visitor—he heard something rather startling. The barber mentioned a German family who had just left the Lido after a brief stay, and rattled on in his obsequious way: "The signore is not leaving—he has no fear of the sickness, has he?" Aschenbach looked at him. "The sickness?" he repeated. Whereat the prattler fell silent, became very busy all at once, affected not to hear. When Aschenbach persisted he said he really knew nothing at all about it, and tried in a fresh burst of eloquence to drown the embarrassing subject.

That was one forenoon. After luncheon Aschenbach had himself ferried across to Venice, in a dead calm, under a burning sun; driven by his mania, he was following the Polish young folk, whom he had seen with their companion, taking the way to the landing-stage. He did not find his idol on the Piazza. But as he sat there at tea, at a little round table on the shady side, suddenly he noticed a peculiar odour, which, it seemed to him now, had been in the air for days without his being aware: a sweetish, medicinal smell, associated with wounds and disease and suspect cleanliness. He sniffed and pondered and at length recognized it; finished his tea and left the square at the end facing the cathedral. In the narrow space the stench grew stronger. At the street corners placards were stuck up, in which the city authorities warned the population against the danger of certain infections of the gastric system, prevalent during the heated season; advising them not to eat oysters or other shell-fish and not to use the canal waters. The ordinance showed every sign of minimizing an existing situation. Little groups of people stood about silently in the squares and on the bridges; the traveller moved among them, watched and listened and thought.

He spoke to a shopkeeper lounging at his door among dangling coral necklaces and trinkets of artificial amethyst, and asked him about the disagreeable odour. The man looked at him, heavy-eyed, and hastily pulled himself together. "Just a formal precaution, signore," he said, with a gesture. "A police regulation we have to put up with. The air is sultry—the sirocco is not wholesome, as the signore knows. Just a precautionary measure, you understand—probably unnecessary. . . ." Aschenbach thanked him and passed on. And on the boat that bore him back to the Lido he smelt the germicide again.

On reaching his hotel he sought the table in the lobby and buried himself in the newspapers. The foreign-language sheets had nothing. But in the German papers certain rumours were mentioned, statistics given, then officially denied, then the good faith of the denials called in question. The departure of the German and Austrian contingent was thus made plain. As for other nationals, they knew or suspected nothing—they were still undisturbed. Aschenbach tossed the newspapers back on the table. "It ought to be kept quiet," he thought, aroused. "It should not be talked about." And he felt in his heart a curious elation at these events impending in the world about him. Passion is like crime: it does not thrive on the established order and the common round; it welcomes every blow dealt the bourgeois structure, every weakening of the social fabric, because therein it feels a sure hope of its own advantage. These things that were going on in the unclean alleys of Venice, under cover of an official hushing-up policy—they gave Aschenbach a dark satisfaction. The city's evil secret mingled with the one in the depths of his heart—and he would have staked all he possessed to keep it, since in his infatuation he cared for nothing but to keep Tadzio here, and owned to himself not without horror, that he could not exist were the lad to pass from his sight.

He was no longer satisfied to owe his communion with his charmer to chance and the routine of hotel life; he had begun to follow and waylay him. On Sundays, for example, the Polish family never appeared on the beach. Aschenbach guessed they went to mass at San Marco and pursued them thither. He passed from the glare of the Piazza into the golden twilight of the holy place and found him he sought bowed in worship over a prie-dieu. He kept in the background, standing on the fissured mosaic pavement among the devout populace, that knelt and muttered and made the sign of the cross; and the crowded splendour of the oriental temple weighed voluptuously on his sense. A heavily ornate priest intoned and gesticulated before the altar, where little candle-flames flickered helplessly in the reek of incense-breathing smoke; and with that cloying sacrificial smell another seemed to mingle—the odour of the sickened city. But through all the glamour and glitter Aschenbach saw the exquisite creature there in front turn his head, seek out and meet his lover's eye.

The crowd streamed out through the portals into the brilliant square thick with fluttering doves, and the fond fool stood aside in the vestibule on the watch. He saw the Polish family leave the church. The children took ceremonial leave of their mother, and she turned towards the Piazzetta on her way home, while his charmer and the cloistered sisters, with their governess, passed beneath the clock tower into the Merceria. When they were a few paces on, he followed—he stole behind them on their walk through the city. When they paused, he did so too; when they turned round, he fled into inns and courtyards to let them pass.

Once he lost them from view, hunted feverishly over bridges and in filthy *culs-de-sac,* only to confront them suddenly in a narrow passage whence there was no escape, and experience a moment of panic fear. Yet it would be untrue to say he suffered. Mind and heart were drunk with passion, his footsteps guided by the dæmonic power whose pastime it is to trample on human reason and dignity.

Tadzio and his sisters at length took a gondola. Aschenbach hid behind a portico or fountain while they embarked, and directly they pushed off did the same. In a furtive whisper he told the boatman he would tip him well to follow at a little distance the other gondola, just rounding a corner, and fairly sickened at the man's quick, sly grasp and ready acceptance of the go-between's rôle.

Leaning back among soft, black cushions he swayed gently in the wake of the other black-snouted bark, to which the strength of his passion chained him. Sometimes it passed from his view, and then he was assailed by an anguish of unrest. But his guide appeared to have long practice in affairs like these; always, by dint of short cuts or deft manœuvres, he contrived to overtake the coveted sight. The air was heavy and foul, the sun burnt down through a slate-coloured haze. Water slapped gurgling against wood and stone. The gondolier's cry, half warning, half salute, was answered with singular accord from far within the silence of the labyrinth. They passed little gardens, high up the crumbling wall, hung with clustering white and purple flowers that sent down an odour of almonds. Moorish lattices showed shadowy in the gloom. The marble steps of a church descended into the canal, and on them a beggar squatted, displaying his misery to view, showing the whites of his eyes, holding out his hat for alms. Farther on a dealer in antiquities cringed before his lair, inviting the passer-by to enter and be duped. Yes, this was Venice, this the fair frailty that fawned and that betrayed, half fairy-tale, half snare; the city in whose stagnating air the art of painting once put forth so lusty a growth, and where musicians were moved to accords so weirdly lulling and lascivious. Our adventurer felt his senses wooed by this voluptuousness of sight and sound, tasted his secret knowledge that the city sickened and hid its sickness for love of gain, and bent an ever more unbridled leer on the gondola that glided on before him.

It came at last to this—that his frenzy left him capacity for nothing else but to pursue his flame; to dream of him absent, to lavish, loverlike, endearing terms on his mere shadow. He was alone, he was a foreigner, he was sunk deep in this belated bliss of his—all which enabled him to pass unblushing through experiences well-nigh unbelievable. One night, returning late from Venice, he paused by his beloved's chamber door in the second storey, leaned his head against the panel, and remained there long, in utter drunkenness, powerless to tear himself away, blind to the danger of being caught in so mad an attitude.

And yet there were not wholly lacking moments when he paused and reflected, when in consternation he asked himself what path was this on which he had set his foot. Like most other men of parts and attainments, he had an aristocratic interest in his forbears, and when he achieved a success he liked to think he had gratified them, compelled their admiration and regard. He thought of them now, involved as he was in this illicit adventure, seized of these exotic excesses of feeling; thought of their stern self-command and decent manliness, and gave a melancholy smile. What would they have said? What, indeed, would they have said to his entire life, that varied to the point of degeneracy from theirs? This life in the bonds of art, had not he himself, in the days of youth and in the very spirit of those bourgeois forefathers, pronounced mocking judgment upon it? And yet, at bottom, it had been so like their own! It had been a service, and he a soldier, like some of them; and art was war—a grilling, exhausting struggle that nowadays wore one out before one could grow old. It had been a life of self-conquest, a life against odds, dour, steadfast, abstinent; he had made it symbolical of the kind of over-strained heroism the time admired, and he was entitled to call it manly, even courageous. He wondered if such a life might not be somehow specially pleasing in the eyes of the god who had him in his power. For Eros had received most countenance among the most valiant nations—

yes, were we not told that in their cities prowess made him flourish exceedingly? And many heroes of olden time had willingly borne his yoke, not counting any humiliation such if it happened by the god's decree; vows, prostrations, self-abasements, these were no source of shame to the lover; rather they reaped him praise and honour.

Thus did the fond man's folly condition his thoughts; thus did he seek to hold his dignity upright in his own eyes. And all the while he kept doggedly on the traces of the disreputable secret the city kept hidden at its heart, just as he kept his own—and all that he learned fed his passion with vague, lawless hopes. He turned over newspapers at cafés, bent on finding a report on the progress of the disease; and in the German sheets, which had ceased to appear on the hotel table, he found a series of contradictory statements. The deaths, it was variously asserted, ran to twenty, to forty, to a hundred or more; yet in the next day's issue the existence of the pestilence was, if not roundly denied, reported as a matter of a few sporadic cases such as might be brought into a seaport town. After that the warnings would break out again, and the protests against the unscrupulous game the authorities were playing. No definite information was to be had.

And yet our solitary felt he had a sort of first claim on a share in the unwholesome secret; he took a fantastic satisfaction in putting leading questions to such persons as were interested to conceal it, and forcing them to explicit untruths by way of denial. One day he attacked the manager, that small, soft-stepping man in the French frock-coat, who was moving about among the guests at luncheon, supervising the service and making himself socially agreeable. He paused at Aschenbach's table to exchange a greeting, and the guest put a question, with a negligent, casual air: "Why in the world are they forever disinfecting the city of Venice?" "A police regulation," the adroit one replied; "a precautionary measure, intended to protect the health of the public during this unseasonably warm and sultry weather." "Very praiseworthy of the police," Aschenbach gravely responded. After a further exchange of meteorological commonplaces the manager passed on.

It happened that a band of street musicians came to perform in the hotel gardens that evening after dinner. They grouped themselves beneath an iron stanchion supporting an arc-light, two women and two men, and turned their faces, that shone white in the glare, up towards the guests who sat on the hotel terrace enjoying this popular entertainment along with their coffee and iced drinks. The hotel lift-boys, waiters, and office staff stood in the doorway and listened; the Russian family displayed the usual Russian absorption in their enjoyment—they had their chairs put down into the garden to be nearer the singers and sat there in a half-circle with gratitude painted on their features, the old serf in her turban erect behind their chairs.

These strolling players were adepts at mandolin, guitar, harmonica, even compassing a reedy violin. Vocal numbers alternated with instrumental, the younger woman, who had a high shrill voice, joining in a love-duet with the sweetly falsettoing tenor. The actual head of the company, however, and incontestably its most gifted member, was the other man, who played the guitar. He was a sort of baritone buffo; with no voice to speak of, but possessed of a pantomimic gift and remarkable burlesque *élan*. Often he stepped out of the group and advanced towards the terrace, guitar in hand, and his audience rewarded his sallies with bursts of laughter. The Russians in their parterre seats were beside themselves with delight over this display of southern vivacity; their shouts and screams of applause encouraged him to bolder and bolder flights.

Aschenbach sat near the balustrade, a glass of pomegranate-juice and soda-water sparkling ruby-red before him, with which he now and then moistened his lips. His nerves drank in thirstily the unlovely sounds, the vulgar and sentimental tunes, for passion paralyses good taste and makes its victim accept with rapture what a man in his senses would either laugh at or turn from with disgust. Idly he sat and watched the antics of the buffoon with his face set in a fixed and painful smile, while inwardly his whole being was rigid with the intensity of the regard he bent on Tadzio, leaning over the railing six paces off.

He lounged there, in the white belted suit he sometimes wore at dinner, in all his innate, inevitable grace, with his left arm on the balustrade, his legs crossed, the right hand on the supporting hip; and looked down on the strolling singers with an expression that was hardly a smile, but rather a distant curiosity and polite toleration. Now and then he straightened himself and with a charming movement of both arms drew down his white blouse through his leather belt, throwing out his chest. And sometimes—Aschenbach saw it with triumph, with horror, and a sense that his reason was tottering—the lad would cast a glance, that might be slow and cautious, or might be sudden and swift, as though to take him by surprise, to the place where his lover sat. Aschenbach did not meet the glance. An ignoble caution made him keep his eyes in leash. For in the rear of the terrace sat Tadzio's mother and governess; and matters had gone so far that he feared to make himself conspicuous. Several times, on the beach, in the hotel lobby, on the Piazza, he had seen, with a stealing numbness, that they called Tadzio away from his neighborhood. And his pride revolted at the affront, even while conscience told him it was deserved.

The performer below presently began a solo, with guitar accompaniment, a street song in several stanzas, just then the rage all over Italy. He delivered it in a striking and dramatic recitative, and his company joined in the refrain. He was a man of slight build, with a thin, undernourished face; his shabby felt hat rested on the back of his neck, a great mop of red hair sticking out in front; and he stood there on the gravel in advance of his troupe, in an impudent, swaggering posture, twanging the strings of his instrument and flinging a witty and rollicking recitative up to the terrace, while the veins of his forehead swelled with the violence of his effort. He was scarcely a Venetian type, belonging rather to the race of Neapolitan jesters, half bully, half comedian, brutal, blustering, an unpleasant customer, and entertaining to the last degree. The words of his song were trivial and silly, but on his lips, accompanied with gestures of head, hands, arms, and body, with leers and winks and the loose play of the tongue in the corner of his mouth, they took on meaning, an equivocal meaning, yet vaguely offensive. He wore a white sports shirt with a suit of ordinary clothes, and a strikingly large and naked-looking Adam's apple rose out of the open collar. From that pale, snub-nosed face it was hard to judge of his age; vice sat on it, it was furrowed with grimacing, and two deep wrinkles of defiance and self-will, almost of desperation, stood oddly between the red brows, above the grinning, mobile mouth. But what more than all drew upon him the profound scrutiny of our solitary watcher was that this suspicious figure seemed to carry with it its own suspicious odour. For whenever the refrain occurred and the singer, with waving arms and antic gestures, passed in his grotesque march immediately beneath Aschenbach's seat, a strong smell of carbolic was wafted up to the terrace.

After the song he began to take up money, beginning with the Russian family, who gave liberally, and then mounting the steps to the terrace. But here he became as cringing as he had before been forward. He glided between the tables, bowing and scraping, showing his strong white teeth in a servile smile, though the two deep furrows on the brow were still very marked. His audience looked at the strange creature as he went about collecting his livelihood, and their curiosity was not unmixed with disfavor. They tossed coins with their finger-tips into his hat and took care not to touch it. Let the enjoyment be never so great, a sort of embarrassment always comes when the comedian oversteps the physical distance between himself and respectable people. This man felt it and sought to make his peace by fawning. He came along the railing to Aschenbach, and with him came that smell no one else seemed to notice.

"Listen!" said the solitary, in a low voice, almost mechanically; "they are disinfecting Venice—why?" The mountebank answered hoarsely: "Because of the police. Orders, signore. On account of the heat and the sirocco. The sirocco is oppressive. Not good for the health." He spoke as though surprised that anyone could ask, and with the flat of his hand he demonstrated how oppressive the sirocco was. "So there is no plague in Venice?" Aschenbach asked the question between his teeth, very low. The man's expressive face fell, he put on a look of comical innocence. "A plague? What sort of plague? Is the sirocco a plague? Or perhaps our police are a plague! You are making fun of us, signore! A plague! Why should there be? The police make regulations on account of the heat and the weather. . . ." He gestured. "Quite," said Aschenbach, once more, soft and low; and dropping an unduly large coin into the man's hat dismissed him with a sign. He bowed very low and left. But he had not reached the steps when two of the hotel servants flung themselves on him and began to whisper, their faces close to his. He shrugged, seemed to be giving assurances, to be swearing he had said nothing. It was not hard to guess the import of his words. They let him go at last and he went back into the garden, where he conferred briefly with his troupe and then stepped forward for a farewell song.

It was one Aschenbach had never to his knowledge heard before, a rowdy air, with words in impossible dialect. It had a laughing-refrain in which the other three artists joined at the top of their lungs. The refrain had neither words nor accompaniment, it was nothing but rhythmical, modulated, natural laughter, which the soloist in particular knew how to render with most deceptive realism. Now that he was farther off his audience, his self-assurance had come back, and this laughter of his rang with a mocking note. He would be overtaken, before he reached the end of the last line of each stanza; he would catch his breath, lay his hand over his mouth, his voice would quaver and his shoulders shake, he would lose power to contain himself longer. Just at the right moment each time, it came whooping, bawling, crashing out of him, with a verisimilitude that never failed to set his audience off in profuse and unpremeditated mirth that seemed to add gusto to his own. He bent his knees, he clapped his thigh, he held his sides, he looked ripe for bursting. He no longer laughed, but yelled, pointing his finger at the company there above as though there could be in all the world nothing so comic as they; until at last they laughed in hotel, terrace, and garden, down to the waiters, lift-boys, and servants—laughed as though possessed.

Aschenbach could no longer rest in his chair, he sat poised for flight. But the combined effect of the laughing, the hospital odour in his nostrils, and the nearness of the beloved was to hold him in a spell; he felt unable to stir. Under cover of the general commotion he looked across at Tadzio and saw that the lovely boy returned his gaze with a seriousness that seemed the copy of his own; the general hilarity, it seemed to say, had no power over him, he kept aloof. The grey-haired man was overpowered, disarmed by this docile, childlike deference; with difficulty he refrained from hiding his face in his hands. Tadzio's habit, too, of drawing himself up and taking a deep sighing breath struck him as being due to an oppression of the chest. "He is sickly, he will never live to grow up," he thought once again, with that dispassionate vision to which his madness of desire sometimes so strangely gave way. And compassion struggled with the reckless exultation of his heart.

The players, meanwhile, had finished and gone; their leader bowing and scraping, kissing his hands and adorning his leave-taking with antics that grew madder with the applause they evoked. After all the others were outside, he pretended to run backwards full tilt against a lamp-post and slunk to the gate apparently doubled over with pain. But there he threw off his buffoon's mask, stood erect, with an elastic straightening of his whole figure, ran out his tongue impudently at the guests on the terrace, and vanished in the night. The company dispersed. Tadzio had long since left the balustrade. But he, the lonely man, sat for long, to the waiters' great annoyance, before the dregs of pomegranate-juice in his glass. Time passed, the night went on. Long ago, in his parental home, he had watched the sand filter through an hourglass—he could still see, as though it stood before him, the fragile, pregnant little toy. Soundless and fine the rust-red streamlet ran through the narrow neck, and made, as it declined in the upper cavity, an exquisite little vortex.

The very next afternoon the solitary took another step in pursuit of his fixed policy of baiting the outer world. This time he had all possible success. He went, that is, into the English travel bureau in the Piazza, changed some money at the desk, and posing as the suspicious foreigner, put his fateful question. The clerk was a tweed-clad young Britisher, with his eyes set close together, his hair parted in the middle, and radiating that steady reliability which makes his like so strange a phenomenon in the *gamin,* agile-witted south. He began: "No ground for alarm, sir. A mere formality. Quite regular in view of the unhealthy climatic conditions." But then, looking up, he chanced to meet with his own blue eyes the stranger's weary, melancholy gaze, fixed on his face. The Englishman coloured. He continued in a lower voice, rather confused: "At least, that is the official explanation, which they see fit to stick to. I may tell you there's a bit more to it than that." And then, in his good, straightforward way, he told the truth.

For the past several years Asiatic cholera had shown a strong tendency to spread. Its source was the hot, moist swamps of the delta of the Ganges, where it bred in the mephitic air of that primeval island-jungle, among whose bamboo thickets the tiger crouches, where life of every sort flourishes in rankest abundance, and only man avoids the spot. Thence the pestilence had spread throughout Hindustan, raging with great violence; moved eastward to China, westward to Afghanistan and Persia; following the great caravan routes, it brought terror to Astrakhan, terror to Moscow. Even while Europe trembled lest the spectre be seen striding westward across country, it was carried by sea from Syrian ports and appeared simultaneously at several points on the Mediterranean littoral; raised its head in Toulon and Malaga, Palermo and Naples, and soon got a firm hold in Calabria and Apulia. Northern Italy had been spared—so far. But in May the horrible vibrions were found on the same day in two bodies: the emaciated, blackened corpses of a bargee and a woman who kept a green-grocer's shop. Both cases were hushed up. But in a week there were ten more—twenty, thirty in different quarters of the town. An Austrian provincial, having come to Venice on a few days' pleasure trip, went home and died with all the symptoms of the plague. Thus was explained the fact that the German-language papers were the first to print the news of the Venetian outbreak. The Venetian authorities published in reply a statement to the effect that the state of the city's health had never been better; at the same time instituting the most necessary precautions. But by that time the food supplies—milk, meat, or vegetables—had probably been contaminated, for death unseen and unacknowledged was devouring and laying waste in the narrow streets, while a brooding, unseasonable heat warmed the waters of the canals and encouraged the spread of the pestilence. Yes, the disease seemed to flourish and wax strong, to redouble its generative powers. Recoveries were rare. Eighty out of every hundred died, and horribly, for the onslaught was of the extremest violence, and not infrequently of the "dry" type, the most malignant form of the contagion. In this form the victim's body loses power to expel the water secreted by the blood-vessels, it shrivels up, he passes with hoarse cries from convulsion to convulsion, his blood grows thick like pitch, and he suffocates in a few hours. He is fortunate indeed, if, as sometimes happens, the disease, after a slight *malaise,* takes the form of a profound unconsciousness, from which the sufferer seldom or never rouses. By the beginning of June the quarantine buildings of the *ospedale civico* had quietly filled up, the two orphan asylums were entirely occupied, and there was a hideously brisk traffic between the *Nuovo Fundamento* and the island of San Michele, where the cemetery was. But the city was not swayed by high-minded motives or regard for international agreements. The authorities were more actuated by fear of being out of pocket, by regard for the new exhibition of paintings just opened in the Public Gardens, or by apprehension of the large losses the hotels and the shops that catered to foreigners would suffer in case of panic and blockade. And the fears of the people supported the persistent official policy of silence and denial. The city's first medical officer, an honest and competent man, had indignantly resigned his office and been privily replaced by a more compliant person. The fact was known; and this corruption in high places played its part, together with the suspense as to where the walking terror might strike next, to demoralize the baser elements in the city and encourage those antisocial forces which shun the light of day. There was intemperance, indecency, increase of crime. Evenings one saw many drunken people which was unusual. Gangs of men in surly mood made the streets unsafe, theft and assault were said to be frequent, even murder; for in two cases persons supposedly victims of the plague were proved to have been poisoned by their own families. And professional vice was rampant, displaying excesses heretofore unknown and only at home much farther south and in the east.

Such was the substance of the Englishman's tale. "You would do well," he concluded, "to leave today instead of tomorrow. The blockade cannot be more than a few days off."

"Thank you," said Aschenbach, and left the office.

The Piazza lay in sweltering sunshine. Innocent foreigners sat before the cafés or stood in front of the cathedral, the centre of clouds of doves that, with fluttering wings, tried to shoulder each other away and pick the kernels of maize from the extended hand. Aschenbach strode up and down the spacious flags, feverishly excited, triumphant in possession of the truth at last, but with a sickening taste in his mouth and a fantastic horror at his heart. One decent, expiatory course lay open to him; he considered it. Tonight, after dinner, he might approach the lady of the pearls and address her in words which he precisely formulated in his mind: "Madame, will you permit an entire stranger to serve you with a word of advice and warning which self-interest prevents others from uttering? Go away. Leave here at once, without delay, with Tadzio and your daughters. Venice is in the grip of pestilence." Then might he lay his hand in farewell upon the head of that instrument of a mocking deity; and thereafter himself flee the accursed morass. But he knew that he was far indeed from any serious desire to take such a step. It would restore him, would give him back himself once more; but he who is beside himself revolts at the idea of self-possession. There crossed his mind the vision of a white building with inscriptions on it, glittering in the sinking sun—he recalled how his mind had dreamed away into their transparent mysticism; recalled the strange pilgrim apparition that had wakened in the aging man a lust for strange countries and fresh sights. And these memories, again, brought in their train the thought of returning home, returning to reason, self-mastery, an ordered existence, to the old life of effort. Alas! the bare thought made him wince with a revulsion that was like physical nausea. "It must be kept quiet," he whispered fiercely. "I will not speak!" The knowledge that he shared the city's secret, the city's guilt—it put him beside himself, intoxicated him as a small quantity of wine will a man suffering from brain-fag. His thoughts dwelt upon the image of the desolate and calamitous city, and he was giddy with fugitive, mad, unreasoning hopes and visions of a monstrous sweetness. That tender sentiment he had a moment ago evoked, what was it compared with such images as these? His art, his moral sense, what were they in the balance beside the boons that chaos might confer? He kept silence, he stopped on.

That night he had a fearful dream—if dream be the right word for a mental and physical experience which did indeed befall him in deep sleep, as a thing quite apart and real to his senses, yet without his seeing himself as present in it. Rather its theatre seemed to be his own soul, and the events burst in from outside, violently overcoming the profound resistance of his spirit; passed him through and left him, left the whole cultural structure of a lifetime trampled on, ravaged, and destroyed.

The beginning was fear; fear and desire, with a shuddering curiosity. Night reigned, and his senses were on the alert; he heard loud, confused noises from far away, clamour and hubbub. There was a rattling, a crashing, a low dull thunder; shrill halloos and a kind of howl with a long-drawn *u*-sound at the end. And with all these, dominating them all, flute-notes of the cruellest sweetness, deep and cooing, keeping shamelessly on until the listener felt his very entrails betwitched. He heard a voice, naming, though darkly, that which was to come: "The stranger god!" A glow lighted up the surrounding mist and by it he recognized a mountain scene like that about his country home. From the wooded heights, from among the tree-trunks and crumbling moss-covered rocks, a troop came tumbling and raging down, a whirling rout of men and animals, and overflowed the hillside with flames and human forms, with clamour and the reeling dance. The females stumbled over the long, hairy pelts that dangled from their girdles; with heads flung back they uttered loud hoarse cries and shook their tambourines high in air; brandished naked daggers or torches vomiting trails of sparks. They shrieked, holding their breasts in both hands; coiling snakes with quivering tongues they clutched about their waists. Horned and hairy males, girt about the loins with hides, drooped heads and lifted arms and thighs in unison, as they beat on brazen vessels that gave out droning thunder, or thumped madly on drums. There were troops of beardless youths armed with garlanded staves; these ran after goats and thrust their staves against the creatures' flanks, then clung to the plunging horns and let themselves be borne off with triumphant shouts. And one and all the mad rout yelled that cry, composed of soft consonants with a long-drawn *u*-sound at the end, so sweet and wild it was together, and like nothing ever heard before! It would ring through the air like the bellow of a challenging stag, and be given back many-tongued; or they would use it to goad each other on to dance with wild excess of tossing limbs—they never let it die. But the deep, beguiling notes of the flute wove in and out and over all. Beguiling too it was to him who struggled in the grip of these sights and sounds, shamelessly awaiting the coming feast and the uttermost surrender. He trembled, he shrank, his will was steadfast to preserve and uphold his own god against this stranger who was sworn enemy to dignity and self-control. But the mountain wall took up the noise and howling and gave it back manifold; it rose high, swelled to a madness that carried him away. His senses reeled in the steam of panting bodies, the acrid stench from the goats, the odour as of stagnant waters—and another, too familiar smell—of wounds, uncleanness, and disease. His heart throbbed to the drums, his brain reeled, a blind rage seized him, a whirling lust, he craved with all his soul to join the ring that formed about the obscene symbol of the godhead, which they were unveiling and elevating, monstrous and wooden, while from full throats they yelled their rallying-cry. Foam dripped from their lips, they drove each other on with lewd gesturings and beckoning hands. They laughed, they howled, they thrust their pointed staves into each other's flesh and licked the blood as it ran down. But now the dreamer was in them and of them, the stranger god was his own. Yes, it was he who was flinging himself upon the animals, who bit and tore and swallowed smoking gobbets of flesh——while on the trampled moss there now began the rites in honour of the god, an orgy of promiscuous embraces—and in his very soul he tasted the bestial degradation of his fall.

The unhappy man woke from this dream shattered, unhinged, powerless in the demon's grip. He no longer avoided men's eyes nor cared whether he exposed himself to suspicion. And anyhow, people were leaving; many of the bathing-cabins stood empty, there were many vacant places in the dining-room, scarcely any foreigners were seen in the streets. The truth seemed to have leaked out; despite all efforts to the contrary, panic was in the air. But the lady of the pearls stopped on with her family; whether because the rumours had not reached her or because she was too proud and fearless to heed them. Tadzio remained; and it seemed at times to Aschenbach, in his obsessed state, that death and fear together might clear the island of all other souls and leave him there alone with him he coveted. In the long mornings on the beach his heavy gaze would rest, a fixed and reckless stare, upon the lad; towards nightfall, lost to shame, he would follow him through the city's narrow streets where horrid death stalked too, and at such time it seemed to him as though the moral law were fallen in ruins and only the monstrous and perverse held out a hope.

Like any lover, he desired to please; suffered agonies at the thought of failure, and brightened his dress with smart ties and handkerchiefs and other youthful touches. He added jewellery and perfumes and spent hours each day over his toilette, appearing at dinner elaborately arrayed and tensely excited. The presence of the youthful beauty that had bewitched him filled him with disgust of his own aging body; the sight of his own sharp features and grey hair plunged him in hopeless mortification; he made desperate efforts to recover the appearance and freshness of his youth and began paying frequent visits to the hotel barber. Enveloped in the white sheet, beneath the hands of that garrulous personage, he would lean back in the chair and look at himself in the glass with misgiving.

"Grey," he said, with a grimace.

"Slightly," answered the man. "Entirely due to neglect, to a lack of regard for appearances. Very natural, of course, in men of affairs, but, after all, not very sensible, for it is just such people who ought to be above vulgar prejudice in matters like these. Some folk have very strict ideas about the use of cosmetics; but they never extend them to the teeth, as they logically should. And very disgusted other people would be if they did. No, we are all as old as we feel, but no older, and grey hair can misrepresent a man worse than dyed. You, for instance, signore, have a right to your natural colour. Surely you will permit me to restore what belongs to you?"

"How?" asked Aschenbach.

For answer the oily one washed his client's hair in two waters, one clear and one dark, and lo, it was as black as in the days of his youth. He waved it with the tongs in wide, flat undulations, and stepped back to admire the effect.

"Now if we were just to freshen up the skin a little," he said.

And with that he went on from one thing to another, his enthusiasm waxing with each new idea. Aschenbach sat there comfortably; he was incapable of objecting to the process—rather as it went forward it roused his hopes. He watched it in the mirror and saw his eyebrows grow more even and arching, the eyes gain in size and brilliance, by dint of a little application below the lids. A delicate carmine glowed on his cheeks where the skin had been so brown and leathery. The dry, anæmic lips grew full, they turned the colour of ripe strawberries, the lines round eyes and mouth were treated with a facial cream and gave place to youthful bloom. It was a young man who looked back at him from the glass—Aschenbach's heart leaped at the sight. The artist in cosmetic at last professed himself satisfied; after the manner of such people, he thanked his client profusely for what he had done himself. "The merest trifle, the merest, signore," he said as he added the final touches. "Now the signore can fall in love as soon as he likes." Aschenbach went off as in a dream, dazed between joy and fear, in his red neck-tie and broad straw hat with its gay striped band.

A lukewarm storm-wind had come up. It rained a little now and then, the air was heavy and turbid and smelt of decay. Aschenbach, with fevered cheeks beneath the rouge, seemed to hear rushing and flapping sounds in his ears, as though storm-spirits were abroad—unhallowed ocean harpies who follow those devoted to destruction, snatch away and defile their viands. For the heat took away his appetite and thus he was haunted with the idea that his food was infected.

One afternoon he pursued his charmer deep into the stricken city's huddled heart. The labyrinthine little streets, squares, canals, and bridges, each one so like the next, at length quite made him lose his bearings. He did not even know the points of the compass; all his care was not to lose sight of the figure after which his eyes thirsted. He slunk under walls, he lurked behind buildings or people's backs; and the sustained tension of his senses and emotions exhausted him more and more, though for a long time he was unconscious of fatigue. Tadzio walked behind the others, he let them pass ahead in the narrow alleys, and as he sauntered slowly after, he would turn his head and assure himself with a glance of his strange, twilit grey eyes that his lover was still following. He saw him—and he did not betray him. The knowledge enraptured Aschenbach. Lured by those eyes, led on the leading-string of his own passion and folly, utterly lovesick, he stole upon the footsteps of his unseemly hope—and at the end found himself cheated. The Polish family crossed a small vaulted bridge, the height of whose archway hid them from his sight, and when he climbed it himself they were nowhere to be seen. He hunted in three directions—straight ahead and on both sides the narrow, dirty quay—in vain. Worn quite out and unnerved, he had to give over the search.

His head burned, his body was wet with clammy sweat, he was plagued by intolerable thirst. He looked about for refreshment, of whatever sort, and found a little fruit-shop where he bought some strawberries. They were overripe and soft; he ate them as he went. The street he was on opened out into a little square, one of those charmed, forsaken spots he liked; he recognized it as the very one where he had sat weeks ago and conceived his abortive plan of flight. He sank down on the steps of the well and leaned his head against its stone rim. It was quiet here. Grass grew between the stones, and rubbish lay about. Tall, weather-beaten houses bordered the square, one of them rather palatial, with vaulted windows, gaping now, and little lion balconies. In the ground floor of another was an apothecary's shop. A waft of carbolic acid was borne on a warm gust of wind.

There he sat, the master; this was he who had found a way to reconcile art and honours; who had written *The Abject,* in a style of classic purity renounced bohemianism and all its works, all sympathy with the abyss and the troubled depths of the outcast human soul. This was he who had put knowledge underfoot to climb so high; who had outgrown the ironic pose and adjusted himself to the burdens and obligations of fame; whose renown had been officially recognized and his name ennobled, whose style was set for a model in the schools. There he sat. His eyelids were closed, there was only a swift, sidelong glint of the eyeballs now and again, something between a question and a leer; while the rouged and flabby mouth uttered single words of the sentences shaped in his disordered brain by the fantastic logic that governs our dreams.

"For mark you, Phædrus, beauty alone is both divine and visible; and so it is the sense way, the artist's way, little Phædrus, to the spirit. But, now tell me, my dear boy, do you believe that such a man can ever attain wisdom and true manly worth, for whom the path to the spirit must lead through the senses? Or do you rather think—for I leave the point to you—that it is a path of perilous sweetness, a way of transgression, and must surely lead him who walks in it astray? For you know that we poets cannot walk the way of beauty without Eros as our companion and guide. We may be heroic after our fashion, disciplined warriors of our craft, yet are we all the women, for we exult in passion, and love is still our desire—our craving and our shame. And from this you will perceive that we poets can be neither wise nor worthy citizens. We must needs be wanton, must needs rove at large in the realm of feeling. Our magisterial style is all folly and pretence, our honourable repute a farce, the crowd's belief in us is merely laughable. And to teach youth, or the populace, by means of art is a dangerous practice and ought to be forbidden. For what good can an artist be as a teacher, when from his birth up he is headed direct for the pit? We may want to shun it and attain to honour in the world; but however we turn, it draws us still. So, then, since knowledge might destroy us, we will have none of it. For knowledge, Phædrus, does not make him who possesses it dignified or austere. Knowledge is all-knowing, understanding, forgiving; it takes up no position, sets no store by form. It has compassion with the abyss—it *is* the abyss. So we reject it, firmly, and henceforward our concern shall be with beauty only. And by beauty we mean simplicity, largeness, and renewed severity of discipline; we mean a return to detachment and to form. But detachment, Phædrus, and preoccupation with form lead to intoxication and desire, they may lead the noblest among us to frightful emotional excesses, which his own stern cult of the beautiful would make him the first to condemn. So they too, they too, lead to the bottomless pit. Yes, they lead us thither, I say, us who are poets—who by our natures are prone not to excellence but to excess. And now, Phædrus, I will go. Remain here; and only when you can no longer see me, then do you depart also."

A few days later Gustave Aschenbach left his hotel rather later than usual in the morning. He was not feeling well and had to struggle against spells of giddiness only half physical in their nature, accompanied by a swiftly mounting dread, a sense of futility and hopelessness—but whether this referred to himself or to the outer world he could not tell. In the lobby he saw a quantity of luggage lying strapped and ready; asked the porter whose it was, and received in answer the name he already knew he should hear—that of the Polish family. The expression of his ravaged features did not change; he only gave that quick lift of the head with which we sometimes receive the uninteresting answer to a casual query. But he put another: "When?" "After luncheon," the man replied. He nodded, and went down to the beach.

It was an unfriendly scene. Little crisping shivers ran all across the wide stretch of shallow water between the shore and the first sand-bank. The whole beach, once so full of colour and life, looked now autumnal, out of season; it was nearly deserted and not even very clean. A camera on a tripod stood at the edge of the water, apparently abandoned; its black cloth snapped in the freshening wind.

Tadzio was there, in front of his cabin, with the three or four playfellows still left him. Aschenbach set up his chair some halfway between the cabins and the water, spread a rug over his knees, and sat looking on. The game this time was unsupervised, the elders being probably busy with their packing, and it looked rather lawless and out-of-hand. Jaschiu, the sturdy lad in the belted suit, with the black, brilliantined hair, became angry at a handful of sand thrown in his eyes; he challenged Tadzio to a fight, which quickly ended in the downfall of the weaker. And perhaps the coarser nature saw here a chance to avenge himself at last, by one cruel act, for his long weeks of subserviency: the victor would not let the vanquished get up, but remained kneeling on Tadzio's back, pressing Tadzio's face into the sand—for so long a time that it seemed the exhausted lad might even suffocate. He made spasmodic efforts to shake the other off, lay still, and then began a feeble twitching. Just as Aschenbach was about to spring indignantly to the rescue, Jaschiu let his victim go. Tadzio, very pale, half sat up, and remained so, leaning on one arm, for several minutes, with darkening eyes and rumpled hair. Then he rose and walked slowly away. The others called him, at first gaily, then imploringly; he would not hear. Jaschiu was evidently overtaken by swift remorse; he followed his friend and tried to make his peace, but Tadzio motioned him back with a jerk of one shoulder and went down to the water's edge. He was barefoot and wore his striped linen suit with the red breast-knot.

There he stayed a little, with bent head, tracing figures in the wet sand with one toe; then stepped into the shallow water, which at its deepest did not wet his knees; waded idly through it and reached the sand-bar. Now he paused again, with his face turned seaward; and next began to move slowly leftwards along the narrow strip of sand the sea left bare. He paced there, divided by an expanse of water from the shore, from his mates by his moody pride; a remote and isolated figure, with floating locks, out there in sea and wind, against the misty inane. Once more he paused to look: with a sudden recollection, or by an impulse, he turned from the waist up, in an exquisite movement, one hand resting on his hip, and looked over his shoulder at the shore. The watcher sat just as he had sat that time in the lobby of the hotel when first the twilit grey eyes had met his own. He rested his head against the chair-back and followed the movements of the figure out there, then lifted it, as it were in answer to Tadzio's gaze. It sank on his breast, the eyes looked out beneath their lids, while his whole face took on the relaxed and brooding expression of deep slumber. It seemed to him the pale and lovely Summoner out there smiled at him and beckoned; as though, with the hand he lifted from his hip, he pointed outward as he hovered on before into an immensity of richest expectation. And, as so often before, he rose to follow.

Some minutes passed before anyone hastened to the aid of the elderly man sitting there collapsed in his chair. They bore him to his room. And before nightfall a shocked and respectful world received the news of his decease.

1911

TONIO KRÖGER

The winter sun, poor ghost of itself, hung milky and wan behind layers of cloud above the huddled roofs of the town. In the gabled streets it was wet and windy and there came in gusts a sort of soft hail, not ice, not snow.

School was out. The hosts of the released streamed over the paved court and out at the wrought-iron gate, where they broke up and hastened off right and left. Elder pupils held their books in a strap high on the left shoulder and rowed, right arm against the wind, towards dinner. Small people trotted gaily off, splashing the slush with their feet, the tools of learning rattling amain in their walrus-skin satchels. But one and all pulled off their caps and cast down their eyes in awe before the Olympian hat and ambrosial beard of a master moving homewards with measured stride. . . .

"Ah, there you are at last, Hans," said Tonio Kröger. He had been waiting a long time in the street and went up with a smile to the friend he saw coming out of the gate in talk with other boys and about to go off with them. . . . "What?" said Hans, and looked at Tonio. "Right-oh! We'll take a little walk, then."

Tonio said nothing and his eyes were clouded. Did Hans forget, had he only just remembered that they were to take a walk together today? And he himself had looked forward to it with almost incessant joy.

"Well, good-bye, fellows," said Hans Hansen to his comrades.

"I'm taking a walk with Kröger." And the two turned to their left, while the others sauntered off in the opposite direction.

Hans and Tonio had time to take a walk after school because in neither of their families was dinner served before four o'clock. Their fathers were prominent business men, who held public office and were of consequence in the town. Hans's people had owned for some generations the big wood-yards down by the river, where powerful machine-saws hissed and spat and cut up timber; while Tonio was the son of Consul Kröger, whose grain-sacks with the firm name in great black letters you might see any day driven through the streets; his large, old ancestral home was the finest house in all the town. The two friends had to keep taking off their hats to their many acquaintances; some folk did not even wait for the fourteen-year-old lads to speak first, as by rights they should.

Both of them carried their satchels across their shoulders and both were well and warmly dressed: Hans in a short sailor jacket, with the wide blue collar of his sailor suit turned out over shoulders and back, and Tonio in a belted grey overcoat. Hans wore a Danish sailor cap with black ribbons, beneath which streamed a shock of straw-coloured hair. He was uncommonly handsome and well built, broad in the shoulders and narrow in the hips, with keen, far-apart, steel-blue eyes; while beneath Tonio's round fur cap was a brunette face with the finely chiselled features of the south; the dark eyes, with delicate shadows and too heavy lids, looked dreamily and a little timorously on the world. Tonio's walk was idle and uneven, whereas the other's slim legs in their black stockings moved with an elastic, rhythmic tread.

Tonio did not speak. He suffered. His rather oblique brows were drawn together in a frown, his lips were rounded to whistle, he gazed into space with his head on one side. Posture and manner were habitual.

Suddenly Hans shoved his arm into Tonio's, with a sideways look—he knew very well what the trouble was. And Tonio, though he was silent for the next few steps, felt his heart soften.

"I hadn't forgotten, you see, Tonio," Hans said, gazing at the pavement, "I only thought it wouldn't come off today because it was so wet and windy. But I don't mind that at all, and it's jolly of you to have waited. I thought you had gone home, and I was cross. . . ."

Everything in Tonio leaped and jumped for joy at the words.

"All right; let's go over the wall," he said with a quaver in his voice. "Over the Millwall and the Holstenwall, and I'll go as far as your house with you, Hans. Then I'll have to walk back alone, but that doesn't matter; next time you can go round my way."

At bottom he was not really convinced by what Hans said; he quite knew the other attached less importance to this walk than he did himself. Yet he saw Hans was sorry for his remissness and willing to be put in a position to ask pardon, a pardon that Tonio was far indeed from withholding.

The truth was, Tonio loved Hans Hansen, and had already suffered much on his account. He who loves the more is the inferior and must suffer; in this hard and simple fact his fourteen-year-old soul had already been instructed by life; and he was so organized that he received such experiences consciously, wrote them down as it were inwardly, and even, in a certain way, took pleasure in them, though without ever letting them mould his conduct, indeed, or drawing any practical advantage from them. Being what he was, he found this knowledge far more important and far more interesting than the sort they made him learn in schools; yes, during his lesson hours in the vaulted Gothic classrooms he was mainly occupied in feeling his way about among these intuitions of his and penetrating them. The process gave him the same kind of satisfaction as that he felt when he moved about in his room with his violin—for he played the violin—and made the tones, brought out as softly as ever he knew how, mingle with the plashing of the fountain that leaped and danced down there in the garden beneath the branches of the old walnut tree.

The fountain, the old walnut tree, his fiddle, and away in the distance the North Sea, within sound of whose summer murmurings he spent his holidays—these were the things he loved, within these he enfolded his spirit, among these things his inner life took its course. And they were all things whose names were effective in verse and occurred pretty frequently in the lines Tonio Kröger sometimes wrote.

The fact that he had a note-book full of such things, written by himself, leaked out through his own carelessness and injured him no little with the masters as well as among his fellows. On the one hand, Consul Kröger's son found their attitude both cheap and silly, and despised his schoolmates and his masters as well, and in his turn (with extraordinary penetration) saw through and disliked their personal weaknesses and bad breeding. But then, on the other hand, he himself felt his verse-making extravagant and out of place and to a certain extent agreed with those who considered it an unpleasing occupation. But that did not enable him to leave off.

As he wasted his time at home, was slow and absent-minded at school, and always had bad marks from the masters, he was in the habit of bringing home pitifully poor reports, which troubled and angered his father, a tall, fastidiously dressed man, with thoughtful blue eyes, and always a wild flower in his buttonhole. But for his mother, she cared nothing about the reports—Tonio's beautiful black-haired mother, whose name was Consuelo, and who was so absolutely different from the other ladies in the town, because father had brought her long ago from some place far down on the map.

Tonio loved his dark, fiery mother, who played the piano and mandolin so wonderfully, and he was glad his doubtful standing among men did not distress her. Though at the same time he found his father's annoyance a more dignified and respectable attitude and despite his scoldings understood him very well, whereas his mother's blithe indifference always seemed just a little wanton. His thoughts at times would run something like this: "It is true enough that I am what I am and will not and cannot alter: heedless, self-willed, with my mind on things nobody else thinks of. And so it is right they should scold and punish me and not smother things all up with kisses and music. After all, we are not gypsies living in a green wagon; we're respectable people, the family of Consul Kröger." And not seldom he would think: "Why is it I am different, why do I fight everything, why am I at odds with the masters and like a stranger among the other boys? The good scholars, and the solid majority—they don't find the masters funny, they don't write verses, their thoughts are all about things that people do think about and can talk about out loud. How regular and comfortable they must feel, knowing that everybody knows just where they stand! It must be nice! But what is the matter with me, and what will be the end of it all?"

These thoughts about himself and his relation to life played an important part in Tonio's love for Hans Hansen. He loved him in the first place because he was handsome; but in the next because he was in every respect his own opposite and foil. Hans Hansen was a capital scholar, and a jolly chap to boot, who was head at drill, rode and swam to perfection, and lived in the sunshine of popularity. The masters were almost tender with him, they called him Hans and were partial to him in every way; the other pupils curried favour with him; even grown people stopped him on the street, twiched the shock of hair beneath his Danish sailor cap, and said: "Ah, here you are, Hans Hansen, with your pretty blond hair! Still head of the school? Remember me to your father and mother, that's a fine lad!"

Such was Hans Hansen; and ever since Tonio Kröger had known him, from the very minute he set eyes on him, he had burned inwardly with a heavy, envious longing. "Who else has blue eyes like yours, or lives in such friendliness and harmony with all the world? You are always spending your time with some right and proper occupation. When you have done your prep you take your riding-lesson, or make things with a fret-saw; even in the holidays, at the seashore, you row and sail and swim all the time, while I wander off somewhere and lie down in the sand and stare at the strange and mysterious changes that whisk over the face of the sea. And all that is why your eyes are so clear. To be like you . . ."

He made no attempt to be like Hans Hansen, and perhaps hardly even seriously wanted to. What he did ardently, painfully want was that just as he was, Hans Hansen should love him; and he wooed Hans Hansen in his own way, deeply, lingeringly, devotedly, with a melancholy that gnawed and burned more terribly than all the sudden passion one might have expected from his exotic looks.

And he wooed not in vain. Hans respected Tonio's superior power of putting certain difficult matters into words; moreover, he felt the lively presence of an uncommonly strong and tender feeling for himself; he was grateful for it, and his response gave Tonio much happiness—though also many pangs of jealousy and disillusion over his futile efforts to establish a communion of spirit between them. For the queer thing was that Tonio, who after all envied Hans Hansen for being what he was, still kept on trying to draw him over to his own side; though of course he could succeed in this at most only at moments and superficially. . . .

"I have just been reading something so wonderful and splendid . . ." he said. They were walking and eating together out of a bag of fruit toffees they had bought at Iverson's sweet-shop in Mill Street for ten pfennigs. "You must read it, Hans, it is Schiller's *Don Carlos* . . . I'll lend it you if you like. . . ."

"Oh, no," said Hans Hansen, "you needn't, Tonio, that's not anything for me. I'll stick to my horse books. There are wonderful cuts in them, let me tell you. I'll show them to you when you come to see me. They are instantaneous photography—the horse in motion; you can see him trot and canter and jump, in all positions, that you never can get to see in life, because they happen so fast. . . ."

"In all positions?" asked Tonio politely. "Yes, that must be great. But about *Don Carlos*—it is beyond anything you could possibly dream of. There are places in it that are so lovely they make you jump . . . as though it were an explosion—"

"An explosion?" asked Hans Hansen. "What sort of an explosion?"

"For instance, the place where the king has been crying because the marquis betrayed him . . . but the marquis did it only out of love for the prince, you see, he sacrifices himself for his sake. And the word comes out of the cabinet into the antechamber that the king has been weeping. 'Weeping? The king been weeping?' All the courtiers are fearfully upset, it goes through and through you, for the king has always been so frightfully stiff and stern. But it is so easy to understand why he cried, and I feel sorrier for him than for the prince and the marquis put together. He is always so alone, nobody loves him, and then he thinks he has found one man, and then *he* betrays him. . . ."

Hans Hansen looked sideways into Tonio's face, and something in it must have won him to the subject, for suddenly he shoved his arm once more into Tonio's and said:

"How had he betrayed him, Tonio?"

Tonio went on.

"Well," he said, "you see all the letters for Brabant and Flanders—"

"There comes Irwin Immerthal," said Hans.

Tonio stopped talking. If only the earth would open and swallow Immerthal up! "Why does he have to come disturbing us? If he only doesn't go with us all the way and talk about the riding-lessons!" For Irwin Immerthal had riding-lessons too. He was the son of the bank president and lived close by, outside the city wall. He had already been home and left his bag, and now he walked towards them through the avenue. His legs were crooked and his eyes like slits.

" 'lo, Immerthal," said Hans. I'm taking a little walk with Kröger. . . ."

"I have to go into town on an errand," said Immerthal. "But I'll walk a little way with you. Are those fruit toffees you've got? Thanks, I'll have couple. Tomorrow we have our next lesson, Hans." He meant the riding-lesson.

"What larks!" said Hans. "I'm going to get the leather gaiters for a present, because I was top lately in our papers."

"You don't take riding-lessons, I suppose, Kröger?" asked Immerthal, and his eyes were only two gleaming cracks.

"No . . ." answered Tonio, uncertainly.

"You ought to ask your father," Hans Hansen remarked, "so you could have lessons too, Kröger."

"Yes . . ." said Tonio. He spoke hastily and without interest; his throat had suddenly contracted, because Hans had called him by his last name. Hans seemed conscious of it too, for he said by way of explanation: "I call you Kröger because your first name is so crazy. Don't mind my saying so, I can't do with it all. Tonio—why, what sort of name is that? Though of course I know it's not your fault in the least."

"No, they probably called you that because it sounds so foreign and sort of something special," said Immerthal, obviously with intent to say just the right thing.

Tonio's mouth twitched. He pulled himself together and said:

"Yes, it's a silly name—Lord knows I'd rather be called Heinrich or Wilhelm. It's all because I'm named after my mother's brother Antonio. She comes from down there, you know. . . ."

There he stopped and let the others have their say about horses and saddles. Hans had taken Immerthal's arm; he talked with a fluency that *Don Carlos* could never have roused in him. . . . Tonio felt a mounting desire to weep pricking his nose from time to time; he had hard work to control the trembling of his lips.

Hans could not stand his name—what was to be done? He himself was called Hans, and Immerthal was called Irwin; two good, sound, familiar names, offensive to nobody. And Tonio was foreign and queer. Yes, there was always something queer about him, whether he would or no, and he was alone, the regular and usual would none of him; although after all he was no gypsy in a green wagon, but the son of Consul Kröger, a member of the Kröger family. But why did Hans call him Tonio as long as they were alone and then feel ashamed as soon as anybody else was by? Just now he had won him over, they had been close together, he was sure. "How had he betrayed him, Tonio?" Hans asked, and took his arm. But he had breathed easier directly Immerthal came up, he had dropped him like a shot, even gratuitously taunted him with his outlandish name. How it hurt to have to see through all this! . . . Hans Hansen did like him a little, when they were alone, that he knew. But let a third person come, he was ashamed, and offered up his friend. And again he was alone. He thought of King Philip. The king had wept. . . .

"Goodness, I have to go," said Irwin Immerthal. "Good-bye, and thanks for the toffee." He jumped upon a bench that stood by the way, ran along it with his crooked legs, jumped down, and trotted off.

"I like Immerthal," said Hans, with emphasis. He had a spoilt and arbitrary way of announcing his likes and dislikes, as though graciously pleased to confer them like an order on this person and that. . . . He went on talking about the riding-lessons where he had left off. Anyhow, it was not very much farther to his house; the walk over the walls was not a long one. They held their caps and bent their heads before the strong, damp wind that rattled and groaned in the leafless trees. And Hans Hansen went on talking, Tonio throwing in a forced yes or no from time to time. Hans talked eagerly, had taken his arm again; but the contact gave Tonio no pleasure. The nearness was only apparent, not real; it meant nothing. . . .

They struck away from the walls close to the station, where they saw a train puff busily past, idly counted the coaches, and waved to the man who was perched on top of the last one bundled in a leather coat. They stopped in front of the Hansen villa on the Lindenplatz, and Hans went into detail about what fun it was to stand on the bottom rail of the garden gate and let it swing on its creaking hinges. After that they said good-bye.

"I must go in now," said Hans. "Good-bye, Tonio. Next time I'll take you home, see if I don't."

"Good-bye, Hans," said Tonio. "It was a nice walk."

They put out their hands, all wet and rusty from the garden gate. But as Hans looked into Tonio's eyes, he bethought himself, a look of remorse came over his charming face.

"And I'll read *Don Carlos* pretty soon, too," he said quickly. "That bit about the king in his cabinet must be nuts." Then he took his bag under his arm and ran off through the front garden. Before he disappeared he turned and nodded once more.

And Tonio went off as though on wings. The wind was at his back; but it was not the wind alone that bore him along so lightly.

Hans would read *Don Carlos,* and then they would have something to talk about, and neither Irwin Immerthal nor another could join in. How well they understood each other! Perhaps—

who knew?—some day he might even get Hans to write poetry! . . . No, no, that he did not ask. Hans must not become like Tonio, he must stop just as he was, so strong and bright, everybody loved him as he was, and Tonio most of all. But it would do him no harm to read *Don Carlos*. . . . Tonio passed under the squat old city gate, along by the harbour, and up the steep, wet, windy gabled street to his parents' house. His heart beat richly: longing was awake in it, and a gently envy; a faint contempt, and no little innocent bliss.

Ingeborg Holm, blonde little Inge, the daughter of Dr. Holm, who lived on Market Square opposite the tall old Gothic fountain with its manifold spires—she it was Tonio Kröger loved when he was sixteen years old.

Strange how things come about! He had seen her a thousand times; then one evening he saw her again; saw her in a certain light, talking with a friend in a certain saucy way, laughing and tossing her head; saw her lift her arm and smooth her back hair with her schoolgirl hand, that was by no means particularly fine or slender, in such a way that the thin white sleeve slipped down from her elbow; heard her speak a word or two, a quite indifferent phrase, but with a certain intonation, with a warm ring in her voice; and his heart throbbed with ecstasy, far stronger than that he had once felt when he looked at Hans Hansen long ago, when he was still a little, stupid boy.

That evening he carried away her picture in his eye: the thick blond plait, the longish, laughing blue eyes, the saddle of pale freckles across the nose. He could not go to sleep for hearing that ring in her voice; he tried in a whisper to imitate the tone in which she had uttered the commonplace phrase, and felt a shiver run through and through him. He knew by experience that this was love. And he was accurately aware that love would surely bring him much pain, affliction, and sadness, that it would certainly destroy his peace, filling his heart to overflowing with melodies which would be no good to him because he would never have the time or tranquillity to give them permanent form.

Yet he received this love with joy, surrendered himself to it, and cherished it with all the strength of his being; for he knew that love made one vital and rich, and he longed to be vital and rich, far more than he did to work tranquilly on anything to give it permanent form.

Tonio Kröger fell in love with merry Ingeborg Holm in Frau Consul Hustede's drawing-room on the evening when it was emptied of furniture for the weekly dancing-class. It was a private class, attended only by members of the first families; it met by turns in the various parental houses to receive instruction from Knaak, the dancing-master, who came from Hamburg expressly for the purpose.

François Knaak was his name, and what a man he was! *"J'ai l'honneur de me vous représenter,"* he would say, *"mon nom est Knaak.* . . . This is not said during the bowing, but after you have finished and are standing up straight again. In a low voice, but distinctly. Of course one does not need to introduce oneself in French every day in the week, but if you can do it correctly and faultlessly in French you are not likely to make a mistake when you do it in German." How marvellously the silky black frock-coat fitted his chubby hips! His trouser-legs fell down in soft folds upon his patent-leather pumps with their wide satin bows, and his brown eyes glanced about him with languid pleasure in their own beauty.

All this excess of self-confidence and good form was positively overpowering. He went trippingly—and nobody tripped like him, so elastically, so weavingly, rockingly, royally—up to the mistress of the house, made a bow, waited for a hand to be put forth. This vouchsafed, he gave murmurous voice to his gratitude, stepped buoyantly back, turned on his left foot, swiftly drawing the right one backwards on its toe-tip, and moved away, with his hips shaking.

When you took leave of a company you must go backwards out at the door; when you fetched a chair, you were not to shove it along the floor or clutch it by one leg; but gently, by the back, and set it down without a sound. When you stood, you were not to fold your hands on your tummy or seek with your tongue the corners of your mouth. If you did, Herr Knaak had a way of showing you how it looked that filled you with disgust for that particular gesture all the rest of your life.

This was deportment. As for dancing, Herr Knaak was, if possible, even more of a master at that. The salon was emptied of furniture and lighted by a gas-chandelier in the middle of the ceiling and candles on the mantel-shelf. The floor was strewn with talc, and the pupils stood about in a dumb semicircle. But in the next room, behind the portières, mothers and aunts sat on plush-upholstered chairs and watched Herr Knaak through their lorgnettes, as in little springs and hops, curtsying slightly, the hem of his frock-coat held up on each side by two fingers, he demonstrated the single steps of the mazurka. When he wanted to dazzle his audience completely he would suddenly and unexpectedly spring from the ground, whirling his two legs about each other with bewildering swiftness in the air, as it were trilling with them, and then, with a subdued bump, which nevertheless shook everything within him to its depths, return to earth.

"What an unmentionable monkey!" thought Tonio Kröger to himself. But he saw the absorbed smile on jolly little Inge's face as she followed Herr Knaak's movements; and that, though not that alone, roused in him something like admiration of all this wonderfully controlled corporeality. How tranquil, how imperturbable was Herr Knaak's gaze! His eyes did not plumb the depth of things to the place where life becomes complex and melancholy; they knew nothing save that they were beautiful brown eyes. But that was just why his bearing was so proud. To be able to walk like that, one must be stupid; then one was loved, then one was lovable. He could so well understand how it was that Inge, blonde, sweet little Inge, looked at Herr Knaak as she did. But would never a girl look at him like that?

Oh, yes, there would, and did. For instance, Magdalena Vermehren, Attorney Vermehren's daughter, with the gentle mouth and the great, dark, brilliant eyes, so serious and adoring. She often fell down in the dance; but when it was "ladies' choice" she came up to him; she knew he wrote verses and twice she had asked him to show them to her. She often sat at a distance, with drooping head, and gazed at him. He did not care. It was Inge he loved, blonde, jolly Inge, who most assuredly despised him for his poetic effusions . . . he looked at her, looked at her narrow blue eyes full of fun and mockery, and felt an envious longing; to be shut away from her like this, to be forever strange—he felt it in his breast, like a heavy, burning weight.

"First couple *en avant,*" said Herr Knaak; and no words can tell how marvellously he pronounced the nasal. They were to practise the quadrille, and to Tonio Kröger's profound alarm he found himself in the same set with Inge Holm. He avoided her where he could, yet somehow was forever near her; kept his eyes away from her person and yet found his gaze ever on her. There she came, tripping up hand-in-hand with red-headed Ferdinand Matthiessen; she flung back her braid, drew a deep breath, and took her place opposite Tonio. Herr Heinzelmann, at the piano, laid bony hands upon the keys, Herr Knaak waved his arm, the quadrille began.

She moved to and fro before his eyes, forwards and back, pacing and swinging; he seemed to catch a fragrance from her hair or the folds of her thin white frock, and his eyes grew sadder and sadder. "I love you, dear, sweet Inge," he said to himself, and put into his words all the pain he felt to see her so intent upon the dance with not a thought of him. Some lines of an exquisite poem by Storm came into his mind: "I would sleep, but thou must dance." It seemed against all sense, and most depressing, that he must be dancing when he was in love. . . .

"First couple *en avant,*" said Herr Knaak; it was the next figure. *"Compliment! Moulinet des dames! Tour de main!"* and he swallowed the silent *e* in the *"de,"* with quite indescribable ease and grace.

"Second couple *en avant!"* This was Tonio Kröger and his partner. *"Compliment!"* And Tonio Kröger bowed. *"Moulinet des dames!"* And Tonio Kröger, with bent head and gloomy brows, laid his hand on those of the four ladies, on Ingeborg Holm's hand, and danced the *moulinet.*

Roundabout rose a tittering and laughing. Herr Knaak took a ballet pose conventionally expressive of horror. "Oh, dear! Oh, dear!" he cried. "Stop! Stop! Kröger among the ladies! *En arrière,* Fräulein Kröger, step back, *fi donc!* Everybody else understood it but you. Shoo! Get out! Get away!" He drew out his yellow silk handkerchief and flapped Tonio Kröger back to his place.

Everyone laughed, the girls and the boys and the ladies beyond the portières; Herr Knaak had made something too utterly funny out of the little episode, it was as amusing as a play. But Herr Heinzelmann at the piano sat and waited, with a dry, business-like air, for a sign to go on; he was hardened against Herr Knaak's effects.

Then the quadrille went on. And the intermission followed. The parlourmaid came clinking in with a tray of wine-jelly glasses, the cook followed in her wake with a load of plum-cake. But Tonio Kröger stole away. He stole out into the corridor and stood there, his hands behind his back, in front of a window with the blind down. He never thought that one could not see through the blind and that it was absurd to stand there as though one were looking out.

For he was looking within, into himself, the theatre of so much pain and longing. Why, why was he here? Why was he not sitting by the window in his own room, reading Storm's *Immensee* and lifting his eyes to the twilight garden outside, where the old walnut tree moaned? That was the place for him! Others might dance, others bend their fresh and lively minds upon the pleasure in hand! . . . But no, no, after all, his place was here, where he could feel near Inge even although he stood lonely and aloof, seeking to distinguish the warm notes of her voice amid the buzzing, clattering, and laughter within. Oh, lovely Inge, blonde Inge of the narrow, laughing blue eyes! So lovely and laughing as you are one can only be if one does not read *Immensee* and never tries to write things like it. And that was just the tragedy!

Ah, she *must* come! She *must* notice where he had gone, must feel how he suffered! She must slip out to him, even pity must bring her, to lay her hand on his shoulder and say: "Do come back to us, ah, don't be sad—I love you, Tonio." He listened behind him and waited in frantic suspense. But not in the least. Such things did not happen on this earth.

Had she laughed at him too like all the others? Yes, she had, however gladly he would have denied it for both their sakes. And yet it was only because he had been so taken up with her that he had danced the *moulinet des dames*. Suppose he had—what did that matter? Had not a magazine accepted a poem of his a little while ago—even though the magazine had failed before his poem could be printed? The day was coming when he would be famous, when they would print everything he wrote; and *then* he would see if that made any impression on Inge Holm! No, it would make no impression at all; that was just it. Magdalena Vermehren, who was always falling down in the dances, yes, she would be impressed. But never Ingeborg Holm, never blue-eyed, laughing Inge. So what was the good of it?

Tonio Kröger's heart contracted painfully at the thought. To feel stirring within you the wonderful and melancholy play of strange forces and to be aware that those others you yearn for are blithely inaccessible to all that moves you—what a pain is this! And yet! He stood there aloof and alone, staring hopelessly at a drawn blind and making, in his distraction, as though he could look out. But yet he was happy. For he lived. His heart was full; hotly and sadly it beat for thee, Ingeborg Holm, and his soul embraced thy blonde, simple, pert, commonplace little personality in blissful self-abnegation.

Often after that he stood thus, with burning cheeks, in lonely corners, whither the sound of music, the tinkling of glasses and fragrance of flowers came but faintly, and tried to distinguish the ringing tones of thy voice amid the distant happy din; stood suffering for thee—and still was happy! Often it angered him to think that he might talk with Magdalena Vermehren, who always fell down in the dance. She understood him, she laughed or was serious in the right places; while Inge the fair, let him sit never so near her, seemed remote and estranged, his speech not being her speech. And still—he was happy. For happiness, he told himself, is not in being loved—which is a satisfaction of the vanity and mingled with disgust. Happiness is in loving, and perhaps in snatching fugitive little approaches to the beloved object. And he took inward note of this thought, wrote it down in his mind; followed out all its implications and felt it to the depths of his soul.

"Faithfulness," thought Tonio Kröger. "Yes, I will be faithful, I will love thee, Ingeborg, as long as I live!" He said this in the honesty of his intentions. And yet a still small voice whispered misgivings in his ear: after all, he had forgotten Hans Hansen utterly, even though he saw him every day! And the hateful, the pitiable fact was that this still, small, rather spiteful voice was right: time passed and the day came when Tonio Kröger was no longer so unconditionally ready as once he had been to die for the lively Inge, because he felt in himself desires and powers to accomplish in his own way a host of wonderful things in this world.

And he circled with watchful eye the sacrificial altar, where flickered the pure, chaste flame of his love; knelt before it and tended and cherished it in every way, because he so wanted to be faithful. And in a little while, unobservably, without sensation or stir, it went out after all.

But Tonio Kröger still stood before the cold altar, full of regret and dismay at the fact that faithfulness was impossible upon this earth. Then he shrugged his shoulders and went his way.

He went the way that go he must, a little idly, a little irregularly, whistling to himself, gazing into space with his head on one side; and if he went wrong it was because for some people there is no such thing as a right way. Asked what in the world he meant to become, he gave various answers, for he was used to say (and had even already written it) that he bore within himself the possibility of a thousand ways of life, together with the private conviction that they were all sheer impossibilities.

Even before he left the narrow streets of his native city, the threads that bound him to it had gently loosened. The old Kröger family gradually declined, and some people quite rightly considered Tonio Kröger's own existence and way of life as one of the signs of decay. His father's mother, the head of the family, had died, and not long after his own father followed, the tall, thoughtful, carefully dressed gentleman with the field-flower in his buttonhole. The great Kröger house, with all its stately tradition, came up for sale, and the firm was dissolved. Tonio's mother, his beautiful, fiery mother, who played the piano and mandolin so wonderfully and to whom nothing mattered at all, she married again after a year's time; married a musician, moreover, a virtuoso with an Italian name, and went away with him into remote blue distances. Tonio Kröger found this a little irregular, but who was he to call her to order, who wrote poetry himself and could not even give an answer when asked what he meant to do in life?

And so he left his native town and its tortuous, gabled streets with the damp wind whistling through them; left the fountain in the garden and the ancient walnut tree, familiar friends of his youth; left the sea too, that he loved so much, and felt no pain to go. For he was grown up and sensible and had come to realize how things stood with him; he looked down on the lowly and vulgar life he had led so long in these surroundings.

He surrendered utterly to the power that to him seemed the highest on earth, to whose service he felt called, which promised him elevation and honours: the power of intellect, the power of the Word, that lords it with a smile over the unconscious and inarticulate. To this power he surrendered with all the passion of youth, and it rewarded him with all it had to give, taking from him inexorably, in return, all that it is wont to take.

It sharpened his eyes and made him see through the large words which puff out the bosoms of mankind; it opened for him men's souls and his own, made him clairvoyant, showed him the inwardness of the world and the ultimate behind men's words and deeds. And all that he saw could be put in two words: the comedy and the tragedy of life.

And then, with knowledge, its torment and its arrogance, came solitude; because he could not endure the blithe and innocent with their darkened understanding, while they in turn were troubled by the sign on his brow. But his love of the word kept growing sweeter and sweeter, and his love of form; for he used to say (and had already said it in writing) that knowledge of the soul would unfailingly make us melancholy if the pleasures of expression did not keep us alert and of good cheer.

He lived in large cities and in the south, promising himself a luxuriant ripening of his art by southern suns; perhaps it was the blood of his mother's race that drew him thither. But his heart being dead and loveless, he fell into adventures of the flesh, descended into the depths of lust and searing sin, and suffering unspeakably thereby. It might have been his father in him, that tall, thoughtful, fastidiously dressed man with the wild flower in his buttonhole, that made him suffer so down there in the south; now and again he would feel a faint, yearning memory of a certain joy that was of the soul; once it had been his own, but now, in all his joys, he could not find it again.

Then he would be seized with disgust and hatred of the senses; pant after purity and seemly peace, while still he breathed the air of art, the tepid, sweet air of permanent spring, heavy with fragrance where it breeds and brews and burgeons in the mysterious bliss of creation. So for all result he was flung to and fro forever between two crass extremes: between icy intellect and scorching sense, and what with his pangs of conscience led an exhausting life, rare, extraordinary, excessive, which at bottom he, Tonio Kröger, despised. "What a labyrinth!" he sometimes thought. "How could I possibly have got into all these fantastic adventures? As though I had a wagonful of travelling gypsies for my ancestors!"

But as his health suffered from these excesses, so his artistry was sharpened; it grew fastidious, precious, *raffiné,* morbidly sensitive in questions of tact and taste, rasped by the banal. His first appearance in print elicited much applause; there was joy among the elect, for it was a good and workmanlike performance, full of humour and acquaintance with pain. In no long time his name—the same by which his masters had reproached him, the same he had signed to his earliest verses on the walnut tree and the fountain and the sea, those syllables compact of the north and the south, that good middle-class name with the exotic twist to it—became a synonym for excellence; for the painful thoroughness of the experiences he had gone through, combined with a tenacious ambition and a persistent industry, joined battle with the irritable fastidiousness of his taste and under grinding torments issued in work of a quality quite uncommon.

He worked, not like a man who works that he may live; but as one who is bent on doing nothing but work; having no regard for himself as a human being but only as a creator; moving about grey and unobtrusive among his fellows like an actor without his make-up, who counts for nothing as soon as he stops representing something else. He worked withdrawn out of sight and sound of the small fry, for whom he felt nothing but contempt, because to them a talent was a social asset like another; who, whether they were poor or not, went about ostentatiously shabby or else flaunted startling cravats, all the time taking jolly good care to amuse themselves, to be artistic and charming without the smallest notion of the fact that good work only comes out under pressure of a bad life; that he who lives does not work; that one must die to life in order to be utterly a creator.

"Shall I disturb you?" asked Tonio Kröger on the threshold of the atelier. He held his hat in his hand and bowed with some ceremony, although Lisabeta Ivanovna was a good friend of his, to whom he told all his troubles.

"Mercy on you, Tonio Kröger! Don't be so formal," answered she, with her lilting intonation. "Everybody knows you were taught good manners in your nursery." She transferred her brush to her left hand, that held the palette, reached him her right, and looked him in the face, smiling and shaking her head.

"Yes, but you are working," he said. "Let's see. Oh, you've been getting on," and he looked at the colour-sketches leaning against chairs at both sides of the easel and from them to the large canvas covered with a square linen mesh, where the first patches of colour were beginning to appear among the confused and schematic lines of the charcoal sketch.

This was in Munich, in a back building in Schellingstrasse, several storeys up. Beyond the wide window facing the north were blue sky, sunshine, birds twittering; the young sweet breath of spring streaming through an open pane mingled with the smells of paint and fixative. The afternoon light, bright golden, flooded the spacious emptiness of the atelier; it made no secret of the bad flooring or the rough table under the window, covered with little bottles, tubes, and brushes; it illumined the unframed studies on the unpapered walls, the torn silk screen that shut off a charmingly furnished little living-corner near the door; it shone upon the inchoate work on the easel, upon the artist and the poet there before it.

She was about the same age as himself—slightly past thirty. She sat there on a low stool, in her dark-blue apron, and leant her chin in her hand. Her brown hair, compactly dressed, already a little grey at the sides, was parted in the middle and waved over the temples, framing a sensitive, sympathetic, dark-skinned face, which was Slavic in its facial structure, with flat nose, strongly accentuated cheek-bones, and little bright black eyes. She sat there measuring her work with her head on one side and her eyes screwed up; her features were drawn with a look of misgiving, almost of vexation.

He stood beside her, his right hand on his hip, with the other furiously twirling his brown moustache. His dress, reserved in cut and a soothing shade of grey, was punctilious and dignified to the last degree. He was whistling softly to himself, in the way he had, and his slanting brows were gathered in a frown. The dark-brown hair was parted with severe correctness, but the laboured forehead beneath showed a nervous twitching, and the chiselled southern features were sharpened as though they had been gone over again with a graver's tool. And yet the mouth—how gently curved it was, the chin how softly formed! . . . After a little he drew his hand across his brow and eyes and turned away.

"I ought not to have come," he said.

"And why not, Tonio Kröger?"

"I've just got up from my desk, Lisabeta, and inside my head it looks just the way it does on this canvas. A scaffolding, a faint first draft smeared with corrections and a few splotches of colour; yes, and I come up here and see the same thing. And the same conflict and contradiction in the air," he went on, sniffing, "that has been torturing me at home. It's extraordinary. If you are possessed by an idea, you find it expressed everywhere, you even *smell* it. Fixative and the breath of spring; art and—what? Don't say nature, Lisabeta, 'nature' isn't exhausting. Ah, no, I ought to have gone for a walk, though it's doubtful if it would have made me feel better. Five minutes ago, not far from here, I met a man I know, Adalbert, the novelist. 'God damn the spring!' says he in the aggressive way he has. 'It is and always has been the most ghastly time of the year. Can you get hold of a single sensible idea, Kröger? Can you sit still and work out even the smallest effect, when your blood tickles till it's positively indecent and you are teased by a whole host of irrelevant sensations that when you look at them turn out to be unworkable trash? For my part, I am going to a café. A café is neutral territory, the change of the seasons doesn't affect it; it represents, so to speak, the detached and elevated sphere of the literary man, in which one is only capable of refined ideas.' And he went into the café . . . and perhaps I ought to have gone with him."

Lisabeta was highly entertained.

"I like that, Tonio Kröger. That part about the indecent tickling is good. And he is right too, in a way, for spring is really not very conducive to work. But now listen. Spring or no spring, I will just finish this little place—work out this little effect, as your friend Adalbert would say. Then we'll go into the 'salon' and have tea, and you can talk yourself out, for I can perfectly well see you are too full for utterance. Will you just compose yourself somewhere—on that chest, for instance, if you are not afraid for your aristocratic garments—"

"Oh, leave my clothes alone, Lisabeta Ivanovna! Do you want me to go about in a ragged velveteen jacket or a red waistcoat? Every artist is as bohemian as the deuce, inside! Let him at least wear proper clothes and behave outwardly like a respectable being. No, I am not too full for utterance," he said as he watched her mixing her paints. "I've told you, it is only that I have a problem and a conflict, that sticks in my mind and disturbs me at my work. . . . Yes, what was it we were just saying? We were talking about Adalbert, the novelist, that stout and forthright man. 'Spring is the most ghastly time of the year,' says he, and goes into a café. A man has to know what he needs, eh? Well, you see he's not the only one; the spring makes me nervous, too; I get dazed with the triflingness and sacredness of the memories and feelings it evokes; only that I don't succeed in looking down on it; for the truth is it makes me ashamed; I quail before its sheer naturalness and triumphant youth. And I don't know whether I should envy Adalbert or despise him for his ignorance. . . .

"Yes, it is true; spring is a bad time for work; and why? Because we are feeling too much. Nobody but a beginner imagines that he who creates must feel. Every real and genuine artist smiles at such naïve blunders as that. A melancholy enough smile, perhaps, but still a smile. For what an artist talks about is never the main point; it is the raw material, in and for itself indifferent, out of which, with bland and serene mastery, he creates the work of art. If you care too much about what you have to say, if your heart is too much in it, you can be pretty sure of making a mess. You get pathetic, you wax sentimental; something dull and doddering, without roots or outlines, with no sense of humour—something tiresome and banal grows under your hand, and you get nothing out of it but apathy in your audience and disappointment and misery in yourself. For so it is, Lisabeta; feeling, warm, heartfelt feeling, is always banal and futile; only the irritations and icy ecstasies of the artist's corrupted nervous system are artistic. The artist must be unhuman, extra-human; he must stand in a queer aloof relationship to our humanity; only so is he in a position, I ought to say only so would he be tempted, to represent it, to present it, to portray it to good effect. The very gift of style, of form and expression, is nothing else than this cool and fastidious attitude towards humanity; you might say there has to be this impoverishment and devastation as a preliminary condition. For sound natural feeling, say what you like, has no taste. It is all up with the artist as soon as he becomes a man and begins to feel. Adalbert knows that; that's why he betook himself to the café, the neutral territory—God help him!"

"Yes, God help him, Batuschka," said Lisabeta, as she washed her hands in a tin basin. "You don't need to follow his example."

"No, Lisabeta, I am not going to; and the only reason is that I am now and again in a position to feel a little ashamed of the springtime of my art. You see sometimes I get letters from strangers, full of praise and thanks and admiration from people whose feelings I have touched. I read them and feel touched myself at these warm if ungainly emotions I have called up; a sort of pity steals over me at this naïve enthusiasm; and I positively blush at the thought of how these good people would freeze up if they were to get a look behind the scenes. What they, in their innocence, cannot comprehend is that a properly constituted, healthy, decent man never writes, acts, or composes—all of which does not hinder me from using his admiration for my genius to goad myself on; nor from taking it in deadly earnest and aping the airs of a great man. Oh, don't talk to me, Lisabeta. I tell you I am sick to death of depicting humanity without having any part or lot in it. . . . Is an artist a male, anyhow? Ask the females! It seems to me we artists are all of us something like those unsexed papal singers . . . we sing like angels; but—"

"Shame on you, Tonio Kröger. But come to tea. The water is just on the boil, and here are some *papyros*. You were talking about singing soprano, do go on. But really you ought to be ashamed of yourself. If I did not know your passionate devotion to your calling and how proud you are of it—"

"Don't talk about 'calling,' Lisabeta Ivanovna. Literature is not a calling, it is a curse, believe me! When does one begin to feel the curse? Early, horribly early. At a time when one ought by rights still to be living in peace and harmony with God and the world. It begins by your feeling yourself set apart, in a curious sort of opposition to the nice, regular people; there is a gulf of ironic sensibility, of knowledge, scepticism, disagreement between you and the others; it grows deeper and deeper, you realize that you are alone; and from then on any *rapprochement* is simply hopeless! What a fate! That is, if you still have enough heart, enough warmth of affections, to feel how frightful it is! . . . Your self-consciousness is kindled, because you among thousands feel the sign on your brow and know that everyone else sees it. I once knew an actor, a man of genius, who had to struggle with a morbid self-consciousness and instability. When he had no rôle to play, nothing to represent, this man, consummate artist but impoverished human being, was overcome by an exaggerated consciousness of his ego. A genuine artist—not one who has taken up art as a profession like another, but artist foreordained and damned—you can pick out, without boasting very sharp perceptions, out of a group of men. The sense of being set apart and not belonging, of being known and observed, something both regal and incongruous shows in his face. You might see something of the same sort on the features of a prince walking through a crowd in ordinary clothes. But no civilian clothes are any good here, Lisabeta. You can disguise yourself, you can dress up like an attaché or a lieutenant of the guard on leave; you hardly need to give a glance or speak a word before everyone knows you are not a human being, but something else: something queer, different, inimical.

"But what is it, to be an artist? Nothing shows up the general human dislike of thinking, and man's innate craving to be comfortable, better than his attitude to this question. When these worthy people are affected by a work of art, they say humbly that that sort of thing is a 'gift.' And because in their innocence they assume that beautiful and uplifting results must have beautiful and uplifting causes, they never dream that the 'gift' in question is a very dubious affair and rests upon extremely sinister foundations. Everybody knows that artists are 'sensitive' and easily wounded; just as everybody knows that ordinary people, with a normal bump of self-confidence, are not. Now you see, Lisabeta, I cherish at the bottom of my soul all the scorn and suspicion of the artist gentry—translated into terms of the intellectual—that my upright old forbears there on the Baltic would have felt for any juggler or mountebank that entered their houses.

Listen to this. I know a banker, grey-haired business man, who has a gift for writing stories. He employs this gift in his idle hours, and some of his stories are of the first rank. But despite—I say despite—this excellent gift his withers are by no means unwrung: on the contrary, he has had to serve a prison sentence, on anything but trifling grounds. Yes, it was actually first *in prison* that he became conscious of his gift, and his experiences as a convict are the main theme in all his works. One might be rash enough to conclude that a man has to be at home in some kind of jail in order to become a poet. But can you escape the suspicion that the source and essence of his being an artist had less to do with his life in prison than they had with the reasons that *brought him there?* A banker who writes—that is a rarity, isn't it? But a banker who isn't a criminal, who is irreproachably respectable, and yet writes—he doesn't exist. Yes, you are laughing, and yet I am more than half serious. No problem, none in the world, is more tormenting than this of the artist and his human aspect. Take the most miraculous case of all, take the most typical and therefore the most powerful of artists, take such a morbid and profoundly equivocal work as *Tristan and Isolde,* and look at the effect it has on a healthy young man of thoroughly normal feelings. Exaltation, encouragement, warm, downright enthusiasm, perhaps incitement to 'artistic' creation of his own. Poor young dilettante! In us artists it looks fundamentally different from what he wots of, with his 'warm heart' and 'honest enthusiasm.' I've seen women and youths go mad over artists . . . and I *knew* about them . . . ! The origin, the accompanying phenomena, and the conditions of the artist life—good Lord, what I haven't observed about them, over and over!"

"Observed, Tonio Kröger? If I may ask, only 'observed'?"

He was silent, knitting his oblique brown brows and whistling softly to himself.

"Let me have your cup, Tonio. The tea is weak. And take another cigarette. Now, you perfectly know that you are looking at things as they do not necessarily have to be looked at. . . ."

"That is Horatio's answer, dear Lisabeta. ' 'Twere to consider too curiously, to consider so.' "

"I mean, Tonio Kröger, that one can consider them just exactly as well from another side. I am only a silly painting female, and if I can contradict you at all, if I can defend your own profession a little against you, it is not by saying anything new, but simply by reminding you of some things you very well know yourself: of the purifying and healing influence of letters, the subduing of the passions by knowledge and eloquence; literature as the guide to understanding, forgiveness, and love, the redeeming power of the word, literary art as the noblest manifestation of the human mind, the poet as the most highly developed of human beings, the poet as saint. Is it to consider things not curiously enough, to consider them so?"

"You may talk like that, Lisabeta Ivanovna, you have a perfect right. And with reference to Russian literature, and the words of your poets, one can really worship them; they really come close to being that elevated literature you are talking about. But I am not ignoring your objections, they are part of the things I have in my mind today. . . . Look at me, Lisabeta. I don't look any too cheerful, do I? A little old and tired and pinched, eh? Well, now to come back to the 'knowledge.' Can't you imagine a man, born orthodox, mild-mannered, well-meaning, a bit sentimental, just simply over-stimulated by his psychological clairvoyance, and going to the dogs? Not to let the sadness of the world unman you; to read, mark, learn, and put to account even the most torturing things and to be of perpetual good cheer, in the sublime consciousness of moral superiority over the horrible invention of existence—yes, thank you! But despite all the joys of expression once in a while the thing gets on your nerves. *'Tout comprendre c'est tout pardonner.'* I don't know about that. There is something I call being sick of knowledge, Lisabeta; when it is enough for you to see through a thing in order to be sick to death of it, and not in the least in a forgiving mood. Such was the case of Hamlet the Dane, that typical literary man. He knew what it meant to be called to knowledge without being born to it. To see things clear, if even through your tears, to recognize, notice, observe—and have to put it all down with a smile, at the very moment when hands are clinging, and lips meeting, and the human gaze is blinded with feeling—it is infamous, Lisabeta, it is indecent, outrageous—but what good does it do to be outraged?

"Then another and no less charming side of the thing, of course, is your ennui, your indifferent and ironic attitude towards truth. It is a fact that there is no society in the world so dumb and hopeless as a circle of literary people who are hounded to death as it is. All knowledge is old and tedious to them. Utter some truth that it gave you considerable youthful joy to conquer and possess—and they will all chortle at you for your naïveté. Oh, yes, Lisabeta, literature is a wearing job. In human society, I do assure you, a reserved and sceptical man can be taken for stupid, whereas he is really only arrogant and perhaps lacks courage. So much for 'knowledge.' Now for the 'Word.' It isn't so much a matter of the 'redeeming power' as it is of putting your emotions on ice and serving them up chilled! Honestly, don't you think there's a good deal of cool cheek in the prompt and superficial way a writer can get rid of his feelings by turning them into literature? If your heart is too full, if you are overpowered with the emotions of some sweet or exalted moment—nothing simpler! Go to the literary man, he will put it all straight for you instanter. He will analyse and formulate your affair, label it and express it and discuss it and polish it off and make you indifferent to it for time and eternity—and not charge you a farthing. You will go home quite relieved, cooled off, enlightened; and wonder what it was all about and why you were so mightily moved. And will you seriously enter the lists in behalf of this vain and frigid charlatan? What is uttered, so runs this *credo,* is finished and done with. If the whole world could be expressed, it would be saved, finished and done. . . . Well and good. But I am not a nihilist—"

"You are not a—" said Lisabeta. . . . She was lifting a teaspoonful of tea to her mouth and paused in the act to stare at him.

"Come, come, Lisabeta, what's the matter? I say I am not a nihilist, with respect, that is, to lively feeling. You see, the literary man does not understand that life may go on living, unashamed, even after it has been expressed and therewith finished. No matter how much it has been redeemed by becoming literature, it keeps right on sinning—for all action is sin in the mind's eye—

"I'm nearly done, Lisabeta. Please listen. I love life—this is an admission. I present it to you, you may have it. I have never made it to anyone else. People say—people have even written and printed—that I hate life, or fear or despise or abominate it. I liked to hear this, it has always flattered me; but that does not make it true. I love life. You smile; and I know why, Lisabeta. But I implore you not to take what I am saying for literature. Don't think of Cæsar Borgia or any drunken philosophy that has him for a standard-bearer. He is nothing to me, your Cæsar Borgia. I have no opinion of him, and I shall never comprehend how one can honour the extraordinary and dæmonic as an ideal. No, life as the eternal antinomy of mind and art does not represent itself to us as a vision of savage greatness and ruthless beauty; we who are set apart and different do not conceive it as, like us, unusual; it is the normal, respectable, and admirable that is the kingdom of our longing: life, in all its seductive banality! That man is very far from being an artist, my dear, whose last and deepest enthusiasm is the *raffiné,* the eccentric and satanic; who does not know a longing for the innocent, the simple, and the living, for a little friendship, devotion, familiar human happiness—the gnawing, surreptitious hankering, Lisabeta, for the bliss of the commonplace. . . .

"A genuine human friend. Believe me, I should be proud and happy to possess a friend among men. But up to now all the friends I have had have been dæmons, kobolds, impious monsters, and spectres dumb with excess of knowledge—that is to say, literary men.

"I may be standing upon some platform, in some hall in front of people who have come to listen to me. And I find myself looking round among my hearers, I catch myself secretly peering about the auditorium, and all the while I am thinking who it is that has come here to listen to me, whose grateful applause is in my ears, with whom my art is making me one. . . . I do not find what I seek, Lisabeta, I find the herd. The same old community, the same old gathering of early Christians, so to speak: people with fine souls in uncouth bodies, people who are always falling down in the dance, if you know what I mean; the kind to whom poetry serves as a sort of mild revenge on life. Always and only the poor and suffering, never any of the others, the blue-eyed ones, Lisabeta—they do not need mind. . . .

"And, after all, would it not be a lamentable lack of logic to want it otherwise? It is against all sense to love life and yet bend all the powers you have to draw it over to your own side, to the side of finesse and melancholy and the whole sickly aristocracy of letters. The kingdom of art increases and that of health and innocence declines on this earth. What there is left of it ought to be carefully preserved; one ought not to tempt people to read poetry who would much rather read books about the instantaneous photography of horses.

"For, after all, what more pitiable sight is there than life led astray by art? We artists have a consummate contempt for the dilettante, the man who is leading a living life and yet thinks he can be an artist too if he gets the chance. I am speaking from personal experience, I do assure you. Suppose I am in a company in a good house, with eating and drinking going on, and plenty of conversation and good feeling: I am glad and grateful to be able to lose myself among good regular people for a while. Then all of a sudden—I am thinking of something that actually happened—an officer gets up, a lieutenant, a stout, good-looking chap, whom I could never have believed guilty of any conduct unbecoming his uniform, and actually in good set terms asks the company's permission to read some verses of his own composition. Everybody looks disconcerted, they laugh and tell him to go on, and he takes them at their word and reads from a sheet of paper he has up to now been hiding in his coat-tail pocket—something about love and music, as deeply felt as it is inept. But I ask you: a lieutenant! A man of the world! He surely did not need to. . . . Well, the inevitable result is long faces, silence, a little artificial applause, everybody thoroughly uncomfortable. The first sensation I am conscious of is guilt—I feel partly responsible for the disturbance this rash youth has brought upon the company; and no wonder, for I, as a member of the same guild, am a target for some of the unfriendly glances. But next minute I realize something else: this man for whom just now I felt the greatest respect has suddenly sunk in my eyes. I feel a benevolent pity. Along with some other brave and good-natured gentlemen I go up and speak to him. 'Congratulations, Herr Lieutenant,' I say, 'that is a very pretty talent you have. It was charming.' And I am within an ace of clapping him on the shoulder. But is that the way one is supposed to feel towards a lieutenant—benevolent? . . . It was his own fault. There he stood, suffering embarrassment for the mistake of thinking that one may pluck a single leaf from the laurel tree of art without paying for it with his life. No, there I go with my colleague, the convict banker—but don't you find, Lisabeta, that I have quite a Hamlet-like flow of oratory today?"

"Are you done, Tonio Kröger?"

"No. But there won't be any more."

"And quite enough too. Are you expecting a reply?"

"Have you one ready?"

"I should say. I have listened to you faithfully, Tonio, from beginning to end, and I will give you the answer to everything you have said this afternoon and the solution of the problem that has been upsetting you. Now: the solution is that you, as you sit there, are, quite simply, a bourgeois."

"Am I?" he asked a little crestfallen.

"Yes, that hits you hard, it must. So I will soften the judgment just a little. You are a bourgeois on the wrong path, a bourgeois *manqué.*"

Silence. Then he got up resolutely and took his hat and stick.

"Thank you, Lisabeta Ivanovna; now I can go home in peace. I am expressed."

Towards autumn Tonio Kröger said to Lisabeta Ivanovna:

"Well, Lisabeta, I think I'll be off. I need a change of air. I must get away, out into the open."

"Well, well, well, little Father! Does it please your Highness to go down to Italy again?"

"Oh, get along with your Italy, Lisabeta. I'm fed up with Italy, I spew it out of my mouth. It's a long time since I imagined I could belong down there. Art, eh? Blue-velvet sky, ardent wine, the sweets of sensuality. In short, I don't want it—I decline with thanks. The whole *bellezza* business makes me nervous. All those frightfully animated people down there with their black animal-like eyes; I don't like them either. These Romance peoples have no soul in their eyes. No, I'm going to take a trip to Denmark."

"To Denmark?"

"Yes. I'm quite sanguine of the results. I happen never to have been there, though I lived all my youth so close to it. Still I have always known and loved the country. I suppose I must have this northern tendency from my father, for my mother was really more for the *bellezza,* in so far, that is, as she cared very much one way or the other. But just take the books that are written up there, that clean, meaty, whimsical Scandinavian literature. Lisabeta, there's nothing like it, I love it. Or take the Scandinavian meals, those incomparable meals, which can only be digested in strong sea air (I don't know whether I can digest them in any sort of air); I know them from my home too, because we ate that way up there. Take even the names, the given names that people rejoice in up north; we have a good many of them in my part of the country too: Ingeborg, for instance, isn't it the purest poetry—like a harp-tone? And then the sea—up there it's the Baltic! . . . In a word, I am going, Lisabeta, I want to see the Baltic again and read the books and hear the names on their native heath; I want to stand on the terrace at Kronberg, where the ghost appeared to Hamlet, bringing despair and death to that poor, noble-souled youth. . . ."

"How are you going, Tonio, if I may ask? What route are you taking?"

"The usual one," he said, shrugging his shoulders, and blushed perceptibly. "Yes, I shall touch my—my point of departure, Lisabeta, after thirteen years, and that may turn out rather funny."

She smiled.

"That is what I wanted to hear, Tonio Kröger. Well, be off, then, in God's name. Be sure to write to me, do you hear? I shall expect a letter full of your experiences in—Denmark."

And Tonio Kröger travelled north. He travelled in comfort (for he was wont to say that anyone who suffered inwardly more than other people had a right to a little outward ease); and he did not stay until the towers of the little town he had left rose up in the grey air. Among them he made a short and singular stay.

The dreary afternoon was merging into evening when the train pulled into the narrow, reeking shed, so marvellously familiar. The volumes of thick smoke rolled up to the dirty glass roof and wreathed to and fro there in long tatters, just as they had, long ago, on the day when Tonio Kröger, with nothing but derision in his heart, had left his native town.— He arranged to have his luggage sent to his hotel and walked out of the station.

There were the cabs, those enormously high, enormously wide black cabs drawn by two horses, standing in a rank. He did not take one, he only looked at them, as he looked at everything: the narrow gables, and the pointed towers peering above the roofs close at hand; the plump, fair, easy-going populace, with their broad yet rapid speech. And a nervous laugh mounted in him, mysteriously akin to a sob.— He walked on, slowly, with the damp wind constantly in his face, across the bridge, with the mythological statues on the railings, and some distance along the harbour.

Good Lord, how tiny and close it all seemed! The comical little gabled streets were climbing up just as of yore from the port to the town! And on the ruffled waters the smoke-stacks and masts of the ships dipped gently in the wind and twilight. Should he go up that next street, leading, he knew, to a certain house? No, tomorrow. He was too sleepy. His head was heavy from the journey, and slow, vague trains of thought passed through his mind.

Sometimes in the past thirteen years, when he was suffering

from indigestion, he had dreamed of being back home in the echoing old house in the steep, narrow street. His father had been there too, and reproached him bitterly for his dissolute manner of life, and this, each time, he had found quite as it should be. And now the present refused to distinguish itself in any way from one of those tantalizing dream-fabrications in which the dreamer asks himself if this be delusion or reality and is driven to decide for the latter, only to wake up after all in the end. . . . He paced through the half-empty streets with his head inclined against the wind, moving as though in his sleep in the direction of the hotel, the first hotel in the town, where he meant to sleep. A bow-legged man, with a pole at the end of which burned a tiny fire, walked before him with a rolling, seafaring gait and lighted the gas-lamps.

What was at the bottom of this? What was it burning darkly beneath the ashes of his fatigue, refusing to burst out into a clear blaze? Hush, hush, only no talk. Only don't make words! He would have liked to go on so, for a long time, in the wind, through the dusky, dreamily familiar streets—but everything was so little and close together here. You reached your goal at once.

In the upper town there were arc-lamps, just lighted. There was the hotel with the two black lions in front of it; he had been afraid of them as a child. And there they were, still looking at each other as though they were about to sneeze; only they seemed to have grown much smaller. Tonio Kröger passed between them into the hotel.

As he came on foot, he was received with no great ceremony. There was a porter, and a lordly gentleman dressed in black, to do the honours; the latter, shoving back his cuffs with his little fingers, measured him from the crown of his head to the soles of his boots, obviously with intent to place him, to assign him to his proper category socially and hierarchically speaking and then mete out the suitable degree of courtesy. He seemed not to come to any clear decision and compromised on a moderate display of politeness. A mild-mannered waiter with yellow-white side-whiskers, in a dress suit shiny with age, and rosettes on his soundless shoes, led him up two flights into a clean old room furnished in patriarchal style. Its windows gave on a twilit view of courts and gables, very mediæval and picturesque, with the fantastic bulk of the old church close by. Tonio Kröger stood awhile before this window; then he sat down on the wide sofa, crossed his arms, drew down his brows, and whistled to himself.

Lights were brought and his luggage came up. The mild-mannered waiter laid the hotel register on the table, and Tonio Kröger, his head on one side, scrawled something on it that might be taken for a name, a station, and a place of origin. Then he ordered supper and went on gazing into space from his sofa-corner. When it stood before him he let it wait long untouched, then took a few bites and walked up and down an hour in his room, stopping from time to time and closing his eyes. Then he very slowly undressed and went to bed. He slept long and had curiously confused and ardent dreams.

It was broad day when he woke. Hastily he recalled where he was and got up to draw the curtains; the pale-blue sky, already with a hint of autumn, was streaked with frayed and tattered cloud; still, above his native city the sun was shining.

He spent more care than usual upon his toilette, washed and shaved and made himself fresh and immaculate as though about to call upon some smart family where a well-dressed and flawless appearance was *de rigueur;* and while occupied in this wise he listened to the anxious beating of his heart.

How bright it was outside! He would have liked better a twilight air like yesterday's, instead of passing through the streets in the broad sunlight, under everybody's eye. Would he meet people he knew, be stopped and questioned and have to submit to be asked how he had spent the last thirteen years? No, thank goodness, he was known to nobody here; even if anybody remembered him, it was unlikely he would be recognized—for certainly he had changed in the meantime! He surveyed himself in the glass and felt a sudden sense of security behind his mask, behind his work-worn face, that was older than his years. . . . He sent for breakfast, and after that he went out; he passed under the disdainful eye of the porter and the gentleman in black, through the vestibule and between the two lions, and so into the street.

Where was he going? He scarcely knew. It was the same as yesterday. Hardly was he in the midst of this long-familiar scene, this stately conglomeration of gables, turrets, arcades, and fountains, hardly did he feel once more the wind in his face, that strong current wafting a faint and pungent aroma from far-off dreams, when the same mistiness laid itself like a veil about his senses. . . . The muscles of his face relaxed, and he looked at men and things with a look grown suddenly calm. Perhaps right there, on that street corner, he might wake up after all. . . .

Where was he going? It seemed to him the direction he took had a connection with his sad and strangely rueful dreams of the night. . . . He went to Market Square, under the vaulted arches of the Rathaus, where the butchers were weighing out their wares red-handed, where the tall old Gothic fountain stood with its manifold spires. He paused in front of a house, a plain narrow building, like many another, with a fretted baroque gable; stood there lost in contemplation. He read the plate on the door, his eyes rested a little while on each of the windows. Then slowly he turned away.

Where did he go? Towards home. But he took a roundabout way outside the walls—for he had plenty of time. He went over the Millwall and over the Holstenwall, clutching his hat, for the wind was rushing and moaning through the trees. He left the wall near the station, where he saw a train puffing busily past, idly counted the coaches, and looked after the man who sat perched upon the last. In the Lindenplatz he stopped at one of the pretty villas, peered long into the garden and up at the windows, lastly conceived the idea of swinging the gate to and fro upon its hinges till it creaked. Then he looked awhile at his moist, rust-stained hand and went on, went through the squat old gate, along the harbour, and up the steep, windy street to his parents' house.

It stood aloof from its neighbors, its gable towering above them; grey and sombre, as it had stood these three hundred years;

and Tonio Kröger read the pious, half-illegible motto above the entrance. Then he drew a long breath and went in.

His heart gave a throb of fear, lest his father might come out of one of the doors on the ground floor, in his office coat, with the pen behind his ear, and take him to task for his excesses. He would have found the reproach quite in order; but he got past unchidden. The inner door was ajar, which appeared to him reprehensible though at the same time he felt as one does in certain broken dreams, where obstacles melt away of themselves, and one presses onward in marvellous favour with fortune. The wide entry, paved with great square flags, echoed to his tread. Opposite the silent kitchen was the curious projecting structure, of rough boards, but cleanly varnished, that had been the servants' quarters. It was quite high up and could only be reached by a sort of ladder from the entry. But the great cupboards and carven presses were gone. The son of the house climbed the majestic staircase, with his hand on the white-enamelled, fret-work balustrade. At each step he lifted his hand, and put it down again with the next as though testing whether he could call back his ancient familiarity with the stout old railing. . . . But at the landing of the entresol he stopped. For on the entrance door was a white plate; and on it in black letters he read: "Public Library."

"Public Library?" thought Tonio Kröger. What were either literature or the public doing here? He knocked . . . heard a "come in," and obeying it with gloomy suspense gazed upon a scene of most unhappy alteration.

The storey was three rooms deep, and all the doors stood open. The walls were covered nearly all the way up with long rows of books in uniform bindings, standing in dark-coloured bookcases. In each room a poor creature of a man sat writing behind a sort of counter. The farthest two just turned their heads, but the nearest got up in haste and, leaning with both hands on the table, stuck out his head, pursed his lips, lifted his brows, and looked at the visitor with eagerly blinking eyes.

"I beg pardon," said Tonio Kröger without turning his eyes from the book-shelves. "I am a stranger here, seeing the sights.

So this is your Public Library? May I examine your collection a little?"

"Certainly, with pleasure," said the official, blinking still more violently. "It is open to everybody. . . . Pray look about you. Should you care for a catalogue?"

"No, thanks," answered Tonio Kröger, "I shall soon find my way about." And he began to move slowly along the walls, with the appearance of studying the rows of books. After a while he took down a volume, opened it, and posted himself at the window.

This was the breakfast-room. They had eaten here in the morning instead of in the big dining-room upstairs, with its white statues of gods and goddesses standing out against the blue walls. . . . Beyond there had been a bedroom, where his father's mother had died—only after a long struggle, old as she was, for she had been of a pleasure-loving nature and clung to life. And his father too had drawn his last breath in the same room; that tall, correct, slightly melancholy and pensive gentleman with the wild flower in his buttonhole. . . . Tonio had sat at the foot of his death-bed, quite given over to unutterable feelings of love and grief. His mother had knelt at the bedside, his lovely, fiery mother, dissolved in hot tears, and after that she had withdrawn with her artist into the far blue south. . . . And beyond still, the small third room, likewise full of books and presided over by a shabby man—that had been for years on end his own. Thither he had come after school and a walk—like today's; against that wall his table had stood with the drawer where he had kept his first clumsy, heartfelt attempts at verse. . . . The walnut tree . . . a pang went through him. He gave a sidewise glance out at the window. The garden lay desolate, but there stood the old walnut tree where it used to stand, groaning and creaking heavily in the wind. And Tonio Kröger let his gaze fall upon the book he had in his hands, an excellent piece of work, and very familiar. He followed the black lines of print, the paragraphs, the flow of words that flowed with so much art, mounting in the ardour of creation to a certain climax and effect and then as artfully breaking off.

"Yes, that was well done," he said; put back the book and turned away. Then he saw that the functionary still stood bolt-upright, blinking with a mingled expression of zeal and misgiving. "A capital collection, I see," said Tonio Kröger. "I have already quite a good idea of it. Much obliged to you. Good-bye." He went out; but it was a poor exit, and he felt sure the official would stand there perturbed and blinking for several minutes.

He felt no desire for further researches. He had been home. Strangers were living upstairs in the large rooms behind the pillared hall; the top of the stairs was shut off by a glass door which used not to be there, and on the door was a plate. He went away, down the steps, across the echoing corridor, and left his parental home. He sought a restaurant, sat down in a corner, and brooded over a heavy, greasy meal. Then he returned to his hotel.

"I am leaving," he said to the fine gentleman in black. "This afternoon." And he asked for his bill, and for a carriage to take him down to the harbour where he should take the boat for Copenhagen. Then he went up to his room and sat there stiff and still, with his cheek on his hand, looking down on the table before him with absent eyes. Later he paid his bill and packed his things. At the appointed hour the carriage was announced and Tonio Kröger went down in travel array.

At the foot of the stairs the gentleman in black was waiting.

"Beg pardon," he said, shoving back his cuffs with his little fingers. . . . "Beg pardon, but we must detain you just a moment. Herr Seehaase, the proprietor, would like to exchange two words with you. A matter of form. . . . He is back there. . . . If you will have the goodness to step this way. . . . It is *only* Herr Seehaase, the proprietor."

And he ushered Tonio Kröger into the background of the vestibule. . . . There, in fact, stood Herr Seehaase. Tonio Kröger recognized him from old time. He was small, fat, and bow-legged. His shaven side-whisker was white, but he wore the same old low-cut dress coat and little velvet cap embroidered in green.

He was not alone. Beside him, at a little high desk fastened into the wall, stood a policeman in a helmet, his gloved right hand resting on a document in coloured inks; he turned towards Tonio Kröger with his honest, soldierly face as though he expected Tonio to sink into the earth at his glance.

Tonio Kröger looked at the two and confined himself to waiting.

"You came from Munich?" the policeman asked at length in a heavy, good-natured voice.

Tonio Kröger said he had.

"You are going to Copenhagen?"

"Yes, I am on the way to a Danish seashore resort."

"Seashore resort? Well, you must produce your papers," said the policeman. He uttered the last word with great satisfaction.

"Papers . . . ?" He had no papers. He drew out his pocket-book and looked into it; but aside from notes there was nothing there but some proof-sheets of a story which he had taken along to finish reading. He hated relations with officials and had never got himself a passport. . . .

"I am sorry," he said, "but I don't travel with papers."

"Ah!" said the policeman. "And what might be your name?"

Tonio replied.

"Is that a fact?" asked the policeman, suddenly erect, and expanding his nostrils as wide as he could. . . .

"Yes, that is a fact," answered Tonio Kröger.

"And what are you, anyhow?"

Tonio Kröger gulped and gave the name of his trade in a firm voice. Herr Seehaase lifted his head and looked him curiously in the face.

"H'm," said the policeman. "And you give out that you are not identical with an individdle named"—he said "individdle" and then, referring to his document in coloured inks, spelled out an involved, fantastic name which mingled all the sounds of all the races—Tonio Kröger forgot it next minute—"of unknown parentage and unspecified means," he went on, "wanted by the Munich police for various shady transactions, and probably in flight towards Denmark?"

"Yes, I give out all that, and more," said Tonio Kröger, wriggling his shoulders. The gesture made a certain impression.

"What? Oh, yes, of course," said the policeman. "You say you can't show any papers—"

Herr Seehaase threw himself into the breach.

"It is only a formality," he said pacifically, "nothing else. You must bear in mind the official is only doing his duty. If you could only identify yourself somehow—some document . . ."

They were all silent. Should he make an end of the business, by revealing to Herr Seehaase that he was no swindler without specified means, no gypsy in a green wagon, but the son of the late Consul Kröger, a member of the Kröger family? No, he felt no desire to do that. After all, were not these guardians of civic order within their right? He even agreed with them—up to a point. He shrugged his shoulders and kept quiet.

"What have you got, then?" asked the policeman. "In your portfoly, I mean?"

"Here? Nothing. Just a proof-sheet," answered Tonio Kröger.

"Proof-sheet? What's that? Let's see it."

And Tonio Kröger handed over his work. The policeman spread it out on the shelf and began reading. Herr Seehaase drew up and shared it with him. Tonio Kröger looked over their shoulders to see what they read. It was a good moment, a little effect he had worked out to a perfection. He had a sense of self-satisfaction.

"You see," he said, "there is my name. I wrote it, and it is going to be published, you understand."

"All right, that will answer," said Herr Seehaase with decision, gathered up the sheets and gave them back. "That will have to answer, Petersen," he repeated crisply, shutting his eyes and shaking his head as though to see and hear no more. "We must not keep the gentleman any longer. The carriage is waiting. I implore you to pardon the little inconvenience, sir. The officer has only done his duty, but I told him at once he was on the wrong track. . . ."

"Indeed!" thought Tonio Kröger.

The officer seemed still to have his doubts; he muttered something else about individdle and document. But Herr Seehaase, overflowing with regrets, led his guest through the vestibule, accompanied him past the two lions to the carriage, and himself, with many respectful bows, closed the door upon him. And then the funny, high, wide old cab rolled and rattled and bumped down the steep, narrow street to the quay.

And such was the manner of Tonio Kröger's visit to his ancestral home.

Night fell and the moon swam up with silver gleam as Tonio Kröger's boat reached the open sea. He stood at the prow wrapped in his cloak against a mounting wind, and looked beneath into the dark going and coming of the waves as they hovered and swayed and came on, to meet with a clap and shoot erratically away in a bright gush of foam.

He was lulled in a mood of still enchantment. The episode at the hotel, their wanting to arrest him for a swindler in his own home, had cast him down a little, even although he found it quite in order—in a certain way. But after he came on board he had watched, as he used to do as a boy with his father, the lading of goods into the deep bowels of the boat, amid shouts of mingled Danish and Plattdeutsch; not only boxes and bales, but also a Bengal tiger and a polar bear were lowered in cages with stout iron bars. They had probably come from Hamburg and were destined for a Danish menagerie. He had enjoyed these distractions. And as the boat glided along between flat riverbanks he quite forgot Officer Petersen's inquisition; while all the rest—his sweet, sad, rueful dreams of the night before, the walk he had taken, the walnut tree—had welled up again in his soul. The sea opened out and he saw in the distance the beach where he as a lad had been let to listen to the ocean's summer dreams; saw the flashing of the lighthouse tower and the lights of the Kurhaus where he and his parents had lived. . . . The Baltic! He bent his head to the strong salt wind; it came sweeping on, it enfolded him, made him faintly giddy and a little deaf; and in that mild confusion of the senses all memory of evil, of anguish and error, effort and exertion of the will, sank away into joyous oblivion and were gone. The roaring, foaming, flapping, and slapping all about him came to his ears like the groan and rustle of an old walnut tree, the creaking of a garden gate. . . . More and more the darkness came on.

"The stars! Oh, by Lord, look at the stars!" a voice suddenly said, with a heavy singsong accent that seemed to come out of the inside of a tun. He recognized it. It belonged to a young man with red-blond hair who had been Tonio Kröger's neighbour at dinner in the salon. His dress was very simple, his eyes were red, and he had the moist and chilly look of a person who has just bathed. With nervous and self-conscious movements he had taken unto himself an astonishing quantity of lobster omelet. Now he leaned on the rail beside Tonio Kröger and looked up at the skies, holding his chin between thumb and forefinger. Beyond a doubt he was in one of those rare and festal and edifying moods that cause the barriers between man and man to fall; when the heart opens even to the stranger, and the mouth utters that which otherwise it would blush to speak. . . .

"Look, by dear sir, just look at the stars. There they stahd and glitter; by goodness, the whole sky is full of theb! And I ask you, when you stahd ahd look up at theb, ahd realize that bany of theb are a huddred tibes larger thad the earth, how does it bake you feel? Yes, we have idvehted the telegraph and the telephode and all the triuphs of our bodern tibes. But whed we look up there, after all we have to recogdize and uhderstad that we are worbs, biserable worbs, ahd dothing else. Ab I right, sir, or ab I wrog? Yes, we are worbs," he answered himself, and nodded meekly and abjectly in the direction of the firmament.

"Ah, no, he has no literature in his belly," thought Tonio Kröger. And he recalled something he had lately read, an essay by a famous French writer on cosmological and psychological philosophies, a very delightful *causerie*.

He made some sort of reply to the young man's feeling remarks, and they went on talking, leaning over the rail, and looking into the night with its movement and fitful lights. The young man, it seemed, was a Hamburg merchant on his holiday.

"Y'ought to travel to Copedhagen on the boat, thigks I, and so here I ab, and so far it's been fide. But they shouldn't have given us the lobster obelet, sir, for it's going to be storby—the captain said so hibself—and that's do joke with indigestible food like that in your stobach. . . ."

Tonio Kröger listened to all this engaging artlessness and was privately drawn to it.

"Yes," he said, "all the food up here is too heavy. It makes one lazy and melancholy."

"Belancholy?" repeated the young man, and looked at him, taken aback. Then he asked, suddenly: "You are a stradger up here, sir?"

"Yes, I come from a long way off," answered Tonio Kröger vaguely, waving his arm.

"But you're right," said the youth; "Lord kdows you are right about the belancholy. I am dearly always belancholy, but specially on evedings like this when there are stars in the sky." And he supported his chin again with his thumb and forefinger.

"Surely this man writes verses," thought Tonio Kröger; "business man's verses, full of deep feeling and singlemindedness."

Evening drew on. The wind had grown so violent as to prevent them from talking. So they thought they would sleep a bit, and wished each other good-night.

Tonio Kröger stretched himself out on the narrow cabin bed, but he found no repose. The strong wind with its sharp tang had power to rouse him; he was strangely restless with sweet anticipations. Also he was violently sick with the motion of the ship as she glided down a steep mountain of wave and her screw vibrated as in agony, free of the water. He put on all his clothes again and went up to the deck.

Clouds raced across the moon. The sea danced. It did not come on in full-bodied, regular waves; but far out in the pale and flickering light the water was lashed, torn, and tumbled; leaped upward like great licking flames; hung in jagged and fantastic shapes above dizzy abysses, where the foam seemed to be tossed by the playful strength of colossal arms and flung upward in all directions. The ship had a heavy passage; she lurched and stamped and groaned through the welter; and far down in her bowels the tiger and the polar bear voiced their acute discomfort. A man in an oilskin, with the hood drawn over his head and a lantern strapped to his chest, went straddling painfully up and down the deck. And at the stern, leaning far out, stood the young man from Hamburg suffering the worst. "Lord!" he said, in a hollow, quavering voice, when he saw Tonio Kröger. "Look at the uproar of the elebents, sir!" But he could say no more—he was obliged to turn hastily away.

Tonio Kröger clutched at a taut rope and looked abroad into the arrogance of the elements. His exultation outvied storm and wave; within himself he chanted a song to the sea, instinct with love of her: "O thou wild friend of my youth, Once more I behold thee—" But it got no further, he did not finish it. It was not fated to receive a final form nor in tranquillity to be welded to a perfect whole. For his heart was too full. . . .

Long he stood; then stretched himself out on a bench by the pilot-house and looked up at the sky, where stars were flickering. He even slept a little. And when the cold foam splashed his face it seemed in his half-dreams like a caress.

Perpendicular chalk-cliffs, ghostly in the moonlight, came in sight. They were nearing the island of Möen. Then sleep came again, broken by salty showers of spray that bit into his face and made it stiff. . . . When he really roused, it was broad day, fresh and palest grey, and the sea had gone down. At breakfast he saw the young man from Hamburg again, who blushed rosy-red for shame of the poetic indiscretions he had been betrayed into by the dark, ruffled up his little red-blond moustache with all five fingers, and called out a brisk and soldierly good-morning—after that he studiously avoided him.

And Tonio Kröger landed in Denmark. He arrived in Copenhagen, gave tips to everybody who laid claim to them, took a room at a hotel, and roamed the city for three days with an open guide-book and the air of an intelligent foreigner bent on improving his mind. He looked at the king's New Market and the "Horse" in the middle of it, gazed respectfully up the columns of the Frauenkirch, stood long before Thorwaldsen's noble and beautiful statuary, climbed the round tower, visited castles, and spent two lively evenings in the Tivoli. But all this was not exactly what he saw.

The doors of the houses—so like those in his native town, with open-work gables of baroque shape—bore names known to him of old; names that had a tender and precious quality, and withal in their syllables an accent of plaintive reproach, of repining after the lost and gone. He walked, he gazed, drawing deep, lingering draughts of moist sea air; and everywhere he saw eyes as blue, hair as blond, faces as familiar, as those that had visited his rueful dreams the night he had spent in his native town. There in the open street it befell him that a glance, a ringing word, a sudden laugh would pierce him to his marrow.

He could not stand the bustling city for long. A restlessness, half memory and half hope, half foolish and half sweet, possessed him; he was moved to drop this rôle of ardent inquiring tourist and lie somewhere, quite quietly, on a beach. So he took ship once more and travelled under a cloudy sky, over a black water, northwards along the coast of Seeland towards Helsingör. Thence he drove, at once, by carriage, for three-quarters of an hour, along and above the sea, reaching at length his ultimate goal, the little white "bath-hotel" with green blinds. It stood surrounded by a settlement of cottages, and its shingled turret tower looked out on the beach and the Swedish coast. Here he left the carriage, took possession of the light room they had ready for him, filled shelves and presses with his kit, and prepared to stop awhile.

It was well on in September; not many guests were left in Aalsgaard. Meals were served on the ground floor, in the great beamed dining-room, whose lofty windows led out upon the veranda and the sea. The landlady presided, an elderly spinster with white hair and faded eyes, a faint colour in her cheek and a feeble twittering voice. She was forever arranging her red hands to look well upon the table-cloth. There was a short-necked old gentleman, quite blue in the face, with a grey sailor beard; a fish-dealer he was, from the capital, and strong at the German. He seemed entirely congested and inclined to apoplexy; breathed in short gasps, kept putting his beringed first finger to one nostril, and snorting violently to get a passage of air through the other. Notwithstanding, he addressed himself constantly to the whisky-bottle, which stood at his place at luncheon and dinner, and breakfast as well. Besides him the company consisted only of three tall American youths with their governor or tutor, who kept adjusting his glasses in unbroken silence. All day long he played football with his charges, who had narrow, taciturn faces and reddish-yellow hair parted in the middle. "Please pass the *wurst,*" said one. "That's not *wurst,* it's *schinken,*" said the other, and this was the extent of their conversation, as the rest of the time they sat there dumb, drinking hot water.

Tonio Kröger could have wished himself no better table-companions. He revelled in the peace and quiet, listened to the Danish palatals, the clear and the clouded vowels in which the fish-dealer and the landlady desultorily conversed; modestly exchanged views with the fish-dealer on the state of the barometer, and then left the table to go through the veranda and onto the beach once more, where he had already spent long, long morning hours.

Sometimes it was still summery there. The sea lay idle and smooth, in stripes of blue and russet and bottle-green, played all across with glittering silvery lights. The seaweed shrivelled in the sun and the jelly-fish lay steaming. There was a faintly stagnant smell and a whiff of tar from the fishing-boat against which Tonio Kröger leaned, so standing that he had before his eyes not the Swedish coast but the open horizon, and in his face the pure, fresh breath of the softly breathing sea.

Then grey, stormy days would come. The waves lowered their heads like bulls and charged against the beach; they ran and ramped high up the sands and left them strewn with shining wet sea-grass, driftwood, and mussels. All abroad beneath an overcast sky extended ranges of billows, and between them foaming valleys palely green; but above the spot where the sun hung behind the cloud a patch like white velvet lay on the sea.

Tonio Kröger stood wrapped in wind and tumult, sunk in the continual dull, drowsy uproar that he loved. When he turned away it seemed suddenly warm and silent all about him. But he was never unconscious of the sea at his back; it called, it lured, it beckoned him. And he smiled.

He went landward, by lonely meadow-paths, and was swallowed up in the beech-groves that clothed the rolling landscape near and far. Here he sat down on the moss, against a tree, and gazed at the strip of water he could see between the trunks. Sometimes the sound of surf came on the wind—a noise like boards collapsing at a distance. And from the tree-tops over his head a cawing—hoarse, desolate, forlorn. He held a book on his knee, but did not read a line. He enjoyed profound forgetfulness, hovered disembodied above space and time; only now and again his heart would contract with a fugitive pain, a stab of longing and regret, into whose origin he was too lazy to inquire.

Thus passed some days. He could not have said how many and had no desire to know. But then came one on which something happened; happened while the sun stood in the sky and people were about; and Tonio Kröger, even, felt no vast surprise.

The very opening of the day had been rare and festal. Tonio Kröger woke early and suddenly from his sleep, with a vague and exquisite alarm; he seemed to be looking at a miracle, a magic illumination. His room had a glass door and balcony facing the sound; a thin white gauze curtain divided it into living- and sleeping-quarters, both hung with delicately tinted paper and furnished with an airy good taste that gave them a sunny and friendly look. But now to his sleep-drunken eyes it lay bathed in a serene and roseate light, an unearthly brightness that gilded walls and furniture and turned the gauze curtain to radiant pink cloud. Tonio Kröger did not at once understand. Not until he stood at the glass door and looked out did he realize that this was the sunrise.

For several days there had been clouds and rain; but now the sky was like a piece of pale-blue silk, spanned shimmering above sea and land, and shot with light from red and golden clouds. The sun's disk rose in splendour from a crisply glittering sea that seemed to quiver and burn beneath it. So began the day. In a joyous daze Tonio Kröger flung on his clothes, and breakfasting in the veranda before everybody else, swam from the little wooden bathhouse some distance out into the sound, then walked for an hour along the beach. When he came back, several omnibuses were before the door, and from the dining-room he could see people in the parlour next door where the piano was, in the veranda, and on the terrace in front; quantities of people sitting at little tables enjoying beer and sandwiches amid lively discourse. There were whole families, there were old and young, there were even a few children.

At second breakfast—the table was heavily laden with cold viands, roast, pickled, and smoked—Tonio Kröger inquired what was going on.

"Guests," said the fish-dealer. "Tourists and ball-guests from Helsingör. Lord help us, we shall get no sleep this night! There will be dancing and music, and I fear me it will keep up till late. It is a family reunion, a sort of celebration and excursion combined; they all subscribe to it and take advantage of the good weather. They came by boat and bus and they are having breakfast. After that they go on with their drive, but at night they will all come back for a dance here in the hall. Yes, damn it, you'll see we shan't get a wink of sleep."

"Oh, it will be a pleasant change," said Tonio Kröger.

After that there was nothing more said for some time. The landlady arranged her red fingers on the cloth, the fish-dealer blew through his nostril, the Americans drank hot water and made long faces.

Then all at once a thing came to pass: *Hans Hansen and Ingeborg Holm walked through the room.*

Tonio Kröger, pleasantly fatigued after his swim and rapid walk, was leaning back in his chair and eating smoked salmon on toast; he sat facing the veranda and the ocean. All at once the door opened and the two entered hand-in-hand—calmly and unhurried. Ingeborg, blonde Inge, was dressed just as she used to be at Herr Knaak's dancing-class. The light flowered frock reached down to her ankles and it had a tulle fichu draped with a pointed opening that left her soft throat free. Her hat hung by its ribbons over her arm. She, perhaps, was a little more grown up than she used to be, and her wonderful plait of hair was wound round her head; but Hans Hansen was the same as ever. He wore his sailor overcoat with gilt buttons, and his wide blue sailor collar lay across his shoulders and back; the sailor cap with its short ribbons he was dangling carelessly in his hand. Ingeborg's narrow eyes were turned away; perhaps she felt shy before the company at table. But Hans Hansen turned his head straight towards them, and measured one after another defiantly with his steel-blue eyes; challengingly, with a sort of contempt. He even dropped Ingeborg's hand and swung his cap harder than ever, to show what manner of man he was. Thus the two, against the silent, blue-dyed sea, measured the length of the room and passed through the opposite door into the parlour.

This was at half past eleven in the morning. While the guests of the house was still at table the company in the veranda broke up and went away by the side door. No one else came into the dining-room. The guests could hear them laughing and joking as they got into the omnibuses, which rumbled away one by one. . . . "So they are coming back?" asked Tonio Kröger.

"That they are," said the fish-dealer. "More's the pity. They have ordered music, let me tell you—and my room is right above the dining-room."

"Oh, well, it's a pleasant change," repeated Tonio Kröger. Then he got up and went away.

That day he spent as he had the others, on the beach and in the wood, holding a book on his knee and blinking in the sun. He had but one thought; they were coming back to have a dance in the hall, the fish-dealer had promised they would; and he did nothing but be glad of this, with a sweet and timorous gladness such as he had not felt through all these long dead years. Once he happened, by some chance association, to think of his friend

Adalbert, the novelist, the man who had known what he wanted and betaken himself to the café to get away from the spring. Tonio Kröger shrugged his shoulders at the thought of him.

Luncheon was served earlier than usual, also supper, which they ate in the parlour because the dining-room was being got ready for the ball, and the whole house flung in disorder for the occasion. It grew dark; Tonio Kröger sitting in his room heard on the road and in the house the sounds of approaching festivity. The picknickers were coming back; from Helsingör, by bicycle and carriage, new guests were arriving; a fiddle and a nasal clarinet might be heard practising down in the dining-room. Everything promised a brilliant ball. . . .

Now the little orchestra struck up a march; he could hear the notes, faint but lively. The dancing opened with a polonaise. Tonio Kröger sat for a while and listened. But when he heard the march-time go over into a waltz he got up and slipped noiselessly out of his room.

From his corridor it was possible to go by the side stairs to the side entrance of the hotel and thence to the veranda without passing through a room. He took this route, softly and stealthily as though on forbidden paths, feeling along through the dark, relentlessly drawn by this stupid jigging music, that now came up to him loud and clear.

The veranda was empty and dim, but the glass door stood open into the hall, where shone two large oil lamps, furnished with bright reflectors. Thither he stole on soft feet; and his skin prickled with the thievish pleasure of standing unseen in the dark and spying on the dancers there in the brightly lighted room. Quickly and eagerly he glanced about for the two whom he sought. . . .

Even though the ball was only half an hour old, the merriment seemed in full swing; however, the guests had come hither already warm and merry, after a whole day of carefree, happy companionship. By bending forward a little, Tonio Kröger could see into the parlour from where he was. Several old gentlemen sat there smoking, drinking, and playing cards; others were with their wives on the plush-upholstered chairs in the foreground watching the dance. They sat with their knees apart and their hands resting on them, puffing out their cheeks with a prosperous air; the mothers, with bonnets perched on their parted hair, with their hands folded over their stomachs and their heads on one side, gazed into the whirl of dancers. A platform had been erected on the long side of the hall, and on it the musicians were doing their utmost. There was even a trumpet, that blew with a certain caution, as though afraid of its own voice, and yet after all kept breaking and cracking. Couples were dipping and circling about, others walked arm-in-arm up and down the room. No one wore ballroom clothes; they were dressed as for an outing in the summertime: the men in countrified suits which were obviously their Sunday wear; the girls in light-coloured frocks with bunches of field-flowers in their bodices. Even a few children were there, dancing with each other in their own way, even after the music stopped. There was a long-legged man in a coat with a little swallow-tail, a provincial lion with an eye-glass and frizzed hair, a post-office clerk or some such thing; he was like a comic figure stepped bodily out of a Danish novel; and he seemed to be the leader and manager of the ball. He was everywhere at once, bustling, perspiring, officious, utterly absorbed; setting down his feet, in shiny, pointed, military half-boots, in a very artificial and involved manner, toes first; waving his arms to issue an order, clapping his hands for the music to begin; here, there, and everywhere, and glancing over his shoulder in pride at his great bow of office, the streamers of which fluttered grandly in his rear.

Yes, there they were, those two, who had gone by Tonio Kröger in the broad light of day; he saw them again—with a joyful start he recognized them almost at the same moment. Here was Hans Hansen by the door, quite close; his legs apart, a little bent over, he was eating with circumspection a large piece of sponge-cake, holding his hand cupwise under his chin to catch the crumbs. And there by the wall sat Ingeborg Holm, Inge the fair; the post-office clerk was just mincing up to her with an exaggerated bow and asking her to dance. He laid one hand on his back and gracefully shoved the other into his bosom. But she was shaking her head in token that she was a little out of breath and must rest awhile, whereat the post-office clerk sat down by her side.

Tonio Kröger looked at them both, these two for whom he had in time past suffered love—at Hans and Ingeborg. They were Hans and Ingeborg not so much by virtue of individual traits and similarity of costume as by similarity of race and type. This was the blond, fair-haired breed of the steel-blue eyes, which stood to him for the pure, the blithe, the untroubled in life; for a virginal aloofness that was at once both simple and full of pride. . . . He looked at them. Hans Hansen was standing there in his sailor suit, lively and well built as ever, broad in the shoulders and narrow in the hips; Ingeborg was laughing and tossing her head in a certain high-spirited way she had; she carried her hand, a schoolgirl hand, not at all slender, not at all particularly aristocratic, to the back of her head in a certain manner so that the thin sleeve fell away from her elbow—and suddenly such a pang of home-sickness shook his breast that involuntarily he drew farther back into the darkness lest someone might see his features twitch.

"Had I forgotten you?" he asked. "No, never. Not thee, Hans, not thee, Inge the fair! It was always you I worked for; when I heard applause I always stole a look to see if you were there. . . . Did you read *Don Carlos,* Hans Hansen, as you promised me at the garden gate? No, don't read it! I do not ask it any more. What have you to do with a king who weeps for loneliness? You must not cloud your clear eyes or make them dreamy and dim by peering into melancholy poetry. . . . To be like you! To begin again, to grow up like you, regular like you, simple and normal and cheerful, in conformity and understanding with God and man, beloved of the innocent and happy. To take you, Ingeborg Holm, to wife, and have a son like you, Hans Hansen—to live free from the curse of knowledge and the torment of creation, live and praise God in blessed mediocrity! Begin again? But it would do no good. It would turn out the same—everything would turn out the same as it did before. For some go of necessity astray, because for them there is no such thing as a right path."

The music ceased; there was a pause in which refreshments were handed round. The post-office assistant tripped about in person with a trayful of herring salad and served the ladies; but before Ingeborg Holm he even went down on one knee as he passed her the dish, and she blushed for pleasure.

But now those within began to be aware of a spectator behind the glass door; some of the flushed and pretty faces turned to measure him with hostile glances; but he stood his ground. Ingeborg and Hans looked at him too, at almost the same time, both with that utter indifference in their eyes that looks so like contempt. And he was conscious too of a gaze resting on him from a different quarter; turned his head and met with his own the eyes that had sought him out. A girl stood not far off, with a fine, pale little face—he had already noticed her. She had not danced much, she had few partners, and he had seen her sitting there against the wall, her lips closed in a bitter line. She was standing alone now too; her dress was a thin light stuff, like the others, but beneath the transparent frock her shoulders showed angular and poor, and the thin neck was thrust down so deep between those meagre shoulders that as she stood there motionless she might almost be thought a little deformed. She was holding her hands in their thin mitts across her flat breast, with the finger-tips touching; her head was drooped, yet she was looking up at Tonio Kröger with black swimming eyes. He turned away. . . .

Here, quite close to him, were Ingeborg and Hans. He had sat down beside her—she was perhaps his sister—and they ate and drank together surrounded by other rosy-cheeked folk; they chattered and made merry, called to each other in ringing voices, and laughed aloud. Why could he not go up and speak to them? Make some trivial remark to him or her, to which they might at least answer with a smile? It would make him happy—he longed to do it; he would go back more satisfied to his room if he might feel he had established a little contact with them. He thought out what he might say; but he had not the courage to say it. Yes, this too was just as it had been: they would not understand him, they would listen like strangers to anything he was able to say. For their speech was not his speech.

It seemed the dance was about to begin again. The leader developed a comprehensive activity. He dashed hither and thither, adjuring everybody to get partners; helped the waiters to push chairs and glasses out of the way, gave orders to the musicians, even took some awkward people by the shoulders and shoved them aside. . . . What was coming? They formed squares of four couples each. . . . A frightful memory brought the colour to Tonio Kröger's cheeks. They were forming for a quadrille.

The music struck up, the couples bowed and crossed over. The leader called off; he called off—Heaven save us—in French! And pronounced the nasals with great distinction. Ingeborg Holm danced close by, in the set nearest the glass door. She moved to and fro before him, forwards and back, pacing and turning; he caught a waft from her hair or the thin stuff of her frock, and it made him close his eyes with the old, familiar feeling, the fragrance and bitter-sweet enchantment he had faintly felt in all these days, that now filled him utterly with irresistible sweetness. And what was the feeling? Longing, tenderness? Envy? Self-contempt? . . . *Moulinet des dames!* "Did you laugh, Ingeborg the blonde, did you laugh at me when I disgraced myself by dancing the *moulinet?* And would you still laugh today even after I have become something like a famous man? Yes, that you would, and you would be right to laugh. Even if I in my own person had written the nine symphonies and *The World as Will and Idea* and painted the Last Judgment, you would still be eternally right to laugh. . . . " As he looked at her he thought of a line of verse once so familiar to him, now long forgotten: "I would sleep, but thou must dance." How well he knew it, that melancholy northern mood it evoked—its heavy inarticulateness. To sleep. . . . To long to be allowed to live the life of simple feeling, to rest sweetly and passively in feeling alone, without compulsion to act and achieve—and yet to be forced to dance, dance the cruel and perilous sword-dance of art; without even being allowed to forget the melancholy conflict within oneself; to be forced to dance, the while one loved. . . .

A sudden wild extravagance had come over the scene. The sets had broken up, the quadrille was being succeeded by a galop, and all the couples were leaping and gliding about. They flew past Tonio Kröger to a maddeningly quick tempo, crossing, advancing, retreating, with quick, breathless laughter. A couple came rushing and circling towards Tonio Kröger; the girl had a pale, refined face and lean, high shoulders. Suddenly, directly in front of him, they tripped and slipped and stumbled. . . . The pale girl fell, so hard and violently it almost looked dangerous; and her partner with her. He must have hurt himself badly, for he quite forgot her, and, half rising, began to rub his knee and grimace; while she, quite dazed, it seemed, still lay on the floor. Then Tonio Kröger came forward, took her gently by the arms, and lifted her up. She looked dazed, bewildered, wretched; then suddenly her delicate face flushed pink.

"Tak, O, mange tak!" she said, and gazed up at him with dark, swimming eyes.

"You should not dance any more, Fräulein," he said gently. Once more he looked round at *them,* at Ingeborg and Hans, and then he went out, left the ball and the veranda and returned to his own room.

He was exhausted with jealousy, worn out with the gaiety in which he had had no part. Just the same, just the same as it had always been. Always with burning cheeks he had stood in his dark corner and suffered for you, you blond, you living, you happy ones! And then quite simply gone away. Somebody *must* come now! Ingeborg *must* notice he had gone, must slip after him, lay a hand on his shoulder and say: "Come back and be happy. I love you!" But she came not at all. No, such things did not happen. Yes, all was as it had been, and he too was happy, just as he had been. For his heart was alive. But between that past and this present what had happened to make him become that which he now was? Icy desolation, solitude: mind, and art, forsooth!

He undressed, lay down, put out the light. Two names he whispered into his pillow, the few chaste northern syllables that meant for him his true and native way of love, of longing and happiness; that meant to him life and home, meant simple and heartfelt feeling. He looked back on the years that had passed. He thought of the dreamy adventures of the senses, nerves, and mind in which he had been involved; saw himself eaten up with intellect and introspection, ravaged and paralysed by insight, half worn out by the fevers and frosts of creation, helpless and in anguish of conscience between two extremes, flung to and fro between austerity and lust; *raffiné,* impoverished, exhausted by frigid and artificially heightened ecstasies; erring, forsaken, martyred, and ill—and sobbed with nostalgia and remorse.

Here in his room it was still and dark. But from below life's lulling, trivial waltz-rhythm came faintly to his ears.

Tonio Kröger sat up in the north, composing his promised letter to his friend Lisabeta Ivanovna.

"Dear Lisabeta down there in Arcady, whither I shall shortly return," he wrote: "Here is something like a letter, but it will probably disappoint you, for I mean to keep it rather general. Not that I have nothing to tell; for indeed, in my way, I have had experiences; for instance, in my native town they were even going to arrest me . . . but of that by word of mouth. Sometimes now I have days when I would rather state things in general terms than go on telling stories.

"You probably still remember, Lisabeta, that you called me a *bourgeois, a bourgeois manqué?* You called me that in an hour when, led on by other confessions I had previously let slip, I confessed to you my love of life, or what I call life. I ask myself if you were aware how very close you came to the truth, how much my love of 'life' is one and the same thing as my being a *bourgeois.* This journey of mine has given me much occasion to ponder the subject.

"My father, you know, had the temperament of the north:

solid, reflective, puritanically correct, with a tendency to melancholia. My mother, of indeterminate foreign blood, was beautiful, sensuous, naïve, passionate, and careless at once, and, I think, irregular by instinct. The mixture was no doubt extraordinary and bore with it extraordinary dangers. The issue of it, a *bourgeois* who strayed off into art, a bohemian who feels nostalgic yearnings for respectability, an artist with a bad conscience. For surely it is my *bourgeois* conscience makes me see in the artist life, in all irregularity and all genius, something profoundly suspect, profoundly disreputable; that fills me with this lovelorn *faiblesse* for the simple and good, the comfortably normal, the average unendowed respectable human being.

"I stand between two worlds. I am at home in neither, and I suffer in consequence. You artists call me a *bourgeois,* and the *bourgeois* try to arrest me. . . . I don't know which makes me feel worse. The *bourgeois* are stupid; but you adorers of the beautiful, who call me phlegmatic and without aspirations, you ought to realize that there is a way of being an artist that goes so deep and is so much a matter of origins and destinies that no longing seems to it sweeter and more worth knowing than longing after the bliss of the commonplace.

"I admire those proud, cold beings who adventure upon the paths of great and dæmonic beauty and despise 'mankind'; but I do not envy them. For if anything is capable of making a poet of a literary man, it is my *bourgeois* love of the human, the living and usual. It is the source of all warmth, goodness, and humour; I even almost think it is itself that love of which it stands written that one may speak with the tongues of men and of angels and yet having it not is as sounding brass and tinkling cymbals.

"The work I have so far done is nothing or not much—as good as nothing. I will do better, Lisabeta—this is a promise. As I write, the sea whispers to me and I close my eyes. I am looking into a world unborn and formless, that needs to be ordered and shaped; I see into a whirl of shadows of human figures who beckon to me to weave spells to redeem them: tragic and laughable figures and some that are both together—and to these I am drawn. But my deepest and secretest love belongs to the blond and blue-eyed, the fair and living, the happy, lovely, and commonplace.

"Do not chide this love, Lisabeta; it is good and fruitful. There is longing in it, and a gentle envy; a touch of contempt and no little innocent bliss."

1903

MARIO AND THE MAGICIAN

The atmosphere of Torre di Venere remains unpleasant in the memory. From the first moment the air of the place made us uneasy, we felt irritable, on edge; then at the end came the shocking business of Cipolla, that dreadful being who seemed to incorporate, in so fateful and so humanly impressive a way, all the peculiar evilness of the situation as a whole. Looking back, we had the feeling that the horrible end of the affair had been preordained and lay in the nature of things; that the children had to be present at it was an added impropriety, due to the false colours in which the weird creature presented himself. Luckily for them, they did not know where the comedy left off and the tragedy began; and we let them remain in their happy belief that the whole thing had been a play up till the end.

Torre di Venere lies some fifteen kilometres from Portoclemente, one of the most popular summer resorts on the Tyrrhenian Sea. Portoclemente is urban and elegant and full to overflowing for months on end. Its gay and busy main street of shops and hotels runs down to a wide sandy beach covered with tents and pennanted sand-castles and sunburnt humanity, where at all times a lively social bustle reigns, and much noise. But this same spacious and inviting fine-sanded beach, this same border of pine grove and near, presiding mountains, continues all the way along the coast. No wonder then that some competition of a quiet kind should have sprung up further on. Torre di Venere—the tower that gave the town its name is gone long since, one looks for it in vain—is an offshoot of the larger resort, and for some years remained an idyll for the few, a refuge for more unworldly spirits. But the usual history of such places repeated itself: peace has had to retire further along the coast, to Marina Petriera and dear knows where else. We all know how the world at once seeks peace and puts her to flight—rushing upon her in the fond idea that they two will wed, and where she is, there it can be at home. It will even set up its Vanity Fair in a spot and be capable of thinking that peace is still by its side. Thus Torre—though its atmosphere so far is more modest and contemplative than that of Portoclemente—has been quite taken up, by both Italians and foreigners. It is no longer the thing to go to Portoclemente—though still so much the thing that it is as noisy and crowded as ever. One goes next door, so to speak: to Torre. So much more refined, even, and cheaper to boot. And the attractiveness of these qualities persists, though the qualities themselves long ago ceased to be evident. Torre has got a Grand Hotel. Numerous pensions have sprung up, some modest, some pretentious. The people who own or rent the villas and pinetas overlooking the sea no longer have it all their own way on the beach. In July and August it looks just like the beach at Portoclemente: it swarms with a screaming, squabbling, merrymaking crowd, and the sun, blazing down like mad, peels the skin off their necks. Garish little flat-bottomed boats rock on the glittering blue, manned by children, whose mothers hover afar and fill the air with anxious cries of Nino! and Sandro! and Bice! and Maria! Pedlars step across the legs of recumbent sun-bathers, selling flowers and corals, oysters, lemonade, and *cornetti al burro,* and crying their wares in the breathy, full-throated southern voice.

Such was the scene that greeted our arrival in Torre: pleasant enough, but after all, we thought, we had come too soon. It was the middle of August, the Italian season was still at its height, scarcely the moment for strangers to learn to love the special charms of the place. What an afternoon crowd in the cafés on the front! For instance, in the Esquisito, where we sometimes sat and were served by Mario, that very Mario of whom I shall have presently to tell. It is well-nigh impossible to find a table; and the various orchestras contend together in the midst of one's conversation with bewildering effect. Of course, it is in the afternoon that people come over from Portoclemente. The excursion is a favourite one for the restless denizens of that pleasure resort, and a Fiat motor-bus plies to and fro, coating inch-thick with dust the oleander and laurel hedges along the highroad—a notable if repulsive sight.

Yes, decidedly one should go to Torre in September, when the great public has left. Or else in May, before the water is warm enough to tempt the Southerner to bathe. Even in the before and after seasons Torre is not empty, but life is less national and more subdued. English, French, and German prevail under the tent-awnings and in the pension dining-rooms; whereas in August—in the Grand Hotel, at least, where, in default of private addresses, we had engaged rooms—the stranger finds the field so occupied by Florentine and Roman society that he feels quite isolated and even temporarily *déclassé*.

We had, rather to our annoyance, this experience on the evening we arrived, when we went in to dinner and were shown to our table by the waiter in charge. As a table, it had nothing against it, save that we had already fixed our eyes upon those on the veranda beyond, built out over the water, where little red-shaded lamps glowed—and there were still some tables empty, though it was as full as the dining-room within. The children went into raptures at the festive sight, and without more ado we announced our intention to take our meals by preference in the veranda. Our words, it appeared, were prompted by ignorance; for we were informed, with somewhat embarrassed politeness, that the cosy nook outside was reserved for the clients of the hotel: *ai nostri clienti*. Their clients? But we were their clients. We were not tourists or trippers, but boarders for a stay of some three or four weeks. However, we forbore to press for an explanation of the difference between the likes of us and that clientèle to whom it was vouchsafed to eat out there in the glow of the red lamps, and took our dinner by the prosaic common light of the dining-room chandelier—a thoroughly ordinary and monotonous hotel bill of fare, be it said. In Pensione Eleonora, a few steps landward, the table, as we were to discover, was much better.

And thither it was that we moved, three or four days later, before we had had time to settle in properly at the Grand Hotel. Not on account of the veranda and the lamps. The children, straightway on the best of terms with waiters and pages, absorbed in the joys of life on the beach, promptly forgot those colourful seductions. But now there arose, between ourselves and the veranda clientèle—or perhaps more correctly with the compliant management—one of those little unpleasantnesses which can quite spoil the pleasure of a holiday. Among the guests were some high Roman aristocracy, a Principe X and his family. These grand folk occupied rooms close to our own, and the Principessa, a great and a passionately maternal lady, was thrown into a panic by the vestiges of a whooping-cough which our little ones had lately got over, but which now and then still faintly troubled the unshatterable slumbers of our youngest-born. The nature of this illness is not clear, leaving some play for the imagination. So we took no offence at our elegant neighbour for clinging to the widely held view that whooping-cough is acoustically contagious and quite simply fearing lest her children yield to the bad example set by ours. In the fullness of her feminine self-confidence she protested to the management, which then, in the person of the proverbial frock-coated manager, hastened to represent to us, with many expressions of regret, that under the circumstances they were obliged to transfer us to the annexe. We did our best to assure him that the disease was in its very last stages, that it was actually over, and presented no danger of infection to anybody. All that we gained was permission to bring the case before the hotel physician—not one chosen by us—by whose verdict we must then abide. We agreed, convinced that thus we should at once pacify the Princess and escape the trouble of moving. The doctor appeared, and behaved like a faithful and honest servant of science. He examined the child and gave his opinion: the disease was quite over, no danger of contagion was present. We drew a long breath and considered the incident closed—until the manager announced that despite the doctor's verdict it would still be necessary for us to give up our rooms and retire to the *dépendance*. Byzantinism like this outraged us. It is not likely that the Principessa was responsible for the wilful breach of faith. Very likely the fawning management had not even dared to tell her what the physician said. Anyhow, we made it clear to his understanding that we preferred to leave the hotel altogether and at once—and packed our trunks. We could do so with a light heart, having already set up casual friendly relations with Casa Eleonora. We had noticed its pleasant exterior and formed the acquaintance of its proprietor, Signora Angiolieri, and her husband: she slender and black-haired, Tuscan in type, probably at the beginning of the thirties, with the dead ivory complexion of the southern woman, he quiet and bald and carefully dressed. They owned a larger establishment in Florence and presided only in summer and early autumn over the branch in Torre di Venere. But earlier, before her marriage, our new landlady had been companion, fellow-traveller, wardrobe mistress, yes, friend, of Eleonora Duse and manifestly regarded that period as the crown of her career. Even at our first visit she spoke of it with animation. Numerous photographs of the great actress, with affectionate inscriptions, were displayed about the drawing-room, and other souvenirs of their life together adorned the little tables and étagères. This cult of a so interesting past was calculated, of course, to heighten the advantages of the signora's present business. Nevertheless our pleasure and interest were quite genuine as we were conducted through the house by its owner and listened to her sonorous and staccato Tuscan voice relating anecdotes of that immortal mistress, depicting her suffering saintliness, her genius, her profound delicacy of feeling.

Thither, then, we moved our effects, to the dismay of the staff of the Grand Hotel, who, like all Italians, were very good to children. Our new quarters were retired and pleasant, we were within easy reach of the sea through the avenue of young plane trees that ran down to the esplanade. In the clean, cool dining-room Signora Angiolieri daily served the soup with her own hands, the service was attentive and good, the table capital. We even discovered some Viennese acquaintances, and enjoyed chatting with them after luncheon, in front of the house. They, in their turn, were the means of our finding others—in short, all seemed for the best, and we were heartily glad of the change we had made. Nothing was now wanting to a holiday of the most gratifying kind.

And yet no proper gratification ensued. Perhaps the stupid occasion of our change of quarters pursued us to the new ones we had found. Personally, I admit that I do not easily forget these collisions with ordinary humanity, the naïve misuse of power, the injustice, the sycophantic corruption. I dwelt upon the incident too much, it irritated me in retrospect—quite futilely, of course, since such phenomena are only all too natural and all too much the rule. And we had not broken off relations with the Grand Hotel. The children were as friendly as ever there, the porter mended their toys, and we sometimes took tea in the garden. We even saw the Principessa. She would come out, with her firm and delicate tread, her lips emphatically corallined, to look after her children, playing under the supervision of their English governess. She did not dream that we were anywhere near, for so soon as she appeared in the offing we sternly forbade our little one even to clear his throat.

The heat—if I may bring it in evidence—was extreme. It was African. The power of the sun, directly one left the border of the indigo-blue wave, was so frightful, so relentless, that the mere thought of the few steps between the beach and luncheon was a burden, clad though one might be only in pyjamas. Do you care for that sort of thing? Weeks on end? Yes, of course, it is proper to the south, it is classic weather, the sun of Homer, the climate wherein human culture came to flower—and all the rest of it. But after a while it is too much for me, I reach a point where I begin to find it dull. The burning void of the sky, day after day, weighs one down; the high coloration, the enormous naïveté of the unrefracted light—they do, I dare say, induce light-heartedness, a carefree mood born of immunity from downpours and other meteorological caprices. But slowly, slowly, there makes itself felt a lack: the deeper, more complex needs of the northern soul remain unsatisfied. You are left barren—even it may be, in time, a little contemptuous. True without that stupid business of the whooping-cough I might not have been feeling these things. I was annoyed, very likely I wanted to feel them and so half-unconsciously seized upon an idea lying ready to hand to induce, or if not to induce, at least to justify and strengthen, my attitude. Up to this point, then, if you like, let us grant some ill will on our part. But the sea; and the mornings spent extended upon the fine sand in face of its eternal splendours—no, the sea could not conceivably induce such feelings. Yet it was none the less true that, despite all previous experience, we were not at home on the beach, we were not happy.

It was too soon, too soon. The beach, as I have said, was still in the hands of the middle-class native. It is a pleasing breed to look at, and among the young we saw much shapeliness and charm. Still, we were necessarily surrounded by a great deal of very average humanity—a middle-class mob, which, you will admit, is not more charming under this sun than under one's own native sky. The voices these women have! It was sometimes hard to believe that we were in the land which is the western cradle of the art of song. *"Fuggièro!"* I can still hear that cry, as for twenty mornings long I heard it close behind me, breathy, full-throated, hideously stressed, with a harsh open *e,* uttered in accents of mechanical despair. *"Fuggièro! Rispondi almeno!"* Answer when I call you! The *sp* in *rispondi* was pronounced like *shp,* as Germans pronounce it; and this, on top of what I felt already, vexed my sensitive soul. The cry was addressed to a repulsive youngster whose sunburn had made disgusting raw sores on his shoulders. He outdid anything I have ever seen for ill-breeding, refractoriness, and temper and was a great coward to boot, putting the whole beach in an uproar, one day, because of his outrageous sensitiveness to the slightest pain. A sand-crab had pinched his toe in the water, and the minute injury made him set up a cry of heroic proportions—the shout of an antique hero in his agony—that pierced one to the marrow and called up visions of some frightful tragedy. Evidently he considered himself not only wounded, but poisoned as well; he crawled out on the sand and lay in apparently intolerable anguish, groaning *"Ohi!"* and *"Ohimè!"* and threshing about with arms and legs to ward off his mother's tragic appeals and the questions of the bystanders. An audience gathered round. A doctor was fetched—the same who had pronounced objective judgment on our whooping-cough—and here again acquitted himself like a man of science. Good-naturedly he reassured the boy, telling him that he was not hurt at all, he should simply go into the water again to relieve the smart. Instead of which, Fuggièro was borne off the beach, followed by a concourse of people. But he did not fail to appear next morning, nor did he leave off spoiling our children's sand-castles. Of course, always by accident. In short, a perfect terror.

And this twelve-year-old lad was prominent among the influences that, imperceptibly at first, combined to spoil our holiday and render it unwholesome. Somehow or other, there was a stiffness, a lack of innocent enjoyment. These people stood on their dignity—just why, and in what spirit, it was not easy at first to tell. They displayed much self-respectingness; towards each other and towards the foreigner their bearing was that of a person newly conscious of a sense of honour. And wherefore? Gradually we realized the political implications and understood that we were in the presence of a national ideal. The beach, in fact, was alive with patriotic children—a phenomenon as unnatural as it was depressing. Children are a human species and a society apart, a nation of their own, so to speak. On the basis of their common form of life, they find each other out with the greatest ease, no matter how different their small vocabularies. Ours soon played with natives and foreigners alike. Yet they were plainly both puzzled and disappointed at times. There were wounded sensibilities, displays of assertiveness—or rather hardly assertiveness, for it was too self-conscious and too didactic to deserve the name. There were quarrels over flags, disputes about authority and precedence. Grownups joined in, not so much to pacify as to render judgment and enunciate principles. Phrases were dropped about the greatness and dignity of Italy, solemn phrases that spoilt the fun. We saw our two little ones retreat, puzzled and hurt, and were put to it to explain the situation. These people, we told them, were just passing through a certain stage, something rather like an illness, perhaps; not very pleasant, but probably unavoidable.

We had only our own carelessness to thank that we came to blows in the end with this "stage"—which, after all, we had seen and sized up long before now. Yes, it came to another "cross-purposes," so evidently the earlier ones had not been sheer accident. In a word, we became an offence to the public morals. Our small daughter—eight years old, but in physical development a good year younger and thin as a chicken—had had a good long bathe and gone playing in the warm sun in her wet costume. We told her that she might take off her bathing-suit, which was stiff with sand, rinse it in the sea, and put it on again, after which she must take care to keep it cleaner. Off goes the costume and she runs down naked to the sea, rinses her little jersey, and comes back. Ought we to have foreseen the outburst of anger and resentment which her conduct, and thus our conduct, called forth? Without delivering a homily on the subject, I may say that in the last decade our attitude towards the nude body and our feelings regarding it have undergone, all over the world, a fundamental change. There are things we "never think about" any more, and among them is the freedom we had permitted to this by no means provocative little childish body. But in these parts it was taken as a challenge. The patriotic children hooted. Fuggièro whistled on his fingers. The sudden buzz of conversation among the grown people in our neighbourhood boded no good. A gentleman in city togs, with a not very apropos bowler hat on the back of his head, was assuring his outraged womenfolk that he proposed to take punitive measures; he stepped up to us, and a philippic descended on our unworthy heads, in which all the emotionalism of the sense-loving south spoke in the service of morality and discipline. The offence against decency of which we had been guilty was, he said, the more to be condemned because it was also a gross ingratitude and an insulting breach of his country's hospitality. We had criminally injured not only the letter and spirit of the public bathing regulations, but also the honour of Italy; he, the gentleman in the city togs, knew how to defend that honour and proposed to see to it that our offence against the national dignity should not go unpunished.

We did our best, bowing respectfully, to give ear to this eloquence. To contradict the man, overheated as he was, would probably be to fall from one error into another. On the tips of our tongues we had various answers: as, that the word "hospitality," in its strictest sense, was not quite the right one, taking all the circumstances into consideration. We were not literally the guests of Italy, but of Signora Angiolieri, who had assumed the rôle of dispenser of hospitality some years ago on laying down that of familiar friend to Eleonora Duse. We longed to say that surely this beautiful country had not sunk so low as to be reduced to a state of hypersensitive prudishness. But we confined ourselves to assuring the gentleman that any lack of respect, any provocation on our parts, had been the furthest from our thoughts. And as a mitigating circumstance we pointed out the tender age and physical slightness of the little culprit. In vain. Our protests were waved away, he did not believe in them; our defence would not hold water. We must be made an example of. The authorities were notified, by telephone, I believe, and their representatives appeared on the beach. He said the case was *"molto grave."* We had to go with him to the Municipio up in the Piazza, where a higher official confirmed the previous verdict of *"molto grave,"* launched into a stream of the usual didactic phrases—the selfsame tune and words as the man in the bowler hat—and levied a fine and ransom of fifty lire. We felt that the adventure must willy-nilly be worth to us this much of a contribution to the economy of the Italian government; paid, and left. Ought we not at this point to have left Torre as well?

If we only had! We should thus have escaped that fatal Cipolla. But circumstances combined to prevent us from making up our minds to a change. A certain poet says that it is indolence that makes us endure uncomfortable situations. The *aperçu* may serve as an explanation for our inaction. Anyhow, one dislikes voiding the field immediately upon such an event. Especially if sympathy from other quarters encourages one to defy it. And in the Villa Eleonora they pronounced as with one voice upon the injustice of our punishment. Some Italian after-dinner acquaintances found that the episode put their country in a very bad light, and proposed taking the man in the bowler hat to task, as one fellow-citizen to another. But the next day he and his party had vanished from the beach. Not on our account, of course. Though it might be that the consciousness of his impending departure had added energy to his rebuke; in any case his going was a relief. And, furthermore, we stayed because our stay had by now become remarkable in our own eyes, which is worth something in itself, quite apart from the comfort or discomfort involved. Shall we strike sail, avoid a certain experience so soon as it seems not expressly calculated to increase our enjoyment or our self-esteem? Shall we go away whenever life looks like turning in the slightest uncanny, or not quite normal, or even rather painful and mortifying? No, surely not. Rather stay and look matters in the face, brave them out; perhaps precisely in so doing lies a lesson for us to learn. We stayed on and reaped as the awful reward of our constancy the unholy and staggering experience with Cipolla.

I have not mentioned that the after season had begun, almost on the very day we were disciplined by the city authorities. The worshipful gentleman in the bowler hat, our denouncer, was not the only person to leave the resort. There was a regular exodus, on every hand you saw luggage-carts on their way to the station. The beach denationalized itself. Life in Torre, in the cafés and the pinetas, became more homelike and more European. Very likely we might even have eaten at a table in the glass veranda, but we refrained, being content at Signora Angiolieri's—as content, that is, as our evil star would let us be. But at the same time with this turn for the better came a change in the weather: almost to an hour it showed itself in harmony with the holiday calendar of the general public. The sky was overcast; not that it grew any cooler, but the unclouded heat of the entire eighteen days since our arrival, and probably long before that, gave place to a stifling sirocco air, while from time to time a little ineffectual rain sprinkled the velvety surface of the beach. Add to which, that two-thirds of our intended stay at Torre had passed. The colourless, lazy sea, with sluggish jellyfish floating in its shallows, was at least a change. And it would have been silly to feel retrospective longings after a sun that had caused us so many sighs when it burned down in all its arrogant power.

At this juncture, then, it was that Cipolla announced himself. Cavaliere Cipolla he was called on the posters that appeared one day stuck up everywhere, even in the dining-room of Pensione Eleonora. A travelling virtuoso, an entertainer, *"forzatore, illusionista, prestidigatore,"* as he called himself, who proposed to wait upon the highly respectable population of Torre di Venere with a display of extraordinary phenomena of a mysterious and staggering kind. A conjuror! The bare announcement was enough to turn our children's heads. They had never seen anything of the sort, and now our present holiday was to afford them this new excitement. From that moment on they besieged us with prayers to take tickets for the performance. We had doubts, from the first, on the score of the lateness of the hour, nine o'clock; but gave way, in the idea that we might see a little of what Cipolla had to offer, probably no great matter, and then go home. Besides, of course, the children could sleep late next day. We bought four tickets of Signora Angiolieri herself, she having taken a number of the stalls on commission to sell them to her guests. She could not vouch for the man's performance, and we had no great expectations. But we were conscious of a need for diversion, and the children's violent curiosity proved catching.

The Cavaliere's performance was to take place in a hall where during the season there had been a cinema with a weekly programme. We had never been there. You reached it by following the main street under the wall of the *"palazzo,"* a ruin with a "For sale" sign, that suggested a castle and had obviously been built in lordlier days. In the same street were the chemist, the hairdresser, and all the better shops; it led, so to speak, from the feudal past the bourgeois into the proletarian, for it ended off between two rows of poor fishing-huts, where old women sat mending nets before the doors. And here, among the proletariat, was the hall, not much more, actually than a wooden shed, though a large one, with a turreted entrance, plastered on either side with layers of gay placards. Some while after dinner, then, on the appointed evening, we wended our way thither in the dark, the children dressed in their best and blissful with the sense of so much irregularity. It was sultry, as it had been for days; there was heat lightning now and then, and a little rain; we proceeded under umbrellas. It took us a quarter of an hour.

Our tickets were collected at the entrance, our places we had to find ourselves. They were in the third row left, and as we sat down we saw that, late though the hour was for the performance, it was to be interpreted with even more laxity. Only very slowly did an audience—who seemed to be relied upon to come late—begin to fill the stalls. These comprised the whole auditorium; there were no boxes.This tardiness gave us some concern. The children's cheeks were already flushed as much with fatigue as with excitement. But even when we entered, the standing-room at the back and in the side aisles was already well occupied. There stood the manhood of Torre di Venere, all and sundry, fisherfolk, rough-and-ready youths with bare forearms crossed over their striped jerseys. We were well pleased with the presence of this native assemblage, which always adds colour and animation to occasions like the present; and the children were frankly delighted. For they had friends among these people—acquaintances picked up on afternoon strolls to the further ends of the beach. We would be turning homeward, at the hour when the sun dropped into the sea, spent with the huge effort it had made and gilding with reddish gold the oncoming surf; and we would come upon bare-legged fisherfolk standing in rows, bracing and hauling with long-drawn cries as they drew in the nets and harvested in dripping baskets their catch, often so scanty, of *frutto di mare*. The children looked on, helped to pull, brought out their little stock of Italian words, made friends. So now they exchanged nods with the "standing-room" clientèle; there was Guiscardo, there Antonio, they knew them by name and waved and called across in half-whispers, getting answering nods and smiles that displayed rows of healthy white teeth. Look, there is even Mario, Mario from the Esquisito, who brings us the chocolate. He wants to see the conjuror, too, and he must have come early, for he is almost in front; but he does not see us, he is not paying attention; that is a way he has, even though he is a waiter. So we wave instead to the man who lets out the little boats on the beach; he is there too, standing at the back.

It had got to a quarter past nine, it got to almost half past. It was natural that we should be nervous. When would the children get to bed? It had been a mistake to bring them, for now it would be very hard to suggest breaking off their enjoyment before it had got well under way. The stalls had filled in time; all Torre, apparently was there: the guests of the Grand Hotel, the guests of the Villa Eleonora, familiar faces from the beach. We heard English and German and the sort of French that Rumanians speak with Italians. Madame Angiolieri herself sat two rows behind us, with her quiet, bald-headed spouse, who kept stroking his moustache with the two middle fingers of his right hand. Everybody had come late, but nobody too late. Cipolla made us wait for him.

He made us wait. That is probably the way to put it. He heightened the suspense by his delay in appearing. And we could see the point of this, too—only not when it was carried to extremes. Towards half past nine the audience began to clap—an amiable way of expressing justifiable impatience, evincing as it does an eagerness to applaud. For the little ones, this was a joy in itself—all children love to clap. From the popular sphere came loud cries of *"Pronti!" Cominciamo!"* And lo, it seemed now as easy to begin as before it had been hard. A gong sounded, greeted by the standing rows with a many voiced "Ah-h!" and the curtains parted. They revealed a platform furnished more like a schoolroom than like the theatre of a conjuring performance—largely because of the blackboard in the left foreground. There was a common yellow hat-stand, a few ordinary straw-bottomed chairs, and further back a little round table holding a water carafe and glass, also a tray with a liqueur glass and a flask of pale yellow liquid. We had still a few seconds of time to let these things sink in. Then, with no darkening of the house, Cavaliere Cipolla made his entry.

He came forward with a rapid step that expressed his eagerness to appear before his public and gave rise to the illusion that he had already come a long way to put himself at their service—whereas, of course, he had only been standing in the wings. His costume supported the fiction. A man of an age hard to determine, but by no means young; with a sharp, ravaged face, piercing eyes, compressed lips, small black waxed moustache, and a so-called imperial in the curve between mouth and chin. He was dressed for the street with a sort of complicated evening elegance, in a wide black pelerine with velvet collar and satin lining; which, in the hampered state of his arms, he held together in front with his white-gloved hands. He had a white scarf round his neck; a top hat with a curving brim sat far back on his head. Perhaps more than anywhere else the eighteenth century is still alive in Italy, and with it the charlatan and mountebank type so characteristic of the period. Only there, at any rate, does one still encounter really well-preserved specimens. Cipolla had in his whole appearance much of the historic type; his very clothes helped to conjure up the traditional figure with its blatantly, fantastically foppish air. His pretentious costume sat upon him, or rather hung upon him, most curiously, being in one place drawn too tight, in another a mass of awkward folds. There was something not quite in order about his figure, both front and back—that was plain later on. But I must emphasize the fact that there was not a trace of personal jocularity or clownishness in his pose, manner, or behaviour. On the contrary, there was complete seriousness, an absence of any humorous appeal; occasionally even a cross-grained pride, along with that curious, self-satisfied air so characteristic of the deformed. None of all this, however, prevented his appearance from being greeted with laughter from more than one quarter of the hall.

All the eagerness had left his manner. The swift entry had been merely an expression of energy, not of zeal. Standing at the footlights he negligently drew off his gloves, to display long yellow hands, one of them adorned with a seal ring with a lapislazuli in a high setting. As he stood there, his small hard eyes, with flabby pouches beneath them, roved appraisingly about the hall, not quickly, rather in a considered examination, pausing here and there upon a face with his lips clipped together, not speaking a word. Then with a display of skill as surprising as it was casual, he rolled his gloves into a ball and tossed them across a considerable distance into the glass on the table. Next from an inner pocket he drew forth a packet of cigarettes; you could see by the wrapper that they were the cheapest sort the government sells. With his fingertips he pulled out a cigarette and lighted it, without looking, from a quick-firing benzine lighter. He drew the smoke deep into his lungs and let it out again, tapping his foot, with both lips drawn in an arrogant grimace and the grey smoke streaming out between broken and saw-edged teeth.

With a keenness equal to his own his audience eyed him. The youths at the rear scowled as they peered at this cocksure creature to search out his secret weaknesses. He betrayed none. In fetching out and putting back the cigarettes his clothes got in his way. He had to turn back his pelerine, and in so doing revealed a riding-whip with a silver claw-handle that hung by a leather thong from his left forearm and looked decidedly out of place. You could see that he had on not evening clothes but a frock-coat, and under this, as he lifted it to get at his pocket, could be seen a striped sash worn about the body. Somebody behind me whispered that this sash went with his title of Cavaliere. I give the information for what it may be worth—personally, I never heard that the title carried such insignia with it. Perhaps the sash was sheer pose, like the way he stood there, without a word, casually and arrogantly puffing smoke into his audience's face.

People laughed, as I said. The merriment had become almost general when somebody in the "standing seats," in a loud, dry voice, remarked: *"Buona sera."*

Cipolla cocked his head. "Who was that?" asked he, as though he had been dared. "Who was that just spoke? Well? First so bold and now so modest? *Paura,* eh?" He spoke with a rather high, asthmatic voice, which yet had a metallic quality. He waited.

"That was me," a youth at the rear broke into the stillness, seeing himself thus challenged. He was not far from us, a handsome fellow in a woollen shirt, with his coat hanging over one shoulder. He wore his surly, wiry hair in a high, dishevelled mop, the style affected by the youth of the awakened Fatherland; it gave him an African appearance that rather spoiled his looks. *"Bè!* That was me. It was your business to say it first, but I was trying to be friendly."

More laughter. The chap had a tongue in his head. *"Ha sciolto la scilinguágnolo,"* I heard near me. After all, the retort was deserved.

"Ah, bravo!" answered Cipolla. "I like you, *giovanotto.* Trust me, I've had my eye on you for some time. People like you are just in my line. I can use them. And you are the pick of the lot, that's plain to see. You do what you like. Or is it possible you have ever not done what you liked—or even, maybe, what you didn't like? What somebody else liked, in short? Hark ye, my friend, that might be a pleasant change for you, to divide up the willing and the doing and stop tackling both jobs at once. Division of labour, *sistema americano, sa!* For instance, suppose you were to show your tongue to this select and honourable audience here—your whole tongue, right down to the roots?"

"No, I won't," said the youth, hostilely. "Sticking out your tongue shows a bad bringing-up."

"Nothing of the sort," retorted Cipolla. "You would only be *doing* it. With all due respect to your bringing-up, I suggest that before I count ten, you will perform a right turn and stick out your tongue at the company here further than you knew yourself that you could stick it out."

He gazed at the youth, and his piercing eyes seemed to sink deeper into their sockets. *"Uno!"* said he. He had let his riding-whip slide down his arm and made it whistle once through the air. The boy faced about and put out his tongue, so long, so extendedly, that you could see it was the very uttermost in tongue which he had to offer. Then turned back, stony-faced, to his former position.

"That was me," mocked Cipolla, with a jerk of his head towards the youth. *"Bè!* That was me." Leaving the audience to enjoy its sensations, he turned towards the little round table, lifted the bottle, poured out a small glass of what was obviously cognac, and tipped it up with a practised hand.

The children laughed with all their hearts. They had understood practically nothing of what had been said, but it pleased them hugely that something so funny should happen, straightaway, between that queer man up there and somebody out of the audience. They had no preconception of what an "evening" would be like and were quite ready to find this a priceless beginning. As for us, we exchanged a glance and I remember that involuntarily I made with my lips the sound that Cipolla's whip had made when it cut the air. For the rest, it was plain that people did not know what to make of a preposterous beginning like this to a sleight-of-hand performance. They could not see why the *giovanotto,* who after all in a way had been their spokesman, should suddenly have turned on them to vent his incivility. They felt that he had behaved like a silly ass and withdrew their countenances from him in favour of the artist, who now came back from his refreshment table and addressed them as follows:

"Ladies and gentlemen," said he, in his wheezing, metallic voice, "you saw just now that I was rather sensitive on the score of the rebuke this hopeful young linguist saw fit to give me"—*"questo linguista di belle speranze"* was what he said, and we all laughed at the pun. "I am a man who sets some store by himself, you may take it from me. And I see no point in being wished a good-evening unless it is done courteously and in all seriousness. For anything else there is no occasion. When a man wishes me a good-evening he wishes himself one, for the audience will have one only if I do. So this lady-killer of Torre di Venere" (another thrust) "did well to testify that I have one tonight and that I can dispense with any wishes of his in the matter. I can boast of having good evenings almost without exception. One not so good does come my way now and again, but very seldom. My calling is hard and my health not of the best. I have a little physical defect which prevented me from doing my bit in the war for the greater glory of the Fatherland. It is perforce with my mental and spiritual parts that I conquer life—which after all only means conquering oneself. And I flatter myself that my achievements have aroused interest and respect among the educated public. The leading newspapers have lauded me, the *Corriere della Sera* did me the courtesy of calling me a phenomenon, and in Rome the brother of the *Duce* honoured me by his presence at one of my evenings. I should not have thought that in a relatively less important place" (laughter here, at the expense of poor little Torre) "I should have to give up the small personal habits which brilliant and elevated audiences had been ready to overlook. Nor did I think I had to stand being heckled by a person who seems to have been rather spoilt by the favours of the fair sex." All this of course at the expense of the youth whom Cipolla never tired of presenting in the guise of *donnaiuolo* and rustic Don Juan. His persistent thin-skinnedness and animosity were in striking contrast to the self-confidence and the worldly success he boasted of. One might have assumed that the *giovanotto* was merely the chosen butt of Cipolla's customary professional sallies, had not the very pointed witticisms betrayed a genuine antagonism. No one looking at the physical parts of the two men need have been at a loss for the explanation, even if the deformed man had not constantly played on the other's supposed success with the fair sex. "Well," Cipolla went on, "before beginning our entertainment this evening, perhaps you will permit me to make myself comfortable."

And he went towards the hat-stand to take off his things.

"Parla benissimo," asserted somebody in our neighbourhood. So far, the man had done nothing; but what he had said was accepted as an achievement, by means of that he had made an impression. Among southern peoples speech is a constituent part of the pleasure of living, it enjoys far livelier social esteem than in the north. That national cement, the mother tongue, is paid symbolic honours down here, and there is something blithely

symbolical in the pleasure people take in their respect for its forms and phonetics. They enjoy speaking, they enjoy listening; and they listen with discrimination. For the way a man speaks serves as a measure of his personal rank; carelessness and clumsiness are greeted with scorn, elegance and mastery are rewarded with social éclat. Wherefore the small man too, where it is a question of getting his effect, chooses his phrase nicely and turns it with care. On this count, then, at least, Cipolla had won his audience; though he by no means belonged to the class of men which the Italian, in a singular mixture of moral and æsthetic judgments, labels *"simpatico."*

After removing his hat, scarf, and mantle he came to the front of the stage, settling his coat, pulling down his cuffs with their large cuff-buttons, adjusting his absurd sash. He had very ugly hair; the top of his head, that is, was almost bald, while a narrow, black-varnished frizz of curls ran from front to back as though stuck on; the side hair, likewise blackened, was brushed forward to the corners of the eyes—it was, in short, the hairdressing of an old-fashioned circus-director, fantastic, but entirely suited to his outmoded personal type and worn with so much assurance as to take the edge off the public's sense of humour. The little physical defect of which he had warned us was now all too visible, though the nature of it was even now not very clear; the chest was too high, as is usual in such cases, but the corresponding malformation of the back did not sit between the shoulders, it took the form of a sort of hips or buttocks hump, which did not indeed hinder his movements but gave him a grotesque and dipping stride at every step he took. However, by mentioning his deformity beforehand he had broken the shock of it, and a delicate propriety of feeling appeared to reign throughout the hall.

"At your service," said Cipolla. "With your kind permission, we will begin the evening with some arithmetical tests."

Arithmetic? That did not sound much like sleight-of-hand. We began to have our suspicions that the man was sailing under a false flag, only we did not yet know which was the right one. I felt sorry on the children's account; but for the moment they were content simply to be there.

The numerical test which Cipolla now introduced was as simple as it was baffling. He began by fastening a piece of paper to the upper right-hand corner of the blackboard; then lifting it up, he wrote something underneath. He talked all the while, relieving the dryness of his offering by a constant flow of words, and showed himself a practised speaker, never at a loss for conversational turns of phrase. It was in keeping with the nature of his performance, and at the same time vastly entertained the children, that he went on to eliminate the gap between stage and audience, which had already been bridged over by the curious skirmish with the fisher lad; he had representatives from the audience mount the stage, and himself descended the wooden steps to seek personal contact with his public. And again, with individuals, he fell into his former taunting tone. I do not know how far that was a deliberate feature of his system; he preserved a serious, even a peevish air, but his audience, at least the more popular section, seemed convinced that that was all part of the game. So then, after he had written something and covered the writing by the paper, he desired that two persons should come up on the platform and help to perform the calculations. They would not be difficult, even for people not clever at figures. As usual, nobody volunteered, and Cipolla took care not to molest the more select portion of his audience. He kept to the populace. Turning to two sturdy young louts standing behind us, he beckoned them to the front, encouraging and scolding by turns. They should not stand there gaping, he said, unwilling to oblige the company. Actually he got them in motion; with clumsy tread they came down the middle aisle, climbed the steps, and stood in front of the blackboard, grinning sheepishly at their comrades' shouts and applause. Cipolla joked with them for a few minutes, praised their heroic firmness of limb and the size of their hands, so well calculated to do this service for the public. Then he handed one of them the chalk and told him to write down the numbers as they were called out. But now the creature declared that he could not write! *"Non so scrivere,"* said he in his gruff voice, and his companion added that neither did he.

God knows whether they told the truth or whether they wanted to make game of Cipolla. Anyhow, the latter was far from sharing the general merriment which their confession aroused. He was insulted and disgusted. He sat there on a straw-bottomed chair in the centre of the stage with his legs crossed, smoking a fresh cigarette out of his cheap packet; obviously it tasted the better for the cognac he had indulged in while the yokels were stumping up the steps. Again he inhaled the smoke and let it stream out between curling lips. Swinging his leg, with his gaze sternly averted from the two shamelessly chuckling creatures and from the audience as well, he stared into space as one who withdraws himself and his dignity from the contemplation of an utterly despicable phenomenon.

"Scandalous," said he, in a sort of icy snarl. "Go back to your places! In Italy everybody can write—in all her greatness there is no room for ignorance and unenlightenment. To accuse her of them, in the hearing of this international company, is a cheap joke, in which you yourselves cut a very poor figure and humiliate the government and the whole country as well. If it is true that Torre di Venere is indeed the last refuge of such ignorance, then I must blush to have visited the place—being, as I already was, aware of its inferiority to Rome in more than one respect—"

Here Cipolla was interrupted by the youth with the Nubian coiffure and his jacket across his shoulder. His fighting spirit, as we now saw, had only abdicated temporarily, and he now flung himself into the breach in defence of his native heath. "That will do," said he loudly. "That's enough jokes about Torre. We all come from the place and we won't stand strangers making fun of it. These two chaps are our friends. Maybe they are no scholars, but even so they may be straighter than some folks in the room who are so free with their boasts about Rome, though they did not build it either."

That was capital. The young man had certainly cut his eyeteeth. And this sort of spectacle was good fun, even though it still further delayed the regular performance. It is always fascinating to listen to an altercation. Some people it simply amuses, they take a sort of kill-joy pleasure in not being principals. Others feel upset and uneasy, and my sympathies are with these latter, although on the present occasion I was under the impression that all this was part of the show—the analphabetic yokels no less than the *giovanotto* with the jacket. The children listened well pleased. They understood not at all, but the sound of the voices made them hold their breath. So this was a "magic evening"—at least it was the kind they have in Italy. They expressly found it "lovely." Cipolla had stood up and with two of his scooping strides was at the footlights.

"Well, well, see who's here!" said he with grim cordiality. "An old acquaintance! A young man with his heart at the end of his tongue" (he used the word *linguaccia,* which means a coated tongue, and gave rise to much hilarity). "That will do, my friends," he turned to the yokels. "I do not need you now, I have business with this deserving young man here, *con questo torregiano di Venere,* this tower of Venus, who no doubt expects the gratitude of the fair as a reward for his prowess—"

"Ah, non scherziamo! We're talking earnest," cried out the youth. His eyes flashed, and he actually made as though to pull off his jacket and proceed to direct methods of settlement.

Cipolla did not take him too seriously. We had exchanged apprehensive glances; but he was dealing with a fellow-countryman and had his native soil beneath his feet. He kept quite cool and showed complete mastery of the situation. He looked at his audience, smiled, and made a sideways motion of the head towards the young cockerel as though calling the public to witness how the man's bumptiousness only served to betray the simplicity of his mind. And then, for the second time, something strange happened, which set Cipolla's calm superiority in an uncanny light, and in some mysterious and irritating way turned all the explosiveness latent in the air into matter for laughter.

Cipolla drew still nearer to the fellow, looking him in the eye with a peculiar gaze. He even came half-way down the steps that led into the auditorium on our left, so that he stood directly in front of the trouble-maker, on slightly higher ground. The riding-whip hung from his arm.

"My son, you do not feel much like joking," he said. "It is only too natural, for anyone can see that you are not feeling too well. Even your tongue, which leaves something to be desired on the score of cleanliness, indicates acute disorder of the gastric system. An evening entertainment is no place for people in your state; you yourself, I can tell, were of several minds whether you would not do better to put on a flannel bandage and go to bed. It was not good judgment to drink so much of that very sour white wine this afternoon. Now you have such a colic you would like to double up with the pain. Go ahead, don't be embarrassed. There is a distinct relief that comes from bending over, in cases of intestinal cramp."

He spoke thus, word for word, with quiet impressiveness and a kind of stern sympathy, and his eyes, plunged the while deep in the young man's, seemed to grow very tired and at the same time burning above their enlarged tear-ducts—they were the strangest eyes, you could tell that not manly pride alone was preventing the young adversary from withdrawing his gaze. And presently, indeed, all trace of its former arrogance was gone from the bronzed young face. He looked open-mouthed at the Cavaliere and the open mouth was drawn in a rueful smile.

"Double over," repeated Cipolla. "What else can you do? With a colic like that you *must* bend. Surely you will not struggle against the performance of a perfectly natural action just because somebody suggests it to you?"

Slowly the youth lifted his forearms, folded and squeezed them across his body; it turned a little sideways, then bent, lower and lower, the feet shifted, the knees turned inward, until he had become a picture of writhing pain, until he all but grovelled upon the ground. Cipolla let him stand for some seconds thus, then made a short cut through the air with his whip and went with his scooping stride back to the little table, where he poured himself out a cognac.

"Il boit beaucoup," asserted a lady behind us. Was that the only thing that struck her? We could not tell how far the audi-

ence grasped the situation. The fellow was standing upright again, with a sheepish grin—he looked as though he scarcely knew how it had all happened. The scene had been followed with tense interest and applauded at the end; there were shouts of *"Bravo, Cipolla!"* and *"Bravo, giovanotto!"* Apparently the issue of the duel was not looked upon as a personal defeat for the young man. Rather the audience encouraged him as one does an actor who succeeds in an unsympathetic rôle. Certainly his way of screwing himself up with cramp had been highly picturesque, its appeal was directly calculated to impress the gallery—in short, a fine dramatic performance. But I am not sure how far the audience were moved by that natural tactfulness in which the south excels, or how far it penetrated into the nature of what was going on.

The Cavaliere, refreshed, had lighted another cigarette. The numerical tests might now proceed. A young man was easily found in the back row who was willing to write down on the blackboard the numbers as they were dictated to him. Him too we knew; the whole entertainment had taken on an intimate character through our acquaintance with so many of the actors. This was the man who worked at the greengrocer's in the main street; he had served us several times, with neatness and dispatch. He wielded the chalk with clerkly confidence, while Cipolla descended to our level and walked with his deformed gait through the audience, collecting numbers as they were given, in two, three, and four places, and calling them out to the grocer's assistant, who wrote them down in a column. In all this, everything on both sides was calculated to amuse, with its jokes and its oratorical asides. The artist could not fail to hit on foreigners, who were not ready with their figures, and with them he was elaborately patient and chivalrous, to the great amusement of the natives, whom he reduced to confusion in their turn, by making them translate numbers that were given in English or French. Some people gave dates concerned with great events in Italian history. Cipolla took them up at once and made patriotic comments. Somebody shouted "Number one!" The Cavaliere, incensed at this as at every attempt to make game of him, retorted over his shoulder that he could not take less than two-place figures. Whereupon another joker cried out "Number two!" and was greeted with the applause and laughter which every reference to natural functions is sure to win among southerners.

When fifteen numbers stood in a long straggling row on the board, Cipolla called for a general adding-match. Ready reckoners might add in their heads, but pencil and paper were not forbidden. Cipolla, while the work went on, sat on his chair near the blackboard, smoked and grimaced, with the complacent, pompous air cripples so often have. The five-place addition was soon done. Somebody announced the answer, somebody else confirmed it, a third had arrived at a slightly different result, but the fourth agreed with the first and second. Cipolla got up, tapped some ash from his coat, and lifted the paper at the upper right-hand corner of the board to display the writing. The correct answer, a sum close on a million, stood there; he had written it down beforehand.

Astonishment, and loud applause. The children were overwhelmed. How had he done that, they wanted to know. We told them it was a trick, not easily explainable offhand. In short, the man was a conjuror. This was what a sleight-of-hand evening was like, so now they knew. First the fisherman had cramp, and then the right answer was written down beforehand—it was all simply glorious, and we saw with dismay that despite the hot eyes and the hand of the clock at almost half past ten, it would be very hard to get them away. There would be tears. And yet it was plain that this magician did not "magick"—at least not in the accepted sense, of manual dexterity—and that the entertainment was not at all suitable for children. Again, I do not know, either, what the audience really thought. Obviously there was grave doubt whether its answers had been given of "free choice"; here and there an individual might have answered of his own motion, but on the whole Cipolla certainly selected his people and thus kept the whole procedure in his own hands and directed it towards the given result. Even so, one had to admire the quickness of his calculations, however much one felt disinclined to admire anything else about the performance. Then his patriotism, his irritable sense of dignity—the Cavaliere's own countrymen might feel in their element with all that and continue in a laughing mood; but the combination certainly gave us outsiders food for thought.

Cipolla himself saw to it—though without giving them a name—that the nature of his powers should be clear beyond a doubt to even the least-instructed person. He alluded to them, of course, in his talk—and he talked without stopping—but only in vague, boastful, self-advertising phrases. He went on awhile with experiments on the same lines as the first, merely making them more complicated by introducing operations in multiplying, subtracting, and dividing; then he simplified them to the last degree in order to bring out the method. He simply had numbers "guessed" which were previously written under the paper; and the guess was nearly always right. One guesser admitted that he had had in mind to give a certain number, when Cipolla's whip went whistling through the air, and a quite different one slipped out, which proved to be the "right" one. Cipolla's shoulders shook. He pretended admiration for the powers of the people questioned. But in all his compliments there was something fleering and derogatory; the victims could scarcely have relished them much, although they smiled, and although they might easily have set down some part of the applause to their own credit. Moreover, I had not the impression that the artist was popular with his public. A certain ill will and reluctance were in the air, but courtesy kept such feelings in check, as did Cipolla's competency and his stern self-confidence. Even the riding-whip, I think, did much to keep rebellion from becoming overt.

From tricks with numbers he passed to tricks with cards. There were two packs, which he drew out of his pockets, and so much I still remember, that the basis of the tricks he played with them was as follows: from the first pack he drew three cards and thrust them without looking at them inside his coat. Another person then drew three out of the second pack, and these turned out to be the same as the first three—not invariably all the three, for it did happen that only two were the same. But in the majority of cases Cipolla triumphed, showing his three cards with a little bow in acknowledgment of the applause with which his audience conceded his possession of strange powers—strange whether for good or evil. A young man in the front row, to our right, an Italian, with proud, finely chiselled features, rose up and said that he intended to assert his own will in his choice and consciously to resist any influence, of whatever sort. Under these circumstances, what did Cipolla think would be the result? "You will," answered the Cavaliere, "make my task somewhat more difficult thereby. As for the result, your resistance will not alter it in the least. Freedom exists, and also the will exists; but freedom of the will does not exist, for a will that aims at its own freedom aims at the unknown. You are free to draw or not to draw. But if you draw, you will draw the right cards—the more certainly, the more wilfully obstinate your behaviour."

One must admit that he could not have chosen his words better, to trouble the waters and confuse the mind. The refractory youth hesitated before drawing. Then he pulled out a card and at once demanded to see if it was among the chosen three. "But why?" queried Cipolla. "Why do things by halves?" Then, as the other defiantly insisted, *"E servito,"* said the juggler, with a gesture of exaggerated servility; and held out the three cards fanwise, without looking at them himself. The left-hand card was the one drawn.

Amid general applause, the apostle of freedom sat down. How far Cipolla employed small tricks and manual dexterity to help out his natural talents, the deuce only knew. But even without them the result would have been the same: the curiosity of the entire audience was unbounded and universal, everybody both enjoyed the amazing character of the entertainment and unanimously conceded the professional skill of the performer. *"Lavora bene,"* we heard, here and there in our neighbourhood; it signified the triumph of objective judgment over antipathy and repressed resentment.

After his last, incomplete, yet so much the more telling success, Cipolla had at once fortified himself with another cognac. Truly he did "drink a lot," and the fact made a bad impression. But obviously he needed the liquor and the cigarettes for the replenishment of his energy, upon which, as he himself said, heavy demands were made in all directions. Certainly in the intervals he looked very ill, exhausted and hollow-eyed. Then the little glassful would redress the balance, and the flow of lively, self-confident chatter run on, while the smoke he inhaled gushed out grey from his lungs. I clearly recall that he passed from the card-tricks to parlour games—the kind based on certain powers which in human nature are higher or else lower than human reason: on intuition and "magnetic" transmission; in short, upon a low type of manifestation. What I do not remember is the precise order things came in. And I will not bore you with a description of these experiments; everybody knows them, everybody has at one time or another taken part in this finding of hidden articles, this blind carrying out of a series of acts, directed by a force that proceeds from organism to organism by unexplored paths. Everybody has had his little glimpse into the equivocal, impure, inexplicable nature of the occult, has been conscious of both curiosity and contempt, has shaken his head over the human tendency of those who deal in it to help themselves out with humbuggery, though, after all, the humbuggery is no disproof whatever of the genuineness of the other elements in the dubious amalgam. I can only say here that each single circumstance gains in weight and the whole greatly in impressiveness when it is a man like Cipolla who is the chief actor and guiding spirit in the sinister business. He sat smoking at the rear of the stage, his back to the audience while they conferred. The object passed from hand to hand which it was his task to find, with which he was to perform some action agreed upon beforehand. Then he would start to move zigzag through the hall, with his head thrown back and one hand outstretched, the other clasped in that of a guide who was in the secret but enjoined to keep himself perfectly passive, with his thoughts directed upon the agreed goal. Cipolla moved with the bearing typical in these experiments: now groping upon a false start, now with a quick forward thrust, now pausing as though to listen and by sudden inspiration correcting his course. The rôles seemed reversed, the stream of influence was moving in the contrary direction, as the artist himself pointed out, in his ceaseless flow of discourse. The suffering, receptive, performing part was now his, the will he had before imposed on others was shut out, he acted in obedience to a voiceless common will which was in the air. But he made it perfectly clear that it all came to the same thing. The capacity for self-surrender, he said, for becoming a tool, for the most unconditional and utter self-abnegation, was but the reverse side of that other power to will and to command. Commanding and obeying formed together one single principle, one indissoluble unity; he who knew how to obey knew also how to command, and conversely; the one idea was comprehended in the other, as people and leader were comprehended in one another. But that which was *done,* the highly exacting and exhausting performance, was in every case his, the leader's and mover's, in whom the will became obedience, the obedience will, whose person was the cradle and womb of both, and who thus suffered enormous hardship. Repeatedly he emphasized the fact that his lot was a hard one—presumably to account for his need of stimulant and his frequent recourse to the little glass.

Thus he groped his way forward, like a blind seer, led and sustained by the mysterious common will. He drew a pin set with a stone out of its hiding-place in an English-woman's shoe, carried it, halting and pressing on by turns, to another lady—Signora Angiolieri—and handed it to her on bended knee, with the words it had been agreed he was to utter. "I present you with this in token of my respect," was the sentence. Their sense was obvious, but the words themselves not easy to hit upon, for the reason that they had been agreed on in French; the language complication seemed to us a little malicious, implying as it did a conflict between the audience's natural interest in the success of the miracle, and their desire to witness the humiliation of this presumptuous man. It was a strange sight: Cipolla on his knees before the signora, wrestling, amid efforts at speech, after knowledge of the preordained words. "I must say something," he said, "and I feel clearly what it is I must say. But I also feel that if it passed my lips it would be wrong. Be careful not to help me unintentionally!" he cried out, though very likely that was precisely what he was hoping for. *"Pensez très fort,"* he cried all at once, in bad French, and then burst out with the required words—in Italian, indeed, but with the final substantive pronounced in the sister tongue, in which he was probably far from fluent: he said *vénération* instead of *venerazione,* with an impossible nasal. And this partial success, after the complete success before it, the finding of the pin, the presentation of it on his knees to the right person—was almost more impressive than if he had got the sentence exactly right, and evoked bursts of admiring applause.

Cipolla got up from his knees and wiped the perspiration from his brow. You understand that this experiment with the pin was a single case, which I describe because it sticks in my memory. But he changed his method several times and improvised a number of variations suggested by his contact with his audience; a good deal of time thus went by. He seemed to get particular inspiration from the person of our landlady; she drew him on to the most extraordinary displays of clairvoyance. "It does not escape me, madame," he said to her, "that there is something unusual about you, some special and honourable distinction. He who has eyes to see descries about your lovely brow an aureola—if I mistake not, it once was stronger than now—a slowly paling radiance . . . hush, not a word! Don't help me. Beside you sits your husband—yes?" He turned towards the silent Signor Angiolieri. "You are the husband of this lady, and your happiness is complete. But in the midst of this happiness memories rise . . . the past, signora, so it seems to me, plays an important part in your present. You knew a king . . . has not a king crossed your path in bygone days?"

"No," breathed the dispenser of our midday soup, her golden-brown eyes gleaming in the noble pallor of her face.

"No? No, not a king; I meant that generally, I did not mean literally a king. Not a king, not a prince, and a prince after all, a king of a loftier realm; it was a great artist, at whose side you once—you would contradict me, and yet I am not wholly wrong. Well, then! It was a woman, a great, a world-renowned woman artist, whose friendship you enjoyed in your tender years, whose sacred memory overshadows and transfigures your whole existence. Her name? Need I utter it, whose fame has long been bound up with the Fatherland's, immortal as its own? Eleonora Duse," he finished, softly and with much solemnity.

The little woman bowed her head, overcome. The applause was like a patriotic demonstration. Nearly everyone there knew about Signora Angiolieri's wonderful past; they were all able to confirm the Cavaliere's intuition—not least the present guests of Casa Eleonora. But we wondered how much of the truth he had learned as the result of professional inquiries made on his arrival. Yet I see no reason at all to cast doubt, on rational grounds, upon powers which, before our very eyes, became fatal to their possessor.

At this point there was an intermission. Our lord and master withdrew. Now I confess that almost ever since the beginning of my tale I have looked forward with dread to this moment in it. The thoughts of men are mostly not hard to read; in this case they are very easy. You are sure to ask why we did not choose this moment to go away—and I must continue to owe you an answer. I do not know why. I cannot defend myself. By this time it was certainly eleven, probably later. The children were asleep. The last series of tests had been too long, nature had had her way. They were sleeping in our laps, the little one on mine, the boy on his mother's. That was, in a way, a consolation; but at the same time it was also ground for compassion and a clear leading to take them home to bed. And I give you my word that we wanted to obey this touching admonition, we seriously wanted to. We roused the poor things and told them it was now high time to go. But they were no sooner conscious than they began to resist and implore—you know how horrified children are at the thought of leaving before the end of a thing. No cajoling has any effect, you have to use force. It was so lovely, they wailed. How did we know what was coming next? Surely we could not leave until after the intermission; they liked a little nap now and again—only not go home, only not go to bed, while the beautiful evening was still going on!

We yielded, but only for the moment, of course—so far as we

knew—only for a little while, just a few minutes longer. I cannot excuse our staying, scarcely can I even understand it. Did we think, having once said A, we had to say B—having once brought the children hither we had to let them stay? No, it is not good enough. Were we ourselves so highly entertained? Yes, and no. Our feelings for Cavaliere Cipolla were of a very mixed kind, but so were the feelings of the whole audience, if I mistake not, and nobody left. Were we under the sway of a fascination which emanated from this man who took so strange a way to earn his bread; a fascination which he gave out independently of the programme and even between the tricks and which paralysed our resolve? Again, sheer curiosity may account for something. One was curious to know how such an evening turned out; Cipolla in his remarks having all along hinted that he had tricks in his bag stranger than any he had yet produced.

But all that is not it—or at least it is not all of it. More correct it would be to answer the first question with another. Why had we not left Torre di Venere itself before now? To me the two questions are one and the same, and in order to get out of the impasse I might simply say that I had answered it already. For, as things had been in Torre in general: queer, uncomfortable, troublesome, tense, oppressive, so precisely they were here in this hall tonight. Yes, more than precisely. For it seemed to be the fountainhead of all the uncanniness and all the strained feelings which had oppressed the atmosphere of our holiday. This man whose return to the stage we were awaiting was the personification of all that; and, as we had not gone away in general, so to speak, it would have been inconsistent to do it in the particular case. You may call this an explanation, you may call it inertia, as you see fit. Any argument more to the purpose I simply do not know how to adduce.

Well, there was an interval of ten minutes, which grew into nearly twenty. The children remained awake. They were enchanted by our compliance, and filled the break to their own satisfaction by renewing relations with the popular sphere, with Antonio, Guiscardo, and the canoe man. They put their hands to their mouths and called messages across, appealing to us for the Italian words. "Hope you have a good catch tomorrow, a whole netful!" They called to Mario, Esquisito Mario: *"Mario, una cioccolata e biscotti!"* And this time he heeded and answered with a smile: *"Subito, signorini!"* Later we had reason to recall this kindly, if rather absent and pensive smile.

Thus the interval passed, the gong sounded. The audience, which had scattered in conversation, took their places again, the children sat up straight in their chairs with their hands in their laps. The curtain had not been dropped. Cipolla came forward again, with his dipping stride, and began to introduce the second half of the programme with a lecture.

Let me state once for all that this self-confident cripple was the most powerful hypnotist I have ever seen in my life. It was pretty plain now that he threw dust in the public eye and advertised himself as a prestidigitator on account of police regulations which would have prevented him from making his living by the exercise of his powers. Perhaps this eye-wash is the usual thing in Italy; it may be permitted or even connived at by the authorities. Certainly the man had from the beginning made little concealment of the actual nature of his operations; and this second half of the programme was quite frankly and exclusively devoted to one sort of experiment. While he still practised some rhetorical circumlocutions, the tests themselves were one long series of attacks upon the will-power, the loss or compulsion of volition. Comic, exciting, amazing by turns, by midnight they were still in full swing; we ran the gamut of all the phenomena this natural-unnatural field has to show, from the unimpressive at one end of the scale to the monstrous at the other. The audience laughed and applauded as they followed the grotesque details; shook their heads, clapped their knees, fell very frankly under the spell of this stern, self-assured personality. At the same time I saw signs that they were not quite complacent, not quite unconscious of the peculiar ignominy which lay, for the individual and for the general, in Cipolla's triumphs.

Two main features were constant in all the experiments: the liquor glass and the claw-handled riding-whip. The first was always invoked to add fuel to his demoniac fires; without it, apparently, they might have burned out. On this score we might even have felt pity for the man; but the whistle of his scourge, the insulting symbol of his domination, before which we all cowered, drowned out every sensation save a dazed and outbraved submission to his power. Did he then lay claim to our sympathy to boot? I was struck by a remark he made—it suggested no less. At the climax of his experiments, by stroking and breathing upon a certain young man who had offered himself as a subject and already proved himself a particularly susceptible one, he had not only put him into the condition known as deep trance and extended his insensible body by neck and feet across the backs of two chairs, but had actually sat down on the rigid form as on a bench, without making it yield. The sight of this unholy figure in a frock-coat squatted on the stiff body was horrible and incredible; the audience, convinced that the victim of this scientific diversion must be suffering, expressed its sympathy: *"Ah, poveretto!"* Poor soul, poor soul! *"Poor soul!"* Cipolla mocked them, with some bitterness. "Ladies and gentlemen, you are barking up the wrong tree. *Sono io il poveretto.* I am the person who is suffering, I am the one to be pitied." We pocketed the information. Very good. Maybe the experiment was at his expense, maybe it was he who had suffered the cramp when the *giovanotto* over there had made the faces. But appearances were all against it; and one does not feel like saying *poveretto* to a man who is suffering to bring about the humiliation of others.

I have got ahead of my story and lost sight of the sequence of events. To this day my mind is full of the Cavaliere's feats of endurance; only I do not recall them in their order—which does not matter. So much I do know: that the longer and more circumstantial tests, which got the most applause, impressed me less than some of the small ones which passed quickly over. I remember the young man whose body Cipolla converted into a board, only because of the accompanying remarks which I have quoted. An elderly lady in a cane-seated chair was lulled by Cipolla in the delusion that she was on a voyage to India and gave a voluble account of her adventures by land and sea. But I found this phenomenon less impressive than one which followed immediately after the intermission. A tall, well-built, soldierly man was unable to lift his arm, after the hunchback had told him that he could not and given a cut through the air with his whip. I can still see the face of that stately, mustachioed colonel smiling and clenching his teeth as he struggled to regain his lost freedom of action. A staggering performance! He seemed to be exerting his will, and in vain; the trouble, however, was probably simply that he could not will. There was involved here that recoil of the will upon itself which paralyses choice—as our tyrant had previously explained to the Roman gentleman.

Still less can I forget the touching scene, at once comic and horrible, with Signora Angiolieri. The Cavaliere, probably in his first bold survey of the room, had spied out her ethereal lack of resistance to his power. For actually he bewitched her, literally drew her out of her seat, out of her row, and away with him whither he willed. And in order to enhance his effect, he bade Signor Angiolieri call upon his wife by her name, to throw, as it were, all the weight of his existence and his rights in her into the scale, to rouse by the voice of her husband everything in his spouse's soul which could shield her virtue against the evil assaults of magic. And how vain it all was! Cipolla was standing at some distance from the couple, when he made a single cut with his whip through the air. It caused our landlady to shudder violently and turn her face towards him. "Sofronia!" cried Signor Angiolieri—we had not known that Signora Angiolieri's name was Sofronia. And he did well to call, everybody saw that there was no time to lose. His wife kept her face turned in the direction of the diabolical Cavaliere, who with his ten long yellow fingers was making passes at his victim, moving backwards as he did so, step by step. Then Signora Angiolieri, her pale face gleaming, rose up from her seat, turned right round, and began to glide after him. Fatal and forbidding sight! Her face as though moonstruck, stiff-armed, her lovely hands lifted a little at the wrists, the feet as it were together, she seemed to float slowly out of her row and after the tempter. "Call her, sir, keep on calling," prompted the redoubtable man. And Signor Angiolieri, in a weak voice, called: "Sofronia!" Ah, again and again he called; as his wife went further off he even curved one hand round his lips and beckoned with the other as he called. But the poor voice of love and duty echoed unheard, in vain, behind the lost one's back; the signora swayed along, moonstruck, deaf, enslaved; she glided into the middle aisle and down it towards the fingering hunchback, towards the door. We were driven to the conviction, that she would have followed her master, had he so willed it, to the ends of the earth.

"Accidente!" cried out Signor Angiolieri, in genuine affright, springing up as the exit was reached. But at the same moment the Cavaliere put aside, as it were, the triumphal crown and broke off. "Enough, signora, I thank you," he said, and offered his arm to lead her back to her husband. "Signor," he greeted the latter, "here is your wife. Unharmed, with my compliments, I give her into your hands. Cherish with all the strength of your manhood a treasure which is so wholly yours, and let your zeal be quickened by knowing that there are powers stronger than reason or virtue, and not always so magnanimously ready to relinquish their prey!"

Poor Signor Angiolieri, so quiet, so bald! He did not look as though he would know how to defend his happiness, even against powers much less demoniac than these which were now adding mockery to frightfulness. Solemnly and pompously the Cavaliere retired to the stage, amid applause to which his eloquence gave double strength. It was this particular episode, I feel sure, that set the seal upon his ascendancy. For now he made them dance, yes, literally; and the dancing lent a dissolute, abandoned, topsy-turvy air to the scene, a drunken abdication of the critical spirit which had so long resisted the spell of this man. Yes, he had had to fight to get the upper hand—for instance against the animosity of the young Roman gentleman, whose rebellious spirit threatened to serve others as a rallying-point. But it was precisely upon the importance of example that the Cavaliere was so strong. He had the wit to make his attack at the weakest point and to choose as his first victim that feeble, ecstatic youth whom he had previously made into a board. The master had but to look at him, when this young man would fling himself back as though struck by lightning, place his hands rigidly at his sides, and fall into a state of military somnambulism, in which it was plain to any eye that he was open to the most absurd suggestion that might be made to him. He seemed quite content in his abject state, quite pleased to be relieved of the burden of voluntary choice. Again and again he offered himself as a subject and gloried in the model facility he had in losing consciousness. So now he mounted the platform, and a single cut of the whip was enough to make him dance to the Cavaliere's orders, in a kind of complacent ecstasy, eyes closed, head nodding, lank limbs flying in all directions.

It looked unmistakably like enjoyment, and other recruits were not long in coming forward: two other young men, one humbly and one well dressed, were soon jigging alongside the first. But now the gentleman from Rome bobbed up again, asking defiantly if the Cavaliere would engage to make him dance too, even against his will.

"Even against your will," answered Cipolla, in unforgettable accents. That frightful *"anche se non vuole"* still rings in my ears. The struggle began. After Cipolla had taken another little glass and lighted a fresh cigarette he stationed the Roman at a point in the middle aisle and himself took up a position some distance behind, making his whip whistle through the air as he gave the order: *"Balla!"* His opponent did not stir. *"Balla!"* repeated the Cavaliere incisively, and snapped his whip. You saw the young man move his neck round in his collar; at the same time one hand lifted slightly at the wrist, one ankle turned outward. But that was all, for the time at least; merely a tendency to twitch, now sternly repressed, now seeming about to get the upper hand. It escaped nobody that here a heroic obstinacy, a fixed resolve to resist, must needs be conquered; we were beholding a gallant effort to strike out and save the honour of the human race. He twitched but danced not; and the struggle was so prolonged that the Cavaliere had to divide his attention between it and the stage, turning now and then to make his riding-whip whistle in the direction of the dancers, as it were to keep them in leash. At the same time he advised the audience that no fatigue was involved in such activities, however long they went on, since it was not the automatons up there who danced, but himself. Then once more his eye would bore itself into the back of the Roman's neck and lay siege to the strength of purpose which defied him.

One saw it waver, that strength of purpose, beneath the repeated summons and whip-crackings. Saw with an objective interest which yet was not quite free from traces of sympathetic emotion—from pity, even from a cruel kind of pleasure. If I understand what was going on, it was the negative character of the young man's fighting position which was his undoing. It is likely that not willing is not a practicable state of mind; *not* to want to do something may be in the long run a mental content impossible to subsist on. Between not willing a certain thing and not willing at all—in other words, yielding to another person's will—there may lie too small a space for the idea of freedom to squeeze into. Again, there were the Cavaliere's persuasive words, woven in among the whip-crackings and commands, as he mingled effects that were his own secret with others of a bewilderingly psychological kind. *"Balla!"* said he. "Who wants to torture himself like that? Is forcing yourself your idea of freedom? *Una ballatina!* Why, your arms and legs are aching for it. What a relief to give way to them—there, you are dancing already! That is no struggle any more, it is pleasure!" And so it was. The jerking and twitching of the refractory youth's limbs had at last got the upper hand; he lifted his arms, then his knees, his joints quite suddenly relaxed, he flung his legs and danced, and amid bursts of applause the Cavaliere led him to join the row of puppets on the stage. Up there we could see his face as he "enjoyed" himself; it was clothed in a broad grin and the eyes were half-shut. In a way, it was consoling to see that he was having a better time than he had had in the hour of his pride.

His "fall" was, I may say, an epoch. The ice was completely broken, Cipolla's triumph had reached its height. The Circe's wand, that whistling leather whip with the claw handle, held absolute sway. At one time—it must have been well after midnight—not only were there eight or ten persons dancing on the little stage, but in the hall below a varied animation reigned, and a long-toothed Anglo-Saxoness in a pince-nez left her seat of her own motion to perform a tarantella in the centre aisle. Cipolla was lounging in a cane-seated chair at the left of the stage, gulping down the smoke of a cigarette and breathing it impudently out through his bad teeth. He tapped his foot and shrugged his shoulders, looking down upon the abandoned scene in the hall; now and then he snapped his whip backwards at a laggard upon the stage. The children were awake at the moment. With shame I speak of them. For it was not good to be here, least of all for them; that we had not taken them away can only be explained by saying that we had caught the general devil-may-careness of the hour. By that time it was all one. Anyhow, thank goodness, they lacked understanding for the disreputable side of the entertainment, and in their innocence were perpetually charmed by the unheard-of indulgence which permitted them to be present at such a thing as a magician's "evening." Whole quarter-hours at a time they drowsed on our laps, waking refreshed and rosy-cheeked, with sleep-drunken eyes, to laugh to bursting at the leaps and jumps the magician made those people up there make. They had not thought it would be so jolly; they joined with their clumsy little hands in every round of applause. And jumped for joy upon their chairs, as was their wont, when Cipolla beckoned to their friend Mario from the Esquisito, beckoned to him just like a picture in a book, holding his hand in front of his nose and bending and straightening the forefinger by turns.

Mario obeyed. I can see him now going up the stairs to Cipolla, who continued to beckon him, in that droll, picture-book sort of way. He hesitated for a moment at first; that, too, I recall quite clearly. During the whole evening he had lounged against a wooden pillar at the side entrance, with his arms folded, or else with his hands thrust into his jacket pockets. He was on our left, near the youth with the militant hair, and had followed the performance attentively, so far as we had seen, if with no particular animation and God knows how much comprehension. He could not much relish being summoned thus, at the end of the evening. But it was only too easy to see why he obeyed. After all, obedience was his calling in life; and then, how should a simple lad like him find it within his human capacity to refuse compliance to a man so throned and crowned as Cipolla at that hour? Willy-nilly he left his column and with a word of thanks to those making way for him he mounted the steps with a doubtful smile on his full lips.

Picture a thickset youth of twenty years, with clipt hair, a low forehead, and heavy-lidded eyes of an indefinite grey, shot with green and yellow. These things I knew from having spoken with him, as we often had. There was a saddle of freckles on the flat nose, the whole upper half of the face retreated behind the lower, and that again was dominated by thick lips that parted to show the salivated teeth. These thick lips and the veiled look of the eyes lent the whole face a primitive melancholy—it was that which had drawn us to him from the first. In it was not the faintest trace of brutality—indeed, his hands would have given the lie to such an idea, being unusually slender and delicate even for a southerner. They were hands by which one liked being served.

We knew him humanly without knowing him personally, if I may make that distinction. We saw him nearly every day, and felt a certain kindness for his dreamy ways, which might at times be actual inattentiveness, suddenly transformed into a redeeming zeal to serve. His mien was serious, only the children could bring a smile to his face. It was not sulky, but uningratiating, without intentional effort to please—or, rather, it seemed to give up being pleasant in the conviction that it could not succeed. We should have remembered Mario in any case, as one of those homely recollections of travel which often stick in the mind better than more important ones. But of his circumstances we knew no more than that his father was a petty clerk in the Municipio and his mother took in washing.

His white waiter's-coat became him better than the faded striped suit he wore, with a gay coloured scarf instead of a collar, the ends tucked into his jacket. He neared Cipolla, who however did not leave off that motion of his finger before his nose, so that Mario had to come still closer, right up to the chair-seat and the master's legs. Whereupon the latter spread out his elbows and seized the lad, turning him so that we had a view of his face. Then gazed him briskly up and down, with a careless, commanding eye.

"Well, *ragazzo mio,* how comes it we make acquaintance so late in the day? But believe me, I made yours long ago. Yes, yes, I've had you in my eye this long while and known what good stuff you were made of. How could I go and forget you again? Well, I've had a good deal to think about. . . . Now tell me, what is your name? The first name, that's all I want."

"My name is Mario," the young man answered, in a low voice.

"Ah, Mario. Very good. Yes, yes, there is such a name, quite a common name, a classic name too, one of those which preserve the heroic traditions of the Fatherland. *Bravo! Salve!"* And he flung up his arm slantingly above his crooked shoulder, palm outward, in the Roman salute. He may have been slightly tipsy by now, and no wonder; but he spoke as before, clearly, fluently, and with emphasis. Though about this time there had crept into his voice a gross, autocratic note, and a kind of arrogance was in his sprawl.

"Well, now, Mario *mio,"* he went on, "it's a good thing you came this evening, and that's a pretty scarf you've got on; it is becoming to your style of beauty. It must stand you in good stead with the girls, the pretty pretty girls of Torre—"

From the row of youths, close by the place where Mario had been standing, sounded a laugh. It came from the youth with the militant hair. He stood there, his jacket over his shoulder, and laughed outright, rudely and scornfully.

Mario gave a start. I think it was a shrug, but he may have started and then hastened to cover the movement by shrugging his shoulders, as much as to say that the neckerchief and the fair sex were matters of equal indifference to him.

The Cavaliere gave a downward glance.

"We needn't trouble about him," he said. "He is jealous, because your scarf is so popular with the girls, maybe partly because you and I are so friendly up here. Perhaps he'd like me to put him in mind of his colic—I could do it free of charge. Tell me, Mario. You've come here this evening for a bit of fun—and in the daytime you work in an ironmonger's shop?"

"In a café," corrected the youth.

"Oh, in a café. That's where Cipolla nearly came a cropper! What you are is a cup-bearer, a Ganymede—I like that, it is another classical allusion—*Salvietta!*" Again the Cavaliere saluted, to the huge gratification of his audience.

Mario smiled too. "But before that," he interpolated, in the interest of accuracy, "I worked for a while in a shop in Portoclemente." He seemed visited by a natural desire to assist the prophecy by dredging out its essential features.

"There, didn't I say so? In an ironmonger's shop?"

"They kept combs and brushes," Mario got round it.

"Didn't I say that you were not always a Ganymede? Not always at the sign of the serviette? Even when Cipolla makes a mistake, it is a kind that makes you believe in him. Now tell me: Do you believe in me?"

An indefinite gesture.

"A half-way answer," commented the Cavaliere. "Probably it is not easy to win your confidence. Even for me, I can see, it is not so easy. I see in your features a reserve, a sadness, *un tratto di malinconia* . . . tell me" (he seized Mario's hand persuasively) "have you troubles?"

"*Nossignore,*" answered Mario, promptly and decidedly.

"You have troubles," insisted the Cavaliere, bearing down the denial by the weight of his authority. "Can't I see? Trying to pull the wool over Cipolla's eyes, are you? Of course, about the girls—it is a girl, isn't it? You have love troubles?"

Mario gave a vigorous head-shake. And again the *giovanotto*'s brutal laugh rang out. The Cavaliere gave heed. His eyes were roving about somewhere in the air: but he cocked an ear to the sound, then swung his whip backwards, as he had once or twice before in his conversation with Mario, that none of his puppets might flag in their zeal. The gesture had nearly cost him his new prey: Mario gave a sudden start in the direction of the steps. But Cipolla had him in his clutch.

"Not so fast," said he. "That would be fine, wouldn't it? So you want to skip, do you, Ganymede, right in the middle of the fun, or, rather, when it is just beginning? Stay with me, I'll show you something nice. I'll convince you. You have no reason to worry, I promise you. This girl—you know her and others know her too—what's her name? Wait! I read the name in your eyes, it is on the tip of my tongue and yours too—"

"Silvestra!" shouted the *giovanotto* from below.

The Cavaliere's face did not change.

"Aren't there the forward people?" he asked, not looking down, more as in undisturbed converse with Mario. "Aren't there the young fighting-cocks that crow in season and out? Takes the word out of your mouth, the conceited fool, and seems to think he has some special right to it. Let him be. But Silvestra, your Silvestra—ah, what a girl that is! What a prize! Brings your heart into your mouth to see her walk or laugh or breathe, she is so lovely. And her round arms when she washes, and tosses her head back to get the hair out of her eyes! An angel from paradise!"

Mario started at him, his head thrust forward. He seemed to have forgotten the audience, forgotten where he was. The red rings round his eyes had got larger, they looked as though they were painted on. His thick lips parted.

"And she makes you suffer, this angel," went on Cipolla, "or, rather, you make yourself suffer for her—there is a difference, my lad, a most important difference, let me tell you. There are misunderstandings in love, maybe nowhere else in the world are there so many. I know what you are thinking: what does this Cipolla, with his little physical defect, know about love? Wrong, all wrong, he knows a lot. He has a wide and powerful understanding of its workings, and it pays to listen to his advice. But let's leave Cipolla out, cut him out altogether and think only of Silvestra, your peerless Silvestra! What! Is she to give any young gamecock the preference, so that he can laugh while you cry? To prefer him to a chap like you, so full of feeling and so sympathetic? Not very likely, is it? It is impossible—we know better, Cipolla and she. If I were to put myself in her place and choose between the two of you, a tarry lout like that—a codfish, a sea-urchin—and a Mario, a knight of the serviette, who moves among gentlefolk and hands round refreshments with an air—my word, but my heart would speak in no uncertain tones—it knows to whom I gave it long ago. It is time that he should see and understand, my chosen one! It is time that you see me and recognize me, Mario, my beloved! Tell me, who am I?"

It was grisly, the way the betrayer made himself irresistible, wreathed and coquetted with his crooked shoulder, languished with the puffy eyes, and showed his splintered teeth in a sickly smile. And alas, at his beguiling words, what was come of our Mario? It is hard for me to tell, hard as it was for me to see; for here was nothing less than an utter abandonment of the inmost soul, a public exposure of timid and deluded passion and rapture. He put his hands across his mouth, his shoulders rose and fell with his pantings. He could not, it was plain, trust his eyes and ears for joy, and the one thing he forgot was precisely that he could not trust them. "Silvestra!" he breathed, from the very depths of his vanquished heart.

"Kiss me!" said the hunchback. "Trust me, I love thee. Kiss me here." And with the tip of his index finger, hand, arm, and little finger outspread, he pointed to his cheek, near the mouth. And Mario bent and kissed him.

It had grown very still in the room. That was a monstrous moment, grotesque and thrilling, the moment of Mario's bliss. In that evil span of time, crowded with a sense of the illusiveness of all joy, one sound became audible, and that not quite at once, but on the instant of the melancholy and ribald meeting between Mario's lips and the repulsive flesh which thrust itself forward for his caress. It was the sound of a laugh, from the *giovanotto* on our left. It broke into the dramatic suspense of the moment, coarse, mocking, and yet—or I must have been grossly mistaken—with an undertone of compassion for the poor bewildered, victimized creature. It had a faint ring of that *"Poveretto"* which Cipolla had declared was wasted on the wrong person, when he claimed the pity for his own.

The laugh still rang in the air when the recipient of the caress gave his whip a little swish, low down, close to his chair-leg, and Mario started up and flung himself back. He stood in that posture staring, his hands one over the other on those desecrated lips. Then he beat his temples with his clenched fists, over and over; turned and staggered down the steps, while the audience applauded, and Cipolla sat there with his hands in his lap, his shoulders shaking. Once below, and even while in full retreat, Mario hurled himself round with legs flung wide apart; one arm flew up, and two flat shattering detonations crashed through applause and laughter.

There was instant silence. Even the dancers came to a full stop and stared about, struck dumb. Cipolla bounded from his seat. He stood with his arms spread out, slanting as though to ward everybody off, as though next moment he would cry out: "Stop! Keep back! Silence! What was that?" Then, in that instant, he sank back in his seat, his head rolling on his chest; in the next he had fallen sideways to the floor, where he lay motionless, a huddled heap of clothing, with limbs awry.

The commotion was indescribable. Ladies hid their faces, shuddering, on the breasts of their escorts. There were shouts for a doctor, for the police. People flung themselves on Mario in a mob, to disarm him, to take away the weapon that hung from his fingers—that small, dull-metal, scarcely pistol-shaped tool with hardly any barrel—in how strange and unexpected a direction had fate levelled it!

And now—now finally, at last—we took the children and led them towards the exit, past the pair of *carabinier* just entering. Was that the end, they wanted to know, that they might go in peace? Yes, we assured them, that was the end. An end of horror, a fatal end. And yet a liberation—for I could not, and I cannot, but find it so!

1929

DISORDER AND EARLY SORROW

The principal dish at dinner had been croquettes made of turnip greens. So there follows a trifle, concocted out of those dessert powders we use nowadays, that taste like almond soap. Xaver, the youthful manservant, in his outgrown striped jacket, white woollen gloves, and yellow sandals, hands it round, and the "big folk" take this opportunity to remind their father, tactfully, that company is coming today.

The "big folk" are two, Ingrid and Bert. Ingrid is brown-eyed, eighteen, and perfectly delightful. She is on the eve of her exams, and will probably pass them, if only because she knows how to wind masters, and even headmasters, round her finger. She does not, however, mean to use her certificate once she gets it; having leanings towards the stage, on the ground of her ingratiating smile, her equally ingratiating voice, and a marked and irresistible talent for burlesque. Bert is blond and seventeen. He intends to get done with school somehow, anyhow, and fling himself into the arms of life. He will be a dancer, or a cabaret actor, possibly even a waiter—but not a waiter anywhere else save at Cairo, the night-club, whither he has once already taken flight, at five in the morning, and been brought back crestfallen. Bert bears a strong resemblance to the youthful manservant, Xaver Kleinsgutl, of about the same age as himself; not because he looks common—in features he is strikingly like his father, Professor Cornelius—but by reason of an approximation of types, due in its turn to far-reaching compromises in matters of dress and bearing generally. Both lads wear their heavy hair very long on top, with a cursory parting in the middle, and give their heads the same characteristic toss to throw it off the forehead. When one of them leaves the house, by the garden gate, bareheaded in all weathers, in a blouse rakishly girt with a leather strap, and sheers off bent well over with his head on one side; or else mounts his push-bike—Xaver makes free with his employers', of both sexes, or even, in acutely irresponsible mood, with the Professor's own—Dr. Cornelius from his bedroom window cannot, for the life of him, tell whether he is looking at his son or his servant. Both, he thinks, look like young moujiks. And both are impassioned cigarette-smokers, though Bert has not the means to compete with Xaver, who smokes as many as thirty a day, of a brand named after a popular cinema star. The big folk call their father and mother the "old folk"—not behind their backs, but as a form of address and in all affection: "Hullo, old folks," they will say; though Cornelius is only forty-seven years old and his wife eight years younger. And the Professor's parents, who lead in his household the humble and hesitant life of the really old, are on the big folk's lips the "ancients." As for the "little folk," Ellie and Snapper, who take their meals upstairs with blue-faced Ann—so called because of her prevailing facial hue—Ellie and Snapper follow their mother's example and address their father by his first name, Abel. Unutterably comic it sounds, in its pert, confiding familiarity; particularly on the lips, in the sweet accents, of five-year-old Eleanor, who is the image of Frau Cornelius's baby pictures and whom the Professor loves above everything else in the world.

"Darling old thing," says Ingrid affably, laying her large but shapely hand on his, as he presides in proper middle-class style over the family table, with her on his left and the mother opposite: "Parent mine, may I ever so gently jog your memory, for you have probably forgotten: this is the afternoon we were to have our little jollification, our turkey-trot with eats to match. You haven't a thing to do but just bear up and not funk it; everything will be over by nine o'clock."

"Oh—ah!" says Cornelius, his face falling. "Good!" he goes on, and nods his head to show himself in harmony with the inevitable. "I only meant—is this really the day? Thursday, yes. How time flies! Well, what time are they coming?"

"Half past four they'll be dropping in, I should say," answers Ingrid, to whom her brother leaves the major rôle in all dealings with the father. Upstairs, while he is resting, he will hear scarcely anything, and from seven to eight he takes his walk. He can slip out by the terrace if he likes.

"Tut!" says Cornelius deprecatingly, as who should say: "You exaggerate." But Bert puts in: "It's the one evening in the week Wanja doesn't have to play. Any other night he'd have to leave by half past six, which would be painful for all concerned."

Wanja is Ivan Herzl, the celebrated young leading man at the Stadttheater. Bert and Ingrid are on intimate terms with him, they often visit him in his dressing-room and have tea. He is an artist of the modern school, who stands on the stage in strange and, to the Professor's mind, utterly affected dancing attitudes, and shrieks lamentably. To a professor of history, all highly repugnant; but Bert has entirely succumbed to Herzl's influence, blackens the lower rim of his eyelids—despite painful but fruitless scenes with the father—and with youthful carelessness of the ancestral anguish declares that not only will he take Herzl for his model if he becomes a dancer, but in case he turns out to be a waiter at the Cairo he means to walk precisely thus.

Cornelius slightly raises his brows and makes his son a little bow—indicative of the unassumingness and self-abnegation that befits his age. You could not call it a mocking bow or suggestive in any special sense. Bert may refer it to himself or equally to his so talented friend.

"Who else is coming?" next inquires the master of the house. They mention various people, names all more or less familiar, from the city, from the suburban colony, from Ingrid's school. They still have some telephoning to do, they say. They have to phone Max. This is Max Hergesell, an engineering student; Ingrid utters his name in the nasal drawl which according to her is the traditional intonation of all the Hergesells. She goes on to parody it in the most abandonedly funny and lifelike way, and the parents laugh until they nearly choke over the wretched trifle. For even in these times when something funny happens people have to laugh.

From time to time the telephone bell rings in the Professor's study, and the big folk run across, knowing it is their affair. Many people had to give up their telephones the last time the price rose, but so far the Corneliuses have been able to keep theirs, just as they have kept their villa, which was built before the war, by dint of the salary Cornelius draws as professor of history—a million marks, and more or less adequate to the chances and changes of post-war life. The house is comfortable, even elegant, though sadly in need of repairs that cannot be made for lack of materials, and at present disfigured by iron stoves with long pipes. Even so, it is still the proper setting of the upper middle class, though they themselves look odd enough in it, with their worn and turned clothing and altered way of life. The children, of course, know nothing else; to them it is normal and regular, they belong by birth to the "villa proletariat." The problem of clothing troubles them not at all. They and their like have evolved a costume to fit the time, by poverty out of taste for innovation: in summer it consists of scarcely more than a belted linen smock and sandals. The middle-class parents find things rather more difficult.

The big folk's table-napkins hang over their chair-backs, they talk with their friends over the telephone. These friends are the invited guests who have rung up to accept or decline or arrange; and the conversation is carried on in the jargon of the clan, full of slang and high spirits, of which the old folk understand hardly a word. These consult together meantime about the hospitality to be offered to the impending guests. The Professor displays a middle-class ambitiousness: he wants to serve a sweet—or something that looks like a sweet—after the Italian salad and brown-bread sandwiches. But Frau Cornelius says that would be going too far. The guests would not expect it, she is sure—and the big folk, returning once more to their trifle, agree with her.

The mother of the family is of the same general type as Ingrid, though not so tall. She is languid; the fantastic difficulties of the housekeeping have broken and worn her. She really ought to go and take a cure, but feels incapable; the floor is always swaying under her feet, and everything seems upside down. She speaks of what is uppermost in her mind: the eggs, they simply must be bought today. Six thousand marks apiece they are, and just so many are to be had on this one day of the week at one single shop fifteen minutes' journey away. Whatever else they do, the big folk must go and fetch them immediately after luncheon, with Danny, their neighbour's son, who will soon be calling for them; and Xaver Kleinsgutl will don civilian garb and attend his young master and mistress. For no single household is allowed more than five eggs a week; therefore the young people will enter the shop singly, one after another, under assumed names, and thus wring twenty eggs from the shopkeeper for the Cornelius family. This enterprise is the sporting event of the week for all participants, not excepting the moujik Kleinsgutl, and most of all for Ingrid and Bert, who delight in misleading and mystifying their fellow-men and would revel in the performance even if it did not achieve one single egg. They adore impersonating fictitious characters; they love to sit in a bus and carry on long lifelike conversations in a dialect which they otherwise never speak, the most commonplace dialogue about politics and people and the price of food, while the whole bus listens open-mouthed to this incredibly ordinary prattle, though with a dark suspicion all the while that something is wrong somewhere. The conversation waxes ever more shameless, it enters into revolting detail about these people who do not exist. Ingrid can make her voice sound ever so common and twittering and shrill as she impersonates a shop-girl with an illegitimate child, said child being a son with sadistic tendencies, who lately out in the country treated a cow with such unnatural cruelty that no Christian could have borne to see it. Bert nearly explodes at her twittering, but restrains himself and displays a grisly sympathy; he and the unhappy shop-girl entering into a long, stupid, depraved, and shuddery conversation over the particular morbid cruelty involved, until an old gentleman opposite, sitting with his ticket folded between his index finger and his seal ring, can bear it no more and makes public protest against the nature of the themes these young folk are discussing with such particularity. He uses the Greek plural: "themata." Whereat Ingrid pretends to be dissolving in tears, and Bert behaves as though his wrath against the old gentleman was with difficulty being held in check and would probably burst out before long. He clenches his fists, he gnashes his teeth, he shakes from head to foot; and the unhappy old gentleman, whose intentions had been of the best, hastily leaves the bus at the next stop.

Such are the diversions of the big folk. The telephone plays a prominent part in them: they ring up any and everybody—members of government, opera singers, dignitaries of the Church—in the character of shop assistants, or perhaps as Lord or Lady Doolittle. They are only with difficulty persuaded that they have the wrong number. Once they emptied their parents' card-tray and distributed its contents among the neighbours' letter-boxes, wantonly, yet not without enough impish sense of the fitness of things to make it highly upsetting. God only knowing why certain people should have called where they did.

Xaver comes in to clear away, tossing the hair out of his eyes. Now that he has taken off his gloves you can see the yellow chain-ring on his left hand. And as the Professor finishes his watery eight-thousand-mark beer and lights a cigarette, the little folk can be heard scrambling down the stair, coming, by established custom, for their after-dinner call on Father and Mother. They storm the dining-room, after a struggle with the latch, clutched by both pairs of little hands at once; their clumsy small feet twinkle over the carpet, in red felt slippers with the socks falling down on them. With prattle and shoutings each makes for his own place: Snapper to Mother, to climb on her lap, boast of all he has eaten, and thump his fat little tum; Ellie to her Abel, so much hers because she is so very much his; because she consciously luxuriates in the deep tenderness—like all deep feeling, concealing a melancholy strain—with which he holds her small form embraced; in the love in his eyes as he kisses her little fairy hand or the sweet brow with its delicate tracery of tiny blue veins.

The little folk look like each other, with the strong undefined likeness of brother and sister. In clothing and haircut they are twins. Yet they are sharply distinguished after all, and quite on sex lines. It is a little Adam and a little Eve. Not only is Snapper the sturdier and more compact, he appears consciously to emphasize his four-year-old masculinity in speech, manner, and carriage, lifting his shoulders and letting the little arms hang down quite like a young American athlete, drawing down his mouth when he talks and seeking to give his voice a gruff and forthright ring. But all this masculinity is the result of effort rather than natively his. Born and brought up in these desolate, distracted times, he has been endowed by them with an unstable and hypersensitive nervous system and suffers greatly under life's disharmonies. He is prone to sudden anger and outbursts of bitter tears, stamping his feet at every trifle; for this reason he is his mother's special nursling and care. His round, round eyes are chestnut brown and already inclined to squint, so that he will need glasses in the near future. His little nose is long, the mouth small—the father's nose and mouth they are, more plainly than ever since the Professor shaved his pointed beard and goes smooth-faced. The pointed beard had become impossible—even professors must make some concession to the changing times.

But the little daughter sits on her father's knee, his Eleonorchen, his little Eve, so much more gracious a little being, so much sweeter-faced than her brother—and he holds his cigarette away from her while she fingers his glasses with her dainty wee hands. The lenses are divided for reading and distance, and each day they tease her curiosity afresh.

At bottom he suspects that his wife's partiality may have a firmer basis than his own: that Snapper's refractory masculinity perhaps is solider stuff than his own little girl's more explicit charm and grace. But the heart will not be commanded, that he knows; and once and for all his heart belongs to the little one, as it has since the day she came, since the first time he saw her.

Almost always when he holds her in his arms he remembers that first time: remembers the sunny room in the Women's Hospital, where Ellie first saw the light, twelve years after Bert was born. He remembers how he drew near, the mother smiling the while, and cautiously put aside the canopy of the diminutive bed that stood beside the large one. There lay the little miracle among the pillows: so well formed, so encompassed, as it were, with the harmony of sweet proportions, with little hands that even then, though so much tinier, were beautiful as now; with wide-open eyes blue as the sky and brighter than the sunshine—and almost in that very second he felt himself captured and held fast. This was love at first sight, love everlasting: a feeling unknown, unhoped for, unexpected—in so far as it could be a matter of conscious awareness; it took entire possession of him, and he understood, with joyous amazement, that this was for life.

But he understood more. He knows, does Dr. Cornelius, that there is something not quite right about this feeling, so unaware, so undreamed of, so involuntary. He has a shrewd suspicion that it is not by accident it has so utterly mastered him and bound itself up with his existence; that he had—even subconsciously—been preparing for it, or, more precisely, been prepared for it. There is, in short, something in him which at a given moment was ready to issue in such a feeling; and this something, highly extraordinary to relate, is his essence and quality as a professor of history. Dr. Cornelius, however, does not actually say this, even to himself; he merely realizes it, at odd times, and smiles a private smile. He knows that history professors do not love history because it is something that comes to pass, but only because it is something that *has* come to pass; that they hate a revolution like the present one because they feel it is lawless, incoherent, irrelevant—in a word, unhistoric; that their hearts belong to the coherent, disciplined, historic past. For the temper of timelessness, the temper of eternity—thus the scholar communes with himself when he takes his walk by the river before supper—that temper broods over the past; and it is a temper much better suited to the nervous system of a history professor than are the excesses of the present. The past is immortalized; that is to say, it is dead; and death is the root of all godliness and all abiding significance. Dr. Cornelius, walking alone in the dark, has a profound insight into this truth. It is this conservative instinct of his, his sense of the eternal, that has found in his love for his little daughter a way to save itself from the wounding inflicted by the times. For father love, and a little child on its mother's breast—are not these timeless, and thus very, very holy and beautiful? Yet Cornelius, pondering there in the dark, descries something not perfectly right and good in his love. Theoretically, in the interests of science, he admits it to himself. There is something ulterior about it, in the nature of it; that something is hostility, hostility against the history of today, which is still in the making and thus not history at all, in behalf of the genuine history that has already happened—that is to say, death. Yes, passing strange though all this is, yet it is true; true in a sense, that is. His devotion to this priceless little morsel of life and new growth has something to do with death, it clings to death as against life; and that is neither right nor beautiful—in a sense. Though only the most fanatical asceticism could be capable, on no other ground than such casual scientific perception, of tearing this purest and most precious of feelings out of his heart.

He holds his darling on his lap and her slim rosy legs hang down. He raises his brows as he talks to her, tenderly, with a half-teasing note of respect, and listens enchanted to her high, sweet little voice calling him Abel. He exchanges a look with the mother, who is caressing her Snapper and reading him a gentle lecture. He must be more reasonable, he must learn self-control; today again, under the manifold exasperations of life, he has given way to rage and behaved like a howling dervish. Cornelius casts a mistrustful glance at the big folk now and then, too; he thinks it not unlikely they are not unaware of those scientific preoccupations of his evening walks. If such be the case they do not show it. They stand there leaning their arms on their chair-backs and with a benevolence not untinctured with irony look on at the parental happiness.

The children's frocks are of a heavy, brick-red stuff, embroidered in modern "arty" style. They once belonged to Ingrid and Bert and are precisely alike, save that little knickers come out beneath Snapper's smock. And both have their hair bobbed. Snapper's is a streaky blond, inclined to turn dark. It is bristly and sticky and looks for all the world like a droll, badly fitting wig. But Ellie's is chestnut brown, glossy and fine as silk, as pleasing as her whole little personality. It covers her ears—and these ears are not a pair, one of them being the right size, the other distinctly too large. Her father will sometimes uncover this little abnormality and exclaim over it as though he had never noticed it before, which both makes Ellie giggle and covers her with shame. Her eyes are now golden brown, set far apart and with sweet gleams in them—such a clear and lovely look! The brows above are blond; the nose still unformed, with thick nostrils and almost circular holes; the mouth large and expressive, with a beautifully arching and mobile upper lip. When she laughs, dimples come in her cheeks and she shows her teeth like loosely strung pearls. So far she has lost but one tooth, which her father gently twisted out with his handkerchief after it had grown very wobbling. During this small operation she had paled and trembled very much. Her cheeks have the softness proper to her years, but they are not chubby; indeed, they are rather concave, due to her facial structure, with its somewhat prominent jaw. On one, close to the soft fall of her hair, is a downy freckle.

Ellie is not too well pleased with her looks—a sign that already she troubles about such things. Sadly she thinks it is best to admit it once for all, her face is "homely"; though the rest of her, "on the other hand," is not bad at all. She loves expressions like "on the other hand"; they sound choice and grown-up to her, and she likes to string them together, one after the other: "very likely," "probably," "after all." Snapper is self-critical too, though more in the moral sphere: he suffers from remorse for his attacks of rage and considers himself a tremendous sinner. He is quite certain that heaven is not for such as he; he is sure to go to "the bad place" when he dies, and no persuasions will convince him to the contrary—as that God sees the heart and gladly makes allowances. Obstinately he shakes his head, with the comic, crooked little peruke, and vows there is no place for him in heaven. When he has a cold he is immediately quite choked with mucus; rattles and rumbles from top to toe if you even look at him; his temperature flies up at once and he simply puffs. Nursy is pessimistic on the score of his constitution: such fat-blooded children as he might get a stroke any minute. Once she even thought she saw the moment at hand: Snapper had been in one of his berserker rages, and in the ensuing fit of penitence stood himself in the corner with his back to the room. Suddenly Nursy noticed that his face had gone all blue, far bluer, even, than her own. She raised the alarm, crying out that the child's all too rich blood had at length brought him to his final hour; and Snapper, to his vast astonishment, found himself, so far from being rebuked for evil-doing, encompassed in tenderness and anxiety—until it turned out that his colour was not caused by apoplexy but by the distempering on the nursery wall, which had come off on his tear-wet face.

Nursy has come downstairs too, and stands by the door, sleek-haired, owl-eyed, with her hands folded over her white apron, and a severely dignified manner born of her limited intelligence. She is very proud of the care and training she gives her nurslings and declares that they are "enveloping wonderfully." She has had seventeen suppurated teeth lately removed from her jaws and been measured for a set of symmetrical yellow ones in dark rubber gums; these now embellish her peasant face. She is obsessed with the strange conviction that these teeth of hers are the subject of general conversation, that, as it were, the sparrows on the housetops chatter of them. "Everybody knows I've had a false set put in," she will say; "there has been a great deal of foolish talk about them." She is much given to dark hints and veiled innuendo: speaks, for instance, of a certain Dr. Bleifuss, whom every child knows, and "there are even some in the house who pretend to be him." All one can do with talk like this is charitably to pass it over in silence. But she teaches the children nursery rhymes: gems like:

"Puff, puff, here comes the train!
Puff, puff, toot, toot,
Away it goes again."

Or that gastronomical jingle, so suited, in its sparseness, to the times, and yet seemingly with a blitheness of its own:

"Monday we begin the week,
Tuesday there's a bone to pick.
Wednesday we're half way through,
Thursday what a great to-do!
Friday we eat what fish we're able,
Saturday we dance round the table.
Sunday brings us pork and greens—
Here's a feast for kings and queens!"

Also a certain four-line stanza with a romantic appeal, unutterable and unuttered:

"Open the gate, open the gate
And let the carriage drive in.
Who is it in the carriage sits?
A lordly sir with golden hair."

Or, finally that ballad about golden-haired Marianne who sat on a, sat on a, sat on a stone, and combed out her, combed out her, combed out her hair; and about blood-thirsty Rudolph, who pulled out a, pulled out a, pulled out a knife—and his ensuing direful end. Ellie enunciates all these ballads charmingly, with her mobile little lips, and sings them in her sweet little voice—much better than Snapper. She does everything better than he does, and he pays her honest admiration and homage and obeys her in all things except when visited by one of his attacks. Sometimes she teaches him, instructs him upon the birds in the picture-book and tells him their proper names: "This is a chaffinch, Buddy, this is a bullfinch, this is a cowfinch." He has to repeat them after her. She gives him medical instruction too, teaches him the names of diseases, such as infammation of the lungs, infammation of the blood, infammation of the air. If he does not pay attention and cannot say the words after her, she stands him in the corner. Once she even boxed his ears, but was so ashamed that she stood herself in the corner for a long time. Yes, they are fast friends, two souls with but a single thought, and have all their adventures in common. They come home from a walk and relate as with one voice that they have seen two moolies and a teenty-weenty baby calf. They are on familiar terms with the kitchen, which consists of Xaver and the ladies Hinterhofer, two sisters once of the lower middle class who, in these evil days, are reduced to living *"au pair"* as the phrase goes and officiating as cook and housemaid for their board and keep. The little ones have a feeling that Xaver and the Hinterhofers are on much the same footing with their father and mother as they are themselves. At least sometimes, when they have been scolded, they go downstairs and announce that the master and mistress are cross. But playing with the servants lacks charm compared with the joys of playing upstairs. The kitchen could never rise to the height of the games their father can invent. For instance, there is "four gentlemen taking a walk." When they play it Abel will crook his knees until he is the same height with themselves and go walking with them, hand in hand. They never get enough of this sport; they could walk round and round the dining-room a whole day on end, five gentlemen in all, counting the diminished Abel.

Then there is the thrilling cushion game. One of the children, usually Ellie, seats herself, unbeknownst to Abel, in his seat at table. Still as a mouse she awaits his coming. He draws near with his head in the air, descanting in loud, clear tones upon the surpassing comfort of his chair; and sits down on top of Ellie. "What's this, what's this?" says he. And bounces about, deaf to the smothered giggles exploding behind him. "Why have they put a cushion in my chair? And what a queer, hard, awkward-shaped cushion it is!" he goes on. "Frightfully uncomfortable to sit on!" And keeps pushing and bouncing about more and more on the astonishing cushion and clutching behind him into the rapturous giggling and squeaking, until at last he turns round, and the game ends with a magnificent climax of discovery and recognition. They might go through all this a hundred times without diminishing by an iota its power to thrill.

Today is no time for such joys. The imminent festivity disturbs the atmosphere, and besides there is work to be done, and, above all, the eggs to be got. Ellie has just time to recite "Puff, puff," and Cornelius to discover that her ears are not mates, when they are interrupted by the arrival of Danny, come to fetch Bert and Ingrid. Xaver, meantime, has exchanged his striped livery for an ordinary coat, in which he looks rather rough-and-ready, though as brisk and attractive as ever. So then Nursy and the children ascend to the upper regions, the Professor withdraws to his study to read, as always after dinner, and his wife bends her energies upon the sandwiches and salad that must be prepared. And she has another errand as well. Before the young people arrive she has to take her shopping-basket and dash into town on her bicycle, to turn into provisions a sum of money she has in hand, which she dares not keep lest it lose all value.

Cornelius reads, leaning back in his chair, with his cigar between his middle and index fingers. First he reads Macaulay on the origin of the English public debt at the end of the seventeenth century; then an article in a French periodical on the rapid increase in the Spanish debt towards the end of the sixteenth. Both these for his lecture on the morrow. He intends to compare the astonishing prosperity which accompanied the phenomenon in England with its fatal effects a hundred years earlier in Spain, and to analyse the ethical and psychological grounds of the difference in results. For that will give him a chance to refer back from the England of William III, which is the actual subject in hand, to the time of Philip II and the Counter-Reformation, which is his own special field. He has already written a valuable work on this period; it is much cited and got him his professorship. While his cigar burns down and gets strong, he excogitates a few pensive sentences in a key of gentle melancholy, to be delivered before his class next day: about the practically hopeless struggle carried on by the belated Philip against the whole trend of history: against the new, the kingdom-disrupting power of the Germanic ideal of freedom and individual liberty. And about the persistent, futile struggle of the aristocracy, condemned by God and rejected of man, against the forces of progress and change. He savours his sentences; keeps on polishing them while he puts back the books he has been using; then goes upstairs for the usual pause in his day's work, the hour with drawn blinds and closed eyes, which he so imperatively needs. But today, he recalls, he will rest under disturbed conditions, amid the bustle of preparations for the feast. He smiles to find his heart giving a mild flutter at the thought. Disjointed phrases on the theme of black-clad Philip and his times mingle with a confused consciousness that they will soon be dancing down below. For five minutes or so he falls asleep.

As he lies and rests he can hear the sound of the garden gate and the repeated ringing at the bell. Each time a little pang goes through him, of excitement and suspense, at the thought that the young people have begun to fill the floor below. And each time he smiles at himself again—though even his smile is slightly nervous, is tinged with the pleasurable anticipations people always feel before a party. At half past four—it is already dark—he gets up and washes at the wash-stand. The basin has been out of repair for two years. It is supposed to tip, but has broken away from its socket on one side and cannot be mended because there is nobody to mend it; neither replaced because no shop can supply another. So it has to be hung up above the vent and emptied by lifting in both hands and pouring out the water. Cornelius shakes his head over this basin, as he does several times a day—whenever, in fact, he has occasion to use it. He finishes his toilet with care, standing under the ceiling light to polish his glasses till they shine. Then he goes downstairs.

On his way to the dining-room he hears the gramophone already going, and the sound of voices. He puts on a polite, society air; at his tongue's end is the phrase he means to utter: "Pray don't let me disturb you," as he passes directly into the dining-room for his tea. "Pray don't let me disturb you"—it seems to him precisely the *mot juste;* towards the guests cordial and considerate, for himself a very bulwark.

The lower floor is lighted up, all the bulbs in the chandelier are burning save one that has burned out. Cornelius pauses on a lower step and surveys the entrance hall. It looks pleasant and cosy in the bright light, with its copy of Marées over the brick chimney-piece, its wainscoted walls—wainscoted in soft wood—and red-carpeted floor, where the guests stand in groups, chatting, each with his tea-cup and slice of bread-and-butter spread with anchovy paste. There is a festal haze, faint scents of hair and clothing and human breath come to him across the room, it is all characteristic and familiar and highly evocative. The door into the dressing-room is open, guests are still arriving.

A large group of people is rather bewildering at first sight. The Professor takes in only the general scene. He does not see Ingrid, who is standing just at the foot of the steps, in a dark silk frock with a pleated collar falling softly over the shoulders, and bare arms. She smiles up at him, nodding and showing her lovely teeth.

"Rested?" she asks, for his private ear. With a quite unwarranted start he recognizes her, and she presents some of her friends.

"May I introduce Herr Zuber?" she says. "And this is Fräulein Plaichinger."

Herr Zuber is insignificant. But Fräulein Plaichinger is a perfect Germania, blond and voluptuous, arrayed in floating draperies. She has a snub nose, and answers the Professor's salutation in the high, shrill pipe so many stout women have.

"Delighted to meet you," he says. "How nice of you to come! A classmate of Ingrid's, I suppose?"

And Herr Zuber is a golfing partner of Ingrid's. He is in business; he works in his uncle's brewery. Cornelius makes a few jokes about the thinness of the beer and professes to believe that Herr Zuber could easily do something about the quality if he would. "But pray don't let me disturb you," he goes on, and turns towards the dining-room.

"There comes Max," says Ingrid. "Max, you sweep, what do you mean by rolling up at this time of day?" For such is the way they talk to each other, offensively to an older ear; of social forms, of hospitable warmth, there is no faintest trace. They all call each other by their first names.

A young man comes up to them out of the dressing-room and makes his bow; he has an expanse of white shirt-front and a little black string tie. He is as pretty as a picture, dark, with rosy cheeks, clean-shaven of course, but with just a sketch of side-whisker. Not a ridiculous or flashy beauty, not like a gypsy fiddler, but just charming to look at, in a winning, well-bred way, with kind dark eyes. He even wears his dinner-jacket a little awkwardly.

"Please don't scold me, Cornelia," he says; "it's the idiotic lectures." And Ingrid presents him to her father as Herr Hergesell.

Well, and so this is Herr Hergesell. He knows his manners, does Herr Hergesell, and thanks the master of the house quite ingratiatingly for his invitation as they shake hands. "I certainly seem to have missed the bus," says he jocosely. "Of course I have lectures today up to four o'clock; I would have; and after that I had to go home to change." Then he talks about his pumps, with which he has just been struggling in the dressing-room.

"I brought them with me in a bag," he goes on. "Mustn't tramp all over the carpet in our brogues—it's not done. Well, I was ass enough not to fetch along a shoe-horn, and I find I simply can't get in! What a sell! They are the tightest I've ever had, the numbers don't tell you a thing, and all the leather today is just cast iron. It's not leather at all. My poor finger"—he confidingly displays a reddened digit and once more characterizes the whole thing as a "sell," and a putrid sell into the bargain. He really does talk just as Ingrid said he did, with a peculiar nasal drawl, not affectedly in the least, but merely because that is the way of all the Hergesells.

Dr. Cornelius says it is very careless of them not to keep a shoe-horn in the cloak-room and displays proper sympathy with the mangled finger. "But now you *really* must not let me disturb you any longer," he goes on. *"Auf wiedersehen!"* And he crosses the hall into the dining-room.

There are guests there too, drinking tea; the family table is pulled out. But the Professor goes at once to his own little upholstered corner with the electric light bulb above it—the nook where he usually drinks his tea. His wife is sitting there talking with Bert and two other young men, one of them Herzl, whom Cornelius knows and greets; the other a typical "Wandervogel" named Möller, a youth who obviously neither owns nor cares to own the correct evening dress of the middle classes (in fact, there is no such thing any more), nor to ape the manners of a gentleman (and, in fact, there is no such thing any more either). He has a wilderness of hair, horn spectacles, and a long neck, and wears golf stockings and a belted blouse. His regular occupation, the Professor learns, is banking, but he is by way of being an amateur folk-lorist and collects folk-songs from all localities and in all languages. He sings them, too, and at Ingrid's command has brought his guitar; it is hanging in the dressing-room in an oilcloth case. Herzl, the actor, is small and slight, but he has a strong growth of black beard, as you can tell by the thick coat of powder on his cheeks. His eyes are larger than life, with a deep and melancholy glow. He has put on rouge besides the powder—those dull carmine high-lights on the cheeks can be nothing but a cosmetic. "Queer," thinks the Professor. "You would think a man would be one thing or the other—not melancholic and use face paint at the same time. It's a psychological contradiction. How can a melancholy man rouge? But here we have a perfect illustration of the abnormality of the artist soul-form. It can make possible a contradiction like this—perhaps it even consists in the contradiction. All very interesting—and no reason whatever for not being polite to him. Politeness is a primitive convention—and legitimate. . . . Do take some lemon, Herr Hofschauspieler!"

Court actors and court theatres—there are no such things any more, really. But Herzl relishes the sound of the title, notwithstanding he is a revolutionary artist. This must be another contradiction inherent in his soul-form; so, at least, the Professor assumes, and he is probably right. The flattery he is guilty of is a sort of atonement for his previous hard thoughts about the rouge.

"Thank you so much—it's really too good of you, sir," says Herzl, quite embarrassed. He is so overcome that he almost stammers; only his perfect enunciation saves him. His whole bearing towards his hostess and the master of the house is exaggeratedly polite. It is almost as though he had a bad conscience in respect of his rouge; as though an inward compulsion had driven him to put it on, but now, seeing it through the Professor's eyes, he disapproves of it himself, and thinks, by an air of humility towards the whole of unrouged society, to mitigate its effect.

They drink their tea and chat: about Möller's folk-songs, about Basque folk-songs and Spanish folk-songs; from which they pass to the new production of *Don Carlos* at the Stadttheater, in which Herzl plays the title-rôle. He talks about his own rendering of the part and says he hopes his conception of the character has unity. They go on to criticize the rest of the cast, the setting, and the production as a whole; and Cornelius is struck, rather painfully, to find the conversation trending towards his own special province, back to Spain and the Counter-Reformation. He has done nothing at all to give it this turn, he is perfectly innocent, and hopes it does not look as though he had sought an occasion to play the professor. He wonders, and falls silent, feeling relieved when the little folk come up to the table. Ellie and Snapper have on their blue velvet Sunday frocks; they are permitted to partake in the festivities up to bed-time. They look shy and large-eyed as they say how-do-you-do to the strangers and, under pressure, repeat their names and ages. Herr Möller does nothing but gaze at them solemnly, but Herzl is simply ravished. He rolls his eyes up to heaven and puts his hands over his mouth; he positively blesses them. It all, no doubt, comes from his heart, but he is so addicted to theatrical methods of making an impression and getting an effect that both words and behavior ring frightfully false. And even his enthusiasm for the little folk looks too much like part of his general craving to make up for the rouge on his cheeks.

The tea-table has meanwhile emptied of guests, and dancing is going on in the hall. The children run off, the Professor prepares to retire. "Go and enjoy yourselves," he says to Möller and Herzl, who have sprung from their chairs as he rises from his. They shake hands and he withdraws into his study, his peaceful kingdom, where he lets down the blinds, turns on the desk lamp, and sits down to his work.

It is work which can be done, if necessary, under disturbed conditions: nothing but a few letters and a few notes. Of course, Cornelius's mind wanders. Vague impressions float through it: Herr Hergesell's refractory pumps, the high pipe in that plump body of the Plaichinger female. As he writes, or leans back in his chair and stares into space, his thoughts go back to Herr Möller's collection of Basque folk-songs, to Herzl's posings and humility, to "his" Carlos and the court of Philip II. There is something strange, he thinks, about conversations. They are so ductile, they will flow of their own accord in the direction of one's dominating interest. Often and often he has seen this happen. And while he is thinking, he is listening to the sounds next door—rather subdued, he finds them. He hears only voices, no sound of footsteps. The dancers do not glide or circle round the room; they merely walk about over the carpet, which does not hamper their movements in the least. Their way of holding each other is quite different and strange, and they move to the strains of the gramophone, to the weird music of the new world. He concentrates on the music and makes out that it is a jazz-band record, with various percussion instruments and the clack and clatter of castanets, which, however, are not even faintly suggestive of Spain, but merely jazz like the rest. No, not Spain. . . . His thoughts are back at their old round.

Half an hour goes by. It occurs to him it would be no more than friendly to go and contribute a box of cigarettes to the festivities next door. Too bad to ask the young people to smoke their own—though they have probably never thought of it. He goes into the empty dining-room and takes a box from his supply in the cupboard: not the best ones, nor yet the brand he himself prefers, but a certain long, thin kind he is not averse to getting rid of—after all, they are nothing but youngsters. He takes the box into the hall, holds it up with a smile, and deposits it on the mantel-shelf. After which he gives a look round and returns to his own room.

There comes a lull in dance and music. The guests stand about the room in groups or round the table at the window or are seated in a circle by the fireplace. Even the built-in stairs, with their worn velvet carpet, are crowded with young folk as in an amphitheatre: Max Hergesell is there, leaning back with one elbow on the step above and gesticulating with his free hand as he talks to the shrill, voluptuous Plaichinger. The floor of the hall is nearly empty, save just in the centre: there, directly beneath the chandelier, the two little ones in their blue velvet frocks clutch each other in an awkward embrace and twirl silently round and round, oblivious of all else. Cornelius, as he passes, strokes their hair, with a friendly word; it does not distract them from their small solemn preoccupation. But at his own door he turns to glance round and sees young Hergesell push himself off the stair by his elbow—probably because he noticed the Professor. He comes down into the arena, takes Ellie out of her brother's arms, and dances with her himself. It looks very comic, without the music, and he crouches down just as Cornelius does when he goes walking with the four gentlemen, holding the fluttered Ellie as though she were grown up and taking little "shimmying" steps. Everybody watches with huge enjoyment, the gramophone is put on again, dancing becomes general. The Professor stands and looks, with his hand on the door-knob. He nods and laughs; when he finally shuts himself into his study the mechanical smile still lingers on his lips.

Again he turns over pages by his desk lamp, takes notes, attends to a few simple matters. After a while he notices that the guests have forsaken the entrance hall for his wife's drawing-room, into which there is a door from his own study as well. He hears their voices and the sounds of a guitar being tuned. Herr Möller, it seems, is to sing—and does so. He twangs the strings of his instrument and sings in a powerful bass a ballad in a strange tongue, possibly Swedish. The Professor does not succeed in identifying it, though he listens attentively to the end, after which there is great applause. The sound is deadened by the portière that hangs over the dividing door. The young bank-clerk begins another song. Cornelius goes softly in.

It is half-dark in the drawing-room; the only light is from the shaded standard lamp, beneath which Möller sits, on the divan, with his legs crossed, picking his strings. His audience is grouped easily about; as there are not enough seats, some stand, and more, among them many young ladies, are simply sitting on the floor with their hands clasped round their knees or even with their legs stretched out before them. Hergesell sits thus, in his dinner-jacket, next the piano, with Fräulein Plaichinger beside him. Frau Cornelius is holding both children on her lap as she sits in her easy-chair opposite the singer. Snapper, the Bœotian, begins to talk loud and clear in the middle of the song and has to be intimidated with hushings and finger-shakings. Never, never would Ellie allow herself to be guilty of such conduct. She sits there daintily erect and still on her mother's knee. The Professor tries to catch her eye and exchange a private signal with his little girl; but she does not see him. Neither does she seem to be looking at the singer. Her gaze is directed lower down.

Möller sings the "joli tambour":

"Sire, mon roi, donnez-moi votre fille—"

They are all enchanted. "How good!" Hergesell is heard to say, in the odd, nasally condescending Hergesell tone. The next one is a beggar ballad, to a tune composed by young Möller himself; it elicits a storm of applause:

"Gypsy lassie a-goin' to the fair,
Huzza!
Gypsy laddie a-goin' to be there—
Huzza, diddlety umpty dido!"

Laughter and high spirits, sheer reckless hilarity, reigns after this jovial ballad. "Frightfully good!" Hergesell comments again, as before. Follows another popular song, this time a Hungarian one; Möller sings it in its own outlandish tongue, and most effectively. The Professor applauds with ostentation. It warms his heart and does him good, this outcropping of artistic, historic, and cultural elements all amongst the shimmying. He goes up to young Möller and congratulates him, talks about the songs and their sources, and Möller promises to lend him a certain annotated book of folk-songs. Cornelius is the more cordial because all the time, as fathers do, he has been comparing the parts and achievements of this young stranger with those of his own son, and being gnawed by envy and chagrin. This young Möller, he is thinking, is a capable bank-clerk (though about Möller's capacity he knows nothing whatever) and has this special gift besides, which must have taken talent and energy to cultivate. "And here is my poor Bert, who knows nothing and can do nothing and thinks of nothing except playing the clown, without even talent for that!" He tries to be just; he tells himself that, after all, Bert has innate refinement; that probably there is a good deal more to him than there is to the successful Möller; that perhaps he has even something of the poet in him, and his dancing and table-waiting are due to mere boyish folly and the distraught times. But paternal envy and pessimism win the upper hand; when Möller begins another song, Dr. Cornelius goes back to his room.

He works as before, with divided attention, at this and that, while it gets on for seven o'clock. Then he remembers a letter he may just as well write, a short letter and not very important, but letter-writing is wonderful for the way it takes up the time, and it is almost half past when he has finished. At half past eight the Italian salad will be served; so now is the prescribed moment for the Professor to go out into the wintry darkness to post his letters and take his daily quantum of fresh air and exercise. They are dancing again, and he will have to pass through the hall to get his hat and coat; but they are used to him now, he need not stop and beg them not to be disturbed. He lays away his papers, takes up the letters he has written, and goes out. But he sees his wife sitting near the door of his room and pauses a little by her easy-chair.

She is watching the dancing. Now and then the big folk or some of their guests stop to speak to her; the party is at its height, and there are more onlookers than these two: blue-faced

Ann is standing at the bottom of the stairs, in all the dignity of her limitations. She is waiting for the children, who simply cannot get their fill of these unwonted festivities, and watching over Snapper, lest his all too rich blood be churned to the danger-point by too much twirling round. And not only the nursery but the kitchen takes an interest: Xaver and the two ladies Hinterhofer are standing by the pantry door looking on with relish. Fräulein Walburga, the elder of the two sunken sisters (the culinary section—she objects to being called a cook), is a whimsical, good-natured sort, brown-eyed, wearing glasses with thick circular lenses; the nose-piece is wound with a bit of rag to keep it from pressing on her nose. Fräulein Cecilia is younger, though not so precisely young either. Her bearing is as self-assertive as usual, this being her way of sustaining her dignity as a former member of the middle class. For Fräulein Cecilia feels acutely her descent into the ranks of domestic service. She positively declines to wear a cap or other badge of servitude, and her hardest trial is on the Wednesday evening when she has to serve the dinner while Xaver has his afternoon out. She hands the dishes with averted face and elevated nose—a fallen queen; and so distressing is it to behold her degradation that one evening when the little folk happened to be at table and saw her they both with one accord burst into tears. Such anguish is unknown to young Xaver. He enjoys serving and does it with an ease born of practice as well as talent, for he was once a "piccolo." But otherwise he is a thorough-paced good-for-nothing and windbag—with quite distinct traits of character of his own, as his long-suffering employers are always ready to concede, but perfectly impossible and a bag of wind for all that. One must just take him as he is, they think, and not expect figs from thistles. He is the child and product of the disrupted times, a perfect specimen of his generation, follower of the revolution, Bolshevist sympathizer. The Professor's name for him is the "minuteman," because he is always to be counted on in any sudden crisis, if only it address his sense of humour or love of novelty, and will display therein amazing readiness and resource. But he utterly lacks a sense of duty and can as little be trained to the performance of the daily round and common task as some kinds of dog can be taught to jump over a stick. It goes so plainly against the grain that criticism is disarmed. One becomes resigned. On grounds that appealed to him as unusual and amusing he would be ready to turn out of his bed at any hour of the night. But he simply cannot get up before eight in the morning, he cannot do it, he will not jump over the stick. Yet all day long the evidence of this free and untrammelled existence, the sound of his mouth-organ, his joyous whistle, or his raucous but expressive voice lifted in song, rises to the hearing of the world above-stairs; and the smoke of his cigarettes fills the pantry. While the Hinterhofer ladies work he stands and looks on. Of a morning while the Professor is breakfasting, he tears the leaf off the study calendar—but does not lift a finger to dust the room. Dr. Cornelius has often told him to leave the calendar alone, for he tends to tear off two leaves at a time and thus to add to the general confusion. But young Xaver appears to find joy in this activity, and will not be deprived of it.

Again, he is fond of children, a winning trait. He will throw himself into games with the little folk in the garden, make and mend their toys with great ingenuity, even read aloud from their books—and very droll it sounds in his thick-lipped pronunciation. With his whole soul he loves the cinema; after an evening spent there he inclines to melancholy and yearning and talking to himself. Vague hopes stir in him that some day he may make his fortune in that gay world and belong to it by rights—hopes based on his shock of hair and his physical agility and daring. He likes to climb the ash tree in the front garden, mounting branch by branch to the very top and frightening everybody to death who sees him. Once there he lights a cigarette and smokes it as he sways to and fro, keeping a lookout for a cinema director who might chance to come along and engage him.

If he changed his striped jacket for mufti, he might easily dance with the others and no one would notice the difference. For the big folk's friends are rather anomalous in their clothing: evening dress is worn by a few, but it is by no means the rule. There is quite a sprinkling of guests, both male and female, in the same general style as Möller the ballad-singer. The Professor is familiar with the circumstances of most of this young generation he is watching as he stands beside his wife's chair; he has heard them spoken of by name. They are students at the high school or at the School of Applied Art; they lead, at least the masculine portion, that precarious and scrambling existence which is purely the product of the time. There is a tall, pale, spindling youth, the son of a dentist, who lives by speculation. From all the Professor hears, he is a perfect Aladdin. He keeps a car, treats his friends to champagne suppers, and showers presents upon them on every occasion, costly little trifles in mother-of-pearl and gold. So today he has brought gifts to the young givers of the feast: for Bert a gold lead-pencil, and for Ingrid a pair of earrings of barbaric size, great gold circlets that fortunately do not have to go through the little ear-lobe, but are fastened over it by means of a clip. The big folk come laughing to their parents to display these trophies; and the parents shake their heads even while they admire—Aladdin bowing over and over from afar.

The young people appear to be absorbed in their dancing—if the performance they are carrying out with so much still concentration can be called dancing. They stride across the carpet, slowly, according to some unfathomable prescript, strangely embraced; in the newest attitude, tummy advanced and shoulders high, waggling the hips. They do not get tired, because nobody could. There is no such thing as heightened colour or heaving bosoms. Two girls may dance together or two young men—it is all the same. They move to the exotic strains of the gramophone, played with the loudest needles to procure the maximum of sound: shimmies, foxtrots, one-steps, double foxes, African shimmies, Java dances, and Creole polkas, the wild musky melodies follow one another, now furious, now languishing, a monotonous Negro programme in unfamiliar rhythm, to a clacking, clashing, and strumming orchestral accompaniment.

"What is that record?" Cornelius inquires of Ingrid, as she passes him by in the arms of the pale young speculator, with reference to the piece then playing, whose alternate languors and furies he finds comparatively pleasing and showing a certain resourcefulness in detail.

"*Prince of Pappenheim:* 'Console thee, dearest child,' " she answers, and smiles pleasantly back at him with her white teeth.

The cigarette smoke wreathes beneath the chandelier. The air is blue with a festal haze compact of sweet and thrilling ingredients that stir the blood with memories of green-sick pains and are particularly poignant to those whose youth—like the Professor's own—has been over-sensitive. . . . The little folk are still on the floor. They are allowed to stay up until eight, so great is their delight in the party. The guests have got used to their presence; in their own way, they have their place in the doings of the evening. They have separated, anyhow: Snapper revolves all alone in the middle of the carpet, in his little blue velvet smock, while Ellie is running after one of the dancing couples, trying to hold the man fast by his coat. It is Max Hergesell and Fräulein Plaichinger. They dance well, it is a pleasure to watch them. One has to admit that these mad modern dances, when the right people dance them, are not so bad after all—they have something quite taking. Young Hergesell is a capital leader, dances according to rule, yet with individuality. So it looks. With what aplomb can he walk backwards—when space permits! And he knows how to be graceful standing still in a crowd. And his partner supports him well, being unsuspectedly lithe and buoyant, as fat people often are. They look at each other, they are talking, paying no heed to Ellie, though others are smiling to see the child's persistence. Dr. Cornelius tries to catch up his little sweetheart as she passes and draw her to him. But Ellie eludes him, almost peevishly; her dear Abel is nothing to her now. She braces her little arms against his chest and turns her face away with a persecuted look. Then escapes to follow her fancy once more.

The Professor feels an involuntary twinge. Uppermost in his heart is hatred for this party, with its power to intoxicate and estrange his darling child. His love for her—that not quite disinterested, not quite unexceptionable love of his—is easily wounded. He wears a mechanical smile, but his eyes have clouded, and he stares fixedly at a point in the carpet, between the dancers' feet.

"The children ought to go to bed," he tells his wife. But she pleads for another quarter of an hour; she has promised already, and they do love it so! He smiles again and shakes his head, stands so a moment and then goes across to the cloak-room, which is full of coats and hats and scarves and overshoes. He has trouble in rummaging out his own coat, and Max Hergesell comes out of the hall, wiping his brow.

"Going out, sir?" he asks, in Hergesellian accents, dutifully helping the older man on with his coat. "Silly business this, with my pumps," he says. "They pinch like hell. The brutes are simply too tight for me, quite apart from the bad leather. They press just here on the ball of my great toe"—he stands on one foot and holds the other in his hand—"it's simply unbearable. There's nothing for it but to take them off; my brogues will have to do the business. . . . Oh, let me help you, sir."

"Thanks," says Cornelius. "Don't trouble. Get rid of your own tormentors. . . . Oh, thanks very much!" For Hergesell has gone on one knee to snap the fasteners of his snow-boots.

Once more the Professor expresses his gratitude; he is pleased and touched by so much sincere respect and youthful readiness to serve. "Go and enjoy yourself," he counsels. "Change your shoes and make up for what you have been suffering. Nobody can dance in shoes that pinch. Good-bye, I must be off to get a breath of fresh air."

"I'm going to dance with Ellie now," calls Hergesell after him. "She'll be a first-rate dancer when she grows up, and that I'll swear to."

"Think so?" Cornelius answers, already half out. "Well, you are a connoisseur, I'm sure. Don't get curvature of the spine with stooping."

He nods again and goes. "Fine lad," he thinks as he shuts the door. "Student of engineering. Knows what he's bound for, got a good clear head, and so well set up and pleasant too." And again paternal envy rises as he compares his poor Bert's status with this young man's, which he puts in the rosiest light that his son's may look the darker. Thus he sets out on his evening walk.

He goes up the avenue, crosses the bridge, and walks along the bank on the other side as far as the next bridge but one. The air is wet and cold, with a little snow now and then. He turns up his coat-collar and slips the crook of his cane over the arm behind his back. Now and then he ventilates his lungs with a long deep breath of the night air. As usual when he walks, his mind reverts to his professional preoccupations, he thinks about his lectures and the things he means to say tomorrow about Philip's struggle against the Germanic revolution, things steeped in melancholy and penetratingly just. Above all just, he thinks. For in one's dealings with the young it behoves one to display the scientific spirit, to exhibit the principles of enlightenment—not only for purposes of mental discipline, but on the human and individual side, in order not to wound them or indirectly offend their political sensibilities; particularly in these days, when there is so much tinder in the air, opinions are so frightfully split up and chaotic, and you may so easily incur attacks from one party or the other, or even give rise to scandal, by taking sides on a point of history. "And taking sides is unhistoric anyhow," so he muses. "Only justice, only impartiality is historic." And could not, properly considered, be otherwise. . . . For justice can have nothing of youthful fire and blithe, fresh, loyal conviction. It is by nature melancholy. And, being so, has secret affinity with the lost cause and the forlorn hope rather than with the fresh and blithe and loyal—perhaps this affinity is its very essence and without it it would not exist at all! . . . "And is there then no such thing as justice?" the Professor asks himself, and ponders the question so deeply that he absently posts his letters in the next box and turns round to go home. This thought of his is unsettling and disturbing to the scientific mind—but is it not after all itself scientific, psychological, conscientious, and therefore to be accepted without prejudice, no matter how upsetting? In the midst of which musings Dr. Cornelius finds himself back at his own door.

On the outer threshold stands Xaver, and seems to be looking for him.

"Herr Professor," says Xaver, tossing back his hair, "go upstairs to Ellie straight off. She's in a bad way."

"What's the matter?" asks Cornclius in alarm. "Is she ill?"

"No-o, not to say ill," answers Xaver. "She's just in a bad way and crying fit to bust her little heart. It's along o' that chap with the shirt-front that danced with her—Herr Hergesell. She couldn't be got to go upstairs peaceably, not at no price at all, and she's b'en crying bucketfuls."

"Nonsense," says the Professor, who has entered and is tossing off his things in the cloak-room. He says no more; opens the glass door and without a glance at the guests turns swiftly to the stairs. Takes them two at a time, crosses the upper hall and the small room leading into the nursery. Xaver follows at his heels, but stops at the nursery door.

A bright light still burns within, showing the gay frieze that runs all round the room, the large row of shelves heaped with a confusion of toys, the rocking-horse on his swaying platform, with red-varnished nostrils and raised hoofs. On the linoleum lie other toys—building blocks, railway trains, a little trumpet. The two white cribs stand not far apart, Ellie's in the window corner, Snapper's out in the room.

Snapper is asleep. He has said his prayers in loud, ringing tones, prompted by Nurse, and gone off at once into vehement, profound, and rosy slumber—from which a cannon-ball fired at close range could not rouse him. He lies with both fists flung back on the pillows on either side of the tousled head with its funny crooked little slumber-tossed wig.

A circle of females surrounds Ellie's bed: not only blue-faced Ann is there, but the Hinterhofer ladies too, talking to each other and to her. They make way as the Professor comes up and reveal the child sitting all pale among her pillows, sobbing and weeping more bitterly than he has ever seen her sob and weep in her life. Her lovely little hands lie on the coverlet in front of her, the nightgown with its narrow lace border has slipped down from her shoulder—such a thin, birdlike little shoulder—and the sweet head Cornelius loves so well, set on the neck like a flower on its stalk, her head is on one side, with the eyes rolled up to the corner between wall and ceiling above her head. For there she seems to envisage the anguish of her heart and even to nod to it—either on purpose or because her head wobbles as her body is shaken with the violence of her sobs. Her eyes rain down tears. The bow-shaped lips are parted, like a little *mater dolorosa*'s, and from them issue long, low wails that in nothing resemble the unnecessary and exasperating shrieks of a naughty child, but rise from the deep extremity of her heart and wake in the Professor's own a sympathy that is well-nigh intolerable. He has never seen his darling so before. His feelings find immediate vent in an attack on the ladies Hinterhofer.

"What about the supper?" he asks sharply. "There must be a great deal to do. Is my wife being left to do it alone?"

For the acute sensibilities of the former middle class this is quite enough. The ladies withdraw in righteous indignation, and Xaver Kleingutl jeers at them as they pass out. Having been born to low life instead of achieving it, he never loses a chance to mock at their fallen state.

"Childie, childie," murmurs Cornelius, and sitting down by the crib enfolds the anguished Ellie in his arms. "What is the trouble with my darling?"

She bedews his face with her tears.

"Abel . . . Abel . . ." she stammers between sobs. "Why—isn't Max—my brother? Max ought to be—my brother!"

Alas, alas! What mischance is this? Is this what the party has wrought, with its fatal atmosphere? Cornelius glances helplessly up at blue-faced Ann standing there in all the dignity of her limitations with her hands before her on her apron. She purses up her mouth and makes a long face. "It's pretty young," she says, "for the female instincts to be showing up."

"Hold your tongue," snaps Cornelius, in his agony. He has this much to be thankful for, that Ellie does not turn from him now; she does not push him away as she did downstairs, but clings to him in her need, while she reiterates her absurd, bewildered prayer that Max might be her brother, or with a fresh burst of desire demands to be taken downstairs so that he can dance with her again. But Max, of course, is dancing with Fräulein Plaichinger, that behemoth who is his rightful partner and has every claim upon him; whereas Ellie—never, thinks the Professor, his heart torn with the violence of his pity, never has she looked so tiny and birdlike as now, when she nestles to him shaken with sobs and all unaware of what is happening in her little soul. No, she does not know. She does not comprehend that her suffering is on account of Fräulein Plaichinger, fat, overgrown, and utterly within her rights in dancing with Max Hergesell, whereas Ellie may only do it once, by way of a joke, although she is incomparably the more charming of the two. Yet it would be quite mad to reproach young Hergesell with the state of affairs or to make fantastic demands upon him. No, Ellie's suffering is without help or healing and must be covered up. Yet just as it is without understanding, so it is also without restraint—and that is what makes it so horribly painful. Xaver and blue-faced Ann do not feel this pain, it does not affect them—either because of native callousness or because they accept it as the way of nature. But the Professor's fatherly heart is quite torn by it, and by a distressful horror of this passion, so hopeless and so absurd.

Of no avail to hold forth to poor Ellie on the subject of the perfectly good little brother she already has. She only casts a distraught and scornful glance over at the other crib, where Snapper lies vehemently slumbering, and with fresh tears calls again for Max. Of no avail either the promise of a long, long walk tomorrow, all five gentlemen, round and round the dining-room table; or a dramatic description of the thrilling cushion games they will play. No, she will listen to none of all this, nor to lying down and going to sleep. She will not sleep, she will sit bolt upright and suffer. . . . But on a sudden they stop and listen, Abel and Ellie; listen to something miraculous that is coming to pass, that is approaching by strides, two strides, to the nursery door, that now overwhelmingly appears. . . .

It is Xaver's work, not a doubt of that. He has not remained by the door where he stood to gloat over the ejection of the

Hinterhofers. No, he has bestirred himself, taken a notion; likewise steps to carry it out. Downstairs he has gone, twitched Herr Hergesell's sleeve, and made a thick-lipped request. So here they both are. Xaver, having done his part, remains by the door; but Max Hergesell comes up to Ellie's crib; in his dinner-jacket, with his sketchy side-whisker and charming black eyes; obviously quite pleased with his rôle of swan knight and fairy prince, as one who should say: "See, here am I, now all losses are restored and sorrows end!"

Cornelius is almost as much overcome as Ellie herself.

"Just look," he says feebly, "look who's here. This is uncommonly good of you, Herr Hergesell."

"Not a bit of it," says Hergesell. "Why shouldn't I come to say good-night to my fair partner?"

And he approaches the bars of the crib, behind which Ellie sits struck mute. She smiles blissfully through her tears. A funny, high little note that is half a sigh of relief comes from her lips, then she looks dumbly up at her swan knight with her golden-brown eyes—tear-swollen though they are, so much more beautiful than the fat Plaichinger's. She does not put up her arms. Her joy, like her grief, is without understanding; but she does not do that. The lovely little hands lie quiet on the coverlet, and Max Hergesell stands with his arms leaning over the rail as on a balcony.

"And now," he says smartly, "she need not 'sit the livelong night and weep upon her bed'!" He looks at the Professor to make sure he is receiving due credit for the quotation. "Ha ha!" he laughs, "she's beginning young. 'Console thee, dearest child!' Never mind, you're all right! Just as you are you'll be wonderful! You've only got to grow up. . . . And you'll lie down and go to sleep like a good girl, now I've come to say good-night? And not cry any more, little Lorelei?"

Ellie looks up at him, transfigured. One birdlike shoulder is bare; the Professor draws the lace-trimmed nighty over it. There comes into his mind a sentimental story he once read about a dying child who longs to see a clown he had once, with unforgettable ecstasy, beheld in a circus. And they bring the clown to the bedside marvellously arrayed, embroidered before and behind with silver butterflies; and the child dies happy. Max Hergesell is not embroidered, and Ellie, thank God, is not going to die, she has only been "in a bad way." But, after all, the effect is the same. Young Hergesell leans over the bars of the crib and rattles on, more for the father's ear than the child's, but Ellie does not know that—and the father's feelings towards him are a most singular mixture of thankfulness, embarrassment, and hatred.

"Good night, little Lorelei," says Hergesell, and gives her his hand through the bars. Her pretty, soft, white little hand is swallowed up in the grasp of his big, strong, red one. "Sleep well," he says, "and sweet dreams! But don't dream about me—God forbid! Not at your age—ha ha!" And then the fairy clown's visit is at an end. Cornelius accompanies him to the door. "No, no, positively, no thanks called for, don't mention it," he large-heartedly protests; and Xaver goes downstairs with him, to help serve the Italian salad.

But Dr. Cornelius returns to Ellie, who is now lying down, with her cheek pressed into her flat little pillow.

"Well, wasn't that lovely?" he says as he smooths the covers. She nods, with one last little sob. For a quarter of an hour he sits beside her and watches while she falls asleep in her turn, beside the little brother who found the right way so much earlier than she. Her silky brown hair takes the enchanting fall it always does when she sleeps; deep, deep lie the lashes over the eyes that late so abundantly poured forth their sorrow; the angelic mouth with its bowed upper lip is peacefully relaxed and a little open. Only now and then comes a belated catch in her slow breathing.

And her small hands, like pink and white flowers, lie so quietly, one on the coverlet, the other on the pillow by her face—Dr. Cornelius, gazing, feels his heart melt with tenderness as with strong wine.

"How good," he thinks, "that she breathes in oblivion with every breath she draws! That in childhood each night is a deep wide gulf between one day and the next. Tomorrow, beyond all doubt, young Hergesell will be a pale shadow, powerless to darken her little heart. Tomorrow, forgetful of all but present joy, she will walk with Abel and Snapper, all five gentlemen, round and round the table, will play the ever-thrilling cushion game."

Heaven be praised for that!

1925

A MAN AND HIS DOG

HE COMES ROUND THE CORNER

When spring, the fairest season of the year, does honour to its name, and when the trilling of the birds rouses me early because I have ended the day before at a seemly hour, I love to rise betimes and go for a half-hour's walk before breakfast. Strolling hatless in the broad avenue in front of my house, or through the parks beyond, I like to enjoy a few draughts of the young morning air and taste its blithe purity before I am claimed by the labours of the day. Standing on the front steps of my house, I give a whistle in two notes, tonic and lower fourth, like the beginning of the second phrase of Schubert's Unfinished Symphony; it might be considered the musical setting of a two-syllabled name. Next moment, and while I walk towards the garden gate, the faintest tinkle sounds from afar, at first scarcely audible, but growing rapidly louder and more distinct; such a sound as might be made by a metal licence-tag clicking against the trimmings of a leather collar. I face about, to see Bashan rounding the corner of the house at top speed and charging towards me as though he meant to knock me down. In the effort he is making he has dropped his lower lip, baring two white teeth that glitter in the morning sun.

He comes straight from his kennel, which stands at the back of the house, between the props of the veranda floor. Probably, until my two-toned call set him in this violent motion, he had been lying there snatching a nap after the adventures of the night. The kennel has curtains of sacking and is lined with straw; indeed, a straw or so may be clinging to Bashan's sleep-rumpled coat or even sticking between his toes—a comic sight, which reminds me of a painstakingly imagined production of Schiller's *Die Räuber* that I once saw, in which old Count Moor came out of the Hunger Tower tricot-clad, with a straw sticking pathetically between his toes. Involuntarily I assume a defensive position to meet the charge, receiving it on my flank, for Bashan shows every sign of meaning to run between my legs and trip me up. However at the last minute, when a collision is imminent, he always puts on the brakes, executing a half-wheel which speaks for both his mental and his physical self-control. And then, without a sound—for he makes sparing use of his sonorous and expressive voice—he dances wildly round me by way of greeting, with immoderate plungings and waggings which are not confined to the appendage provided by nature for the purpose but bring his whole hind quarters as far as his ribs into play. He contracts his whole body into a curve, he hurtles into the air in a flying leap, he turns round and round on his own axis—and curiously enough, whichever way I turn, he always contrives to execute these manœuvres behind my back. But the moment I stoop down and put out my hand he jumps to my side and stands like a statue, with his shoulder against my shin, in a slantwise posture, his strong paws braced against the ground, his face turned upwards so that he looks at me upside-down. And his utter immobility, as I pat his shoulder and murmur encouragement, is as concentrated and fiercely passionate as the frenzy before it had been.

Bashan is a short-haired German pointer—speaking by and large, that is, and not too literally. For he is probably not quite orthodox, as a pure matter of points. In the first place, he is a little too small. He is, I repeat, definitely undersized for a proper pointer. And then his forelegs are not absolutely straight, they have just the suggestion of an outward curve—which also detracts from his qualifications as a blood-dog. And he has a tendency to a dewlap, those folds of hanging skin under the muzzle, which in Bashan's case are admirably becoming but again would be frowned on by your fanatic for pure breeding, as I understand that a pointer should have taut skin round the neck. Bashan's colouring is very fine: His coat is a rusty brown with black stripes and a good deal of white on chest, paws, and under side. The whole of his snub nose seems to have been dipped in black paint. Over the broad top of his head and on his cool hanging ears the black and brown combine in a lovely velvety pattern. Quite the prettiest thing about him, however, is the whorl or stud or little tuft at the centre of the convolution of white hairs on his chest, which stands out like the boss on an ancient breastplate. Very likely even his splendid coloration is a little too marked and would be objected to by those who put the laws of breeding above the value of personality, for it would appear that the classic pointer type should have a coat of one colour or at most with spots of a different one, but never stripes. Worst of all, from the point of view of classification, is a hairy growth hanging from his muzzle and the corners of his mouth; it might with some justice be called a moustache and goatee, and when you concentrate on it, close at hand or even at a distance, you cannot help thinking of an airedale or a schnauzer.

But classifications aside, what a good and good-looking animal Bashan is, as he stands there straining against my knee, gazing up at me with all his devotion in his eyes! They are particularly fine eyes, too, both gentle and wise, if just a little too prominent and glassy. The iris is the same colour as his coat, a rusty brown; it is only a narrow rim, for the pupils are dilated into pools of blackness and the outer edge merges into the white of the eye wherein it swims. His whole head is expressive of honesty and intelligence, of manly qualities corresponding to his physical structure: his arched and swelling chest where the ribs stand out under the smooth and supple skin; the narrow haunches, the veined, sinewy legs, the strong, well-shaped paws. All these bespeak virility and a stout heart; they suggest hunting blood and peasant stock—yes, certainly the hunter and game dog do after all predominate in Bashan, he is genuine pointer, no matter if he does not owe his existence to a snobbish system of inbreeding. All this, probably, is what I am really telling him as I pat his shoulder-blade and address him with a few disjointed words of encouragement.

So he stands and looks and listens, gathering from what I say and the tone of it that I distinctly approve of his existence—the very thing which I am at pains to imply. And suddenly he thrusts out his head, opening and shutting his lips very fast, and makes a snap at my face as though he meant to bite off my nose. It is a gesture of response to my remarks, and it always makes me recoil with a laugh, as Bashan knows beforehand that it will. It is a kiss in the air, half caress, half teasing, a trick he has had since puppyhood, which I have never seen in any of his predecessors. And he immediately begs pardon for the liberty, crouching, wagging his tail, and behaving funnily embarrassed. So we go out through the garden gate and into the open.

We are encompassed with a roaring like that of the sea; for we live almost directly on the swift-flowing river that foams over shallow ledges at no great distance from the popular avenue. In between lie a fenced-in grass plot planted with maples, and a raised pathway skirted with huge aspen trees, bizarre and willowlike of aspect. At the beginning of June their seed-pods strew the ground far and wide with woolly snow. Upstream, in the direction of the city, construction troops are building a pontoon bridge. Shouts of command and the thump of heavy boots on the planks sound across the river; also, from the further bank, the noise of industrial activity, for there is a locomotive foundry a little way downstream. Its premises have been lately enlarged to meet increased demands, and light streams all night long from its lofty windows. Beautiful glittering new engines roll to and fro on trial runs; a steam whistle emits wailing head-tones from time to time; muffled thunderings of unspecified origin shatter the air, smoke pours out of the many chimneys to be caught up by the wind and borne away over the wooded country beyond the river, for it seldom or never blows over to our side. Thus in our half-suburban, half-rural seclusion the voice of nature mingles with that of man, and over all lies the bright-eyed freshness of the new day.

It might be about half past seven by official time when I set out; by sun-time, half past six. With my hands behind my back I stroll in the tender sunshine down the avenue, cross-hatched by the long shadows of the poplar trees. From where I am I cannot see the river, but I hear its broad and even flow. The trees whisper gently, song-birds fill the air with their penetrating chirps and warbles, twitters and trills; from the direction of the sunrise a plane is flying under the humid blue sky, a rigid, mechanical bird with a droning hum that rises and falls as it steers a free course above river and fields. And Bashan is delighting my eyes with the beautiful long leaps he is making across the low rail of the grass-plot on my left. Backwards and forwards he leaps—as a matter of fact he is doing it because he knows I like it; for I have often urged him on by shouting and striking the railing, praising him when he fell in with my whim. So now he comes up to me after nearly every jump to hear how intrepidly and elegantly he jumps. He even springs up into my face and slavers all over the arm I put out to protect it. But the jumping is also to be conceived as a sort of morning exercise, and morning toilet as well, for it smooths his ruffled coat and rids it of old Moor's straws.

It is good to walk like this in the early morning, with senses rejuvenated and spirit cleansed by the night's long healing draught of Lethe. You look confidently forward to the day, yet pleasantly hesitate to begin it, being master as you are of this little untroubled span of time between, which is your good reward for good behaviour. You indulge in the illusion that your life is habitually steady, simple, concentrated, and contemplative, that you belong entirely to yourself—and this illusion makes you quite happy. For a human being tends to believe that the mood of the moment, be it troubled or blithe, peaceful or stormy, is the true, native, and permanent tenor of his existence; and in particular he likes to exalt every happy chance into an inviolable rule and to regard it as the benign order of his life—whereas the truth is that he is condemned to improvisation and morally lives from hand to mouth all the time. So now, breathing the morning air, you stoutly believe that you are virtuous and free; while you ought to know—and at bottom do know—that the world is spreading its snares round your feet, and that most likely tomorrow you will be lying in your bed until nine, because you sought it at two in the morning hot and befogged with impassioned discussion. Never mind. Today you, a sober character, an early riser, you are the right master for that stout hunter who has just cleared the railings again out of sheer joy in the fact that today you apparently belong to him alone and not to the world.

We follow the avenue for about five minutes, to the point where it ceases to be an avenue and becomes a gravelly waste along the river-bank. From this we turn away to our right and strike into another covered with finer gravel, which has been laid out like the avenue and like it provided with a cycle-path, but is not yet built up. It runs between low-lying, wooded lots of land, towards the slope which is the eastern limit of our river neighbourhood and Bashan's theatre of action. On our way we cross another road, equally embryonic, running along between fields and meadows. Further up, however, where the tram stops, it is quite built up with flats. We descend by a gravel path into a well-laid-out, parklike valley, quite deserted, as indeed the whole region is at this hour. Paths are laid out in curves and rondels, there are benches to rest on, tidy playgrounds, with wide plots of lawn with fine old trees whose boughs nearly sweep the grass, covering all but a glimpse of trunk. They are elms, beeches, limes, and silvery willows, in well-disposed groups. I enjoy to the full the well-landscaped quality of the scene, where I may walk no more disturbed than if it belonged to me alone. Nothing has been forgotten—there are even cement gutters in the gravel paths that lead down the grassy slopes. And the abundant greenery discloses here and there a charming distant vista of one of the villas that bound the spot on two sides.

Here for a while I stroll along the paths, and Bashan revels in the freedom of unlimited level space, galloping across and across the lawns like mad with his body inclined in a centrifugal plane; sometimes, barking with mingled pleasure and exasperation, he pursues a bird which flutters as though spellbound, but perhaps on purpose to tease him, along the ground just in front of his nose. But if I sit down on a bench he is at my side at once and takes up a position on one of my feet. For it is a law of his being that he only runs about when I am in motion too; that when I settle down he follows suit. There seems no obvious reason for this practice; but Bashan never fails to conform to it.

I get an odd, intimate, and amusing sensation from having him sit on my foot and warm it with the blood-heat of his body. A pervasive feeling of sympathy and good cheer fills me, as almost invariably when in his company and looking at things from his angle. He has a rather rustic slouch when he sits down; his shoulder-blades stick out and his paws turn negligently in. He looks smaller and squatter than he really is, and the little white boss on his chest is advanced with comic effect. But all these faults are atoned for by the lofty and dignified carriage of the head, so full of concentration. All is quiet, and we two sit there absolutely still in our turn. The rushing of the water comes to us faint and subdued. And the senses become alert for all the tiny, mysterious little sounds that nature makes: the lizard's quick dart, the note of a bird, the burrowing of a mole in the earth. Bashan pricks up his ears—in so far as the muscles of naturally drooping ears will allow them to be pricked. He cocks his head to hear the better; and the nostrils of his moist black nose keep twitching sensitively as he sniffs.

Then he lies down, but always in contact with my foot. I see him in profile, in that age-old, conventionalized pose of the beast-god, the sphinx: head and chest held high, forelegs close to the body, paws extended in parallel lines. He has got overheated, so he opens his mouth, and at once all the intelligence of his face gives way to the merely animal, his eyes narrow and blink and his rosy tongue lolls out between his strong white pointed teeth.

HOW WE GOT BASHAN

In the neighbourhood on Tölz there is a mountain inn, kept by a pleasingly buxom, black-eyed damsel, with the assistance of a growing daughter, equally buxom and black-eyed. This damsel it was who acted as go-between in our introduction to Bashan and our subsequent acquisition of him. Two years ago now that was; he was six months old at the time. Anastasia—for so the damsel was called—knew that we had had to have our last dog shot; Percy by name, a Scotch collie by breeding and a harmless, feeble-minded aristocrat who in his old age fell victim to a painful and disfiguring skin disease which obliged us to put him away. Since that time we had been without a guardian. She telephoned from her mountain height to say that she had taken to board a dog that was exactly what we wanted and that it might be inspected at any time. The children clamoured to see it, and our own curiosity was scarcely behind theirs; so the very next afternoon we climbed up to Anastasia's inn, and found her in her roomy kitchen full of warm and succulent steam, preparing her lodgers' supper. Her face was brick-red, her brow was wet, the sleeves were rolled back on her plump arms, and her frock was open at the throat. Her young daughter went to and fro, an industrious kitchen-maid. They were glad to see us and thoroughly approved of our having lost no time in coming. We looked about; whereupon Resi, the daughter, led us up to the kitchen table and, squatting with her hands on her knees, addressed a few encouraging words beneath it. Until then, in the flickering half-light, we had seen nothing; but now we perceived something standing there, tied by a bit of rope to the table-leg: an object that must have made any soul alive burst into half-pitying laughter.

Gaunt and knock-kneed he stood there with his tail between his hind legs, his four paws planted together, his back arched, shaking. He may have been frightened, but one had the feeling that he had not enough on his bones to keep him warm; for indeed the poor little animal was a skeleton, a mere rack of bones with a spinal column, covered with a rough fell and stuck up on four sticks. He had laid back his ears—which muscular contraction never fails to extinguish every sign of intelligence and cheer in the face of any dog. In him, who was still entirely puppy, the effect was so consummate that he stood there expressive of nothing but wretchedness, stupidity, and a mute appeal for our forbearance. And his hirsute appendages, which he has to this day, were then out of all proportion to his size and added a final touch of sour hypochondria to his appearance.

We all stooped down and began to coax and encourage this picture of misery. The children were delighted and sympathetic at once, and their shouts mingled with the voice of Anastasia as, standing by her cooking-stove, she began to furnish us with the particulars of her charge's origins and history. He was named, provisionally, Lux, she said, in her pleasant, level voice; and was the offspring of irreproachable parents. She had herself known the mother and of the father had heard nothing but good. Lux had seen the light on a farm in Hugelfing; and it was only due to a combination of circumstances that his owners were willing to part with him cheaply. They had brought him to her inn because there he might be seen by a good many people. They had come in a cart, Lux bravely running the whole twenty kilometres behind the wheels. She, Anastasia, had thought of us at once, knowing that we were on the look-out for a good dog and feeling certain that we should want him. If we so decided, it would be a good thing all round. She was sure we should have great joy of him, he in his turn would have found a good home and be no longer lonely in the world, and she, Anastasia, would know that he was well taken care of. We must not be prejudiced by the figure he cut at the moment; he was upset by his strange surroundings and uncertain of himself, but his good breeding would come out strong before long. His father and mother were of the best.

Ye-es—but perhaps not quite well matched?

On the contrary; that is, they were both of them good stock. He had excellent points—she, Anastasia, would vouch for that. He was not spoilt, either, his needs were modest—and that meant a great deal, nowadays. In fact, up to now he had had nothing to eat but potato-parings. She suggested that we take him home on trial; if we found that we did not take to him she would receive him back and refund the modest sum that was asked for him. She made free to say this, not minding at all if we took her up. Because, knowing the dog and knowing us, both parties, as it were, she was convinced that we should grow to love him, and never dream of giving him up.

All this she said and a great deal more in the same strain in her easy, comfortable, voluble way, working the while over her stove, where the flames shot up suddenly now and then as though we were in a witches' kitchen. She even came and opened Lux's jaws with both hands to show us his beautiful teeth and—for some reason or other—the pink grooves in the roof of his mouth. We asked knowingly if he had had distemper; she replied with a little impatience that she really could not say. Our next question—how large would he get—she answered more glibly: he would be about the size of our departed Percy, she said. There were more questions and answers; a good deal of warm-hearted urging from Anastasia, prayers and pleas from the children, and on our side a feeble lack of resolution. At last we begged for a little time to think things over; she agreed, and we went thoughtfully valleywards, exchanging impressions as we went.

But of course the children had lost their hearts to the wretched little quadruped under the table; in vain we affected to jeer at their lack of judgment and taste, feeling the pull at our own heart-strings. We saw that we should not be able to get him out of our heads; we asked ourselves what would become of him if we scorned him. Into what hands would he fall? The question called up a horrid memory, we saw again the knacker from whom we had rescued Percy with a few timely and merciful bullets and an honourable grave by the garden fence. If we wanted to abandon Lux to an uncertain and perhaps gruesome fate, then we should never have seen him at all, never cast eyes upon his infant whiskered face. We knew him now, we felt a responsibility which we could disclaim only by an arbitrary exercise of authority.

So it was that the third day found us climbing up those same gentle foothills of the Alps. Not that we had decided to buy—no, we only saw that, as things stood, the matter could hardly have any other outcome.

This time we found Frau Anastasia and her daughter drinking coffee, one at each end of the long kitchen table, while between them he sat who bore provisionally the name of Lux, in his very attitude as he sits today, slouching over with his shoulder-blades stuck out and his paws turned in. A bunch of wild flowers in his worn leather collar gave him a festive look, like a rustic bridegroom or a village lad in his Sunday best. The daughter, looking very trim herself in the tight bodice of her peasant costume, said that she had adorned him thus to celebrate his entry into his new home. Mother and daughter both told us they had never been more certain of anything in their lives than that we would come back to fetch him—they knew that we would come this very day.

So there was nothing more to say. Anastasia thanked us in her pleasant way for the purchase price—ten marks—which we handed over. It was clear that she had asked it in our interest rather than in hers or that of the dog's owners; it was by way of giving Lux a positive value, in terms of money, in our eyes. We quite understood, and paid it gladly. Lux was untied from his table-leg and the end of the rope laid in my hand; we crossed Anastasia's door-step followed by the warmest, most cordial assurances and good wishes.

But the homeward way, which it took us an hour to cover, was scarcely a triumphal procession. The bridegroom soon lost his bouquet, while everybody we met either laughed or else jeered at his appearance—and we met a good many people, for our route lay through the length of the market town at the foot of the hill. The last straw was that Lux proved to be suffering from an apparently chronic diarrhœa, which obliged us to make frequent pauses under the villagers' eyes. At such times we formed a circle round him to shield his weakness from unfriendly eyes—asking ourselves whether this was not distemper already making its appearance. Our anxiety was uncalled-for: the future was to prove that we were dealing with a sound and cleanly constitution, which has been proof against distemper and all such ailments up to this day.

Directly we got home we summoned the maids to make acquaintance with the new member of the family and express their modest judgment of his worth. They had evidently been prepared to praise; but, reading our own insecurity in our eyes, they laughed loudly, turning their backs upon the appealing object and waving him off with their hands. We doubted whether they could understand the nature of our financial transaction with the benevolent Anastasia and in our weakness declared that we had had him as a present. Then we led Lux into the veranda and regaled him with a hearty meal of scraps.

He was too frightened to eat. He sniffed at the food we urged upon him, but was evidently, in his modesty, unable to believe that these cheese-parings and chicken-bones were meant for him. But he did not reject the sack stuffed with seaweed which we had prepared for him on the floor. He lay there with his paws drawn up under him, while within we took counsel and eventually came to a conclusion about the name he was to bear in the future.

On the following day he still refused to eat; then came a period when he gulped down everything that came within reach of his muzzle; but gradually he settled down to a regular and more fastidious regimen, this result roughly corresponding with his adjustment to his new life in general, so that I will not dwell further upon it. The process of adaptation suffered an interruption one day—Bashan disappeared. The children had taken him into the garden and let him off the lead for better freedom of action. In a momentary lapse of vigilance he had escaped through the hole under the garden gate and gained the outer world. We were grieved and upset at his loss—at least the masters of the house were, for the maids seemed inclined to take light-heartedly the loss of a dog which we had received as a gift; perhaps they did not even consider it a loss. We telephoned wildly to Anastasia's inn, hoping he might find his way thither. In vain, nobody had seen him; two days passed before we heard that Anastasia had word from Hugelfing that Lux had put in an appearance at his first home some hour and a half before. Yes, he was there, his native idealism had drawn him back to the world of his early potato-parings; through wind and weather he had trotted alone the twelve or fourteen miles which he had first covered between the hind wheels of the farmer's cart. His former owners had to use it again to deliver him into Anastasia's hands once more. On the second day after that we went up to reclaim the wanderer, whom we found as before, tied to the table-leg, jaded and dishevelled, bemired from the mud of the roads. He did show signs of being glad to see us again—but then, why had he gone away?

The time came when it was plain that he had forgotten the farm—yet without having quite struck root with us; so that he was a masterless soul and like a leaf carried by the wind. When we took him walking we had to keep close watch, for he tended to snap the frail bond of sympathy which was all that as yet united us and to lose himself unobtrusively in the woods, where, being quite on his own, he would certainly have reverted to the condition of his wild forbears. Our care preserved him from this dark fate, we held him fast upon his civilized height and to his position as the comrade of man, which his race in the course of millennia has achieved. And then a decisive event, our removal to the city—or a suburb of it—made him wholly dependent upon us and definitely a member of the family.

NOTES ON BASHAN'S CHARACTER AND MANNER OF LIFE

A man in the Isar valley had told me that this kind of dog can become a nuisance, by always wanting to be with his master. Thus I was forewarned against taking too personally Bashan's persistent faithfulness to myself, and it was easier for me to discourage it a little and protect myself at need. It is a deep-lying patriarchal instinct in the dog which leads him—at least in the more manly, outdoor breeds—to recognize and honour in the man of the house and head of the family his absolute master and overlord, protector of the hearth; and to find in the relation of vassalage to him the basis and value of his own existence, whereas his attitude towards the rest of the family is much more independent. Almost from the very first day Bashan behaved in this spirit towards me, following me with his trustful eyes that seemed to be begging me to order him about—which I was chary of doing, for time soon showed that obedience was not one of his strong points—and dogging my footsteps in the obvious conviction that sticking to me was the natural order of things. In the family circle he always sat at my feet, never by any chance at anyone else's. And when we were walking, if I struck off on a path by myself, he invariably followed me and not the others. He insisted on being with me when I worked; if the garden door was closed he would disconcert me by jumping suddenly in at the window, bringing much gravel in his train and flinging himself down panting beneath my desk.

But the presence of any living thing—even a dog—is something of which we are very conscious; we attend to it in a way that is disturbing when we want to be alone. Thus Bashan could become a quite tangible nuisance. He would come up to me wagging his tail, look at me with devouring gaze, and prance provocatively. On the smallest encouragement he would put his forepaws on the arm of my chair, lean against me, and make me laugh with his kisses in the air. Then he would examine the things on my desk, obviously under the impression that they must be good to eat since he so often found me stooped above them; and so doing would smudge my freshly written page with his broad, hairy hunter's paws. I would sharply call him to order and he would lie down on the floor and go to sleep. But when he slept he dreamed, making running motions with all four paws and barking in a subterranean but perfectly audible sort of way. I quite comprehensibly found this distracting; in the first place the sound was uncannily ventriloquistic, in the second it gave me a guilty feeling. For this dream life was obviously an artificial substitute for real running, hunting, and open-air activity; it was supplied to him by his own nature because his life with me did not give him as much of it as his blood and his senses required. I felt touched; but since there was nothing for it, I was constrained in the name of my higher interests to throw off the incubus, telling myself that Bashan brought altogether too much mud into the room and also that he damaged the carpet with his claws.

So then the fiat went forth that he might not be with me or in the house when I was there—though of course there might be exceptions to the rule. He was quick to understand and submit to the unnatural prohibition, as being the inscrutable will of his lord and master. The separation from me—which in winter often lasted the greater part of the day—was in his mind only a separation, not a divorce or severance of connections. He may not be with me, because I have so ordained. But the not being with me is a kind of negative being-with-me, just in that it is carrying out my command. Hence we can hardly speak of an independent existence carried on by Bashan during the hours when he is not by my side. Through the glass door of my study I can see him on the grass plot in front of the house, playing with children and putting on an absurd avuncular air. He repeatedly comes to the door and sniffs at the crack—he cannot see me through the muslin curtains—to assure himself of my presence within; then he sits down and mounts guard with his back to the door. Sometimes I see him from my window prosing along on the elevated path between the aspen trees; but this is only to pass the time, the excursion is void of all pride or joy in life; in fact, it is unthinkable that Bashan should devote himself to the pleasures of the chase on his own account, though there is nothing to prevent him from doing so and my presence, as will be seen, is not always an unmixed advantage.

Life for him begins when I issue from the house—though, alas, it does not always begin even then! For the question is, when I do go out, which way am I going to turn: to the right, down the avenue, the road towards the open and our hunting-ground, or towards the left and the place where the trams stop, to ride into town? Only in the first case is there any sense in accompanying me. At first he used to follow me even when I turned left; when the tram thundered up he would look at it with amazement and then, suppressing his fears, land with one blind and devoted leap among the crowd on the platform. Thence being dislodged by the popular indignation, he would gallop along on the ground behind the roaring vehicle which so little resembled the cart he once knew. He would keep up with it as long as he could, his breath getting shorter and shorter. But the city traffic bewildered his rustic brains; he got between people's legs, strange dogs fell on his flank, he was confused by a volume and variety of smells, the like of which he had never imagined, irresistibly distracted by house-corners impregnated with lingering ancient scents of old adventures. He would fall behind; sometimes he would overtake the tram again, sometimes not; sometimes he overtook the wrong one, which looked just the same, ran blindly in the wrong direction, further and further into a mad, strange world. Once he only came home after two days' absence, limping and starved to death, and, seeking the peace of the last house on the river-bank, found that his lord and master had been sensible enough to get there before him.

This happened two or three times. Then he gave it up and definitely declined to go with me when I turned to the left. He always knows instantly whether I have chosen the wild or the world, directly I get outside the door. He springs up from the mat in the entrance where he has been waiting for me and in that moment divines my intentions; my clothes betray me, the cane I carry, probably even my bearing: my cold and negligent glance or on the other hand the challenging eye I turn upon him. He understands. In the one case he tumbles over himself down the steps, he whirls round and round like a stone in a sling as in dumb rejoicing he runs before me to the gate. In the other he crouches, lays back his ears, the light goes out of his eyes, the fire I have kindled by my appearance dies down to ashes, and he puts on the guilty look which men and animals alike wear when they are unhappy.

Sometimes he cannot believe his eyes, even though they plainly tell him that there is no hope for the chase today. His yearning has been too strong. He refuses to see the signs, the urban walking-stick, the careful city clothes. He presses beside me through the gate, turns round like lightning, and tries to make me turn right, by running off at a gallop in that direction, twisting his head round, and ignoring the fatal negative which I oppose to his efforts. When I actually turn to the left he comes back and walks with me along the hedge, with little snorts and head-tones which seem to emerge from the high tension of his interior. He takes to jumping to and fro over the park railings, although they are rather high for comfort and he gives little moans as he leaps, being evidently afraid of hurting himself. He jumps with a sort of desperate gaiety which is bent on ignoring reality; also in the hope of beguiling me by his performance. For there is still a little—a very little—hope that I may still leave the highroad at the end of the park and turn left after all by the roundabout way past the pillarbox, as I do when I have letters to post. But I do that very seldom; so when the last hope has fled, then Bashan sits down and lets me go my way.

There he sits, in that clumsy rustic posture of his, in the middle of the road and looks after me as far as he can see me. If I turn my head he pricks up his ears, but he does not follow; even if I whistled he would not, for he knows it would be useless. When I turn out of the avenue I can still see him sitting there, a small, dark, clumsy figure in the road, and it goes to my heart, I have pangs of conscience as I mount the tram. He has waited so long—and we all know what torture waiting can be! His whole life is waiting—waiting for the next walk in the open, a waiting that begins as soon as he is rested from the last one. Even his night consists of waiting; for his sleep is distributed throughout the whole twenty-four hours of the day, with many a little nap on the grass in the garden, the sun shining down warm on his coat, or behind the curtains of his kennel, to break up and shorten the empty spaces of the day. Thus his night sleep is broken too, not continuous, and manifold instincts urge him abroad in the darkness; he dashes to and fro all over the garden—and he waits. He waits for the night watchman to come on his rounds with his lantern and when he hears the recurrent heavy tread heralds it, against his own better knowledge, with a terrific outburst of barking. He waits for the sky to grow pale, for the cocks to crow at the nursery-gardener's close by; for the morning breeze to rise among the tree-tops—and for the kitchen door to be opened, so that he may slip in and warm himself at the stove.

Still, the night-time martyrdom must be mild compared with what Bashan has to endure in the day. And particularly when the weather is fine, either winter or summer, when the sunshine lures one abroad and all the muscles twitch with the craving for violent motion—and the master, without whom it is impossible to conceive doing anything—simply will not leave his post behind the glass door. All that agile little body, feverishly alive with pulsating life, is rested through and through, is worn out with resting; sleep is not to be thought of. He comes up on the terrace outside my door, lets himself down with a sigh that seems to come from his very heart, and rests his head on his paws, rolling his eyes up patiently to heaven. That lasts but a few seconds, he cannot stand the position any more, he sickens of it. One other thing there is to do. He can go down again and lift his leg against one of the little formal arbor-vitæ trees that flank the rose-bed—it is the one to the right that suffers from his attentions, wasting away so that it has to be replanted every year. He does go down, then, and performs this action, not because he needs to, but just to pass the time. He stands there a long time, with very little to show for it, however—so long that the hind leg in the air begins to tremble and he has to give a little hop to regain his balance. On four legs once more he is no better off than he was. He stares stupidly up into the boughs of the ash trees, where two birds are flitting and chirping; watches them dart off like arrows and turns away as though in contempt of such light-headedness. He stretches, fit to tear himself apart. The stretching is very thorough; it is done in two sections, thus: first the forelegs, lifting the hind ones into the air; second the rear quarters, by sprawling them out on the ground; both actions being accompanied by tremendous yawning. Then that is over too, cannot be spun out any longer, and if you have just finished an exhaustive stretching you cannot do it over again just at once. He stands still and looks gloomily at the ground. Then he begins to turn round on himself, slowly and consideringly, as though he wanted to lie down, yet was not quite certain of the best way to do it. Finally he decides not to; he moves off sluggishly to the middle of the grass-plot, and once there flings himself violently on his back and scrubs to and fro as though to cool off on the shaven turf. Quite a blissful sensation, this, it seems, for his paws jerk and he snaps in all directions in a delirium of release and satisfaction. He drains this joy down to its vapid dregs, aware that it is fleeting, that you cannot roll and tumble more than ten seconds at most, and that no sound and soul-contenting weariness will result from it, but only a flatness and returning boredom, such as always follows when one tries to drug oneself. He lies there on his side with his eyes rolled up, as though he were dead. Then he gets up and shakes himself, shakes as only his like can shake without fearing concussion of the brain; shakes until everything rattles, until his ears flop together under his chin and foam flies from his dazzling white teeth. And then? He stands perfectly still in his tracks, rigid, dead to the world, without the least idea what to do next. And then, driven to extremes, he climbs the steps once more, comes up to the glass door, lifts his paw and scratches—hesitantly, with his ears laid back, the complete beggar. He scratches only once, quite faintly; but this timidly lifted paw, this single, faint-hearted scratch, to which he has come because he simply cannot think of anything else, are too moving. I get up and open the door, though I know it can lead to no good. And he begins to dance and jump, challenging me to be a man and come abroad with him. He rumples the rugs, upsets the whole room and makes an end of all my peace and quiet. But now judge for yourself if, after I have seen Bashan wait like this, I can find it easy to go off in the tram and leave him, a pathetic little dot at the end of the poplar avenue!

In the long twilights of summer, things are not quite so bad: there is a good chance that I will take an evening walk in the open and thus even after long waiting he will come into his own and with good luck be able to start a hare. But in winter if I go off in the afternoon it is all over for the day, all hope must be buried for another four-and-twenty hours. For night will have fallen; if I go out again our hunting-grounds will lie in inaccessible darkness and I must bend my steps towards the traffic, the lighted streets, and city parks up the river—and this does not suit Bashan's simple soul. He came with me at first, but soon gave it up and stopped at home. Not only that space and freedom were lacking; he was afraid of the bright lights in the darkness, he shied at every bush, at every human form. A policeman's flapping cloak could make him swerve aside with a yelp or even lead him to attack the officer with a courage born of desperation; when the latter, frightened in his turn, would let loose a stream of abuse to our address. Unfortunate episodes mounted up when Bashan and I went out together in the dark and the damp. And speaking of policemen reminds me that there are three classes of human beings whom Bashan does especially abhor: policemen, monks, and chimney-sweeps. He cannot stand them, he assails them with a fury of barking wherever he sees them or when they chance to pass the house.

And winter is of course the time of year when freedom and sobriety are with most difficulty preserved against snares; when it is hardest to lead a regular, retired, and concentrated existence; when I may even seek the city a second time in the day. For the evening has its social claims, pursuing which I may come back at midnight, with the last tram, or losing that am driven to return on foot, my head in a whirl with ideas and wine and smoke, full of roseate views of the world and of course long past the point of normal fatigue. And then the embodiment of that other, truer, soberer life of mine, my own hearthstone, in person, as it were, may come to meet me; not wounded, not reproachful, but on the contrary giving me joyous welcome and bringing me back to my own. I mean, of course, Bashan. In pitchy darkness, the river roaring in my ears, I turn into the poplar avenue, and after the first few steps I am enveloped in a soundless storm of prancings and swishings; on the first occasion I did not know what was happening. "Bashan?" I inquire into the blackness. The prancings and swishings redouble—is this a dancing dervish or a Berserk warrior here on my path? But not a sound; and directly I stand still, I feel those honest, wet and muddy paws on the lapels of my raincoat, and a snapping and flapping in my face, which I draw back even as I stoop down to pat the lean shoulder, equally wet with snow or rain. Yes, the good soul has come to meet the tram. Well informed as always upon my comings and goings, he has got up at what he judged to be the right time, to fetch me from the station. He may have been waiting a long while, in snow or rain, yet his joy at my final appearance knows no resentment at my faithlessness, though I have neglected him all day and brought his hopes to naught. I pat and praise him, and as we go home together I tell him what a fine fellow he is and promise him (that is to say, not so much him as myself) that tomorrow, no matter what the weather, we two will follow the chase together. And resolving thus, I feel my worldly preoccupations melt away; sobriety returns; for the image I have conjured up of our hunting-ground and the charms of its solitude is linked in my mind with the call to higher, stranger, more obscure concerns of mine.

There are still other traits of Bashan's character which I should like to set down here, so that the gentle reader may get as lively and speaking an image of him as is anyway possible. Perhaps the best way would be for me to compare him with our deceased Percy; for a better-defined contrast than that between these two never existed within the same species. First and foremost we must remember that Bashan was entirely sound in mind, whereas Percy, as I have said, and as often happens among aristocratic canines, had always been mad, through and through, a perfectly typical specimen of frantic over-breeding. I have referred to this subject before, in a somewhat wider connection; here I only want, for purposes of comparison, to speak of Bashan's infinitely simpler, more ordinary mentality, expressed for instance in the way he would greet you, or in his behaviour on our walks. His manifestations were always within the bounds of a hearty and healthy common sense; they never even bordered on the hysterical, whereas Percy's on all such occasions overstepped them in a way that was at times quite shocking.

And even that does not quite cover the contrast between these two creatures; the truth is more complex and involved still. Bashan is coarser-fibred, true, like the lower classes; but like them also he is not above complaining. His noble predecessor, on the other hand, united more delicacy and a greater capacity for suffering, with an infinitely firmer and prouder spirit; despite all his foolishness he far excelled in self-discipline the powers of Bashan's peasant soul. In saying this I am not defending any aristocratic system of values. It is simply to do honour to truth and actuality that I want to bring out the mixture of softness and hardiness, delicacy and firmness in the two natures. Bashan, for instance, is quite able to spend the coldest winter night out of doors, behind the sacking curtains of his kennel. He has a weakness of the bladder which makes it impossible for him to remain seven hours shut up in a room; we have to fasten him out, even in the most inhospitable weather, and trust to his robust constitution. Sometimes after a particularly bitter and foggy winter night he comes into the house with his moustache and whiskers like delicately frosted wires; with a little cold, even, and coughing in the odd, one-syllabled way that dogs have. But in a few hours he has got all over it and takes no harm at all. Whereas we should never have dared to expose our silken-haired Percy to such rigours. Yet Bashan is afraid of the slightest pain, behaving so abjectly that one would feel disgusted if the plebeian simplicity of his behaviour did not make one laugh instead. When he goes stalking in the underbrush, I constantly hear him yelping because he has been scratched by a thorn or a branch has struck him in the face. If he hurts his foot or skins his belly a little, jumping over a fence, he sets up a cry like an antique hero in his death-agony; comes to me hobbling on three legs, howling and lamenting in an abandonment of self-pity—the more piercingly, the more sympathy he gets—and this although in fifteen minutes he will be running and jumping again as though nothing had happened.

With Percival it was otherwise; he clenched his jaws and was still. He was afraid of the dog-whip, as Bashan is too; and tasted it, alas, more often than the latter, for in his day I was younger and quicker-tempered and his witlessness often assumed a vicious aspect which cried out for chastisement and drove me on to administer it. When I was quite beside myself and took down the lash from the nail where it hung, Percy might crawl under a table or a bench. But not a sound would escape him under punishment; even at a second flailing he would give vent only to a fervent moan if it stung worse than usual—whereas the baseborn Bashan will howl abjectly if I so much as raise my arm. In short, no sense of honour, no strictness with himself. And anyhow, it seldom comes to corporal punishment, for I long ago ceased to make demands upon him contrary to his nature, of a kind which would lead to conflict between us.

For example, I never ask him to learn tricks; it would be of no use. He is not talented, no circus dog, no trained clown. He is a sound, vigorous young hunter, not a professor. I believe I remarked that he is a capital jumper. No obstacle too great, if the incentive be present: if he cannot jump it he will scrabble up somehow and let himself fall on the other side—at least, he conquers it one way or another. But it must be a genuine obstacle, not to be jumped through or crawled under; otherwise he would think it folly to jump. A wall, a ditch, a fence, a thickset hedge, are genuine obstacles; a crosswise bar, a stick held out, are not, and you cannot jump over them without going contrary to reason and looking silly. Which Bashan refuses to do. He refuses. Try to make him jump over some such unreal obstacle; in the end you will be reduced to taking him by the scruff of the neck, in your anger, and flinging him over, while he whimpers and yaps. Once on the other side he acts as though he had done just what you wanted and celebrates the event in a frenzy of barking and capering. You may coax or you may punish; you cannot break down his reasonable resistance to performing a mere trick. He is not unaccommodating, he sets store by his master's approval, he will jump over a hedge at my will or my command, and not only when he feels like it himself, and enjoys very much the praise I bestow. But over a bar or a stick he will not jump, he will crawl underneath—if he were to die for it. A hundred times he will beg for forgiveness, forbearance, consideration; he fears pain, fears it to the point of being abject. But no fear and no pain can make him capable of a performance which in itself would be child's-play for him, but for which he obviously lacks all mental equipment. When you confront him with it, the question is not whether he will jump or not; that is already settled, and the command means nothing to him but a beating. To demand of him what reason forbids him to understand and hence to do is simply in his eyes to seek a pretext for blows, strife, and disturbance of friendly relations—it is merely the first step towards all these things. Thus Bashan looks at it, so far as I can see, and I doubt whether one may properly charge him with obstinacy. Obstinacy may be broken down, in the last analysis it cries out to be broken down; but Bashan's resistance to performing a trick he would seal with his death.

Extraordinary creature! So close a friend and yet so remote; so different from us, in certain ways, that our language has not power to do justice to his canine logic. For instance, what is the meaning of that frightful circumstantiality—unnerving alike to the spectator and to the parties themselves—attendant on the meeting of dog and dog; or on their first acquaintance or even on their first sight of each other? My excursions with Bashan have made me witness to hundreds of such encounters, or, I might better say, forced me to be an embarrassed spectator at them. And every time, for the duration of the episode, my old familiar Bashan was a stranger to me, I found it impossible to enter into his feelings or behaviour or understand the tribal laws which governed them. Certainly the meeting in the open of two dogs, strangers to each other, is one of the most painful, thrilling, and pregnant of all conceivable encounters; it is surrounded by an atmosphere of the last uncanniness, presided over by a constraint for which I have no preciser name; they simply cannot pass each other, their mutual embarrassment is frightful to behold.

I am not speaking of the case where one of the parties is shut up behind a hedge or a fence. Even then it is not easy to interpret their feelings—but at least the situation is less acute. They sniff each other from far off, and Bashan suddenly seeks shelter in my neighbourhood, whining a little to give vent to a distress and oppression which simply no words can describe. At the same time the imprisoned stranger sets up a violent barking, ostensibly in his character as a good watch-dog, but passing over unconsciously into a whimpering much like Bashan's own, an unsatisfied, envious, distressful whine. We draw near. The strange dog is waiting for us, close to the hedge, grousing and bemoaning his impotence; jumping at the barrier and giving every sign—how seriously one cannot tell—of intending to tear Bashan to pieces if only he could get at him. Bashan might easily stick close to me and pass him by; but he goes up to the hedge. He has to, he would even if I forbade him; to remain away would be to transgress a code older and more inviolable than any prohibition of mine. He advances, then, and with a modest and inscrutable bearing performs that rite which he knows will soothe and appease the other—even if temporarily—so long as the stranger performs it too, though whining and complaining in the act. Then they both chase wildly along the hedge, each on his own side, as close as possible, neither making a sound. At the end of the hedge they both face about and dash back again. But in full career both suddenly halt and stand as though rooted to the spot; they stand still, facing the hedge, and put their noses together through it. For some space of time they stand thus, then resume their curious, futile race shoulder to shoulder on either side of the barrier. But in the end my dog avails himself of his freedom and moves off—a frightful moment for the prisoner! He cannot stand it, he finds it namelessly humiliating that the other should dream of simply going off like that. He raves and slavers and contorts himself in his rage; runs like one mad up and down his enclosure; threatens to jump the hedge and have the faithless Bashan by the throat; he yells insults behind the retreating back. Bashan hears it all, it distresses him, as his manner shows. But he does not turn round, he jogs along beside me, while the cursings in our rear die down into whinings and are still.

Such the procedure when one of the parties is shut up. Embarrassments multiply when both of them are free. I do not relish describing the scene: it is one of the most painful and equivocal imaginable. Bashan has been bounding light-heartedly beside me; he comes up close, he fairly forces himself upon me, with a sniffling and whimpering that seem to come from his very depths. I still do not know what moves his utterance, but I recognize it at once and gather that there is a strange dog in the offing. I look about—yes, there he comes, and even at this distance his strained and hesitating mien betrays that he has already seen Bashan. I am scarcely less upset than they; I find the meeting most undesirable. "Go away," I say to Bashan. "Why do you glue yourself to my leg? Can't you go off and do your business by yourselves?" I try to frighten him off with my cane. For if they start biting—which may easily happen, with reason or without—I shall find it most unpleasant to have them between my feet. "Go away!" I repeat, in a lower voice. But Bashan does not go away, he sticks in his distress the closer to me, making as brief a pause as he can at a tree-trunk to perform the accustomed rite; I can see the other dog doing the same. We are now within twenty paces, the suspense is frightful. The strange dog is crawling on his belly, like a cat, his head thrust out. In this posture he awaits Bashan's approach, poised to spring at the right moment for his throat. But he does not do it, nor does Bashan seem to expect that he will. Or at least he goes up to the crouching stranger, though plainly trembling and heavy-hearted; he would do this, he is obliged to do it, even though I were to act myself and leave him to face the situation alone by striking into a side path. However painful the encounter, he has no choice, avoidance is not to be thought of. He is under a spell, he is bound to the other dog, they are bound to each other with some obscure and equivocal bond which may not be denied. We are now within two paces.

Then the other gets up, without a sound, as though he had never been behaving like a tiger, and stands there just as Bashan is standing, profoundly embarrassed, wretched, at a loss. They cannot pass each other. They probably want to, they turn away their heads, rolling their eyes sideways; evidently the same sense of guilt weighs on them both. They edge cautiously up to each other with a hang-dog air; they stop flank to flank and sniff under each other's tails. At this point the rowing begins, and I speak to Bashan low-voiced and warn him, for now is the decisive moment, now we shall know whether it will come to biting or whether I shall be spared that rude shock. It does come to biting, I do not know how, still less why: quite suddenly they are nothing but a raging tumult and whirling coil out of which issue the frightful guttural noises that animals make when they engage. I may have to engage too, with my cane, to forestall a worse calamity; I may try to get Bashan by the neck or the collar and hold him up at arm's length in the air, the stranger dog hanging on by his teeth. Other horrors there are, too, which I may have to face—and feel them afterwards in all my limbs during the rest of our walk. But it may be too, that after all the preliminaries the affair will pass tamely off and no harm done. At best it is hard to part the two; even if they are not clenched by the teeth, they are held by that inward bond. They may seem to have passed each other, they are no longer flank to flank, but in a straight line with their heads in opposite directions; they may not even turn their heads, but only be rolling their eyes backwards. There may even be a space between them—and yet the painful bond still holds. Neither knows if the right moment for release has come, they would both like to go, yet each seems to have conscientious scruples. Slowly, slowly, the bond loosens, snaps; Bashan bounds lightly away, with, as it were, a new lease on life.

I speak of these things only to show how under stress of circumstance the character of a near friend may reveal itself as strange and foreign. It is dark to me, it is mysterious; I observe it with head-shakings and can only dimly guess what it may mean. And in all other respects I understand Bashan so well, I feel such lively sympathy for all his manifestations! For example, how well I know that whining yawn of his when our walk has been disappointing, too short, or devoid of sporting interest; when I have begun the day late and only gone out for a quarter of an hour before dinner. At such times he walks beside me and yawns—an open, impudent yawn to the whole extent of his jaws, an animal, audible yawn insultingly expressive of his utter boredom. "A fine master I have!" it seems to say. "Far in the night last night I met him at the bridge and now he sits behind his glass door and I wait for him dying of boredom. And when he does go out he only does it to come back again before there is time to start any game. A fine master! Not a proper master at all—really a rotten master, if you ask me!"

Such was the meaning of his yawn, vulgarly plain beyond all misunderstanding. And I admit that he is right, that he has a just grievance, and I put out a hand to pat his shoulder consolingly or to stroke his head. But he is not, under such circumstances, grateful for caresses; he yawns again, if possible more rudely than before, and moves away from my hand, although by nature, in contrast to Percy and in harmony with his own plebeian sentimentality, he sets great store by caresses. He particularly likes having his throat scratched and has a funny way of guiding one's hand to the right place by energetic little jerks of his head. That he has no room just now for endearments is partly due to his disappointment, but also to the fact that when he is in motion—and that means that I also am—he does not care for them. His mood is too manly; but it changes directly I sit down. Then he is all for friendliness again and responds to it with clumsy enthusiasm.

When I sit reading in a corner of the garden wall, or on the lawn with my back to a favourite tree, I enjoy interrupting my intellectual preoccupations to talk and play with Bashan. And what do I say to him? Mostly his own name, the two syllables which are of the utmost personal interest because they refer to himself and have an electric effect upon his whole being. I rouse and stimulate his sense of his own ego by impressing upon him—varying my tone and emphasis—that he *is* Bashan and that Bashan is his name. By continuing this for a while I can actually produce in him a state of ecstasy, a sort of intoxication with his own identity, so that he begins to whirl round on himself and send up loud exultant barks to heaven out of the weight of dignity that lies on his chest. Or we amuse ourselves, I by tapping him on the nose, he by snapping at my hand as though it were a fly. It makes us both laugh, yes, Bashan has to laugh too; and as I laugh I marvel at the sight, to me the oddest and most touching thing in the world. It is moving to see how under my teasing his thin animal cheeks and the corners of his mouth will twitch, and over his dark animal mask will pass an expression like a human smile, or at least some ungainly, pathetic semblance of one. It gives way to a look of startled embarrassment, then transforms the face by appearing again. . . .

But I will go no further nor involve myself in more detail of the kind. Even so I am dismayed at the space I have been led on to give to this little description; for what I had in mind to do was merely to display, as briefly as I might, my hero in his element, on the scene where he is most at home, most himself, and where his gifts show to best advantage; I mean, of course, the chase. But first I must give account to my reader of the theatre of these delights, my landscape by the river and Bashan's hunting-ground. It is a strip of land intimately bound up with his personality, familiar, loved, and significant to me like himself; which fact, accordingly, without further literary justification or embellishment, must serve as the occasion for my description.

THE HUNTING-GROUND

The spacious gardens of the suburb where we live contain many large old trees that rise above the villa roofs and form a striking contrast to the saplings set out at a later period. Unquestionably they are the earliest inhabitants, the pride and adornment of a settlement which is still not very old. They have been carefully protected and preserved, so far as was possible; when any one of them came into conflict with the boundaries of the parcels of land, some venerable silvery moss-grown trunk standing exactly on a border-line, the hedge makes a little curve round it, or an accommodating gap is left in a wall, and the ancient towers up half on public, half on private ground, with bare snow-covered boughs or adorned with its tiny, late-coming leaves.

They are a variety of ash, a tree that loves moisture more than most—and their presence here shows what kind of soil we have. It is not so long since human brains reclaimed it for human habitation; not more than a decade or so. Before that it was a marshy wilderness, a breeding-place for mosquitoes, where willows, dwarf poplars, and other stunted growths mirrored themselves in stagnant pools. The region is subject to floods. There is a stratum of impermeable soil a few yards under the surface; it has always been boggy, with standing water in the hollows. They drained it by lowering the level of the river—engineering is not my strong point, but anyhow it was some such device, by means of which the water which cannot sink into the earth now flows off laterally into the river by several subterranean channels, and the ground is left comparatively dry—but only comparatively, for Bashan and I, knowing it as we do, are acquainted with certain low, retired, and rushy spots, relics of the primeval condition of the region, whose damp coolness defies the summer heat and makes them a grateful place wherein to draw a few long breaths.

The whole district has its peculiarities, indeed, which distinguish it at a glance from the pine forests and moss-grown meadows which are the usual setting of a mountain stream. It has preserved its original characteristics even since it was acquired by the real-estate company; even outside the gardens the original vegetation preponderates over the newly planted. In the avenues and parks, of course, horse-chestnuts and quick-growing maple trees, beeches, and all sorts of ornamental shrubs have been set out; also rows of French poplars standing erect in their sterile masculinity. But the ash trees, as I said, are the aborigines; they are everywhere, and of all ages, century-old giants and tender young seedlings pushing their way by hundreds, like weeds, through the gravel. It is the ash, together with the silver poplar, the aspen, the birch, and the willow, that gives the scene its distinctive look. All these trees have small leaves, and all this small-leaved foliage is very striking by contrast with the huge trunks. But there are elms too, spreading their large, varnished, saw-edged leaves to the sun. And everywhere too are masses of creeper, winding round the young trees in the underbrush and inextricably mingling its leaves with theirs. Little thickets of slim alder trees stand in the hollows. There are few lime trees, no oaks or firs at all, in our domain, though there are some on the slope which bounds it to the east, where the soil changes and with it the character of the vegetation. There they stand out black against the sky, like sentinels guarding our little valley.

It is not more than five hundred yards from slope to river—I have paced it out. Perhaps the strip of river-bank widens a little, further down, but not to any extent; so it is remarkable what landscape variety there is in this small area, even when one makes such moderate use of the playground it affords along the river as do Bashan and I, who rarely spend more than two hours there, counting our going and coming. There is such diversity that we need hardly take the same path twice or ever tire of the view or be conscious of any limitations of space; and this is due to the circumstance that our domain divides itself into three quite different regions or zones. We may confine ourselves to one of these or we may combine all three: they are the neighbourhood of the river and its banks, the neighbourhood of the opposite slope, and the wooded section in the middle.

The wooded zone, the parks, the osier brakes, and the riverside shrubbery take up most of the breadth. I search in vain for a word better than "wood" to describe this strange tract of land. For it is no wood in the usual sense of the word: not a pillared hall of even-sized trunks, carpeted with moss and fallen leaves. The trees in our hunting-ground are of uneven growth and size, hoary giants of willows and poplars, especially along the river, though also deeper in; others ten or fifteen years old, which are probably as large as they will grow; and lastly a legion of slender trees, young ashes, birches, and alders in a nursery garden planted by nature herself. These look larger than they are; and all, as I said, are wound round with creepers which give a look of tropical luxuriance to the scene. But I suspect them of choking the growth of their hosts, for I cannot see that the trunks have grown any thicker in all the years I have known them.

The trees are of few and closely related species. The alder belongs to the birch family, the poplar is after all not very different from a willow. And one might say that they all approach the willow type; foresters tell us that trees tend to adapt themselves to their local conditions, showing a certain conformity, as it were, to the prevailing mode. It is the distorted, fantastic, witchlike silhouette of the willow tree, dweller by still and by flowing waters, that sets the fashion here, with her branches like broom-splints and her crooked-fingered tips; and all the others visibly try to be like her. The silver poplar apes her best; but often it is hard to tell poplar from birch, so much is the latter beguiled by the spirit of the place to take on misshapen forms. Not that there are not also plenty of very shapely and well-grown single specimens of this lovable tree, and enchanting they look in the favouring glow of the late afternoon. In this region the birch appears as a slender silvery bole with a crown of little, separate leaves atop; as a lovely, lithe, and well-grown maiden; it has the prettiest of chalk-white trunks, and its foliage droops like delicate languishing locks of hair. But there are also birches colossal in size, that no man could span with his arms, the bark of which is only white high up, but near the ground has turned black and coarse and is seamed with fissures.

The soil is not like what one expects in a wood. It is loamy, gravelly, even sandy. It seems anything but fertile, and yet, within its nature, is almost luxuriantly so; for it is overgrown with tall, rank grass, often the dry, sharp-cornered kind that grows on dunes. In winter it covers the ground like trampled hay; not seldom it cannot be distinguished from reeds, but in other places it is soft and fat and juicy, and among it grow hemlock, coltsfoot, nettles, all sorts of low-growing things, mixed with tall thistles and tender young tree shoots. Pheasants and other wildfowl hide in this vegetation, which rolls up to and over the gnarled roots of the trees. And everywhere the wild grape and the hop-vine clamber out of the thicket to twine round the trunks in garlands of flapping leaves, or in winter with bare stems like the toughest sort of wire.

Now, all this is not a wood, it is not a park, it is simply an enchanted garden, no more and no less. I will stand for the word—though of course nature here is stingy and sparse and tends to the deformed; a few botanical names exhausting the catalogue of her performance. The ground is rolling, it constantly rises and falls away, so that the view is enclosed on every hand, with a lovely effect of remoteness and privacy. Indeed, if the wood stretched for miles to right and left, as far as it reaches lengthwise, instead of only a hundred and some paces on each side from the middle, one could not feel more secluded. Only by the sense of sound is one made aware of the friendly nearness of the river; you cannot see it, but it whispers gently from the west. There are gorges choked with shrubbery—elder, privet, jasmine, and wild cherry—on close June days the scent is almost overpowering. And again there are low-lying spots, regular gravel-pits, where nothing but a few willow-shoots and a little sage can grow, at the bottom or on the sides.

And all this scene never ceases to exert a strange influence upon me, though it has been my almost daily walk for some years. The fine massed foliage of the ash puts me in mind of a giant fern; these creepers and climbers, this barrenness and this damp, this combination of lush and dry, has a fantastic effect; to convey my whole meaning, it is a little as though I were transported to another geological period, or even to the bottom of the sea—and the fantasy has this much of fact about it, that water did stand here once, for instance in the square low-lying meadow basins thick with shoots of self-sown ash, which now serve as pasture for sheep. One such lies directly behind my house.

The wilderness is crossed in all directions by paths, some of them only lines of trodden grass or gravelly trails, obviously born of use and not laid out—though it would be hard to say who trod them, for only by way of unpleasant exception do Bashan and I meet anyone here. When that happens he stands stock still and gives a little growl which very well expresses my own feelings too. Even on the fine summer Sunday afternoons which bring crowds of people to walk in these parts—for it is always a few degrees cooler here—we remain undisturbed in our fastness. They know it not; the water is the great attraction, as a rule, the river in its course; the human stream gets as close as it can, down to the very edge if there is no flood, rolls along beside it, and then back home again. At most we may come on a pair of lovers in the shrubbery; they look at us wide-eyed and startled out of their nest, or else defiantly as though to ask what objection we have to their presence or their behaviour. All which we disclaim by beating swift retreat, Bashan with the indifference he feels for everything that does not smell like game; I with a face utterly devoid of all expression, either approving or the reverse.

But these woodland paths are not the only way we have of reaching my park. There are streets as well—or rather there are traces, which once were streets, or which once were to have been streets, or which, by God's will, may yet become streets. In other words: there are signs that the pickaxe has been at work, signs of a hopeful real-estate enterprise for some distance beyond the built-up section and the villas. There has been some far-sighted planning on the part of the company which some years ago acquired the land; but their plans went beyond their capacity for carrying them out, for the villas were only a part of what they had in mind. Building-lots were laid out; an area extending for nearly a mile down the river was prepared, and doubtless still remains prepared, to receive possible purchasers and home-loving settlers. The building society conceived things on a rather large scale. They enclosed the river between dykes, they built quays and planted gardens, and, not content with that, they had embarked on clearing the woods, dumped piles of gravel, cut roads through the wilderness, one or two lengthwise and several across the width; fine, well-planned roads, or at last the first steps towards them, made of course gravel, with a wide foot-path and indications of a curb-stone. But no one walks there save Bashan and myself, he on the good stout leather of his four paws, I in hobnailed boots on account of the gravel. For the stately villas projected by the company are still non-existent, despite the good example I set when I built my own house. They have been, I say, non-existent for ten, no, fifteen years; it is no wonder that a kind of blight has settled upon the enterprise and discouragement reigns in the bosom of the building society, a disinclination to go on with their project.

However, things had got so far forward that these streets, though not built up, have all been given names, just as though they were in the centre of the town or in a suburb. I should very much like to know what sort of speculator he was who named them; he seems to have been a literary chap with a fondness for the past: there is an Opitzstrasse, a Flemmingstrasse, a Bürgerstrasse, even an Adalbert-Stifterstrasse—I walk on the last-named with especial reverence in my hobnailed boots. At all the corners stakes have been driven in the ground with street signs affixed to them, as is usual in suburbs where there are no house-corners to receive them; they are the usual little blue enamel plates with white lettering. But alas, they are rather the worse for wear. They have stood here far too long, pointing out the names of vacant sites where nobody wants to live; they are monuments to the failure, the discouragement, and the arrested development of the whole enterprise. They have not been kept up or renewed, the climate has done its worst by them. The enamel has scaled off, the lettering is rusty, there are ugly broken-edged gaps which make the names sometimes almost illegible. One of them, indeed, puzzled me a good deal when I first came here and was spying about the neighbourhood. It was a long name, and the word "street" was perfectly clear, but most of the rest was eaten by rust; there remained only an S at the beginning, an E somewhere about the middle, and another E at the end. I could not reckon with so many unknown quantities. I studied the sign a long time with my hands behind my back, then continued along the foot-path with Bashan. I thought I was thinking about something else, but all the time my brains were privately cudgelling themselves, and suddenly it came over me. I stopped with a start, stood still, and then hastened back, took up my former position, and tested my guess. Yes, it fitted. The name of the street where I was walking was Shakespeare Street.

The streets suit the signboards and the signboards suit the streets—it is a strange and dreamlike harmony in decay. The streets run through the wood they have broken into; but the wood does not remain passive. It does not let the streets stop as they were made, through decade after decade, until at last people come and settle on them. It takes every step to close them again; for what grows here does not mind gravel, it flourishes in it. Purple thistles, blue sage, silvery shoots of willow, and green ash seedlings spring up all over the road and even on the pavement; the streets with the poetic names are going back to the wilderness, whether one likes it or not; in another ten years Opitzstrasse, Flemmingstrasse, and the rest will be closed, they will probably as good as disappear. There is at present no ground for complaint; for from the romantic and picturesque point of view there are no more beautiful streets in the world than they are now. Nothing could be more delightful than strolling through them in their unfinished, abandoned state, if one has/on stout boots and does not mind the gravel. Nothing more agreeable to the eye than looking from the wild garden beneath one's feet to the humid massing of fine-leafed foliage that shuts in the view—foliage such as Claude Lorrain used to paint, three centuries ago. Such as he used to paint, did I say? But surely he painted *this*. He was here, he knew this scene, he studied it. If my building-society man had not confined himself to the literary field, one of these rusty street signs might have borne the name of Claude.

Well, that is our middle or wooded region. But the eastern slope has its own charms not to be despised, either by me or by Bashan, who has his own reasons, which will appear hereafter. I might call this region the zone of the brook; for it takes its idyllic character as landscape from the stream that flows through it, and the peaceful loveliness of its beds of forget-me-not makes it a fit companion-piece to the zone on the other side with its rushing river, whose flowing, when the west wind blows, can be faintly heard even all the way across our hunting-ground. The first of the made cross-roads through the wood runs like a causeway from the poplar avenue to the foot of the hillside, between low-lying pasture-ground on one side and wooded lots of land on the other. And from there a path descends to the left, used by the children to coast on in winter. The brook rises in the level ground at the bottom of this descent. We love to stroll beside it, Bashan and I, on the right or the left bank at will, through the varied territory of our eastern zone. On our left is an extent of wooded meadow, and a nursery-gardening establishment; we can see the backs of the buildings, and sheep cropping the clover, presided over by a rather stupid little girl in a red frock. She keeps propping her hands on her knees and screaming at her charges at the top of her lungs in a harsh, angry, and imperious voice. But she seems to be afraid of the majestic old ram, who looks enormously fat in his thick fleece and who does as he likes regardless of her bullying ways. The child's screams rise to their height when the sheep are thrown into a panic by the appearance of Bashan; and this almost always happens, quite against his will or intent, for he is profoundly indifferent to their existence, behaves as though they were not there, or even deliberately and contemptuously ignores them in an effort to forestall an attack of panic folly on their part. Their scent is strong enough to me, though not unpleasant; but it is not a scent of game, so Bashan takes no interest in harrying them. But let him make a single move, or merely appear on the scene, and the whole flock, but now grazing peacefully over the meadow and bleating in their curiously human voices, some bass, some treble, suddenly collect in a huddled mass of backs and go dashing off, while the imbecile child stoops over and screams at them until her voice cracks and her eyes pop out of her head. Bashan looks up at me as though to say: Am I to blame, did I do anything at all?

But once something quite the opposite happened, that was even more extraordinary and distressing than any panic. A sheep, a quite ordinary specimen, of medium size and the usual sheepish face, save for a narrow-lipped little mouth turned up at the corners into a smile which gave the creature an uncommonly sly and fatuous look—this sheep appeared to be smitten with Bashan's charms. It followed him; it left the flock and the pasture-ground and followed at his heels, wherever he went, smiling with extravagant stupidity. He left the path, and it followed. He ran, it galloped after. He stopped, it did the same, close behind him and smiling its inscrutable smile. Embarrassment and dismay were painted on Bashan's face, and certainly his position was highly distasteful. For good or for ill it lacked any kind of sense or reason. Nothing so consummately silly had ever happened to either of us. The sheep got further and further away from its base, but it seemed not to care for that; it followed the exasperated Bashan apparently resolved to part from him nevermore, but to be at his side whithersoever he went. He stuck close at my side; not so much alarmed—for the which there was no cause—as ashamed of the disgraceful situation. At last, as though he had had enough of it, he stood still, turned round, and gave a menacing growl. The sheep bleated—it was like a man's laugh, a spiteful laugh—and put poor Bashan so beside himself that he ran away with his tail between his legs, the sheep bounding absurdly behind him.

Meanwhile he had got a good way from the flock; the addlepated little girl was screaming fit to burst, and not only bending her knees but jerking them up and down as she screamed till they touched her face, and she looked from a distance like a demented dwarf. A dairymaid in an apron came running, her attention being drawn by the shrieks or in some other way. She had a pitchfork in one hand; with the other she held her breasts, that shook up and down as she ran. She tried to drive back the sheep with the pitchfork—it had started after Bashan again—but unsuccessfully. The sheep did indeed spring away from the fork in the right direction, but then swung round again to follow Bashan's trail. It seemed no power on earth would divert it. But at last I saw what had to be done and turned round. We all marched back, Bashan beside me, behind him the sheep, behind the sheep the maid with the pitchfork, the child in the red frock bouncing and stamping at us all the while. It was not enough to go back to the flock, we had to do the job thoroughly. We went into the farmyard and to the sheep-pen, where the farm girl rolled back the big door with her strong right arm. We all went inside, all of us; and then the rest of us had to slip out again and shut the door in the face of the poor deluded sheep, so that it was taken prisoner. And then, after receiving the farm girl's thanks, Bashan and I might resume our interrupted walk, to the end of which Bashan preserved a sulky and humiliated air.

So much for the sheep. Beyond the farm buildings is an extensive colony of allotments, that looks rather like a cemetery, with its arbours and little summer-houses like chapels and each tiny garden neatly enclosed. The whole colony has a fence round it, with a latticed gate, through which only the owners of the plots have admission. Sometimes I have seen a man with his sleeves rolled up digging his few yards of vegetable-plot—he looked as though he were digging his own grave. Beyond this come open meadows full of mole-hills, reaching to the edge of the middle wooded region; besides the moles, the place abounds in field mice—I mention them on account of Bashan and his multifarious joy of the chase.

But on the other, the right side, the brook and the hillside continue, the latter, as I said, with great variety in its contours. The first part is shadowed and gloomy and set with pines. Then comes a sand-pit which reflects the warm rays of the sun; then a gravel-pit, then a cataract of bricks, as though a house had been demolished up above and the rubble simply flung down the hill, damming the brook at the bottom. But the brook rises until its waters flow over the obstacle and go on, reddened with brick-dust and dyeing the grass along its edge, to flow all the more blithely and pellucidly further on, with the sun making diamonds sparkle on its surface.

I am very fond of brooks, as indeed of all water, from the ocean to the smallest reedy pool. If in the mountains in the summertime my ear but catch the sound of plashing and prattling from afar, I always go to seek out the source of the liquid sounds, a long way if I must; to make the acquaintance and to look in the face of that conversable child of the hills, where he hides. Beautiful are the torrents that come tumbling with mild thunderings down between evergreens and over stony terraces; that form rocky bathing-pools and then dissolve in white foam to fall perpendicularly to the next level. But I have pleasure in the brooks of the flatland too, whether they be so shallow as hardly to cover the slippery, silver-gleaming pebbles in their bed, or as deep as small rivers between overhanging, guardian willow trees, their current flowing swift and strong in the centre, still and gently at the edge. Who would not choose to follow the sound of running waters? Its attraction for the normal man is of a natural, sympathetic sort. For man is water's child, nine-tenths of our body consists of it, and at a certain stage the fœtus possesses gills. For my part I freely admit that the sight of water in whatever form or shape is my most lively and immediate kind of natural enjoyment; yes, I would even say that only in contemplation of it do I achieve true self-forgetfulness and feel my own limited individuality merge into the universal. The sea, still-brooding or coming on in crashing billows, can put me in a state of such profound organic dreaminess, such remoteness from myself, that I am lost to time. Boredom is unknown, hours pass like minutes, in the unity of that companionship. But then, I can lean on the rail of a little bridge over a brook and contemplate its currents, its whirlpools, and its steady flow for as long as you like; with no sense or fear of that other flowing within and about me, that swift gliding away of time. Such love of water and understanding of it make me value the circumstance that the narrow strip of ground where I dwell is enclosed on both sides by water.

But my little brook here is the simplest of its kind, it has no particular or unusual characteristics, it is quite the average brook. Clear as glass, without any guile, it does not dream of seeming deep by being turbid. It is shallow and candid and makes no bones of betraying that there are old tins and the mouldering remains of a laced shoe in its bed. But it is deep enough to serve as a home for pretty, lively, silver-grey little fish, which dart away in zigzags at our approach. In some places it broadens into a pool, and it has willows on its margin, one of which I love to look at as I pass. It stands on the hillside, a little removed from the water; but one of the boughs has bent down and reached across and actually succeeded in plunging its silvery tip into the flowing water. Thus it stands revelling in the pleasure of this contact.

It is pleasant to walk here in the warm breeze of summer. If the weather is very warm Bashan goes into the stream to cool his belly; not more than that, for he never of his own free will wets the upper parts. He stands there with his ears laid back and a look of virtue on his face and lets the water stream round and over him. Then he comes back to me to shake himself, being convinced that this can only be accomplished in my vicinity—although he does it so thoroughly that I receive a perfect shower-bath in the process. It is no good waving him off with my stick or with shoutings. Whatever seems to him natural and right and necessary, that he will do.

The brook flows on westward to the little hamlet that faces north between the wood and the hillside. At the beginning of this hamlet is an inn, and at this point the brook widens into another pool where women kneel to wash their clothes. Crossing the little foot-bridge, you strike into a road going back towards the city between wood and meadow. But on the right of the road is another through the wood, by which in a few minutes you can get back to the river.

And so here we are at the river zone, and the river itself is in front of us, green and roaring and white with foam. It is really nothing more than a mountain torrent; but its ceaseless roaring pervades the whole region round, in the distance subdued, but here a veritable tumult which—if one cannot have the ocean itself—is quite a fair substitute for its awe-inspiring swell. Numberless gulls fill the air with their cries; autumn, winter, and spring they circle screaming round the mouths of the drain-pipes which issue here, seeking their food. In summer they depart once more for the lakes higher up. Wild and half-wild duck also take refuge here in the neighbourhood of the town for the winter months. They rock on the waves, are whirled round and carried off by the current, rise into the air to escape being engulfed, and then settle again on quieter water.

And this river tract also is divided into areas of varying character. At the edge of the wood is the gravelly expanse into which the poplar avenue issues; it extends for nearly a mile downstream, as far as the ferry-house, of which I will speak presently. At this point the underbrush comes nearly down to the river-bed. And all the gravel, as I am aware, constitutes the beginnings of the first and most important of the lengthwise streets, magnificently conceived by the real-estate company as an esplanade, a carriage-road bordered by trees and flowers—where elegantly turned-out riders were to hold sweet converse with ladies leaning back in shiny landaus. Beside the ferry-house, indeed, is a sign, already rickety and rotting, from which one can gather that the site was intended for the erection of a café. Yes, there is the sign—and there it remains, but there is no trace of the little tables, the hurrying waiters and coffee-sipping guests; nobody has bought the site, and the esplanade is nothing but a desert of gravel, where sage and willow-shoots are almost as thick as in Opitz and Flemmingstrasse.

Down close to the river is another, narrower gravel waste, as full of weeds as the bigger one. Along it are grassy mounds supporting telegraph poles. I like to use this as a path, by way of variety—also because it is cleaner, though more difficult, to walk on it than on the actual foot-path, which in bad weather is often very muddy, though it is actually the proper path, extending for miles along the river, finally going off into trails along the bank. It is planted on the river side with young maple and birch trees; on the other side the original inhabitants stand in a row—willows, aspens, and silver poplars of enormous size. The river-bank is steep and high and is ingeniously shored up with withes and concrete to prevent the flooding which threatens two or three times in the year, after heavy rains or when the snows melt in the hills. At several points there are ladderlike wooden steps leading down to the river-bed—an extent of mostly dry gravel, six or eight yards wide. For this mountain torrent behaves precisely as its like do, whether large or small: it may be, according to the conditions up above, either the merest green trickle, hardly covering the stones, where long-legged birds seem to be standing on the water; or it may be a torrent alarming in its power and extent, filling the wide bed with raging fury, whirling round tree-branches and old baskets and dead cats and threatening to commit much damage. Here, too, there is protection against floods in the shape of woven hurdles put in slanting to the stream. When dry, the bed is grown up with wiry grass and wild oats, as well as that omnipresent shrub the blue sage; there is fairly good walking, on the strip of flat stones at the extreme outer edge, and it affords me a pleasant variety, for though the stone is not of the most agreeable to walk on, the close proximity of the river atones for much, and there is even sometimes sand between the gravel and the grass; true, it is mixed with clay, it has not the exquisite cleanness of sea-sand, but after all it is sand. I am taking a walk on the beach that stretches into the distance at the edge of the wave, and there is the sound of the surge and the cry of the gulls, there is that monotony that swallows time and space and shuts one up as in a dream. The river roars eddying over the stones, and half-way to the ferry-house the sound is augmented by a waterfall that comes down by a diagonal canal and tumbles into the larger stream, arching as it falls, shining glassily like a leaping fish, and seething perpetually at its base.

Lovely to walk here when the sky is blue and the ferry-boat flies a flag, perhaps in honour of the fine weather or because it is a feast-day of some sort. There are other boats here too, but the ferry-boat is fast to a wire cable attached to another, thicker cable that is spanned across the stream and runs along it on a little pulley. The current supplies the motive power, the steering is done by hand. The ferryman lives with his wife and child in the ferry-house, which is a little higher up than the upper foot-path; the house has a kitchen-garden and a chicken-house and the man undoubtedly gets it rent-free in his office as ferryman. It is a sort of dwarf villa, rather flimsy, with funny little out-croppings of balconies and bay-windows, and seems to have two rooms below and two above. I like to sit on the little bench on the upper foot-path close to the tiny garden—with Bashan squatting on my foot and the ferryman's chickens stalking round about me, jerking their heads forward with each step. The cock usually comes and perches on the back of the bench with his green bersaglieri tail-feathers hanging down behind; he sits thus beside me and measures me with a fierce side-glance of his red eye. I watch the traffic; it is not crowded, hardly even lively; indeed, the ferry-boat runs only at considerable intervals. The more do I enjoy it when on one side or the other a man appears, or a woman with a basket, and wants to be put across: the "Boat ahoy!" is an age-old, picturesque cry, with a poetry not impaired by the fact that the business is done somewhat differently nowadays. Double flights of steps for those coming and going lead down to the river-bed and to the landings, and there is an electric push-button at the side of each. So when a man appears on the opposite bank and stands looking across the water, he does not put his hands round his mouth and call. He goes up to the push-button, puts out his hand, and pushes. The bell rings shrilly in the ferryman's villa; that is the "Boat ahoy!" even so, and it is poetic still. Then the man waits and looks about. And almost at the moment when the bell rings, the ferryman comes out of his little official dwelling, as though he had been standing behind the door or sitting on a chair waiting for the signal. He comes out, and the way he walks suggests that he has been mechanically put in motion by the ringing of the bell. It is like a shooting-booth when you shoot at the door of a little house and if you hit it a figure comes out, a sentry or a cow-girl. The ferryman crosses his garden at a measured pace, his arms swinging regularly at his sides; over the path and down the steps to the river, where he pushes off the ferry-boat and holds the steering-gear while the little pulley runs along the wire above the stream and the boat is driven across. The man springs in, and once safely on this side hands over his penny and runs briskly up the steps, going off right or left. Sometimes, when the ferryman is not well or is very busy in the house, his wife or even his little child comes out to ferry the stranger across. They can do it as well as he, and so could I, for it is an easy office, requiring no special gift or training. He can reckon himself lucky to have the job and live in the dwarf villa. Anyone, however stupid, could do what he does, and he knows this, of course, and behaves with becoming modesty. On the way back to his house he very politely says: *"Grüss Gott"* to me as I sit there on the bench between Bashan and the cock; you can see that he likes to be on good terms with everybody.

There is a tarry smell, a breeze off the water, a slapping sound against the ferry-boat. What more can one want? Sometimes these things call up a familiar memory: the water is deep, it has a smell of decay—that is the Lagoon, that is Venice. But sometimes there is a heavy storm, a deluge of rain; in my macintosh, my face streaming with wet, I take the upper path, leaning against the strong west wind, which in the poplar avenue has torn the saplings away from their supports. Now one can see why all the trees are bent in one direction and have somewhat lopsided tops. Bashan has to stop often to shake himself, the water flies off him in every direction. The river is quite changed: swollen and dark yellow it rolls threateningly along, rushing and dashing in a furious hurry this way and that; its muddy tide takes up the whole extra bed up to the edge of the undergrowth, pounding against the cement and the willow hurdles—until one is glad of the forethought that put them there. The strange thing about it is that the water is *quiet;* it makes almost no noise at all. And there are no rapids in its course now, the stream is too high for that. You can only see where they were by the fact that its waves are higher and deeper there than elsewhere, and that their crests break backwards instead of forwards like the surf on a beach. The waterfall is insignificant now, its volume is shrunken, no longer vaulted, and the boiling water at its base is almost obliterated by the height of the flood. Bashan's reaction to all this is simple unmitigated astonishment that things can be so changed. He cannot get over it, cannot understand how it is that the dry territory where he is wont to run about has disappeared, is covered by water. He flees up into the undergrowth to get away from the lashing of the flood; looks at me and wags his tail, then back at the water, and has a funny, puzzled way of opening his jaws crookedly, shutting them again and running his tongue round the corner of his mouth. It is not a very refined gesture, in fact rather common, but very speaking, and as human as it is animal—in fact it is just what an ordinary simple-minded man might do in face of a surprising situation, very likely scratching his neck at the same time.

Having gone into some detail in describing the river zone, I believe I have covered the whole region and done all I can to bring it before my reader's eye. I like my description pretty well, but I like the reality of nature even better. It is more vivid and various; just as Bashan himself is warmer, more living and hearty than his imaginary presentment. I am attached to this landscape,

I owe it something, and am grateful, therefore, I have described it. It is my park and my solitude; my thoughts and dreams are mingled and interwoven with images from it, as the tendrils of climbing plants are with the boughs of its trees. I have seen it at all times of day and all seasons of the year: in autumn, when the chemical odour of decaying vegetation fills the air, when all the thistles have shed their down, when the great beeches in my park have spread a rust-coloured carpet of leaves on the meadow and the liquid golden afternoons merge into romantic, theatrical early evenings, with the moon's sickle swimming in the sky, when a milk-brewed mist floats above the lowlands and a crimson sunset burns through the black silhouettes of the tree-branches. In autumn, but in winter too, when the gravel is covered with snow and softly levelled off so that one can walk on it in overshoes; when the river looks black as it flows between sallow frost-bound banks, and the cries of hundreds of gulls fill the air from morning to night. But my freest and most familiar intercourse with it is in the milder months, when no extra clothing is required, to dash out quickly, between two showers, for a quarter of an hour; to bend aside in passing a bough of black alder and get a glimpse of the river as it flows. We may have had guests, and I am left somewhat worn down by conversation, between my four walls, where it seems the breath of the strangers still hovers on the air. Then it is good not to linger but to go out at once and stroll in Gellertstrasse or Stifterstrasse, to draw a long breath and get the air into one's lungs. I look up into the sky, I gaze into the tender depths of the masses of green foliage, and peace returns once more and dwells within my spirit.

And Bashan is always with me. He had not been able to prevent the influx of strange persons into our dwelling though he had lifted up his voice and objected. But it did no good, so he had withdrawn. Now he rejoices to be with me again in our hunting-ground. He runs before me on the gravel path, one ear negligently cocked, with that sidewise gait dogs have, the hind legs not just exactly behind the forelegs. And suddenly I see him gripped, as it were, body and soul, his stump of tail switching furiously, erect in the air. His head goes forward and down, his body lengthens out, he makes short dashes in several directions, and then shoots off in one of them with his nose to the ground. He has struck a scent. He is off after a hare.

THE CHASE

The region round is full of game, and we hunt it; that is, Bashan does and I look on. Thus we go hunting: hares, partridges, field-mice, moles, ducks, and gulls. Neither do we shrink from larger game, we stalk pheasant, even deer, if one of them, in winter, happens to stray into our preserve. It is quite a thrilling sight to see the slender long-legged creature, yellow against the snow, running away, with its white buttocks bobbing up and down, in flight from my little Bashan. He strains every nerve, I look on with the greatest sympathy and suspense. Not that anything would ever come of it, nothing ever has or will. But the lack of concrete results does not affect Bashan's passionate eagerness or mar my own interest at all. We pursue the chase for its own sake, not for the prey nor for any other material advantage. Bashan is, as I have said, the active partner. He does not expect from me anything more than my moral support, having no experience, immediate and personal, that is, of more direct co-operation. I say immediate and personal for it is more than likely that his forbears, at least on the pointer side, know what the chase should really be like. I have sometimes asked myself whether some memory might still linger in him, ready to be awakened by a chance sight or sound. At his level the life of the individual is certainly less sharply distinguished from the race than is the case with human beings, birth and death must be a less far-reaching shock; perhaps the traditions of the stock are preserved unimpaired, so that it would only be an apparent contradiction to speak of inborn experiences, unconscious memories, which, when summoned up, would have the power to confuse the creature as to what were its own individual experiences or give rise to dissatisfaction with them. I indulged in this thought, but finally put it from me, as Bashan obviously put from him the rather brutal episode which gave rise to my speculations.

When we go out to follow the chase it is usually midday, half past eleven or twelve; sometimes, on particularly warm summer days, we go late in the afternoon, six o'clock or so—or perhaps we go then for the second time. But on the afternoon walk things are very different with me—not at all as they were on my careless morning stroll. My freshness and serenity have departed long since, I have been struggling and taking thought, I have overcome difficulties, have had to grit my teeth and tussle with a single detail while at the same time holding a more extended and complex context firmly in mind, concentrating my mental powers upon it down to its furthermost ramifications. And my head is tired. It is the chase with Bashan that relieves and distracts me, gives me new life, and puts me back into condition for the rest of the day, in which there is still something to be done.

Of course we do not select each day a certain kind of game to hunt—only hares, for instance, or only ducks. Actually we hunt everything that comes—I was going to say, within reach of our guns. So that we do not need to go far before starting something, actually the hunt can begin just outside the garden gate; for there are quantities of moles and field-mice in the meadow bottom behind the house. Of course these fur-bearing little creatures are not properly game at all. But their mysterious, burrowing little ways, and especially the slyness and dexterity of the field-mice, which are not blind by day like their brethren the moles, but scamper discreetly about on the ground, whisking into their holes at the approach of danger, so that one cannot even see their legs moving—all this works powerfully upon Bashan's instincts. Besides, they are the only wild creatures he ever catches. A field-mouse, a mole, makes a morsel not to be despised, in these lean days, when he often finds nothing more appetizing than porridge in the dish beside his kennel.

So then I and my walking-stick will scarcely have taken two or three steps up the poplar avenue, and Bashan will have scarcely opened the ball with his usual riotous plunges, when I see him capering off to my right—already he is in the grip of his passion, sees and hears nothing but the maddening invisible activities of the creatures all round him. He slinks through the grass, his whole body tense, wagging his tail and lifting his legs with great caution; stops, with one foreleg and one hind leg in the air, eyes the ground with his head on one side, muzzle pointed, ear muscles stiffly erected—so that his ear-laps fall down in front, each side of his eyes. Then with both fore-paws raised he makes a sudden forwards plunge, and another; looking with a puzzled air at the place where something just now was but is not any more. Then he begins to dig. I feel a strong desire to follow him and see what he gets. But if I did we should never get further, his whole zeal for the chase would be expended here on the spot. So I go on. I need not worry about his losing me. Even if he stops behind a long time and has not seen which way I turned, my trail will be as clear to him as though I were the game he seeks, and he will follow it, head between his paws, even if I am out of sight; already I can hear his licence-tag clinking and his stout paws thudding in my rear. He shoots past me, turns round, and wags his tail to announce that he is on the spot.

But in the woods, or out on the meadows by the brook, I do stop often and watch him digging for a mouse, even though the time allotted for my walk is nearly over. It is so fascinating to see his passionate concentration, I feel the contagion myself and cannot help a fervent wish that he may catch something and I be there to see. The spot where he has chosen to dig looks like any other—perhaps a mossy little mound among the roots at the foot of a birch tree. But he has heard and scented something at that spot, perhaps even viewed it as it whisked away; he is convinced that it is there in its burrow underground, he has only to get at it—and he digs away for dear life, oblivious of all else, not angry, but with the professional passion of the sportsman—it is a magnificent sight. His little striped body, the ribs showing and muscles playing under the smooth skin, is drawn in at the middle, his hind quarters stand up in the air, the stump of a tail vibrating in quick time; his head with his fore-paws is down in the slanting hole he has dug and he turns his face aside as he plies his iron-shod paws. Faster and faster, till earth and little stones and tufts of grass and fragments of tree-roots fly up almost into my face. Sometimes he snorts in the silence, when he has burrowed his nose well into the earth, trying to smell out the motionless, clever, frightened little beast that is besieged down there. It is a muffled snorting; he draws in the air hastily and empties his lungs again the better to scent the fine, keen, far-away, and buried effluvium. How does the creature feel when he hears the snorting? Ah, that is its own affair, or God's, who has made Bashan the enemy of field-mice. Even the emotion of fear is an enhancement of life; and who knows, if there were no Bashan the mouse might find time hang heavy on its hands. Besides, what would be the use of all its beady-eyed cleverness and mining skill, which more than balance what Bashan can do, so that the attacker's success is always more than problematical? In short, I do not feel much pity for the mouse, privately I am on Bashan's side and cannot always stick to my rôle of onlooker. I take my walking-stick and dig out some pebble or gnarled piece of root that is too firmly lodged for him to move. And he sends up a swift, warm glance of understanding to me as he works. With his mouth full of dirt, he chews away at the stubborn earth and the roots running through it, tears out whole chunks and throws them aside, snorts again into his hole and is encouraged by the freshened scent to renew attack on it with his claws.

In nearly every case all this labour is vain. Bashan will give one last cursory look at the scene and then with soil sticking to his nose, and his legs black to the shoulder, he will give it up and trot off indifferently beside me. "No go, Bashan," I say when he looks up at me. "Nothing there," I repeat, shaking my head and shrugging my shoulders to make my meaning clear. But he needs no consolation, he is not in the least depressed by his failure. The chase is the thing, the quarry a minor matter. It was a good effort, he thinks, in so far as he casts his mind back at all to his recent strenuous performance—for already he is bent on a new one, and all three of our zones will furnish him plenty of opportunity.

But sometimes he actually catches the mouse. I have my emotions when that happens, for he gobbles it alive, without compunction, with the fur and the bones. Perhaps the poor little thing was not well enough advised by its instincts, and chose for its hole a place where the earth was too soft and loose and easy to dig. Perhaps its gallery was not long enough and it was too terrified to go on digging, but simply crouched there with its beady eyes popping out of its head for fright, while the horrible snorting came nearer and nearer. And so at last the iron-shod paw laid it bare and scooped it up—out into the light of day, a lost little mouse! It was justified of its fears; luckily these most likely reduced it to a semiconscious state, so that it will hardly have noticed being converted into porridge.

Bashan holds it by the tail and dashes it against the ground, once, twice, thrice; there is the faintest squeak, the very last sound which the god-forsaken little mouse is destined to make on this earth, and now Bashan snaps it up in his jaws, between his strong white teeth. He stands with his forelegs braced apart, his neck bent, and his head stuck out while he chews, shifting the morsel in his mouth and then beginning to munch once more. He crunches the tiny bones, a shred of fur hangs from the corner of his mouth, it disappears and all is over. Bashan begins to execute a dance of joy and triumph round me as I stand leaning on my stick as I have been standing to watch the whole procedure. "You are a fine one!" I say, nodding in grim tribute to his prowess. "You are a murderer, you know, a cannibal!" He only redoubles his activity—he does everything but laugh aloud. So I walk on, feeling rather chilled by what I have seen, yet inwardly amused by the crude humours of life. The event was in the natural order of things, and a mouse lacking in the instinct of self-preservation is on the way to be turned into pulp. But I feel better if I happen not to have assisted the natural order with my stick but to have preserved throughout my attitude of onlooker.

It is startling to have a pheasant burst out of the undergrowth where it was perched asleep or else hoping to be undiscovered, until Bashan's unerring nose ferreted it out. The big, rust-coloured, long-tailed bird rises with a great clapping and flapping and a frightened, angry, cackling cry. It drops its excrement into the brush and takes flight with the absurd headlessness of a chicken to the nearest tree, where it goes on shrieking murder, while Bashan claws at the trunk and barks furiously up at it. "Get up, get up!" he is saying. "Fly away, you silly object of my sporting instincts, that I may chase you!" And the bird cannot resist his loud voice, it rises rustling from the bough and flies on heavy wing through the tree-tops, squawking and complaining, Bashan following below, with ardour, but preserving a stately silence.

This is his joy. He wants and knows no other. For what would happen if he actually caught the pheasant? Nothing at all: I have seen him with one in his claws—he may have stolen upon it while it slept so that the awkward bird could not rise—and he stood over it embarrassed by his triumph, without an idea what to do. The pheasant lay in the grass with its neck and one wing sprawled out and shrieked without stopping—it sounded as though an old woman were being murdered in the bushes, and I hastened up to prevent, if I could, something frightful happening. But I quickly convinced myself that there was no danger. Bashan's obvious helplessness, the half curious, half disgusted look he bent on his capture, with his head on one side, quite reassured me. The old-womanish screaming at his feet got on his nerves, the whole affair made him feel more bothered than triumphant. Perhaps, for his honour as a sportsman, he plucked at the bird—I think I saw him pulling out a couple of feathers with his lips, not using his teeth, and tossing them to one side with an angry shake of the head. But then he moved away and let it go. Not out of magnanimity, but because the affair seemed not to have anything to do with the joyous hunt and so was merely stupid. Never have I seen a more nonplussed bird. It had given itself up for lost, and appeared not to be able to convince itself to the contrary: awhile it lay in the grass as though it were dead. Then it staggered along the ground a little way, fluttered up on a tree, looked like falling off it, but pulled itself together and flew away heavily, with dishevelled plumes. It did not squawk, it kept its bill shut. Without a sound it flew across the park, the river, the woods on the other side, as far away as possible, and certainly it never came back.

But there are plenty of its kind in our hunting-ground and Bashan hunts them in all honour and according to the rules of the game. Eating mice is the only blood-guilt he has on his head and even that is incidental and superfluous. The tracking out, the driving up, the chasing—these are ends in themselves to the sporting spirit, and are plainly so to him, as anybody would see who watched him at his brilliant performance. How beautiful he becomes, how consummate, how ideal! Like a clumsy peasant lad, who will look perfect and statuesque as a huntsman among his native rocks. All that is best in Bashan, all that is genuine and fine, comes out and reaches its flower at these times. Hence his yearning for them, his repining when they fruitlessly slip away. He is no terrier, he is true hunter and pointer, and joy in himself as such speaks in every virile, valiant, native pose he assumes. Not many other things rejoice my eye as does the sight of him going through the brush at a swinging trot, then standing stock-still, with one paw daintily raised and turned in, sagacious, serious, alert, with all his faculties beautifully concentrated. Then suddenly he whimpers. He has trod on a thorn and cries out. Ah, yes, that too is natural, it is amusing to see that he has the courage of his simplicity. It could only passingly mar his dignity, next moment his posture is as fine as ever.

I look at him and recall a time when he lost all his nobility and distinction and reverted to the low physical and moral state in which we found him in the kitchen of that mountain inn and from which he climbed painfully enough to some sort of belief in himself and the world. I do not know what ailed him; he had bleeding from the mouth or nose or throat, I do not know which to this day. Wherever he went he left traces of blood behind: on the grass in our hunting-ground, the straw in his kennel, on the floor in the house—though we could not discover any wound. Sometimes his nose looked as though it had been dipped in red paint. When he sneezed he showered blood all over, and then trod in it and left the marks of his paws about. He was carefully examined without result, and we felt more and more disturbed. Was he tubercular? Or had he some other complaint to which his species was prone? When the mysterious affliction did not pass off after some days, we decided to take him to a veterinary clinic.

Next day at about noon I kindly but firmly adjusted his muzzle, the leather mask which Bashan detests as he does few other things, always trying to get rid of it by shaking his head or rubbing it with his paws. I put him on the plaited leather lead and led him thus harnessed up the poplar avenue, through the English Gardens, and along a city street to the Academy, where we went under the arch and crossed the courtyard. We were received into a waiting-room where several people sat, each holding like me a dog on a lead. They were dogs of all sizes and kinds, gazing dejectedly at each other over their muzzles. There was a matron with her apoplectic pug, a liveried man-servant with a tall, snow-white Russian greyhound, which from time to time gave a hoarse, aristocratic cough; a countryman with a dachshund which seemed to need orthopædic assistance, its legs being entirely crooked and put on all wrong. And many more. The attendant let them in one by one into the consulting-room, and after a while it became the turn of Bashan and me.

The Professor was a man in advanced years, wearing a white surgeon's coat and a gold eye-glass. His hair was curly, and he seemed so mild, expert, and kindly that I would have unhesitatingly entrusted myself and all my family to him in any emergency. During my recital he smiled benevolently at his patient, who sat there looking up at him with equal trustfulness. "He has fine eyes," said he, passing over Bashan's moustaches in silence. He said he would make an examination at once, and poor Bashan, too astounded to offer any resistance, was with the attendant's help stretched out on the table forthwith. And then it was touching to see the physician apply his black stethoscope and auscultate my little man just as I have more than once had it done to me. He listened to his quick-breathing doggish heart, listened to all his organs, in various places. Then with his stethoscope under his arm he examined Bashan's eyes and nose and the cavity of his mouth, and gave a temporary opinion. The dog was a little nervous and anæmic, he said, but otherwise in good condition. The origin of the bleeding was unclear. It might be an epistaxis or a hæmatemesis. But equally well it might be tracheal or pharyngeal hæmorrhage. Perhaps for the present one might characterize it as a case of hæmoptysis. It would be best to keep the animal under careful observation. I might leave it with them and look in at the end of a week.

Thus instructed, I expressed my thanks and took my leave, patting Bashan on the shoulder by way of good-bye. I saw the attendant take the new patient across the courtyard to some back buildings opposite the entrance, Bashan looking back at me with a frightened and bewildered face. And yet he might have felt flattered, as I could not help feeling myself, at having the Professor call him nervous and anæmic. No one could have foretold of him in his cradle that he would one day be called those things or discussed with such gravity and expert knowledge.

But after that my walks abroad were as unseasoned food to the palate; I had little relish of them. No dumb pæan of joy accompanied my going out, no glorious excitement of the chase surrounded my footsteps. The park was a desert, time hung on my hands. During the period of waiting I telephoned several times for news. Answer came through a subordinate that the patient was doing as well as possible under the circumstances—but the circumstances—for better or worse—were never described in more detail. So when the week came round again, I betook myself to the clinic.

Guided by numerous signs and arrows I arrived without difficulty before the entrance of the department where Bashan was lodged, and, warned by another sign on the door, forbore to knock and went straight in. The medium-sized room I found myself in reminded me of a carnivora-house—a similar atmosphere prevailed. Only here the menagerie odour seemed to be kept down by various sweetish-smelling medicinal fumes—a disturbing and oppressive combination. Wire cages ran round the room, most of them occupied. Loud baying greeted me from one of these, at the open door of which a man, who seemed to be the keeper, was busy with rake and shovel. He contented himself with returning my greeting whilst going on with his work, and left me to my own devices.

I had seen Bashan directly I entered the door, and went up to him. He was lying behind his bars on a pile of tan-bark or some such stuff, which contributed its own special odour to the animal and chemical smells in the room. He lay there like a leopard—but a very weary, sluggish, and disgusted leopard. I was startled by the sullen indifference with which he met me. His tail thumped the floor once or twice, weakly; only when I spoke to him did he lift his head from his paws, and even then he let it fall again at once and blinked gloomily to one side. There was an earthenware dish of water at the back of his pen. A framed chart, partly printed and partly written, was fastened to the bars, giving his name, species, sex, and age and showing his temperature curve. "Bastard pointer," it said, "named Bashan. Male. Two years old. Admitted on such and such a day of the month and the year, for observation of occult blood." Underneath followed the fever curve, drawn with a pen and showing small variations; also daily entries of his pulse. Yes, his temperature was taken, and his pulse felt, by a doctor; in this direction everything was being done. But I was distressed about his state of mind.

"Is that one yours?" asked the keeper, who had now come up, his tools in his hands. He had on a sort of gardening apron and was a squat red-faced man with a round beard and rather bloodshot brown eyes that were quite strikingly like a dog's in their humid gaze and faithful expression.

I answered in the affirmative, referred to my telephone conversations and the instructions I had had to come back today, and said I should like to hear how things stood. The man looked at the chart. Yes, the dog was suffering from occult blood, that was always a long business, especially when one did not know where it came from. But was not that always the case? No, they did not really know yet. But the dog was there to be observed, and he would be. And did he still bleed? Yes, now and then he did. And had he fever? I asked, trying to read the chart. No, no fever. His temperature and pulse were quite normal, about ninety beats a minute, he ought to have that much, and if he had not, then they would have to observe him even more carefully. Except for the bleeding, the dog was really doing all right. He had howled at first, of course; he had howled for twenty-four hours, but after that he was used to it. He didn't eat much, for a fact, but then he hadn't much exercise, and perhaps he wasn't a big eater. What did they give him? Soup, said the man. But as he had said, the dog didn't eat much at all. "He seems depressed," I remarked with an assumption of objectivity. Yes, that was true, but it didn't mean much. After all it wasn't very much fun for a dog to lie cooped up like that under observation. They were all depressed, more or less. That is, the good-natured ones, some dogs got mean and treacherous. He could not say that of Bashan. He was a good dog, he would not get mean if he stayed there all his days. I agreed with the man, but I did so with pain and rebellion in my heart. How long then, I asked, did they reckon to keep him here? The man looked at the chart again. Another week, he said, would be needed for the observation, the Herr Professor had said. I'd better come and ask again in another week; that would be two weeks in all, then they would be able to say more about the possibility of getting rid of the hæmorrhages.

I went away, after trying once more to rouse up Bashan by renewed calls and encouragement. In vain. He cared as little for my going as for my coming. He seemed weighed down by bitter loathing and despair. He had the air of saying: "Since you were capable of having me put in this cage, I expect nothing more from you." And, actually, had he not enough ground to despair of reason and justice? What had he done that this should happen to him and that I not only let it happen but took steps to bring it about? And yet my intentions had been of the best. He had bled, and though it seemed to make no difference to him, I thought it sensible that we should call in medical advice, he being a dog in good circumstances. And then we had learned that he was anæmic and nervous—as though he were the daughter of some upper-class family. And then it had to come out like this! How could I explain to him we were treating him with great distinction, in shutting him up like a jaguar, without sun, air, or exercise, and plaguing him every day with a thermometer?

On the way home I asked myself these things; and if before then I had missed Bashan, now worry about him was added to my distress: worry over his state and reproaches to my own address. Perhaps after all I had taken him to the clinic only out of vanity and arrogance. And added to that may I not have secretly wished to get rid of him for a while? Perhaps I had a craving to see what it would be like to be free of his incessant watching of me; to be able to turn calmly to right or left as I pleased, without having to realize that I had been to another living creature the source of joy or of bitter disappointment. Certainly while Bashan was interned I felt a certain inner independence which had long been strange to me. No one exasperated me by looking through the glass door with the air of a martyr. No one put up a hesitating paw to move me to laughter and relenting and persuade me to go out sooner than I wished. Whether I sought the park or kept my room concerned no one at all. It was quiet, pleasant, and had the charm of novelty. But lacking the accustomed spur I hardly went out at all. My health suffered, gradually I approached the condition of Bashan in his cage; and the moral reflection occurred to me that the bonds of sympathy were probably more conducive to my own well-being than the selfish independence for which I had longed.

The second week went by, and on the appointed day I stood with the round-bearded keeper before Bashan's cage. Its inmate lay on his side on the tan-bark, there were bits of it on his coat. He had his head flung back as he lay and was staring with dull, glazed eyes at the bare whitewashed wall. He did not stir. I could scarcely see him breathe; but now and then his chest rose in a long sigh that made the ribs stand out, and fell again with a faint, heart-rending resonance from the vocal cords. His legs seemed to have grown too long, and his paws large out of all proportion, as a result of his extraordinary emaciation. His coat was rough and dishevelled and had, as I said, tan-bark sticking in it. He did not look at me, he seemed not to want to look at anything ever any more.

The bleeding, so the keeper said, had not altogether and entirely disappeared, it came back now and again. Where it came from was still not quite clear; in any case it was harmless. If I liked I could leave the dog here for further observation, to be quite certain, or I could take him home, because the bleeding might disappear just as well there as here. I drew the plaited lead out of my pocket—I had brought it with me—and said that I would take him with me. The keeper thought that was a sensible thing to do. He opened the grating and we summoned Bashan by name, both together and in turn, but he did not come, he kept on staring at the whitewashed wall. But he did not struggle when I put my arm into the cage and pulled him out by the collar. He gave a spring and landed with his four feet on the floor, where he stood with his tail between his legs and his ears laid back, the picture of wretchedness. I picked him up, tipped the keeper, and went to the front office to pay my debt; at the rate of seventy-five pfennigs a day plus the medical examination it came to twelve marks fifty. I led Bashan home, breathing the animal-chemical odours which clung to his coat.

He was broken, in body and in spirit. Animals are more primitive and less inhibited in giving expression to their mental state—there is a sense in which one might say they are more human: descriptive phrases which to us have become mere metaphor still fit them literally, we get a fresh and diverting sense of their meaning when we see it embodied before our eyes. Bashan, as we say, "hung his head"; that is, he did it literally and visibly, till he looked like a worn-out cab-horse, with sores on its legs, standing at the cab-rank, its skin twitching and its poor fly-infested nose weighed down towards the pavement. It was as I have said: those two weeks at the clinic had reduced him to the state he had been in at the beginning. He was the shadow of his former self—if that does not insult the proud and joyous shadow our Bashan once cast. The hospital smell he had brought with him wore off after repeated soapy baths till you got only an occasional whiff; but it was not with him as with human beings: he got no symbolic refreshment from the physical cleansing. The very first day, I took him out to our hunting-grounds, but he followed at my heel with his tongue lolling out; even the pheasants perceived that it was the close season. For days he lay as he had lain in his cage at the clinic, staring with glazed eyes, flabby without and within. He showed no healthy impatience for the chase, did not urge me to go out—indeed it was rather I who had to go and fetch him from his kennel. Even the reckless and indiscriminate way he wolfed his food recalled those early unworthy days. But what a joy to see him slowly finding himself again! Little by little he began to greet me in the morning in his old naïve, impetuous way, storming upon me at my first whistle instead of limping morosely up; putting his fore-paws on my chest and snapping playfully at my face. Gradually there returned to him his old out-of-doors pride and joy in his own physical prowess; once more he delighted my eyes with the bold and beautiful poses he took, the sudden bounds with his feet drawn up, after some creature stirring in the long grass. . . . He forgot. The ugly and to Bashan senseless episode sank into the past, unresolved indeed, unclarified by comprehension, that being of course impossible; it was covered by the lapse of time, as must happen sometimes to human beings. We went on living and what had not been expressed became by degrees forgotten. . . . For several weeks, at lengthening intervals, Bashan's nose showed red. Then the phenomenon disappeared, it was no more, it only had been, and so it was no matter whether it had been an epistaxis or a hæmatemesis.

Well, there! Contrary to my own intentions, I have told the story of the clinic. Perhaps my reader will forgive the lengthy digression and come back to the park and the pleasures of the chase, where we were before the interruption. Do you know that long-drawn wailing howl to which a dog gives vent when he summons up his utmost powers to give chase to a flying hare? In it rage and rapture mingle, desire and the ecstasy of despair. How often have I heard it from Bashan! It is passion itself, deliberate, fostered passion, drunkenly revelled in, shrilling through our woodland scene, and every time I hear it near or far a fearful thrill of pleasure shoots through my limbs. Rejoiced that Bashan will come into his own today, I hasten to his side, to see the chase if I can; when it roars past me I stand spellbound—though the futility of it is clear from the first—and look on with an agitated smile on my face.

And the hare, the common, frightened little hare? The air whistles through its ears, it lays back its head and runs for its life, it scrabbles and bounds with Bashan behind it yelling all he can; its yellow-white scut flies up in the air. And yet at the bottom of its soul, timid as that is and acquainted with fear, it must know that its peril cannot be grave, that it will get away, as its brothers and sisters have done before it, and itself too under like circumstances. Never in his life has Bashan caught one of them, nor will he ever; the thing is as good as impossible. Many dogs, they say, are the death of a hare, a single dog cannot achieve it, even one much speedier and more enduring than Bashan. The hare can "double" and Bashan cannot—and that is all there is to it. For the double is the unfailing natural weapon of those born to seek safety in flight; they always have it by them, to use at the decisive moment; when Bashan's hopes are highest—then they are dashed to the ground, and he is betrayed.

There they come, dashing diagonally through the brush, across the path in front of me, and on towards the river; the hare silently hugging his little trick in his heart, Bashan giving tongue in high head-tones. "Be quiet!" I think. "You are wasting your wind and your lung-power and you ought to save them if you want to catch him up." Thus I think because in my heart I am on Bashan's side, some of his fire has kindled me, I fervently hope he may catch the hare—even at the risk of seeing it torn to shreds before my eyes. How he runs! It is beautiful to see a creature expending the utmost of its powers. He runs better than the hare does, he has stronger muscles, the distance between them visibly diminishes before I lose sight of them. And I make haste too, leaving the path and cutting across the park towards the river-bank, reaching the gravelled street in time to see the chase come raging on—the hopeful, thrilling chase, with Bashan on the hare's very heels; he is still, he runs with his jaw set, the scent just in front of his nose urges him to a final effort.—"One more push, Bashan!" I think, and feel like shouting: "Well run, old chap, remember the double!" But there it is; Bashan does make one more push, and the misfortune is upon us: at that moment the hare gives a quick, easy, almost malicious twitch at right angles to the course, and Bashan shoots past from his rear, howling helplessly and braking his very best so that dirt and pebbles fly into the air. Before he can stop, turn round, and get going in the other direction, yelling all the time as in great mental torment, the hare has gained so much ground that it is out of sight; for while he was braking so desperately Bashan could not watch where it went.

It is no use, I think; it is beautiful but futile; this while the chase fades away through the park. It takes a lot of dogs, five or six, a whole pack. Some of them to take it on the flank, some to cut off its way in front, some to corner it, some to catch it by the neck. And in my excited fancy I see a whole pack of bloodhounds with their tongues out rushing on the hare in their midst.

It is my passion for the chase makes me have these fancies, for what has the hare done to me that I should wish him such a horrible death? Bashan is nearer to me, of course, it is natural that I should feel with him and wish for his success. But the hare is after all a living creature too, and he did not play his trick on my huntsman out of malice, but only from the compelling desire to live yet awhile, nibble young tree-shoots, and beget his kind. It would be different, I go on in my mind, if this cane of mine—I lift it and look at it—were not a harmless stick, but a more serious weapon, effective like lightning and at a distance, with which I could come to Bashan's assistance and hold up the hare in mid career, so that it would turn a somersault and lie dead on the ground. Then we should not need another dog, and it would be Bashan's only task to rouse the game. Whereas as things stand it is Bashan who sometimes rolls over and over in his effort to brake. The hare sometimes does too, but it is nothing to it, it is used to such things, they do not make it feel miserable, whereas it is a shattering experience for Bashan, and might even quite possibly break his neck.

Often such a chase is all over in a few minutes; that is, when the hare succeeds after a short length in ducking into the bushes and hiding, or else by doubling and feinting in throwing off its pursuer, who stands still, hesitating, or makes short springs in this and that direction, while I in my bloodthirstiness shout encouragement and try to show him with my stick the direction the hare took. But often the hunt sways far and wide across the landscape and Bashan's furious baying sounds like a distant bugle-horn, now near, now remote; I go my own way, knowing that he will return. But in what a state he does return, at last! Foam drips from his lips, his ribs flutter, and his loins are lank and expanded, his tongue lolls out of his jaws, which yawn so wide as to distort his features and give his drunken, swimming eyes a weird Mongolian slant. His breath goes like a trip-hammer. "Lie down and rest, Bashan," say I, "or your lungs will burst!" and I wait to give him time to recover. I am alarmed for him when it is cold, when he pumps the air by gasps into his overheated insides and it gushes out again in a white steam; when he swallows whole mouthfuls of snow to quench his furious thirst. He lies there looking helplessly up at me, now and then licking up the slaver from his lips, and I cannot help teasing him a bit about the invariable futility of all his exertions. "Where is the hare, Bashan?" I ask. "Why don't you bring it to me?" He thumps with his tail on the ground when I speak; his sides pump in and out less feverishly, and he gives a rather embarrassed snap—for how can he know that I am mocking him because I feel guilty myself and want to conceal it? For I did not play my part in his enterprise, I was not man enough to hold the hare, as a proper master should have done. He does not know this, and so I can make fun of him and behave as though it were all his fault.

Strange things sometimes happen on these occasions. Never shall I forget the day when the hare ran into my arms. It was on the narrow clayey path above the river. Bashan was in full cry; I came from the wood into the river zone, struck across through the thistles of the gravelly waste, and jumped down the grassy slope to the path just in time to see the hare, with Bashan fifteen paces behind it, come bounding from the direction of the ferry-house towards which I was facing. It leaped right into the path and came towards me. My first impulse was that of the hunter towards his prey: to take advantage of the situation and cut off its escape, driving it back if possible into the jaws of the pursuer joyously yelping behind. I stood fixed to the spot, quite abandoned to the fury of the chase, weighing my cane in my hand as the hare came towards me. A hare's sight is poor, that I knew; hearing and smell are the senses that guide and preserve it. It might have taken me for a tree as I stood there; I hoped and foresaw it would do so and thus fall victim to a frightful error, the possible consequences of which were not very clear to me, though I meant to turn them to our advantage. Whether it did at any time make this mistake is unclear. I think it did not see me at all until the last minute, and what it did was so unexpected as to upset all my plans in a trice and cause a complete and sudden revulsion in my feelings. Was it beside itself with fright? Anyhow, it jumped straight at me, like a dog, ran up my overcoat with its fore-paws and snuggled its head into me, me whom it should most fear, the master of the chase! I stood bent back with my arms raised, I looked down at the hare and it looked up at me. It was only a second, perhaps only part of a second, that this lasted. I saw the hare with such extraordinary distinctness, its long ears, one of which stood up, the other hung down; its large, bright, short-sighted, prominent eyes, its cleft lip and the long hairs of its moustache, the white on its breast and little paws; I felt or thought I felt the throbbing of its hunted heart. And it was strange to see it so clearly and have it so close to me, the little genius of the place, the inmost beating heart of our whole region, this everfleeing little being which I had never seen but for brief moments in our meadows and bottoms, frantically and drolly getting out of the way—and now, in its hour of need, not knowing where to turn, it came to me, it clasped as it were my knees, a human being's knees: not the knees, so it seemed to me, of Bashan's master, but the knees of a man who felt himself master of hares and this hare's master as well as Bashan's. It was, I say, only for the smallest second. Then the hare had dropped off, taken again to its uneven legs, and bounded up the slope on my left; while in its place there was Bashan, Bashan giving tongue in all the horrid head-tones of his hue-and-cry. When he got within reach he was abruptly checked by a deliberate and well-aimed blow from the stick of the hare's master, which sent him yelping down the slope with a temporarily disabled hind quarter. He had to limp painfully back again before he could take up the trail of his by this time vanished prey.

Finally, there are the waterfowl, to our pursuit of which I must devote a few lines. We can only go after them in winter and early spring, before they leave their town quarters—where they stay for their food's sake, and return to their lakes in the mountains. They furnish, of course, much less exciting sport than can be got out of the hares; still, it has its attractions for hunter and hound—or, rather, for the hunter and his master. For me the charm lies in the scenery, the intimate bond with living water; also it is amusing and diverting to watch the creatures swimming and flying and try provisionally to exchange one's personality for theirs and enter into their mode of life.

The ducks lead a quieter, more comfortable, more bourgeois life than do the gulls. They seem to have enough to eat, on the whole, and not to be tormented by the pangs of hunger—their kind of food is regularly to be had, the table, so to speak, always laid. For everything is fish that comes to their net: worms, snails, insects—even the ooze of the river-bed. So they have plenty of time to sit on the stones in the sun, doze with their bills tucked under one wing, and preen their well-oiled plumes, off which the water rolls in drops. Sometimes they take a pleasure-ride on the waves, with their pointed rumps in the air; paddling this way and that and giving little self-satisfied shrugs.

But the nature of gulls is wilder and more strident; there is a dreary monotony about what they do, they are the eternally hungry bird of prey, swooping all day long in hordes across the waterfall, croaking about the drain-pipes that disgorge their brown streams into the river. Single gulls hover and pounce down upon a fish now and then, but this does not go far to satisfy their inordinate mass hunger; they have to fill in with most unappetizing-looking morsels from the drains, snatching them from the water in flight and carrying them off in their crooked beaks. They do not like the river-bank. But when the river is low, they huddle together on the rocks that stick out of the water—the scene is white with them, as the cliffs and islets of northern oceans are white with hosts of nesting eider-duck. I like to watch them rise all together with a great cawing and take to the air, when Bashan barks at them from the bank, across the intervening stream. They need not be frightened, certainly they are in no danger. He has a native aversion to water; but aside from that he would never trust himself to the current, and he is quite right, it is much stronger than he and would soon sweep him away and carry him God knows where. Perhaps into the Danube—but he would only arrive there after having suffered a river-change of a very drastic kind, as we know from seeing the bloated corpses of cats on their way to some distant bourne. Bashan never goes further into the water than the point where it begins to break over the stones. Even when he seems most tense with the pleasure of the chase and looks exactly as though he meant to jump in the very next minute, one knows that under all the excitement his sense of caution is alert and that the dashings and rushings are pure theatre—empty threats, not so much dictated by passion as cold-bloodedly undertaken in order to terrify the web-footed tribe.

But the gulls are too witless and poor-spirited to make light of his performance. He cannot get to them himself, but he sends his voice thundering across the water; it reaches them, and it, too, has actuality; it is an attack which they cannot long resist. They try to at first, they sit still, but a wave of uneasiness goes through the host, they turn their heads, a few lift their wings, and suddenly they all rush up into the air, like a white cloud, whence issue the bitterest, most fatalistic screams, Bashan springing hither and thither on the rocks, to scatter their flight and keep them in motion, for it is motion that he wants, they are not to sit quiet, they must fly, fly up and down the river so that he may chase them.

He scampers along the shore far and wide, for everywhere there are ducks, sitting with their bills tucked in homely comfort under their wings; and wherever he comes they fly up before him. He is like a jolly little hurricane making a clean sweep of the beach. Then they plump down on the water again, where they rock and ride in comfort and safety, or else they fly away over his head with their necks stretched out, while below on the shore he measures the strength of his leg-muscles quite creditably against those of their wings.

He is enchanted, and really grateful to them if they will only fly and give him occasion for this glorious race up and down the beach. It may be that they know what he wants and turn the fact to their own advantage. I saw a mother duck with her brood—this was in spring, all the birds had forsaken the river and only this one was left with her fledglings, not yet able to fly. She had them in a stagnant puddle left by the last flood in the low-lying bed of the shrunken river, and there Bashan found them, while I watched the event from the upper path. He jumped into the puddle and lashed about, furiously barking, driving the family of ducklings into wild disorder. He did them no harm, of course, but he frightened them beyond measure; the ducklings flapped their stumps of wings and scattered in all directions, and the duck was overtaken by an attack of the maternal heroism which will hurl itself blind with valour upon the fiercest foe to protect her brood; more, will even by a frenzied and unnatural display of intrepidity bully the attacker into surrender. She opened her beak to a horrific extent, she ruffled up her feathers, she flew repeatedly into Bashan's face, she made onslaught after onslaught, hissing all the while. The grim seriousness of her behaviour was so convincing that Bashan actually gave ground in confusion, though without definitely retiring from the field, for each time after retreating he would bark and advance anew. Then the mother duck changed her tactics: heroics having failed, she took refuge in strategy. Probably she knew Bashan already and was aware of his foibles and the childish nature of his desires. She left her children in the lurch—or she pretended to; she took to flight, she flew up above the river, "pursued" by Bashan. At least, he thought he was pursuing her, in reality it was she who was leading him on, playing on his childish passion, leading him by the nose. She flew downstream, then upstream, she flew further and further away, Bashan racing equal with her along the bank; they left the pool with the ducklings far behind, and at length both dog and duck disappeared from my sight. Bashan came back to me after a while; the simpleton was quite winded and panting for dear life. But when we passed the pool again on our homeward way, it was empty of its brood.

So much for the mother duck. As for Bashan, he was quite grateful for the sport she had given him. For he hates the ducks who selfishly prefer their bourgeois comfort and refuse to play his game with him, simply gliding off into the water when he comes rushing along, and rocking there in base security before his face and eyes, heedless of his mighty barkings, heedless too—unlike the nervous gulls—of all his feints and plungings. We stand there, Bashan and I, on the stones at the water's edge, and two paces away a duck floats on the wave, floats impudently up and down, her beak pressed coyly against her breast; safe and untouched and sweetly reasonable she bobs up and down out there, let Bashan rave as he will. Paddling against the current, she keeps abreast of us fairly well; yet she is being slowly carried down, closer and closer to one of those beautiful foaming eddies in the stream. In her folly she rides with her tail turned towards it—and now it is only a yard away. Bashan loudly gives tongue, standing with his forelegs braced against the stones; and in my heart I am barking with him, I am on his side and against that impudent, self-satisfied floating thing out there. I wish her ill. Pay attention to our barking, I address her mentally; do not hear the whirlpool roar—and then presently you will find yourself in an unpleasant and undignified situation and I shall be glad! But my malicious hopes are not fulfilled. For at the rapid's very edge she flutters up into the air, flies a few yards upstream, and then, oh, shameless hussy, settles down again.

I recall the feelings of baffled anger with which we looked at that duck—and I am reminded of another occasion, another and final episode in this tale of our hunting-ground. It was attended by a certain satisfaction for my companion and me, but had its painful and disturbing side as well; yes, it even gave rise to some coolness between us, and if I could have foreseen it I would have avoided the spot where it took place.

It was a long way out, beyond the ferry-house, downstream, where the wilds that border the river approach the upper road along the shore. We were going along this, I at an easy pace, Bashan in front with his easy, lop-sided lope. He had roused a hare—or, if you like, it had roused him—had stirred up four pheasants, and now was minded to give his master a little attention. A small bevy of ducks were flying above the river, in v-formation, their necks stretched out. They flew rather high and closer to the other shore, so that they were out of our reach as game, but moving in the same direction as ourselves. They paid no attention to us and we only cast casual glances at them now and then.

Then it happened that opposite to us on the other bank, which like ours was steep here, a man struck out of the bushes, and directly he appeared upon the scene he took up a position which fixed our attention, Bashan's no less than mine, upon him at once. We stopped in our tracks and faced him. He was a fine figure of a man, though rather rough-looking; with drooping moustaches, wearing puttees, a frieze hat cocked down over his forehead, wide velveteen trousers and jerkin to match, over which hung numerous leather straps, for he had a rucksack slung on his back and a gun over his shoulder. Or rather he had had it over his shoulder; for he no sooner appeared than he took it in his hand, laid his cheek along the butt, and aimed it diagonally upwards at the sky. He took a step forwards with one putteed leg, the gun-barrel rested in the hollow of his left hand, with the arm stretched out and the elbow against his side. The other elbow, with the hand on the trigger, stuck out at his side, and we could see his bold, foreshortened face quite clearly as he sighted upwards. It looked somehow very theatrical, this figure standing out above the boulders on the bank, against a background of shrubbery, river, and open sky. But we could have gazed for only a moment when the dull sound of the explosion made me start, I had waited for it with such inward tension.

There was a tiny flash at the same time; it looked pale in the broad daylight; a puff of smoke followed. The man took one slumping pace forwards, like an operatic star, with his face and chest lifted towards the sky, his gun hanging from the strap in his right fist. Something was going on up there where he was looking and where we now looked too. There was a great confusion and scattering, the ducks flew in all directions wildly flapping their wings with a noise like wind in the sails, they tried to volplane down—then suddenly a body fell like a stone onto the water near the other shore.

This was only the first half of the action. But I must interrupt my narrative here to turn the vivid light of my memory upon the figure of Bashan. I can think of large words with which to describe it, phrases we use for great occasions: I could say that he was thunderstruck. But I do not like them, I do not want to use them. The large words are worn out, when the great occasion comes they do not describe it. Better use the small ones and put into them every ounce of their weight. I will simply say that when Bashan heard the explosion, saw its meaning and consequence, he started; and it was the same start which I have seen him give a thousand times when something surprises him, only raised to the *n*th degree. It was a start which flung his whole body backwards with a right-and-left motion, so sudden that it jerked his head against his chest and almost bounced it off his shoulders with the shock; a start which made his whole body seem to be crying out: What! What! What was that? Wait a minute, in the devil's name! *What was that?* He looked and listened with that sort of rage in which extreme astonishment expresses itself; listened within himself and heard things that had always been there, however novel and unheard-of the present form they took. Yes, from this start, which flung him to right and left and halfway round on his axis, I got the impression that he was trying to look at himself, trying to ask: What am I? Who am I? Is this me? At the moment when the duck's body plopped on the water he bounded forwards to the edge of the bank, as though he were going to jump down to the river-bed and plunge in. But he bethought himself of the current and checked his impulse; then, rather shamefaced, devoted himself to staring, as before.

I looked at him, somewhat disturbed. After the duck had fallen I felt that we had had enough and suggested that we go on our way. But he had sat down on his haunches, facing the other shore, his ears erected as high as they would go. When I said: "Well, Bashan, shall we go on?" he turned his head only the briefest second as though saying, with some annoyance: Please don't disturb me! And kept on looking. So I resigned myself, crossed my legs, leaned on my cane, and watched to see what would happen.

The duck—no doubt one of those that had rocked in such pert security on the water in front of our noses—went driving like a wreck on the water, you could not tell which was head and which tail. The river is quieter at this point, its rapids are not so swift as they are further up. But even so, the body was seized by the current, whirled round, and swept away. If the man was not concerned only with sport but had a practical goal in view, then he would better act quickly. And so he did, not losing a moment—it all went very fast. Even as the duck fell he had rushed forward stumbling and almost falling down the slope, with his gun held out at arm's length. Again I was struck with the picturesqueness of the sight, as he came down the slope like a robber or smuggler in a melodrama, in the highly effective scenery of boulder and bush. He held somewhat leftwards, allowing for the current, for the duck was drifting away and he had to head it off. This he did successfully, stretching out the butt end of the gun and bending forward with his feet in the water. Carefully and painstakingly he piloted the duck towards the stones and drew it to shore.

The job was done, the man drew a long breath. He put down his weapon against the bank, took his knapsack from his shoulders, and stuffed the duck inside; buckled it on again, and thus satisfactorily laden and using his gun as a stick, he clambered over the boulders and up the slope.

"Well, he got his Sunday joint," thought I, half enviously, half approvingly. "Come, Bashan, let's go now, it's all over." Bashan got up and turned round on himself, but then he sat down again and looked after the man, even after he had left the scene and disappeared among the bushes. It did not occur to me to ask him twice. He knew where we lived, and he might sit here goggling, after it was all over, as long as he thought well. It was quite a long walk home and I meant to be stirring. So then he came.

He kept beside me on our whole painful homeward way, and did not hunt. Nor did he run diagonally a little ahead, as he does as a rule when not in a hunting mood; he kept behind me, at a jog-trot, and put on a sour face, as I could see when I happened to turn round. I could have borne with that and should not have dreamed of being drawn; I was rather inclined to laugh and shrug my shoulders. But every thirty or forty paces he *yawned*—and that I could not stand. It was that impudent gape of his, expressing the extreme of boredom, accompanied by a throaty little whine which seems to say: Fine master I've got! No master at all! Rotten master, if you ask me!—I am always sensitive to the insulting sound, and this time it was almost enough to shake our friendship to its foundations.

"Go away!" said I. "Get out with you! Go to your new friend with the blunderbuss and attach yourself to him! He does not seem to have a dog, perhaps he could use you in his business. He is only a man in velveteens, to be sure, not a gentleman, but in your eyes he may be one; perhaps he is the right master for you, and I honestly recommend you to suck up to him—now that he has put a flea in your ear to go with your others." (Yes, I actually said that!) "We'll not ask if he has a hunting-licence, or if you won't both get into fine trouble some day at your dirty game—that is your affair, and, as I tell you, my advice is perfectly sincere. You think so much of yourself as a hunter! Did you ever bring me a hare of all those I let you chase? Is it my fault that you do not know how to double, but must come down with your nose in the gravel at the moment when agility is required? Or a pheasant, which in these lean times would be equally welcome? And now you yawn! Get along, I tell you. Go to your master with the puttees and see if he knows how to scratch your neck and make you laugh. I'll wager he does not know how to laugh a decent laugh himself. Do you think he is likely to have you put under scientific observation when you decide to suffer from occult blood, or that when you are his dog you will be pronounced nervous and anæmic? If you do, then you'd better get along. But you may be overestimating the respect which that kind of master would have for you. There are certain distinctions—that kind of man with a gun is very keen on them: native advantages or disadvantages, to make my meaning clearer, troublesome questions of pedigree and breeding, if I must be plain. Not everybody passes these over on grounds of humanity and fine feeling; and if your wonderful master reproaches you with your moustaches the first time you and he have a difference of opinion, then you may remember me and what I am telling you now."

With such biting words did I address Bashan as he slunk behind me on our way home. And though I did not utter but only thought them, for I did not care to look as though I were mad, yet I am convinced that he got my meaning perfectly, at least in its main lines. In short, it was a serious quarrel, and when we got home I deliberately let the gate latch behind me so that he could not slip through and had to climb over the fence. I went into the house without even looking round, and shrugged my shoulders when I heard him yelp because he scratched his belly on the rail.

But all that is long ago, more than six months. Now, like our little clinical episode, it has dropped into the past. Time and forgetfulness have buried it, and on their alluvial deposit where all life lives, we too live on. For a few days Bashan appeared to mope. But long ago he recovered all his joy in the chase, in mice and moles and pheasant, hares and waterfowl. When we return home, at once begins his period of waiting for the next time. I stand at the house door and turn towards him; upon that signal he bounds in two great leaps up the steps and braces his fore-paws against the door, reaching as far up as he can that I may pat him on the shoulder. "Tomorrow, Bashan," say I; "that is, if I am not obliged to pay a visit to the outer world." Then I hasten inside, to take off my hobnailed boots, for the soup stands waiting on the table.

1918

THE BLOOD OF THE WALSUNGS

It was seven minutes to twelve. Wendelin came into the first-floor entrance-hall and sounded the gong. He straddled in his violet knee-breeches on a prayer-rug pale with age and belaboured with his drumstick the metal disk. The brazen din, savage and primitive out of all proportion to its purport, resounded through the drawing-rooms to left and right, the billiard-room, the library, the winter-garden, up and down through the house; it vibrated through the warm and even atmosphere, heavy with exotic perfume. At last the sound ceased, and for another seven minutes Wendelin went about his business while Florian in the dining-room gave the last touches to the table. But on the stroke of twelve the cannibalistic summons sounded a second time. And the family appeared.

Herr Aarenhold came in his little toddle out of the library where he had been busy with his old editions. He was continually acquiring old books, first editions, in many languages, costly and crumbling trifles. Gently rubbing his hands he asked in his slightly plaintive way:

"Beckerath not here yet?"

"No, but he will be. Why shouldn't he? He will be saving a meal in a restaurant," answered Frau Aarenhold, coming noiselessly up the thick-carpeted stairs, on the landing of which stood a small, very ancient church organ.

Herr Aarenhold blinked. His wife was impossible. She was small, ugly, prematurely aged, and shrivelled as though by tropic suns. A necklace of brilliants rested upon her shrunken breast. She wore her hair in complicated twists and knots to form a lofty pile, in which, somewhere on one side, sat a great jewelled brooch, adorned in its turn with a bunch of white aigrettes. Herr Aarenhold and the children had more than once, as diplomatically as possible, advised against this style of coiffure. But Frau Aarenhold clung stoutly to her own taste.

The children came: Kunz and Märit, Siegmund and Sieglinde. Kunz was in a braided uniform, a stunning tanned creature with curling lips and a killing scar. He was doing six weeks' service with his regiment of hussars. Märit made her appearance in an uncorseted garment. She was an ashen, austere blonde of twenty-eight, with a hooked nose, grey eyes like a falcon's, and a bitter, contemptuous mouth. She was studying law and went entirely her own way in life.

Siegmund and Sieglinde came last, hand in hand, from the second floor. They were twins, graceful as young fawns, and with immature figures despite their nineteen years. She wore a Florentine cinquecento frock of claret-coloured velvet, too heavy for her slight body. Siegmund had on a green jacket suit with a tie of raspberry shantung, patent-leather shoes on his narrow feet, and cuff-buttons set with small diamonds. He had a strong growth of black beard but kept it so close-shaven that his sallow face with the heavy gathered brows looked no less boyish than his figure. His head was covered with thick black locks parted far down on one side and growing low on his temples. Her dark brown hair was waved in long, smooth undulations over her ears, confined by a gold circlet. A large pearl—his gift—hung down upon her brow. Round one of his boyish wrists was a heavy gold chain—a gift from her. They were very like each other, with the same slightly drooping nose, the same full lips lying softly together, the same prominent cheek-bones and black, bright eyes. Likest of all were their long slim hands, his no more masculine than hers, save that they were slightly redder. And they went always hand in hand, heedless that the hands of both inclined to moisture.

The family stood about awhile in the lobby, scarcely speaking.

Then Beckerath appeared. He was engaged to Sieglinde. Wendelin opened the door to him and as he entered in his black frock-coat he excused himself for his tardiness. He was a government official and came of a good family. He was short of stature, with a pointed beard and a very yellow complexion, like a canary. His manners were punctilious. He began every sentence by drawing his breath in quickly through his mouth and pressing his chin on his chest.

He kissed Sieglinde's hand and said:

"And you must excuse me too, Sieglinde—it is so far from the Ministry to the Zoo—"

He was not allowed to say thou to her—she did not like it. She answered briskly:

"Very far. Supposing that, in consideration of the fact, you left your office a bit earlier."

Kunz seconded her, his black eyes narrowing to glittering cracks:

"It would no doubt have a most beneficial effect upon our household economy."

"Oh, well—business, you know what it is," von Beckerath said dully. He was thirty-five years old.

The brother and sister had spoken glibly and with point. They may have attacked out of a habitual inward posture of self-defence; perhaps they deliberately meant to wound—perhaps again their words were due to the sheer pleasure of turning a phrase. It would have been unreasonable to feel annoyed. They let his feeble answer pass, as though they found it in character; as though cleverness in him would have been out of place. They went to table; Herr Aarenhold led the way, eager to let von Beckerath see that he was hungry.

They sat down, they unfolded their stiff table-napkins. The immense room was carpeted, the walls were covered with eighteenth-century panelling, and three electric lustres hung from the ceiling. The family table, with its seven places, was lost in the void. It was drawn up close to the large French window, beneath which a dainty little fountain spread its silver spray behind a low lattice. Outside was an extended view of the still wintry garden. Tapestries with pastoral scenes covered the upper part of the walls; they, like the panelling, had been part of the furnishings of a French château. The dining-chairs were low and soft and cushioned with tapestry. A tapering glass vase holding two orchids stood at each place, on the glistening, spotless, faultlessly ironed damask cloth. With careful, skinny hands Herr Aarenhold settled the pince-nez half-way down his nose and with a mistrustful air read the menu, three copies of which lay on the table. He suffered from a weakness of the solar plexus, that nerve centre which lies at the pit of the stomach and may give rise to serious distress. He was obliged to be very careful what he ate.

There was bouillon with beef marrow, sole *au vin blanc,* pheasant, and pineapple.

Nothing else. It was a simple family meal. But it satisfied Herr Aarenhold. It was good, light, nourishing food. The soup was served: a dumb-waiter above the sideboard brought it noiselessly down from the kitchen and the servants handed it round, bending over assiduously, in a very passion of service. The tiny cups were of translucent porcelain, whitish morsels of marrow floated in the hot golden liquid.

Herr Aarenhold felt himself moved to expand a little in the comfortable warmth thus purveyed. He carried his napkin cautiously to his mouth and cast after a means of clothing his thought in words.

"Have another cup, Beckerath," said he. "A working-man has a right to his comforts and his pleasures. Do you really like to eat—really enjoy it, I mean? If not, so much the worse for you. To me every meal is a little celebration. Somebody said that life is pretty nice after all—being arranged so that we can eat four times a day. He's my man! But to do justice to the arrangement one has to preserve one's youthful receptivity—and not everybody can do that. We get old—well, we can't help it. But the thing is to keep things fresh and not get used to them. For instance," he went on, putting a bit of marrow on a piece of roll and sprinkling salt on it, "you are about to change your estate, the plane on which you live is going to be a good deal elevated" (von Beckerath smiled), "and if you want to enjoy your new life, really enjoy it, consciously and artistically, you must take care never to get used to your new situation. Getting used to things is death. It is ennui. Don't give in to it, don't let anything become a matter of course, preserve a childlike taste for the sweets of life. You see . . . for some years now I have been able to command some of the amenities of life" (von Beckerath smiled), "and yet I assure you, every morning that God lets me wake up I have a little thrill because my bed-cover is made of silk. That is what it is to be young. I know perfectly well how I did it; and yet I can look round me and feel like an enchanted prince."

The children exchanged looks, so openly that Herr Aarenhold could not help seeing it; he became visibly embarrassed. He knew that they were united against him, that they despised him: for his origins, for the blood which flowed in his veins and through him in theirs; for the way he had earned his money; for his fads, which in their eyes were unbecoming: for his valetudinarianism, which they found equally annoying; for his weak and whimsical loquacity, which in their eyes traversed the bounds of good taste. He knew all this—and in a way conceded that they were right. But after all he had to assert his personality, he had to lead his own life; and above all he had to be able to talk about it. That was only fair—he had proved that it was worth talking about. He had been a worm, a louse if you like. But just his capacity to realize it so fully, with such vivid self-contempt, had become the ground of that persistent, painful, never-satisfied striving which had made him great. Herr Aarenhold had been born in a remote village in East Prussia, had married the daughter of a well-to-do tradesman, and by means of a bold and shrewd enterprise, of large-scale schemings which had as their object a new and productive coal-bed, he had diverted a large and inexhaustible stream of gold into his coffers.

The fish course came on. The servants hurried with it from the sideboard through the length of the room. They handed round with it a creamy sauce and poured out a Rhine wine that prickled on the tongue. The conversation turned to the approaching wedding.

It was very near, it was to take place in the following week. They talked about the dowry, about plans for the wedding journey to Spain. Actually it was only Herr Aarenhold who talked about them, supported by von Beckerath's polite acquiescence. Frau Aarenhold ate greedily, and as usual contributed nothing to the conversation save some rather pointless questions. Her speech was interlarded with guttural words and phrases from the dialect of her childhood days. Märit was full of silent opposition to the church ceremony which they planned to have; it affronted her highly enlightened convictions. Herr Aarenhold also was privately opposed to the ceremony. Von Beckerath was a Protestant and in Herr Aarenhold's view Protestant ceremonial was without any æsthetic value. It would be different if von Beckerath belonged to the Roman confession. Kunz said nothing, because when von Beckerath was present he always felt annoyed with his mother. And neither Siegmund nor Sieglinde displayed any interest. They held each other's narrow hands between their chairs. Sometimes their gaze sought each other's, melting together in an understanding from which everybody else was shut out. Von Beckerath sat next to Sieglinde on the other side.

"Fifty hours," said Herr Aarenhold, "and you are in Madrid, if you like. That is progress. It took me sixty by the shortest way. I assume that you prefer the train to the sea route via Rotterdam?"

Von Beckerath hastily expressed his preference for the overland route.

"But you won't leave Paris out. Of course, you could go direct to Lyons. And Sieglinde knows Paris. But you should not neglect the opportunity . . . I leave it to you whether or not to stop before that. The choice of the place where the honeymoon begins should certainly be left to you."

Sieglinde turned her head, turned it for the first time towards her betrothed, quite openly and unembarrassed, careless of the lookers-on. For quite three seconds she bent upon the courteous face beside her the wide-eyed, questioning, expectant gaze of her sparkling black eyes—a gaze as vacant of thoughts as any animal's. Between their chairs she was holding the slender hand of her twin; and Siegmund drew his brows together till they formed two black folds at the base of his nose.

The conversation veered and tacked to and fro. They talked of a consignment of cigars which had just come by Herr Aarenhold's order from Havana, packed in zinc. Then it circled round a point of purely abstract interest, brought up by Kunz: namely, whether, if *a* were the necessary and sufficient condition for *b, b* must also be the necessary and sufficient condition for *a*. They argued the matter, they analysed it with great ingenuity, they gave examples; they talked nineteen to the dozen, attacked each other with steely and abstract dialectic, and got no little heated. Märit had introduced a philosophical distinction, that between the actual and the causal principle. Kunz told her, with his nose in the air, that "causal principle" was a pleonasm. Märit, in some annoyance, insisted upon her terminology. Herr Aarenhold straightened himself, with a bit of bread between thumb and forefinger, and prepared to elucidate the whole matter. He suffered a complete rout, the children joined forces to laugh him down. Even his wife jeered at him. "What are you talking about?" she said. "Where did you learn that—you didn't learn much!" Von Beckerath pressed his chin on his breast, opened his mouth, and drew in breath to speak—but they had already passed on, leaving him hanging.

Siegmund began, in a tone of ironic amusement, to speak of an acquaintance of his, a child of nature whose simplicity was such that he abode in ignorance of the difference between dress clothes and dinner jacket. This Parsifal actually talked about a checked dinner jacket. Kunz knew an even more pathetic case—a man who went out to tea in dinner clothes.

"Dinner clothes in the afternoon!" Sieglinde said, making a face. "It isn't even human!"

Von Beckerath laughed sedulously. But inwardly he was remembering that once he himself had worn a dinner coat before six o'clock. And with the game course they passed on to matters of more general cultural interest: to the plastic arts, of which von Beckerath was an amateur, to literature and the theatre, which in the Aarenhold house had the preference—though Siegmund did devote some of his leisure to painting.

The conversation was lively and general and the young people set the key. They talked well, their gestures were nervous and self-assured. They marched in the van of taste, the best was none too good for them. For the vision, the intention, the labouring will, they had no use at all; they ruthlessly insisted upon power achievement, success in the cruel trial of strength. The triumphant work of art they recognized—but they paid it no homage. Herr Aarenhold himself said to von Beckerath:

"You are very indulgent, my dear fellow; you speak up for intentions—but results, *results* are what we are after! You say: 'Of course his work is not much good—but he was only a peasant before he took it up, so his performance is after all astonishing.' Nothing in it. Accomplishment is absolute, not relative. There are no mitigating circumstances. Let a man do first-class work or let him shovel coals. How far should I have got with a good-natured attitude like that? I might have said to myself: 'You're only a poor fish, originally—it's wonderful if you get to be the head of your office.' Well, I'd not be sitting here! I've had to force the world to recognize me, so now I won't recognize anything unless I am forced to!"

The children laughed. At that moment they did not look down on him. They sat there at table, in their low, luxuriously cushioned chairs, with their spoilt, dissatisfied faces. They sat in splendour and security, but their words rang as sharp as though sharpness, hardness, alertness, and pitiless clarity were demanded of them as survival values. Their highest praise was a grudging acceptance, their criticism deft and ruthless; it snatched the weapons from one's hand, it paralysed enthusiasm, made it a laughing-stock. "Very good," they would say of some masterpiece whose lofty intellectual plane would seem to have put it beyond the reach of critique. Passion was a blunder—it made them laugh. Von Beckerath, who tended to be disarmed by his enthusiasms, had hard work holding his own—also his age put him in the wrong. He got smaller and smaller in his chair, pressed his chin on his breast, and in his excitement breathed through his mouth—quite unhorsed by the brisk arrogance of youth. They contradicted everything—as though they found it impossible, discreditable, lamentable, not to contradict. They contradicted most efficiently, their eyes narrowing to gleaming cracks. They fell upon a single word of his, they worried it, they tore it to bits and replaced it by another so telling and deadly that it went straight to the mark and sat in the wound with quivering shaft. Towards the end of luncheon von Beckerath's eyes were red and he looked slightly deranged.

Suddenly—they were sprinkling sugar on their slices of pineapple—Siegmund said, wrinkling up his face in the way he had, as though the sun were making him blink:

"Oh, by the bye, von Beckerath, something else, before we forget it. Sieglinde and I approach you with a request—metaphorically speaking, you see us on our knees. They are giving the *Walküre* tonight. We should like, Sieglinde and I, to hear it once more together—may we? We are of course aware that everything depends upon your gracious favour—"

"How thoughtful!" said Herr Aarenhold.

Kunz drummed the Hunding motif on the cloth.

Von Beckerath was overcome at anybody asking his permission about anything. He answered eagerly:

"But by all means, Siegmund—and you too, Sieglinde; I find your request very reasonable—do go, of course; in fact, I shall be able to go with you. There is an excellent cast tonight."

All the Aarenholds bowed over their plates to hide their laughter. Von Beckerath blinked with his effort to be one of them, to understand and share their mirth.

Siegmund hastened to say:

"Oh, well, actually, it's a rather poor cast, you know. Of course, we are just as grateful to you as though it were good. But I am afraid there is a slight misunderstanding. Sieglinde and I were asking you to permit us to hear the *Walküre* once more *alone* together before the wedding. I don't know if you feel now that—"

"Oh certainly. I quite understand. How charming! Of course you *must* go!"

"Thanks, we are most grateful indeed. Then I will have Percy and Leiermann put in for us. . . ."

"Perhaps I may venture to remark," said Herr Aarenhold, "that your mother and I are driving to dinner with the Erlangers and using Percy and Leiermann. You will have to condescend to the brown coupé and Baal and Lampa."

"And your box?" asked Kunz.

"I took it long ago," said Siegmund, tossing back his head.

They all laughed, all staring at the bridegroom.

Herr Aarenhold unfolded with his finger-tips the paper of a belladonna powder and shook it carefully into his mouth. Then he lighted a fat cigarette, which presently spread abroad a priceless fragrance. The servants sprang forward to draw away his and Frau Aarenhold's chairs. The order was given to serve coffee in the winter-garden. Kunz in a sharp voice ordered his dog-cart brought round; he would drive to the barracks.

Siegmund was dressing for the opera; he had been dressing for an hour. He had so abnormal and constant a need for purification that actually he spent a considerable part of his time before the wash-basin. He stood now in front of his large Empire mirror with the white-enamelled frame; dipped a powder-puff in its embossed box and powdered his freshly shaven chin and cheeks. His beard was so strong that when he went out in the evening he was obliged to shave a second time.

He presented a colourful picture as he stood there, in rose-tinted silk drawers and socks, red morocco slippers, and a wadded house-jacket in a dark pattern with revers of grey fur. For background he had his large sleeping-chamber, full of all sorts of elegant and practical white-enamelled devices. Beyond the windows was a misty view over the tree-tops of the Tiergarten.

It was growing dark. He turned on the circular arrangement of electric bulbs in the white ceiling—they filled the room with soft milky light. Then he drew the velvet curtains across the darkening panes. The light was reflected from the liquid depths of the mirrors in wardrobe, washing-stand, and toilet-table, it flashed from the polished bottles on the tile-inlaid shelves. And Siegmund continued to work on himself. Now and then some thought in his mind would draw his brows together till they formed two black folds over the base of the nose.

His day had passed as his days usually did, vacantly and swiftly. The opera began at half past six and he had begun to change at half past five, so there had not been much afternoon. He had rested on his chaise-longue from two to three, then drunk tea and employed the remaining hour sprawled in a deep leather arm-chair in the study which he shared with Kunz, reading a few pages in each of several new novels. He had found them pitiably weak on the whole; but he had sent a few of them to the binder's to be artistically bound in choice bindings, for his library.

But in the forenoon he had worked. He had spent the hour from ten to eleven in the atelier of his professor, an artist of European repute, who was developing Siegmund's talent for drawing and painting, and receiving from Herr Aarenhold two thousand marks a month for his services. But what Siegmund painted was absurd. He knew it himself; he was far from having any glowing expectations on the score of his talent in this line. He was too shrewd not to know that the conditions of his existence were not the most favourable in the world for the development of a creative gift. The accoutrements of life were so rich and varied, so elaborated, that almost no place at all was left for life itself. Each and every single accessory was so costly and beautiful that it had an existence above and beyond the purpose it was meant to serve—until one's attention was first confused and then exhausted. Siegmund had been born into superfluity, he was perfectly adjusted to it. And yet it was the fact that this superfluity never ceased to thrill and occupy him, to give him constant pleasure. Whether consciously or not, it was with him as with his father, who practised the art of never getting used to anything.

Siegmund loved to read, he strove after the word and the spirit as after a tool which a profound instinct urged him to grasp. But never had he lost himself in a book as one does when that single work seems the most important in the world; unique, a little, all-embracing universe, into which one plunges and submerges oneself in order to draw nourishment out of every syllable. The books and magazines streamed in, he could buy them all, they heaped up about him and even while he read, the number of those still to be read disturbed him. But he had the books bound in stamped leather and labelled with Siegmund Aarenhold's beautiful book-plate; they stood in rows, weighing down his life like a possession which he did not succeed in subordinating to his personality.

The day was his, it was given to him as a gift with all its hours from sunrise to sunset; and yet Siegmund found in his heart that he had no time for a resolve, how much less then for a deed. He was no hero, he commanded no giant powers. The preparation, the lavish equipment for what should have been the serious business of life used up all his energy. How much mental effort had to be expended simply in making a proper toilette! How much time and attention went to his supplies of cigarettes, soaps, and perfumes; how much occasion for making up his mind lay in that moment, recurring two or three times daily, when he had to select his cravat! And it was worth the effort. It was important. The blond-haired citizenry of the land might go about in elastic-sided boots and turn-over collars, heedless of the effect. But he—and most explicitly he—must be unassailable and blameless of exterior from head to foot.

And in the end no one expected more of him. Sometimes there came moments when he had a feeble misgiving about the nature of the "actual"; sometimes he felt that this lack of expectation lamed and dislodged his sense of it. . . . The household arrangements were all made to the end that the day might pass quickly and no empty hour be perceived. The next mealtime always came promptly on. They dined before seven; the evening, when one can idle with a good conscience, was long. The days disappeared, swiftly the seasons came and went. The family spent two summer months at their little castle on the lake, with its large and splendid grounds and many tennis courts, its cool paths through the parks, and shaven lawns adorned by bronze statuettes. A third month was spent in the mountains, in hotels where life was even more expensive than at home. Of late, during the winter, he had had himself driven to school to listen to a course of lectures in the history of art which came at a convenient time. But he had had to leave off because his sense of smell indicated that the rest of the class did not wash often enough.

He spent the hour walking with Sieglinde instead. Always she had been at his side since the very first; she had clung to him since they lisped their first syllables, taken their first steps. He had no friends, never had had one but this, his exquisitely groomed, darkly beautiful counterpart, whose moist and slender hand he held while the richly gilded, empty-eyed hours slipped past. They took fresh flowers with them on their walks, a bunch of violets or lilies of the valley, smelling them in turn or sometimes both together, with languid yet voluptuous abandon. They were like self-centred invalids who absorb themselves in trifles, as narcotics to console them for the loss of hope. With an inward gesture of renunciation they doffed aside the evil-smelling world and loved each other alone, for the priceless sake of their own rare uselessness. But all that they uttered was pointed, neat, and brilliant; it hit off the people they met, the things they saw, everything done by somebody else to the end that it might be exposed to the unerring eye, the sharp tongue, the witty condemnation.

Then von Beckerath had appeared. He had a post in the government and came of a good family. He had proposed for Sieglinde. Frau Aarenhold had supported him, Herr Aarenhold had displayed a benevolent neutrality, Kunz the hussar was his zealous partisan. He had been patient, assiduous, endlessly good-mannered and tactful. And in the end, after she had told him often enough that she did not love him, Sieglinde had begun to look at him searchingly, expectantly, mutely, with her sparkling black eyes—a gaze as speaking and as vacant of thought as an animal's—and had said yes. And Siegmund, whose will was her law, had taken up a position too; slightly to his own disgust he had not opposed the match; was not von Beckerath in the government and a man of good family too? Sometimes he wrinkled his brows over his toilette until they made two heavy black folds at the base of his nose.

He stood on the white bearskin which stretched out its claws beside the bed; his feet were lost in the long soft hair. He sprinkled himself lavishly with toilet water and took up his dress shirt. The starched and shining linen glided over his yellowish torso, which was as lean as a young boy's and yet shaggy with black hair. He arrayed himself further in black silk drawers, black silk socks, and heavy black silk garters with silver buckles, put on the well-pressed trousers of silky black cloth, fastened the white silk braces over his narrow shoulders, and with one foot on a stool began to button his shoes. There was a knock on the door.

"May I come in, Gigi?" asked Sieglinde.

"Yes, come in," he answered.

She was already dressed, in a frock of shimmering sea-green silk, with a square neck outlined by a wide band of beige embroidery. Two embroidered peacocks facing each other above the girdle held a garland in their beaks. Her dark brown hair was unadorned; but a large egg-shaped precious stone hung on a thin pearl chain against her bare skin, the colour of smoked meerschaum. Over her arm she carried a scarf heavily worked with silver.

"I am unable to conceal from you," she said, "that the carriage is waiting." He parried at once:

"And I have no hesitation in replying that it will have to wait patiently two minutes more." It was at least ten. She sat down on the white velvet chaise-longue and watched him at his labours.

Out of a rich chaos of ties he selected a white piqué band and began to tie it before the glass.

"Beckerath," said she, "wears coloured cravats, crossed over the way they wore them last year."

"Beckerath," said he, "is the most trivial existence I have ever had under my personal observation." Turning to her quickly he added: "Moreover, you will do me the favour of not mentioning that German's name to me again this evening."

She gave a short laugh and replied: "You may be sure it will not be a hardship."

He put on the low-cut piqué waistcoat and drew his dress coat over it, the white silk lining caressing his hands as they passed through the sleeves.

"Let me see which buttons you chose," said Sieglinde. They were the amethyst ones; shirt-studs, cuff-links, and waistcoat buttons, a complete set.

She looked at him admiringly, proudly, adoringly, with a world of tenderness in her dark, shining eyes. He kissed the lips lying so softly on each other. They spent another minute on the chaise-longue in mutual caresses.

"Quite, quite soft you are again," said she, stroking his shaven cheeks.

"Your little arm feels like satin," said he, running his hand down her tender forearm. He breathed in the violet odour of her hair.

She kissed him on his closed eyelids; he kissed her on the throat where the pendant hung. They kissed one another's hands. They loved one another sweetly, sensually, for sheer mutual delight in their own well-groomed, pampered, expensive smell. They played together like puppies, biting each other with their lips. Then he got up.

"We mustn't be too late today," said he. He turned the top of the perfume bottle upside down on his handkerchief one last time, rubbed a drop into his narrow red hands, took his gloves, and declared himself ready to go.

He put out the light and they went along the red-carpeted corridor hung with dark old oil paintings and down the steps past the little organ. In the vestibule on the ground floor Wendelin was waiting with their coats, very tall in his long yellow paletot. They yielded their shoulders to his ministrations; Sieglinde's dark head was half lost in her collar of silver fox. Followed by the servant they passed through the stone-paved vestibule into the outer air. It was mild, and there were great ragged flakes of snow in the pearly air. The coupé awaited them. The coachman bent down with his hand to his cockaded hat while Wendelin ushered the brother and sister to their seats; then the door banged shut, he swung himself up to the box, and the carriage was at once in swift motion. It crackled over the gravel, glided through the high, wide gate, curved smoothly to the right, and rolled away.

The luxurious little space in which they sat was pervaded by a gentle warmth. "Shall I shut us in?" Siegmund asked. She nodded and he drew the brown silk curtains across the polished panes.

They were in the city's heart. Lights flew past behind the curtains. Their horses' hoofs rhythmically beat the ground, the carriage swayed noiselessly over the pavement, and round them roared and shrieked and thundered the machinery of urban life. Quite safe and shut away they sat among the wadded brown silk cushions, hand in hand. The carriage drew up and stopped. Wendelin was at the door to help them out. A little group of grey-faced shivering folk stood in the brilliance of the arc-lights and followed them with hostile glances as they passed through the lobby. It was already late, they were the last. They mounted the staircase, threw their cloaks over Wendelin's arms, paused a second before a high mirror, then went through the little door into their box. They were greeted by the last sounds before the hush—voices and the slamming of seats. The lackey pushed their plush-upholstered chairs beneath them; at that moment the lights went down and below their box the orchestra broke into the wild pulsating notes of the prelude.

Night, and tempest. . . . And they, who had been wafted hither on the wings of ease, with no petty annoyances on the way, were in exactly the right mood and could give all their attention at once. Storm, a raging tempest, without in the wood. The angry god's command resounded, once, twice repeated in its wrath, obediently the thunder crashed. The curtain flew up as though blown by the storm. There was the rude hall, dark save for a glow on the pagan hearth. In the centre towered up the trunk of the ash tree. Siegmund appeared in the doorway and leaned against the wooden post beaten and harried by the storm. Draggingly he moved forwards on his sturdy legs wrapped round with hide and thongs. He was rosy-skinned, with a straw-coloured beard; beneath his blond brows and the blond forelock of his wig his blue eyes were directed upon the conductor, with an imploring gaze. At last the orchestra gave way to his voice, which rang clear and metallic, though he tried to make it sound like a gasp. He sang a few bars, to the effect that no matter to whom the hearth belonged he must rest upon it; and at the last word he let himself drop heavily on the bearskin rug and lay there with his head cushioned on his plump arms. His breast heaved in slumber. A minute passed, filled with the singing, speaking flow of the music, rolling its waves at the feet of the events on the stage. . . . Sieglinde entered from the left. She had an alabaster bosom which rose and fell marvellously beneath her muslin robe and deerskin mantle. She displayed surprise at sight of the strange man; pressed her chin upon her breast until it was double, put her lips in position and expressed it, this surprise, in tones which swelled soft and warm from her white throat and were given shape by her tongue and her mobile lips. She tended the stranger; bending over him so that he could see the white flower of her bosom rising from the rough skins, she gave him with both hands the drinking-horn. He drank. The music spoke movingly to him of cool refreshment and cherishing care. They looked at each other with the beginning of enchantment, a first dim recognition, standing rapt while the orchestra interpreted in a melody of profound enchantment.

She gave him mead, first touching the horn with her lips, then watching while he took a long draught. Again their glances met and mingled, while below, the melody voiced their yearning. Then he rose, in deep dejection, turning away painfully, his arms hanging at his sides, to the door, that he might remove from her sight his affliction, his loneliness, his persecuted, hated existence and bear it back into the wild. She called upon him but he did not hear; heedless of self she lifted up her arms and confessed her intolerable anguish. He stopped. Her eyes fell. Below them the music spoke darkly of the bond of suffering that united them. He stayed. He folded his arms and remained by the hearth, awaiting his destiny.

Announced by his pugnacious motif, Hunding entered, paunchy and knock-kneed, like a cow. His beard was black with brown tufts. He stood there frowning, leaning heavily on his spear, and staring ox-eyed at the stranger guest. But as the primitive custom would have it he bade him welcome, in an enormous, rusty voice.

Sieglinde laid the evening meal, Hunding's slow, suspicious gaze moving to and fro between her and the stranger. Dull lout though he was, he saw their likeness: the selfsame breed, that odd, untrammelled rebellious stock, which he hated, to which he felt inferior. They sat down, and Hunding, in two words, introduced himself and accounted for his simple, regular, and orthodox existence. Thus he forced Siegmund to speak of himself—and that was incomparably more difficult. Yet Siegmund spoke, he sang clearly and with wonderful beauty of his life and misfortunes. He told how he had been born with a twin sister—and as people do who dare not speak out, he called himself by a false name. He gave a moving account of the hatred and envy which had been the bane of his life and his strange father's life, how their hall had been burnt, his sister carried off, how they had led in the forest a harried, persecuted, outlawed life; and how finally he had mysteriously lost his father as well. . . . And then Siegmund sang the most painful thing of all: he told of his yearning for human beings, his longing and ceaseless loneliness. He sang of men and women, of friendship and love he had sometimes won, only to be thrust back again into the dark. A curse had lain upon him forever, he was marked by the brand of his strange origins. His speech had not been as others' speech nor theirs as his. What he found good was vexation to them, he was galled by the ancient laws to which they paid honour. Always and everywhere he had lived amid anger and strife, he had borne the yoke of scorn and hatred and contempt—all because he was strange, of a breed and kind hopelessly different from them.

Hunding's reception of all this was entirely characteristic. His reply showed no sympathy and no understanding, but only a sour disgust and suspicion of all Siegmund's story. And finally understanding that the stranger standing here on his own hearth was the very man for whom the hunt had been called up today, he behaved with the four-square pedantry one would have expected of him. With a grim sort of courtesy he declared that for tonight the guest-right protected the fugitive; tomorrow he would have the honour of slaying him in battle. Gruffly he commanded Sieglinde to spice his night-drink for him and to await him in bed within; then after a few more threats he followed her, taking all his weapons with him and leaving Siegmund alone and despairing by the hearth.

Up in the box Siegmund bent over the velvet ledge and leaned his dark boyish head on his narrow red hand. His brows made two black furrows, and one foot, resting on the heel of his patent-leather shoe, was in constant nervous motion. But it stopped as he heard a whisper close to him.

"Gigi!"

His mouth, as he turned, had an insolent line.

Sieglinde was holding out to him a mother-of-pearl box with maraschino cherries.

"The brandy chocolates are underneath," she whispered. But he accepted only a cherry, and as he took it out of the waxed paper she said in his ear:

"She will come back to him again at once."

"I am not entirely unaware of the fact," he said, so loud that several heads were jerked angrily in his direction. . . . Down in the darkness big Siegmund was singing alone. From the depths of his heart he cried out for the sword—for a shining haft to swing on that day when there burst forth at last the bright flame of his anger and rage, which so long had smouldered deep in his heart. He saw the hilt glitter in the tree, saw the embers fade on the hearth, sank back in gloomy slumber—-and started up in joyful amaze when Sieglinde glided back to him in the darkness.

Hunding slept like a stone, a deafened, drunken sleep. Together they rejoiced at the outwitting of the clod; they laughed, and their eyes had the same way of narrowing as they laughed. Then Sieglinde stole a look at the conductor, received her cue, and putting her lips in position sang a long recitative: related the heart-breaking tale of how they had forced her, forsaken, strange and wild as she was, to give herself to the crude and savage Hunding and to count herself lucky in an honourable marriage which might bury her dark origins in oblivion. She sang too, sweetly and soothingly, of the strange old man in the hat and how he had driven the sword-blade into the trunk of the ash tree, to await the coming of him who was destined to draw it out. Passionately she prayed in song that it might be he whom she meant, whom she knew and grievously longed for, the consoler of her sorrows, the friend who should be more than friend, the avenger of her shame, whom once she had lost, whom in her abasement she wept for, her brother in suffering, her saviour, her rescuer. . . .

But at this point Siegmund flung about her his two rosy arms. He pressed her cheek against the pelt that covered his breast and, holding her so, sang above her head—sang out his exultation to the four winds, in a silver trumpeting of sound. His breast glowed hot with the oath that bound him to his mate. All the yearning of his hunted life found assuagement in her; all that love which others had repulsed, when in conscious shame of his dark origins he forced it upon them—in her it found its home. She suffered shame as did he, dishonoured was she like to himself—and now, now their brother-and-sister love should be their revenge!

The storm whistled, a gust of wind burst open the door, a flood of white electric light poured into the hall. Divested of darkness they stood and sang their song of spring and spring's sister, love!

Crouching on the bearskin they looked at each other in the white light, as they sang their duet of love. Their bare arms touched each other as they held each other by the temples and gazed into each other's eyes, and as they sang their mouths were very near. They compared their eyes, their foreheads, their voices—they were the same. The growing, urging recognition wrung from his breast his father's name; she called him by his: Siegmund! Siegmund! He freed the sword, he swung it above his head, and submerged in bliss she told him in song who she was: his twin sister, Sieglinde. In ravishment he stretched out his arms to her, his bride, she sank upon his breast—the curtain fell as the music swelled into a roaring, rushing, foaming whirlpool of passion—swirled and swirled and with one mighty throb stood still.

Rapturous applause. The lights went on. A thousand people got up, stretched unobtrusively as they clapped, then made ready to leave the hall, with heads still turned towards the stage, where the singers appeared before the curtain, like masks hung out in a row at a fair. Hunding too came out and smiled politely, despite all that had just been happening.

Siegmund pushed back his chair and stood up. He was hot; little red patches showed on his cheek-bones, above the lean, sallow, shaven cheeks.

"For my part," said he, "what I want now is a breath of fresh air. Siegmund was pretty feeble, wasn't he?"

"Yes," answered Sieglinde, "and the orchestra saw fit to drag abominably in the Spring Song."

"Frightfully sentimental," said Siegmund, shrugging his narrow shoulders in his dress coat. "Are you coming out?" She lingered a moment, with her elbows on the ledge, still gazing at the stage. He looked at her as she rose and took up her silver scarf. Her soft, full lips were quivering.

They went into the foyer and mingled with the slow-moving throng, downstairs and up again, sometimes holding each other by the hand.

"I should enjoy an ice," said she, "if they were not in all probability uneatable."

"Don't think of it," said he. So they ate bonbons out of their box—maraschino cherries and chocolate beans filled with cognac.

The bell rang and they looked on contemptuously as the crowds rushed back to their seats, blocking the corridors. They waited until all was quiet, regaining their places just as the lights went down again and silence and darkness fell soothingly upon the hall. There was another little ring, the conductor raised his arms and summoned up anew the wave of splendid sound.

Siegmund looked down into the orchestra. The sunken space stood out bright against the darkness of the listening house; hands fingered, arms drew the bows, cheeks puffed out—all these simple folk laboured zealously to bring to utterance the work of a master who suffered and created; created the noble and simple visions enacted above on the stage. Creation? How did one create? Pain gnawed and burned in Siegmund's breast, a drawing anguish which yet was somehow sweet, a yearning—whither, for what? It was all so dark, so shamefully unclear! Two thoughts, two words he had: creation, passion. His temples glowed and throbbed, and it came to him as in a yearning vision that creation was born of passion and was reshaped anew as passion. He saw the pale, spent woman hanging on the breast of the fugitive to whom she gave herself, he saw her love and her destiny and knew that so life must be to be creative. He saw his own life, and knew its contradictions, its clear understanding and spoilt voluptuousness, its splendid security and idle spite, its weakness and wittiness, its languid contempt; his life, so full of words, so void of acts, so full of cleverness, so empty of emotion—and he felt again the burning, the drawing anguish which yet was sweet—whither, and to what end? Creation? Experience? Passion?

The finale of the act came, the curtain fell. Light, applause, general exit. Sieglinde and Siegmund spent the interval as before. They scarcely spoke, as they walked hand-in-hand through the corridors and up and down the steps. She offered him cherries but he took no more. She looked at him, but withdrew her gaze as his rested upon her, walking rather constrained at his side and enduring his eye. Her childish shoulders under the silver web of her scarf looked like those of an Egyptian statue, a little too high and too square. Upon her cheeks burned the same fire he felt in his own.

Again they waited until the crowd had gone in and took their seats at the last possible moment. Storm and wind and driving cloud; wild, heathenish cries of exultation. Eight females, not exactly stars in appearance, eight untrammelled, laughing maidens of the wild, were disporting themselves amid a rocky scene. Brünnhilde broke in upon their merriment with her fears. They skimmed away in terror before the approaching wrath of Wotan, leaving her alone to face him. The angry god nearly annihilated his daughter—but his wrath roared itself out, by degrees grew gentle and dispersed into a mild melancholy, on which note it ended. A noble prospect opened out, the scene was pervaded with epic and religious splendour. Brünnhilde slept. The god mounted the rocks. Great, full-bodied flames, rising, falling, and flickering, glowed all over the boards. The Walküre lay with her coat of mail and her shield on her mossy couch ringed round with fire and smoke, with leaping, dancing tongues, with the magic sleep-compelling fire-music. But she had saved Sieglinde, in whose womb there grew and waxed the seed of that hated unprized race, chosen of the gods, from which the twins had sprung, who had mingled their misfortunes and their afflictions in free and mutual bliss.

Siegmund and Sieglinde left their box; Wendelin was outside, towering in his yellow paletot and holding their cloaks for them to put on. Like a gigantic slave he followed the two dark, slender, fur-mantled, exotic creatures down the stairs to where the carriage waited and the pair of large finely matched glossy thoroughbreds tossed their proud heads in the winter night. Wendelin ushered the twins into their warm little silken-lined retreat, closed the door, and the coupé stood poised for yet a second, quivering slightly from the swing with which Wendelin agilely mounted the box. Then it glided swiftly away and left the theatre behind. Again they rolled noiselessly and easefully to the rhythmic beat of the horses' hoofs, over all the unevennesses of the road, sheltered from the shrill harshness of the bustling life through which they passed. They sat as silent and remote as they had sat in their opera-box facing the stage—almost, one might say, in the same atmosphere. Nothing was there which could alienate them from that extravagant and stormily passionate world which worked upon them with its magic power to draw them to itself.

The carriage stopped; they did not at once realize where they were, or that they had arrived before the door of their parents' house. Then Wendelin appeared at the window, and the porter came out of his lodge to open the door.

"Are my father and mother at home?" Siegmund asked, looking over the porter's head and blinking as though he were staring into the sun.

No, they had not returned from dinner at the Erlangers'. Nor was Kunz at home; Märit too was out, no one knew where, for she went entirely her own way.

In the vestibule they paused to be divested of their wraps; then they went up the stairs and through the first-floor hall into the dining-room. Its immense and splendid spaces lay in darkness save at the upper end, where one lustre burned above a table and Florian waited to serve them. They moved noiselessly across the thick carpet, and Florian seated them in their softly upholstered chairs. Then a gesture from Siegmund dismissed him, they would dispense with his services.

The table was laid with a dish of fruit, a plate of sandwiches, and a jug of red wine. An electric tea-kettle hummed upon a great silver tray, with all appliances about it.

Siegmund ate a caviar sandwich and poured out wine into a slender glass where it glowed a dark ruby red. He drank in quick gulps, and grumblingly stated his opinion that red wine and caviar were a combination offensive to good taste. He drew out his case, jerkily selected a cigarette, and began to smoke, leaning back with his hands in his pockets, wrinkling up his face and twitching his cigarette from one corner of his mouth to the other. His strong growth of beard was already beginning to show again under the high cheek-bones; the two black folds stood out on the base of his nose.

Sieglinde had brewed the tea and added a drop of burgundy. She touched the fragile porcelain cup delicately with her full, soft lips and as she drank she looked across at Siegmund with her great humid black eyes.

She set down her cup and leaned her dark, sweet little head upon her slender hand. Her eyes rested full upon him, with such liquid, speechless eloquence that all she might have said could be nothing beside it.

"Won't you have any more to eat, Gigi?"

"One would not draw," said he, "from the fact that I am smoking, the conclusion that I intend to eat more."

"But you have had nothing but bonbons since tea. Take a peach, at least."

He shrugged his shoulders—or rather he wiggled them like a naughty child, in his dress coat.

"This is stupid. I am going upstairs. Good night."

He drank out his wine, tossed away his table-napkin, and lounged away, with his hands in his pockets, into the darkness at the other end of the room.

He went upstairs to his room, where he turned on the light—not much, only two or three bulbs, which made a wide white circle on the ceiling. Then he stood considering what to do next. The good-night had not been final; this was not how they were used to take leave of each other at the close of the day. She was sure to come to his room. He flung off his coat, put on his fur-trimmed house-jacket, and lighted another cigarette. He lay down on the chaise-longue; sat up again, tried another posture, with his cheek in the pillow; threw himself on his back again and so remained awhile, with his hands under his head.

The subtle, bitterish scent of the tobacco mingled with that of the cosmetics, the soaps, and the toilet waters; their combined perfume hung in the tepid air of the room and Siegmund breathed it in with conscious pleasure, finding it sweeter than ever. Closing his eyes he surrendered to this atmosphere, as a man will console himself with some delicate pleasure of the senses for the extraordinary harshness of his lot.

Then suddenly he started up again, tossed away his cigarette and stood in front of the white wardrobe, which had long mirrors let into each of its three divisions. He moved very close to the middle one and eye to eye he studied himself, conned every feature of his face. Then he opened the two side wings and studied both profiles as well. Long he looked at each mark of his race: the slightly drooping nose, the full lips that rested so softly on each other; the high cheek-bones, the thick black, curling hair that grew far down on the temples and parted so decidedly on one side; finally the eyes under the knit brows, those large black eyes that glowed like fire and had an expression of weary sufferance.

In the mirror he saw the bearskin lying behind him, spreading out its claws beside the bed. He turned round, and there was tragic meaning in the dragging step that bore him towards it—until after a moment more of hesitation he lay down all its length and buried his head in his arm.

For a while he lay motionless, then propped his head on his elbows, with his cheeks resting on his slim reddish hands, and fell again into contemplation of his image opposite him in the mirror. There was a knock on the door. He started, reddened, and moved as though to get up—but sank back again, his head against his outstretched arm, and stopped there, silent.

Sieglinde entered. Her eyes searched the room, without finding him at once. Then with a start she saw him lying on the rug.

"Gigi, what ever are you doing there? Are you ill?" She ran to him, bending over with her hand on his forehead, stroking his hair as she repeated: "You are not ill?"

He shook his head, looking up at her under his brow as she continued to caress him.

She was half ready for bed, having come over in slippers from her dressing-room, which was opposite to his. Her loosened hair flowed down over her open white dressing-jacket; beneath the lace of her chemise Siegmund saw her little breasts, the colour of smoked meerschaum.

"You were so cross," she said. "It was beastly of you to go away like that. I thought I would not come. But then I did, because that was not a proper good-night at all. . . ."

"I was waiting for you," said he.

She was still standing bent over, and made a little moue which brought out markedly the facial characteristics of her race. Then, in her ordinary tone:

"Which does not prevent my present position from giving me a crick in the back."

He shook her off.

"Don't, don't—we must not talk like that—not that way, Sieglinde." His voice was strange, he himself noticed it. He felt parched with fever, his hands and feet were cold and clammy. She knelt beside him on the skin, her hand in his hair. He lifted himself a little to fling one arm round her neck and so looked at her, looked as he had just been looking at himself—at eyes and temples, brow and cheeks.

"You are just like me," said he, haltingly, and swallowed to moisten his dry throat. "Everything about you is just like me—and so—what you have—with Beckerath—the experience—is for me too. That makes things even, Sieglinde—and anyhow, after all, it is, for that matter—it is a revenge, Sieglinde—"

He was seeking to clothe in reason what he was trying to say—yet his words sounded as though he uttered them out of some strange, rash, bewildered dream.

But to her it had no quality of strangeness. She did not blush at his half-spoken, turbid, wild imaginings; his words enveloped her senses like a mist, they drew her down whence they had come, to the borders of a kingdom she had never entered, though sometimes, since her betrothal, she had been carried thither in expectant dreams.

She kissed him on his closed eyelids; he kissed her on her throat, beneath the lace she wore. They kissed each other's hands. They loved each other with all the sweetness of the senses, each for the other's spoilt and costly well-being and delicious fragrance. They breathed it in, this fragrance, with languid and voluptuous abandon, like self-centred invalids, consoling themselves for the loss of hope. They forgot themselves in caresses, which took the upper hand, passing over into a tumult of passion, dying away into a sobbing. . . .

She sat there on the bearskin, with parted lips, supporting herself with one hand, and brushed the hair out of her eyes. He leaned back on his hands against the white dressing-chest, rocked to and fro on his hips, and gazed into the air.

"But Beckerath," said she, seeking to find some order in her thoughts, "Beckerath, Gigi . . . what about him, now?"

"Oh," he said—and for a second the marks of his race stood out strong upon his face—"he ought to be grateful to us. His existence will be a little less trivial, from now on."

1905

TRISTAN

Einfried, the sanatorium. A long, white, rectilinear building with a side wing, set in a spacious garden pleasingly equipped with grottoes, bowers, and little bark pavilions. Behind its slate roofs the mountains tower heavenwards, evergreen, massy, cleft with wooded ravines.

Now as then Dr. Leander directs the establishment. He wears a two-pronged black beard as curly and wiry as horsehair stuffing; his spectacle-lenses are thick, and glitter; he has the look of a man whom science has cooled and hardened and filled with silent, forbearing pessimism. And with this beard, these lenses, this look, and in his short, reserved, preoccupied way, he holds his patients in his spell: holds those sufferers who, too weak to be laws unto themselves, put themselves into his hands that his severity may be a shield unto them.

As for Fräulein von Osterloh, hers it is to preside with unwearying zeal over the housekeeping. Ah, what activity! How she plies, now here, now there, now upstairs, now down, from one end of the building to the other! She is queen in kitchen and storerooms, she mounts the shelves of the linen-presses, she marshals the domestic staff; she ordains the bill of fare, to the end that the table shall be economical, hygienic, attractive, appetizing, and all these in the highest degree; she keeps house diligently, furiously; and her exceeding capacity conceals a constant reproach to the world of men, to no one of whom has it yet occurred to lead her to the altar. But ever on her cheeks there glows, in two round, carmine spots, the unquenchable hope of one day becoming Frau Dr. Leander.

Ozone, and stirless, stirless air! Einfried, whatever Dr. Leander's rivals and detractors may choose to say about it, can be most warmly recommended for lung patients. And not only these, but patients of all sorts, gentlemen, ladies, even children, come to stop here. Dr. Leander's skill is challenged in many different fields. Sufferers from gastric disorders come, like Frau Magistrate Spatz—she has ear trouble into the bargain—people with defective hearts, paralytics, rheumatics, nervous sufferers of all kinds and degrees. A diabetic general here consumes his daily bread amid continual grumblings. There are several gentlemen with gaunt, fleshless faces who fling their legs about in that uncontrollable way that bodes no good. There is an elderly lady, a Frau Pastor Höhlenrauch, who has brought fourteen children into the world and is now incapable of a single thought, yet has not thereby attained to any peace of mind, but must go roving spectre-like all day long up and down through the house, on the arm of her private attendant, as she has been doing this year past.

Sometimes a death takes place among the "severe cases," those who lie in their chambers, never appearing at meals or in the reception-rooms. When this happens no one knows of it, not even the person sleeping next door. In the silence of the night the waxen guest is put away and life at Einfried goes tranquilly on, with its massage, its electric treatment, douches, baths; with its exercises, its steaming and inhaling, in rooms especially equipped with all the triumphs of modern therapeutic.

Yes, a deal happens hereabouts—the institution is in a flourishing way. When new guests arrive, at the entrance to the side wing, the porter sounds the great gong; when these are departures, Dr. Leander, together with Fräulein von Osterloh, conducts the traveller in due form to the waiting carriage. All sorts and kinds of people have received hospitality at Einfried. Even an author is here stealing time from God Almighty—a queer sort of man, with a name like some kind of mineral or precious stone.

Lastly there is, besides Dr. Leander, another physician, who takes care of the slight cases and the hopeless ones. But he bears the name of Müller and is not worth mentioning.

At the beginning of January a business man named Klöterjahn—of the firm of A. C. Klöterjahn & Co.—brought his wife to Einfried. The porter rang the gong, and Fräulein von Osterloh received the guests from a distance in the drawing-room on the ground floor, which, like nearly all the fine old mansion, was furnished in wonderfully pure Empire style. Dr. Leander appeared straightway. He made his best bow, and a preliminary conversation ensued, for the better information of both sides.

Beyond the windows lay the wintry garden, the flowerbeds covered with straw, the grottoes snowed under, the little temples forlorn. Two porters were dragging in the guests' trunks from the carriage drawn up before the wrought-iron gate—for there was no drive up to the house.

"Be careful, Gabriele, *doucement, doucement,* my angel, keep your mouth closed," Herr Klöterjahn had said as he led his wife through the garden; and nobody could look at her without tenderheartedly echoing the caution—though, to be sure, Herr Klöterjahn might quite as well have uttered it all in his own language.

The coachman who had driven the pair from the station to the sanatorium was an uncouth man, and insensitive; yet he sat with his tongue between his teeth as the husband lifted down his wife. The very horses, steaming in the frosty air, seemed to follow the procedure with their eyeballs rolled back in their heads out of sheer concern for so much tenderness and fragile charm.

The young wife's trouble was her trachea; it was expressly so set down in the letter Herr Klöterjahn had sent from the shores of the Baltic to announce their impending arrival to the director of Einfried—the trachea, and not the lungs, thank God! But it is a question whether, if it had been the lungs, the new patient could have looked any more pure and ethereal, any remoter from the concerns of this world, than she did now as she leaned back pale and weary in her chaste white-enamelled arm-chair, beside her robust husband, and listened to the conversation.

Her beautiful white hands, bare save for the simple wedding-ring, rested in her lap, among the folds of a dark, heavy cloth skirt; she wore a close-fitting waist of silver-grey with a stiff collar—it had an all-over pattern of arabesques in high-pile velvet. But these warm, heavy materials only served to bring out the unspeakable delicacy, sweetness, and languor of the little head, to make it look more than ever touching, exquisite, and unearthly. Her light-brown hair was drawn smoothly back and gathered in a knot low in her neck, but near the right temple a single lock fell loose and curling, not far from the place where an odd little vein branched across one well-marked eyebrow, pale blue and sickly amid all that pure, well-nigh transparent spotlessness. That little blue vein above the eye dominated quite painfully the whole fine oval of the face. When she spoke, it stood out still more; yes, even when she smiled—and lent her expression a touch of strain, if not actually of distress, that stirred vague fear in the beholder. And yet she spoke, and she smiled: spoke frankly and pleasantly in her rather husky voice, with a smile in her eyes—though they again were sometimes a little difficult and showed a tendency to avoid a direct gaze. And the corners of her eyes, both sides the base of the slender little nose, were deeply shadowed. She smiled with her mouth too, her beautiful wide mouth, whose lips were so pale and yet seemed to flash—perhaps because their contours were so exceedingly pure and well-cut. Sometimes she cleared her throat, then carried her handkerchief to her mouth and afterwards looked at it.

"Don't clear your throat like that, Gabriele," said Herr Klöterjahn. "You know, darling, Dr. Hinzpeter expressly forbade it, and what we have to do is to exercise self-control, my angel. As I said, it is the trachea," he repeated. "Honestly, when it began, I thought it was the lungs, and it gave me a scare, I do assure you. But it isn't the lungs—we don't mean to let ourselves in for that, do we, Gabriele, my love, eh? Ha ha!"

"Surely not," said Dr. Leander, and glittered at her with his eye-glasses.

Whereupon Herr Klöterjahn ordered coffee, coffee and rolls; and the speaking way he had of sounding the *c* far back in his throat and exploding the *b* in "butter" must have made any soul alive hungry to hear it.

His order was filled; and rooms were assigned to him and his wife, and they took possession with their things.

And Dr. Leander took over the case himself, without calling in Dr. Müller.

The population of Einfried took unusual interest in the fair new patient; Herr Klöterjahn, used as he was to see homage paid her, received it all with great satisfaction. The diabetic general, when he first saw her, stopped grumbling a minute; the gentlemen with the fleshless faces smiled and did their best to keep their legs in order; as for Frau Magistrate Spatz, she made her her oldest friend on the spot. Yes, she made an impression, this woman who bore Herr Klöterjahn's name! A writer who had been sojourning a few weeks in Einfried, a queer sort, he was, with a name like some precious stone or other, positively coloured up when she passed him in the corridor, stopped stock-still and stood there as though rooted to the ground, long after she had disappeared.

Before two days were out, the whole little population knew her history. She came originally from Bremen, as one could tell by certain pleasant small twists in her pronunciation; and it had been in Bremen that, two years gone by, she had bestowed her hand upon Herr Klöterjahn, a successful business man, and become his life-partner. She had followed him to his native town on the Baltic coast, where she had presented him, some ten months before the time of which we write, and under circumstances of the greatest difficulty and danger, with a child, a particularly well-formed and vigorous son and heir. But since that terrible hour she had never fully recovered her strength—granting, that is, that she had ever had any. She had not been long up, still extremely weak, with extremely impoverished vitality, when one day after coughing she brought up a little blood—oh, not much, an insignificant quantity in fact; but it would have been much better to be none at all; and the suspicious thing was, that the same trifling but disquieting incident recurred after another short while. Well, of course, there were things to be done, and Dr. Hinzpeter, the family physician, did them. Complete rest was ordered, little pieces of ice swallowed; morphine administered to check the cough, and other medicines to regulate the heart action. But recovery failed to set in; and while the child, Anton Klöterjahn, junior, a magnificent specimen of a baby, seized on his place in life and held it with prodigious energy and ruthlessness, a low, unobservable fever seemed to waste the young mother daily. It was, as we have heard, an affection of the trachea—a word that in Dr. Hinzpeter's mouth sounded so soothing, so consoling, so reassuring, that it raised their spirits to a surprising degree. But even though it was not the lungs, the doctor presently found that a milder climate and a stay in a sanatorium were imperative if the cure was to be hastened. The reputation enjoyed by Einfried and its director had done the rest.

Such was the state of affairs; Herr Klöterjahn himself related it to all and sundry. He talked with a slovenly pronunciation, in a loud, good-humoured voice, like a man whose digestion is in as capital order as his pocket-book; shovelling out the words pell-mell, in the broad accents of the northern coast-dweller; hurtling some of them forth so that each sound was a little explosion, at which he laughed as at a successful joke.

He was of medium height, broad, stout, and short-legged; his face full and red, with watery blue eyes shaded by very fair lashes; with wide nostrils and humid lips. He wore English side-whiskers and English clothes, and it enchanted him to discover at Einfried an entire English family, father, mother, and three pretty children with their nurse, who were stopping here for the simple and sufficient reason that they knew not where else to go. With this family he partook of a good English breakfast every morning. He set great store by good eating and drinking and proved to be a connoisseur both of food and wines, entertaining the other guests with the most exciting accounts of dinners given in his circle of acquaintance back home, with full descriptions of the choicer and rarer dishes; in the telling his eyes would narrow benignly, and his pronunciation take on certain palatal and nasal sounds, accompanied by smacking noises at the back of his throat. That he was not fundamentally averse to earthly joys of another sort was evinced upon an evening when a guest of the cure, an author by calling, saw him in the corridor trifling in not quite permissible fashion with a chambermaid—a humorous little passage at which the author in question made a laughably disgusted face.

As for Herr Klöterjahn's wife, it was plain to see that she was devotedly attached to her husband. She followed his words and movements with a smile: not the rather arrogant toleration the ailing sometimes bestow upon the well and sound, but the sympathetic participation of a well-disposed invalid in the manifestations of people who rejoice in the blessing of abounding health.

Herr Klöterjahn did not stop long in Einfried. He had brought his wife hither, but when a week had gone by and he knew she was in good hands and well looked after, he did not linger. Duties equally weighty—his flourishing child, his no less flourishing business—took him away; they compelled him to go, leaving her rejoicing in the best of care.

Spinell was the name of that author who had been stopping some weeks in Einfried—Detlev Spinell was his name, and his looks were quite out of the common. Imagine a dark man at the beginning of the thirties, impressively tall, with hair already distinctly grey at the temples, and a round, white, slightly bloated face, without a vestige of beard. Not that it was shaven—that you could have told; it was soft, smooth, boyish, with at most a downy hair here and there. And the effect was singular. His bright, doe-like brown eyes had a gentle expression, the nose was thick and rather too fleshy. Also, Herr Spinell had an upper lip like an ancient Roman's, swelling and full of pores; large, carious teeth, and feet of uncommon size. One of the gentlemen with the rebellious legs, a cynic and ribald wit, had christened him "the dissipated baby"; but the epithet was malicious, and not very apt. Herr Spinell dressed well, in a long black coat and a waistcoat with coloured spots.

He was unsocial and sought no man's company. Only once in a while he might be overtaken by an affable, blithe, expansive mood; and this always happened when he was carried away by an æsthetic fit at the sight of beauty, the harmony of two colours, a vase nobly formed, or the range of mountains lighted by the setting sun. "How beautiful!" he would say, with his head on one side, his shoulders raised, his hands spread out, his lips and nostrils curled and distended. "My God! look, how beautiful!" And in such moments of ardour he was quite capable of flinging his arms blindly round the neck of anybody, high or low, male or female, that happened to be near.

On his table, for anybody to see who entered his room, there always lay the book he had written. It was a novel of medium length, with a perfectly bewildering drawing on the jacket, printed on a sort of filter-paper. Each letter of the type looked like a Gothic cathedral. Fräulein von Osterloh had read it once, in a spare quarter-hour, and found it "very cultured"—which was her circumlocution for inhumanly boresome. Its scenes were laid in fashionable salons, in luxurious boudoirs full of choice *objets d'art,* old furniture, gobelins, rare porcelains, priceless stuffs, and art treasures of all sorts and kinds. On the description of these things was expended the most loving care; as you read you constantly saw Herr Spinell, with distended nostrils, saying: "How beautiful! My God! look, how beautiful!" After all, it was strange he had not written more than this one book; he so obviously adored writing. He spent the greater part of the day doing it, in his room, and sent an extraordinary number of letters to the post, two or three nearly every day—and that made it more striking, even almost funny, that he very seldom received one in return.

Herr Spinell sat opposite Herr Klöterjahn's wife. At the first meal of which the new guests partook, he came rather late into the dining-room, on the ground floor of the side wing, bade good-day to the company generally in a soft voice, and betook himself to his own place, whereupon Dr. Leander perfunctorily presented him to the new-comers. He bowed, and self-consciously began to eat, using his knife and fork rather affectedly with the large, finely shaped white hands that came out from his very narrow coat-sleeves. After a little he grew more at ease and looked tranquilly first at Herr Klöterjahn and then at his wife, by turns. And in the course of the meal Herr Klöterjahn addressed to him sundry queries touching the general situation and climate of Einfried; his wife, in her charming way, added a word or two, and Herr Spinell gave courteous answers. His voice was mild, and really agreeable; but he had a halting way of speaking that almost amounted to an impediment—as though his teeth got in the way of his tongue.

After luncheon, when they had gone into the salon, Dr. Leander came up to the new arrivals to wish them *Mahlzeit,* and Herr Klöterjahn's wife took occasion to ask about their *vis-à-vis*.

"What was the gentleman's name?" she asked. "I did not quite catch it. Spinelli?"

"Spinell, not Spinelli, madame. No, he is not an Italian; he only comes from Lemberg, I believe."

"And what was it you said? He is an author, or something of the sort?" asked Herr Klöterjahn. He had his hands in the pockets of his very easy-fitting English trousers, cocked his head towards the doctor, and opened his mouth, as some people do, to listen the better.

"Yes . . . I really don't know," answered Dr. Leander. "He writes. . . . I believe he has written a book, some sort of novel. I really don't know what."

By which Dr. Leander conveyed that he had no great opinion of the author and declined all responsibility on the score of him.

"But I find that most interesting," said Herr Klöterjahn's wife. Never before had she met an author face to face.

"Oh, yes," said Dr. Leander obligingly. "I understand he has a certain amount of reputation," which closed the conversation.

But a little later, when the new guests had retired and Dr. Leander himself was about to go, Herr Spinell detained him in talk to put a few questions for his own part.

"What was their name?" he asked. "I did not understand a syllable, of course."

"Klöterjahn," answered Dr. Leander, turning away.

"What's that?" asked Herr Spinell.

"Klöterjahn is their name," said Dr. Leander, and went his way. He set no great store by the author.

Have we got as far on as where Herr Klöterjahn went home? Yes, he was back on the shore of the Baltic once more, with his business and his babe, that ruthless and vigorous little being who had cost his mother great suffering and a slight weakness of the trachea; while she herself, the young wife, remained in Einfried and became the intimate friend of Frau Spatz. Which did not prevent Herr Klöterjahn's wife from being on friendly terms with the rest of the guests—for instance with Herr Spinell, who, to the astonishment of everybody, for he had up to now held communion with not a single soul, displayed from the very first an extraordinary devotion and courtesy, and with whom she enjoyed talking, whenever she had any time left over from the stern service of the cure.

He approached her with immense circumspection and reverence, and never spoke save with his voice so carefully subdued that Frau Spatz, with her bad hearing, seldom or never caught anything he said. He tiptoed on his great feet up to the armchair in which Herr Klöterjahn's wife leaned, fragilely smiling; stopped two paces off, with his body bent forward and one leg poised behind him, and talked in his halting way, as though he had an impediment in his speech; with ardour, yet prepared to retire at any moment and vanish at the first sign of fatigue or satiety. But he did not tire her; she begged him to sit down with her and the Rätin; she asked him questions and listened with curious smiles, for he had a way of talking sometimes that was so odd and amusing, different from anything she had ever heard before.

"Why are you in Einfried, really?" she asked. "What cure are you taking, Herr Spinell?"

"Cure? Oh, I'm having myself electrified a bit. Nothing worth mentioning. I will tell you the real reason why I am here, madame. It is a feeling for style."

"Ah?" said Herr Klöterjahn's wife; supported her chin on her hand and turned to him with exaggerated eagerness, as one does to a child who wants to tell a story.

"Yes, madame. Einfried is perfect Empire. It was once a castle, a summer residence, I am told. This side wing is a later addition, but the main building is old and genuine. There are times when I cannot endure Empire, and then times when I simply must have it in order to attain any sense of well-being. Obviously, people feel one way among furniture that is soft and comfortable and voluptuous, and quite another among the straight lines of these tables, chairs, and draperies. This brightness and hardness, this cold, austere simplicity and reserved strength, madame—it has upon me the ultimate effect of an inward purification and rebirth. Beyond a doubt, it is morally elevating."

"Yes, that is remarkable," she said. "And when I try I can understand what you mean."

Whereto he responded that it was not worth her taking any sort of trouble, and they laughed together. Frau Spatz laughed too and found it remarkable in her turn, though she did not say she understood it.

The reception-room was spacious and beautiful. The high, white folding doors that led to the billiard-room were wide open, and the gentlemen with the rebellious legs were disporting themselves within, others as well. On the opposite side of the room a glass door gave on the broad veranda and the garden. Near the door stood a piano. At a green-covered folding table the diabetic general was playing whist with some other gentlemen. Ladies sat reading or embroidering. The rooms were heated by an iron stove, but the chimney-piece, in the purest style, had coals pasted over with red paper to simulate a fire, and chairs were drawn up invitingly.

"You are an early riser, Herr Spinell," said Herr Klöterjahn's wife. "Two or three times already I have chanced to see you leaving the house at half past seven in the morning."

"An early riser? Ah, with a difference, madame, with a vast difference. The truth is, I rise early because I am such a late sleeper."

"You really must explain yourself, Herr Spinell." Frau Spatz too said she demanded an explanation.

"Well, if one is an early riser, one does not need to get up so early. Or so it seems to me. The conscience, madame, is a bad business. I, and other people like me, work hard all our lives to swindle our consciences into feeling pleased and satisfied. We are feckless creatures, and aside from a few good hours we go around weighted down, sick and sore with the knowledge of our own futility. We hate the useful; we know it is vulgar and unlovely, and we defend this position, as a man defends something that is absolutely necessary to his existence. Yet all the while conscience is gnawing at us, to such an extent that we are simply one wound. Added to that, our whole inner life, our view of the world, our way of working, is of a kind—its effect is frightfully unhealthy, undermining, irritating, and this only aggravates the situation. Well, then, there are certain little counter-irritants, without which we would most certainly not hold out. A kind of decorum, a hygienic regimen, for instance, becomes a necessity for some of us. To get up early, to get up ghastly early, take a cold bath, and go out walking in a snowstorm—that may give us a sense of self-satisfaction that lasts as much as an hour. If I were to act out my true character, I should be lying in bed late into the afternoon. My getting up early is all hypocrisy, believe me."

"Why do you say that, Herr Spinell? On the contrary, I call it self-abnegation." Frau Spatz, too, called it self-abnegation.

"Hypocrisy or self-abnegation—call it what you like, madame. I have such a hideously downright nature—"

"Yes, that's it. Surely you torment yourself far too much."

"Yes, madame, I torment myself a great deal."

The fine weather continued. Rigid and spotless white the region lay, the mountains, house and garden, in a windless air that was blinding clear and cast bluish shadows; and above it arched the spotless pale-blue sky, where myriads of bright particles of glittering crystals seemed to dance. Herr Klöterjahn's wife felt tolerably well these days: free of fever, with scarce any cough, and able to eat without too great distaste. Many days she sat taking her cure for hours on end in the sunny cold on the terrace. She sat in the snow, bundled in wraps and furs, and hopefully breathed in the pure icy air to do her trachea good. Sometimes she saw Herr Spinell, dressed like herself, and in fur boots that made his feet a fantastic size, taking an airing in the garden. He walked with tentative tread through the snow, holding his arms in a certain careful pose that was stiff yet not without grace; coming up to the terrace he would bow very respectfully and mount the first step or so to exchange a few words with her.

"Today on my morning walk I saw a beautiful woman—good Lord! how beautiful she was!" he said; laid his head on one side and spread out his hands.

"Really, Herr Spinell. Do describe her to me."

"That I cannot do. Or, rather, it would not be a fair picture. I only saw the lady as I glanced at her in passing, I did not actually see her at all. But that fleeting glimpse was enough to rouse my fancy and make me carry away a picture so beautiful that—good Lord! how beautiful it is!"

She laughed. "Is that the way you always look at beautiful women, Herr Spinell? Just a fleeting glance?"

"Yes, madame; it is a better way than if I were avid of actuality, stared them plump in the face, and carried away with me only a consciousness of the blemishes they in fact possess."

" 'Avid of actuality'—what a strange phrase, a regular literary phrase, Herr Spinell; no one but an author could have said that. It impresses me very much, I must say. There is a lot in it that I dimly understand; there is something free about it, and independent, that even seems to be looking down on reality though it is so very respectable—is respectability itself, as you might say. And it makes me comprehend, too, that there is something else besides the tangible, something more subtle—"

"I know only one face," he said suddenly, with a strange lift in his voice, carrying his closed hands to his shoulders as he spoke and showing his carious teeth in an almost hysterical smile, "I know only one face of such lofty nobility that the mere thought of enhancing it through my imagination would be blasphemous; at which I could wish to look, on which I could wish to dwell, not minutes and not hours, but my whole life long; losing myself utterly therein, forgotten to every earthly thought. . . ."

"Yes, indeed, Herr Spinell. And yet don't you find Fräulein von Osterloh has rather prominent ears?"

He replied only by a profound bow; then, standing erect, let his eyes rest with a look of embarrassment and pain on the strange little vein that branched pale blue and sickly across her pure translucent brow.

An odd sort, a very odd sort. Herr Klöterjahn's wife thought about him sometimes; for she had much leisure for thought. Whether it was that the change of air began to lose its effect or some positively detrimental influence was at work, she began to go backward, the condition of her trachea left much to be desired, she had fever not infrequently, felt tired and exhausted, and could not eat. Dr. Leander most emphatically recommended rest, quiet, caution, care. So she sat, when indeed she was not forced to lie, quite motionless, in the society of Frau Spatz, holding some sort of sewing which she did not sew, and following one or another train of thought.

Yes, he gave her food for thought, this very odd Herr Spinell; and the strange thing was she thought not so much about him as about herself, for he had managed to rouse in her a quite novel interest in her own personality. One day he had said, in the course of conversation:

"No, they are positively the most enigmatic facts in nature—women, I mean. That is a truism, and yet one never ceases to marvel at it afresh. Take some wonderful creature, a sylph, an airy wraith, a fairy dream of a thing, and what does she do? Goes and gives herself to a brawny Hercules at a country fair, or maybe to a butcher's apprentice. Walks about on his arm, even leans her head on his shoulder and looks round with an impish smile as if to say: 'Look on this, if you like, and break your heads over it.' And we break them."

With this speech Herr Klöterjahn's wife had occupied her leisure again and again.

Another day, to the wonderment of Frau Spatz, the following conversation took place:

"May I ask, madame—though you may very likely think me prying—what your name really is?"

"Why, Herr Spinell, you know my name is Klöterjahn!"

"H'm. Yes, I know that—or, rather, I deny it. I mean your own name, your maiden name, of course. You will in justice, madame, admit that anybody who calls you Klöterjahn ought to be thrashed."

She laughed so hard that the little blue vein stood out alarmingly on her brow and gave the pale sweet face a strained expression most disquieting to see.

"Oh, no! Not at all, Herr Spinell! Thrashed, indeed! Is the name Klöterjahn so horrible to you?"

"Yes, madame. I hate the name from the bottom of my heart. I hated it the first time I heard it. It is the abandonment of ugliness; it is grotesque to make you comply with the custom so far as to fasten your husband's name upon you; it is barbarous and vile."

"Well, and how about Eckhof? Is that any better? Eckhof is my father's name."

"Ah, you see! Eckhof is quite another thing. There was a great actor named Eckhof. Eckhof will do nicely. You spoke of your father— Then is your mother—?"

"Yes, my mother died when I was little."

"Ah! Tell me a little more of yourself, pray. But not if it tires you. When it tires you, stop, and I will go on talking about Paris, as I did the other day. But you could speak very softly, or even whisper—that would be more beautiful still. You were born in Bremen?" He breathed, rather than uttered, the question with an expression so awed, so heavy with import, as to suggest that

Bremen was a city like no other on earth, full of hidden beauties and nameless adventures, and ennobling in some mysterious way those born within its walls.

"Yes, imagine," said she involuntarily. "I was born in Bremen."

"I was there once," he thoughtfully remarked.

"Goodness me, you have been there, too? Why, Herr Spinell, it seems to me you must have been everywhere there is between Spitzbergen and Tunis!"

"Yes, I was there once," he repeated. "A few hours, one evening. I recall a narrow old street, with a strange, warped-looking moon above the gabled roofs. Then I was in a cellar that smelled of wine and mould. It is a poignant memory."

"Really? Where could that have been, I wonder? Yes, in just such a grey old gabled house I was born, one of the old merchant houses, with echoing wooden floor and white-painted gallery."

"Then your father is a business man?" he asked hesitatingly.

"Yes, but he is also, and in the first place, an artist."

"Ah! In what way?"

"He plays the violin. But just saying that does not mean much. It is *how* he plays, Herr Spinell—it is that that matters! Sometimes I cannot listen to some of the notes without the tears coming into my eyes and making them burn. Nothing else in the world makes me feel like that. You won't believe it—"

"But I do. Oh, very much I believe it! Tell me, madame, your family is old, is it not? Your family has been living for generations in the old gabled house—living and working and closing their eyes on time?"

"Yes. Tell me why you ask."

"Because it not infrequently happens that a race with sober, practical bourgeois traditions will towards the end of its days flare up in some form of art."

"Is that a fact?"

"Yes."

"It is true, my father is surely more of an artist than some that call themselves so and get the glory of it. I only play the piano a little. They have forbidden me now, but at home, in the old days, I still played. Father and I played together. Yes, I have precious memories of all those years; and especially of the garden, our garden, back of the house. It was dreadfully wild and overgrown, and shut in by crumbling mossy walls. But it was just that gave it such charm. In the middle was a fountain with a wide border of sword-lilies. In the summer I spent long hours there with my friends. We all sat round the fountain on little camp-stools—"

"How beautiful!" said Herr Spinell, and flung up his shoulders. "You sat there and sang?"

"No, we mostly crocheted."

"But still—"

"Yes, we crocheted and chattered, my six friends and I—"

"How beautiful! Good Lord! think of it, *how beautiful!"* cried Herr Spinell again, his face quite distorted with emotion.

"Now, what is it you find so particularly beautiful about that, Herr Spinell?"

"Oh, there being six of them besides you, and your being not one of the six, but a queen among them . . . set apart from your six friends. A little gold crown showed in your hair—quite a modest, unostentatious little crown, still it was there—"

"Nonsense, there was nothing of the sort."

"Yes, there was; it shone unseen. But if I had been there, standing among the shrubbery, one of those times, I should have seen it."

"God knows what you would have seen. But you were not there. Instead of that, it was my husband who came out of the shrubbery one day, with my father. I was afraid they had been listening to our prattle—"

"So it was there, then, madame, that you first met your husband?"

"Yes, there it was I saw him first," she said, in quite a glad, strong voice; she smiled, and as she did so the little blue vein came out and gave her face a constrained and anxious expression. "He was calling on my father on business, you see. Next day he came to dinner, and three days later he proposed for my hand."

"Really? It all happened as fast as that?"

"Yes. Or, rather, it went a little slower after that. For my father was not very much inclined to it, you see, and consented on condition that we wait a long time first. He would rather I had stopped with him, and he had doubts in other ways too. But—"

"But?"

"But I had set my heart on it," she said, smiling; and once more the little vein dominated her whole face with its look of constraint and anxiety.

"Ah, so you set your heart on it."

"Yes, and I displayed great strength of purpose, as you see—"

"As I see. Yes."

"So that my father had to give way in the end."

"And so you forsook him and his fiddle and the old house with the overgrown garden, and the fountain and your six friends, and clave unto Herr Klöterjahn—"

" 'And clave unto'—you have such a strange way of saying things, Herr Spinell. Positively biblical. Yes, I forsook all that; nature has arranged things that way."

"Yes, I suppose that is it."

"And it was a question of my happiness—"

"Of course. And happiness came to you?"

"It came, Herr Spinell, in the moment when they brought little Anton to me, our little Anton, and he screamed so lustily with his strong little lungs—he is very, very strong and healthy, you know—"

"This is not the first time, madame, that I have heard you speak of your little Anton's good health and great strength. He must be quite uncommonly healthy?"

"That he is. And looks so absurdly like my husband!"

"Ah! . . . So that was the way of it. And now you are no longer called by the name of Eckhof, but a different one, and you have your healthy little Anton, and are troubled with your trachea."

"Yes. And you are a perfectly enigmatic man, Herr Spinell, I do assure you."

"Yes. God knows you certainly are," said Frau Spatz, who was present on this occasion.

And that conversation, too, gave Herr Klöterjahn's wife food for reflection. Idle as it was, it contained much to nourish those secret thoughts of hers about herself. Was this the baleful influence which was at work? Her weakness increased and fever often supervened, a quiet glow in which she rested with a feeling of mild elevation, to which she yielded in a pensive mood that was a little affected, self-satisfied, even rather self-righteous. When she had not to keep her bed, Herr Spinell would approach her with immense caution, tiptoeing on his great feet; he would pause two paces off, with his body inclined and one leg behind him, and speak in a voice that was hushed with awe, as though he would lift her higher and higher on the tide of his devotion until she rested on billowy cushions of cloud where no shrill sound nor any earthly touch might reach her. And when he did this she would think of the way Herr Klöterjahn said: "Take care, my angel, keep your mouth closed, Gabriele," a way that made her feel as though he had struck her roughly though well-meaningly on the shoulder. Then as fast as she could she would put the memory away and rest in her weakness and elevation of spirit upon the clouds which Herr Spinell spread out for her.

One day she abruptly returned to the talk they had had about her early life. "Is it really true, Herr Spinell," she asked, "that you would have seen the little gold crown?"

Two weeks had passed since that conversation, yet he knew at once what she meant, and his voice shook as he assured her that he would have seen the little crown as she sat among her friends by the fountain—would have caught its fugitive gleam among her locks.

A few days later one of the guests chanced to make a polite inquiry after the health of little Anton. Herr Klöterjahn's wife gave a quick glance at Herr Spinell, who was standing near, and answered in a perfunctory voice:

"Thanks, how should he be? He and my husband are quite well, of course."

* * *

There came a day at the end of February, colder, purer, more brilliant than any that had come before it, and high spirits held sway at Einfried. The "heart cases" consulted in groups, flushed of cheek, the diabetic general carolled like a boy out of school, and the gentlemen of the rebellious legs cast aside all restraint. And the reason for all these things was that a sleighing party was in prospect, an excursion in sledges into the mountains, with cracking whips and sleigh-bells jingling. Dr. Leander had arranged this diversion for his patients.

The serious cases, of course, had to stop at home. Poor things! The other guests arranged to keep it from them; it did them good to practice this much sympathy and consideration. But a few of those remained at home who might very well have gone. Fräulein von Osterloh was of course excused, she had too much on her mind to permit her even to think of going. She was needed at home, and at home she remained. But the disappointment was general when Herr Klöterjahn's wife announced her intention of stopping away. Dr. Leander exhorted her to come and get the benefit of the fresh air—but in vain. She said she was not up to it, she had a headache, she felt too weak—they had to resign themselves. The cynical gentleman took occasion to say:

"You will see, the dissipated baby will stop at home too."

And he proved to be right, for Herr Spinell gave out that he intended to "work" that afternoon—he was prone thus to characterize his dubious activities. Anyhow, not a soul regretted his absence; nor did they take more to heart the news that Frau Magistrate Spatz had decided to keep her young friend company at home—sleighing made her feel sea-sick.

Luncheon on the great day was eaten as early as twelve o'clock, and immediately thereafter the sledges drew up in front of Einfried. The guests came through the garden in little groups, warmly wrapped, excited, full of eager anticipation. Herr Klöterjahn's wife stood with Frau Spatz at the glass door which gave on the terrace, while Herr Spinell watched the setting-forth from above, at the window of his room. They saw the little struggles that took place for the best seats, amid joking and laughter; and Fräulein von Osterloh, with a fur boa round her neck, running from one sleigh to the other and shoving baskets of provisions under the seats; they saw Dr. Leander, with his fur cap pulled low on his brow, marshalling the whole scene with his spectacle-lenses glittering, to make sure everything was ready. At last he took his own seat and gave the signal to drive off. The horses started up, a few of the ladies shrieked and collapsed, the bells jingled, the short-shafted whips cracked and their long lashes trailed across the snow; Fräulein von Osterloh stood at the gate waving her handkerchief until the train rounded a curve and disappeared; slowly the merry tinkling died away. Then she turned and hastened back through the garden in pursuit of her duties; the two ladies left the glass door, and almost at the same time Herr Spinell abandoned his post of observation above.

Quiet reigned at Einfried. The party would not return before evening. The serious cases lay in their rooms and suffered. Herr Klöterjahn's wife took a short turn with her friend, then they went to their respective chambers. Herr Spinell kept to his, occupied in his own way. Towards four o'clock the ladies were served with half a litre of milk apiece, and Herr Spinell with a light tea. Soon after, Herr Klöterjahn's wife tapped on the wall between her room and Frau Spatz's and called:

"Shan't we go down to the salon, Frau Spatz? I have nothing to do up here."

"In just a minute, my dear," answered she. "I'll just put on my shoes—if you will wait a minute. I have been lying down."

The salon, naturally, was empty. The ladies took seats by the fireplace. The Frau Magistrate embroidered flowers on a strip of canvas; Herr Klöterjahn's wife took a few stitches too, but soon let her work fall in her lap and, leaning on the arm of her chair, fell to dreaming. At length she made some remark, hardly worth the trouble of opening her lips for; the Frau Magistrate asked what she said, and she had to make the effort of saying it all over again, which quite wore her out. But just then steps were heard outside, the door opened, and Herr Spinell came in.

"Shall I be disturbing you?" he asked mildly from the threshold, addressing Herr Klöterjahn's wife and her alone; bending over her, as it were, from a distance, in the tender, hovering way he had.

The young wife answered:

"Why should you? The room is free to everybody—and besides, why would it be disturbing us? On the contrary, I am convinced that I am boring Frau Spatz."

He had no ready answer, merely smiled and showed his carious teeth, then went hesitatingly up to the glass door, the ladies watching him, and stood with his back to them looking out. Presently he half turned round, still gazing into the garden, and said:

"The sun has gone in. The sky clouded over without our seeing it. The dark is coming on already."

"Yes, it is all overcast," replied Herr Klöterjahn's wife. "It looks as though our sleighing party would have some snow after all. Yesterday at this hour it was still broad daylight, now it is already getting dark."

"Well," he said, "after all these brilliant weeks a little dullness is good for the eyes. The sun shines with the same penetrating clearness upon the lovely and the commonplace, and I for one am positively grateful to it for finally going under a cloud."

"Don't you like the sun, Herr Spinell?"

"Well, I am no painter . . . when there is no sun one becomes more profound. . . . It is a thick layer of greyish-white cloud. Perhaps it means thawing weather for tomorrow. But, madame, let me advise you not to sit there at the back of the room looking at your embroidery."

"Don't be alarmed; I am not looking at it. But what else is there to do?"

He had sat down on the piano-stool, resting one arm on the lid of the instrument.

"Music," he said. "If we could only have a little music here. The English children sing darky songs, and that is all."

"And yesterday afternoon Fräulein von Osterloh rendered 'Cloister Bells' at top speed," remarked Herr Klöterjahn's wife.

"But you play, madame!" said he, in an imploring tone. He stood up. "Once you used to play every day with your father."

"Yes, Herr Spinell, in those days I did. In the time of the fountain, you know."

"Play to us today," he begged. "Just a few notes—this once. If you knew how I long for some music—"

"But our family physician, as well as Dr. Leander, expressly forbade it, Herr Spinell."

"But they aren't here—either of them. We are free agents. Just a few bars—"

"No, Herr Spinell, it would be no use. Goodness knows what marvels you expect of me—and I have forgotten everything I knew. Truly, I know scarcely anything by heart."

"Well, then, play that scarcely anything. But there are notes here too. On top of the piano. No, that is nothing. But here is some Chopin."

"Chopin?"

"Yes, the Nocturnes. All we have to do is to light the candles—"

"Pray don't ask me to play, Herr Spinell. I must not. Suppose it were to be bad for me—"

He was silent; standing there in the light of the two candles, with his great feet, in his long black tail-coat, with his beardless face and greying hair. His hands hung down at his sides.

"Then, madame, I will ask no more," he said at length in a low voice. "If you are afraid it will do you harm, then we shall leave the beauty dead and dumb that might have come alive beneath your fingers. You were not always so sensible; at least not when it was the opposite question from what it is today, and you had to decide to take leave of beauty. Then you did not care about your bodily welfare; you showed a firm and unhesitating resolution when you left the fountain and laid aside the little gold crown. Listen," he said, after a pause, and his voice dropped still lower; "If you sit down and play as you used to play when your father stood behind you and brought tears to your eyes with the tones of his violin—who knows but the little gold crown might glimmer once more in your hair. . . ."

"Really," said she, with a smile. Her voice happened to break on the word, it sounded husky and barely audible. She cleared her throat and went on:

"Are those really Chopin's Nocturnes you have there?"

"Yes, here they are open at the place; everything is ready."

"Well, then, in God's name, I will play one," said she. "But only one—do you hear? In any case, one will do you, I am sure."

With which she got up, laid aside her work, and went to the piano. She seated herself on the music-stool, on a few bound volumes, arranged the lights, and turned over the notes. Herr Spinell had drawn up a chair and sat beside her, like a music-master.

She played the Nocturne in E-flat major, opus 9, number 2. If her playing had really lost very much then she must originally have been a consummate artist. The piano was mediocre, but after the first few notes she learned to control it. She displayed a nervous feeling for modulations of timbre and a joy in mobility of rhythm that amounted to the fantastic. Her attack was at once firm and soft. Under her hands the very last drop of sweetness was wrung from the melody; the embellishments seemed to cling with slow grace about her limbs.

She wore the same frock as on the day of her arrival, the dark, heavy bodice with the velvet arabesques in high relief, that gave her head and hands such an unearthly fragile look. Her face did not change as she played, but her lips seemed to become more clear-cut, the shadows deepened at the corners of her eyes. When she finished she laid her hands in her lap and went on looking at the notes. Herr Spinell sat motionless.

She played another Nocturne, and then a third. Then she stood up but only to look on the top of the piano for more music.

It occurred to Herr Spinell to look at the black-bound volumes on the piano-stool. All at once he uttered an incoherent exclamation, his large white hands clutching at one of the books.

"Impossible! No, it cannot be," he said. "But yes, it is. Guess what this is—what was lying here! Guess what I have in my hands."

"What?" she asked.

Mutely he showed her the title-page. He was quite pale; he let the book sink and looked at her, his lips trembling.

"Really? How did that get here? Give it me," was all she said; set the notes on the piano and after a moment's silence began to play.

He sat beside her, bent forward, his hands between his knees, his head bowed. She played the beginning with exaggerated and tormenting slowness, with painfully long pauses between the single figures. The *Sehnsuchtsmotiv,* roving lost and forlorn like a voice in the night, lifted its trembling question. Then silence, a waiting. And lo, an answer: the same timorous, lonely note, only clearer, only tenderer. Silence again. And then, with that marvelous muted *sforzando,* like mounting passion, the love-motif came in; reared and soared and yearned ecstatically upward to its consummation, sank back, was resolved; the cellos taking up the melody to carry it on with their deep, heavy notes of rapture and despair.

Not unsuccessfully did the player seek to suggest the orchestral effects upon the poor instrument at her command. The violin runs of the great climax rang out with brilliant precision. She played with a fastidious reverence, lingering on each figure, bringing out each detail, with the self-forgotten concentration of the priest who lifts the Host above his head. Here two forces, two beings, strove towards each other, in transports of joy and pain; here they embraced and became one in delirious yearning after eternity and the absolute. . . . The prelude flamed up and died away. She stopped at the point where the curtains part, and sat speechless, staring at the keys.

But the boredom of Frau Spatz had now reached that pitch where it distorts the countenance of man, makes the eyes protrude from the head, and lends the features a corpse-like and terrifying aspect. More than that, this music acted on the nerves that controlled her digestion, producing in her dyspeptic organism such *malaise* that she was really afraid she would have an attack.

"I shall have to go up to my room," she said weakly. "Goodbye; I will come back soon."

She went out. Twilight was far advanced. Outside the snow fell thick and soundlessly upon the terrace. The two tapers cast a flickering, circumscribed light.

"The Second Act," he whispered, and she turned the pages and began.

What was it dying away in the distance—the ring of a horn? The rustle of leaves? The rippling of a brook? Silence and night crept up over grove and house; the power of longing had full sway, no prayers or warnings could avail against it. The holy mystery was consummated. The light was quenched; with a strange clouding of the timbre the death-motif sank down: white-veiled desire, by passion driven, fluttered towards love as through the dark it groped to meet her.

Ah, boundless, unquenchable exultation of union in the eternal beyond! Freed from torturing error, escaped from fettering space and time, the Thou and the I, the Thine and the Mine at one forever in a sublimity of bliss! The day might part them with deluding show; but when night fell, then by the power of the potion they would see clear. To him who has looked upon the night of death and known its secret sweets, to him day never can be aught but vain, nor can he know a longing save for night, eternal, real, in which he is made one with love.

O night of love, sink downwards and enfold them, grant them the oblivion they crave, release them from this world of partings and betrayals. Lo, the last light is quenched. Fancy and thought alike are lost, merged in the mystic shade that spread its wings of healing above their madness and despair. "Now, when deceitful daylight pales, when my raptured eye grows dim, then all that from which the light of day would shut my sight, seeking to blind me with false show, to the stanchless torments of my longing soul—then, ah, then, O wonder of fulfilment, even then I am the world!" Followed Brangäna's dark notes of warning, and then those soaring violins so higher than all reason.

"I cannot understand it all, Herr Spinell. Much of it I only divine. What does it mean, this 'even then I am the world'?"

He explained, in a few low-toned words.

"Yes, yes. It means that. How is it you can understand it all so well yet cannot play it?"

Strangely enough, he was not proof against this simple question. He coloured, twisted his hands together, shrank into his chair.

"The two things seldom happen together," he wrung from his lips at last. "No, I cannot play. But go on."

And on they went, into the intoxicated music of the love-mystery. Did love ever die? Tristan's love? The love of thy Isolde, and of mine? Ah, no, death cannot touch that which can never die—and what of him could die, save what distracts and tortures love and severs united lovers? Love joined the two in sweet conjunction, death was powerless to sever such a bond, save only when death was given to one with the very life of the other. Their voices rose in mystic unison, rapt in the wordless hope of that death-in-love, of endless oneness in the wonder-kingdom of the night. Sweet night! Eternal night of love! And all-encompassing land of rapture! Once envisaged or divined, what eye could bear to open again on desolate dawn? Forfend such fears, most gentle death! Release these lovers quite from need of waking. Oh, tumultuous storm of rhythms! Oh, glad chromatic upward surge of metaphysical perception! How find, how bind this bliss so far remote from parting's torturing pangs? Ah, gentle glow of longing, soothing and kind, ah, yielding sweet-sublime, ah, raptured sinking into the twilight of eternity! Thou Isolde, Tristan I, yet no more Tristan, no more Isolde. . . .

All at once something startling happened. The musician broke off and peered into the darkness with her hand above her eyes. Herr Spinell turned round quickly in his chair. The corridor door had opened, a sinister form appeared, leant on the arm of a second form. It was a guest of Einfried, one of those who, like themselves, had been in no state to undertake the sleigh-ride, but had passed this twilight hour in one of her pathetic, instinctive rounds of the house. It was that patient who had borne fourteen children and was no longer capable of a single thought; it was Frau Pastor Höhlenrauch, on the arm of her nurse. She did not look up; with groping step she paced the dim background of the room and vanished by the opposite door, rigid and still, like a lost and wandering soul. Stillness reigned once more.

"That was Frau Pastor Höhlenrauch," he said.

"Yes, that was poor Frau Höhlenrauch," she answered. Then she turned over some leaves and played the finale, played Isolde's song of love and death.

How colourless and clear were her lips, how deep the shadows lay beneath her eyes! The little pale-blue vein in her transparent brow showed fearfully plain and prominent. Beneath her flying fingers the music mounted to its unbelievable climax and was resolved in that ruthless, sudden *pianissimo* which is like having the ground glide from beneath one's feet, yet like a sinking too into the very deeps of desire. Followed the immeasurable plenitude of that vast redemption and fulfilment; it was repeated, swelled into a deafening, unquenchable tumult of immense appeasement that wove and welled and seemed about to die away, only to swell again and weave the *Sehnsuchtsmotiv* into its harmony; at length to breathe an outward breath and die, faint on the air, and soar away. Profound stillness.

They both listened, their heads on one side.

"Those are bells," she said.

"It is the sleighs," he said. "I will go now."

He rose and walked across the room. At the door he halted, then turned and shifted uneasily from one foot to the other. And then, some fifteen or twenty paces from her, it came to pass that he fell upon his knees, both knees, without a sound. His long black coat spread out on the floor. He held his hands clasped over his mouth, and his shoulders heaved.

She sat there with hands in her lap, leaning forward, turned away from the piano, and looked at him. Her face wore a distressed, uncertain smile, while her eyes searched the dimness at the back of the room, searched so painfully, so dreamily, she seemed hardly able to focus her gaze.

The jingling of sleigh-bells came nearer and nearer, there was the crack of whips, a babel of voices.

* * *

The sleighing party had taken place on the twenty-sixth of February, and was talked of for long afterwards. The next day, February twenty-seventh, a day of thaw, that set everything to melting and dripping, splashing and running, Herr Klöterjahn's wife was in capital health and spirits. On the twenty-eighth she brought up a little blood—not much, still it was blood, and accompanied by a far greater loss of strength than ever before. She went to bed.

Dr. Leander examined her, stony-faced. He prescribed according to the dictates of science—morphia, little pieces of ice, absolute quiet. Next day, on account of pressure of work, he turned her case over to Dr. Müller, who took it on in humility and meekness of spirit and according to the letter of his contract—a quiet, pallid, insignificant little man, whose unadvertised activities were consecrated to the care of the slight cases and the hopeless ones.

Dr. Müller presently expressed the view that the separation between Frau Klöterjahn and her spouse had lasted overlong. It would be well if Herr Klöterjahn, in case his flourishing business permitted, were to make another visit to Einfried. One might write him—or even wire. And surely it would benefit the young mother's health and spirits if he were to bring young Anton with him—quite aside from the pleasure it would give the physicians to behold with their own eyes this so healthy little Anton.

And Herr Klöterjahn came. He got Herr Müller's little wire and arrived from the Baltic coast. He got out of the carriage, ordered coffee and rolls, and looked considerably aggrieved.

"My dear sir," he asked, "what is the matter? Why have I been summoned?"

"Because it is desirable that you should be near your wife," Dr. Müller replied.

"Desirable! Desirable! But is it *necessary*? It is a question of expense with me—times are poor and railway journeys cost money. Was it imperative I should take this whole day's journey?

If it were the lungs that are attacked, I should say nothing. But as it is only the trachea, thank God—"

"Herr Klöterjahn," said Dr. Müller mildly, "in the first place the trachea is an important organ. . . ." He ought not to have said "in the first place," because he did not go on to the second.

But there also arrived at Einfried, in Herr Klöterjahn's company, a full-figured personage arrayed all in red and gold and plaid, and she it was who carried on her arm Anton Klöterjahn, junior, that healthy little Anton. Yes, there he was, and nobody could deny that he was healthy even to excess. Pink and white and plump and fragrant, in fresh and immaculate attire, he rested heavily upon the bare red arm of his bebraided body-servant, consumed huge quantities of milk and chopped beef, shouted and screamed, and in every surrendered himself to his instincts.

Our author from the window of his chamber had seen him arrive. With a peculiar gaze, both veiled and piercing, he fixed young Anton with his eye as he was carried from the carriage into the house. He stood there a long time with the same expression on his face.

Herr Spinell was sitting in his room "at work."

His room was like all the others at Einfried—old-fashioned, simple, and distinguished. The massive chest of drawers was mounted with brass lions' heads; the tall mirror on the wall was not a single surface, but made up of many little panes set in lead. There was no carpet on the polished blue paved floor, the stiff legs of the furniture prolonged themselves on it in clear-cut shadows. A spacious writing-table stood at the window, across whose panes the author had drawn the folds of a yellow curtain, in all probability that he might feel more retired.

In the yellow twilight he bent over the table and wrote—wrote one of those numerous letters which he sent weekly to the post and to which, quaintly enough, he seldom or never received an answer. A large, thick quire of paper lay before him, whose upper left-hand corner was a curious involved drawing of a landscape and the name Detlev Spinell in the very latest thing in lettering. He was covering the page with a small, painfully neat, and punctiliously traced script.

"Sir:" he wrote, "I address the following lines to you because I cannot help it; because what I have to say so fills and shakes and tortures me, the words come in such a rush, that I should choke if I did not take this means to relieve myself."

If the truth were told, this about the rush of words was quite simply wide of the fact. And God knows what sort of vanity it was made Herr Spinell put it down. For his words did not come in a rush; they came with such pathetic slowness, considering the man was a writer by trade, you would have drawn the conclusion, watching him, that a writer is one to whom writing comes harder than to anybody else.

He held between two finger-tips one of those curious downy hairs he had on his cheek, and twirled it round and round, whole quarter-hours at a time, gazing into space and not coming forwards by a single line; then wrote a few words, daintily, and struck again. Yet so much was true: that what had managed to get written sounded fluent and vigorous, though the matter was odd enough, even almost equivocal, and at times impossible to follow.

"I feel," the letter went on, "an imperative necessity to make you see what I see; to show you through my eyes, illuminated by the same power of language that clothes them for me, all the things which have stood before my inner eye for weeks, like an indelible vision. It is my habit to yield to the impulse which urges me to put my own experiences into flamingly right and unforgettable words and to give them to the world. And therefore hear me.

"I will do no more than relate what has been and what is: I will merely tell a story, a brief, unspeakably touching story, without comment, blame, or passing of judgment; simply in my own words. It is the story of Gabriele Eckhof, of the woman whom you, sir, call your wife—and mark you this: it is your story, it happened to you, yet it will be I who will for the first time lift it for you to the level of an experience.

"Do you remember the garden, the old, overgrown garden

behind the grey patrician house? The moss was green in the crannies of its weather-beaten wall, and behind the wall dreams and neglect held sway. Do you remember the fountain in the centre? The pale mauve lilies leaned over its crumbling rim, the little stream prattled softly as it fell upon the riven paving. The summer day was drawing to its close.

"Seven maidens sat circlewise round the fountain; but the seventh, or rather the first and only one, was not like the others, for the sinking sun seemed to be weaving a queenly coronal among her locks. Her eyes were like troubled dreams, and yet her pure lips wore a smile.

"They were singing. They lifted their little faces to the leaping streamlet and watched its charming curve droop earthward—their music hovered round it as it leaped and danced. Perhaps their slim hands were folded in their laps the while they sang.

"Can you, sir, recall the scene? Or did you ever see it? No, you saw it not. Your eyes were not formed to see it nor your ears to catch the chaste music of their song. You saw it not, or else you would have forbade your lungs to breathe, your heart to beat. You must have turned aside and gone back to your own life, taking with you what you had seen to preserve it in the depth of your soul to the end of your earthly life, a sacred and inviolable relic. But what did you do?

"That scene, sir, was an end and culmination. Why did you come to spoil it, to give it a sequel, to turn it into the channels of ugly and commonplace life? It was a peaceful apotheosis and a moving, bathed in a sunset beauty of decadence, decay, and death. An ancient stock, too exhausted and refined for life and action, stood there at the end of its days; its latest manifestations were those of art: violin notes, full of that melancholy understanding which is ripeness for death. . . . Did you look into her eyes—those eyes where tears so often stood, lured by the dying sweetness of the violin? Her six friends may have had souls that belonged to life; but hers, the queen's and sister's, death and beauty had claimed for their own.

"You saw it, that deathly beauty; saw, and coveted. The sight of that touching purity moved you with no awe or trepidation.

And it was not enough for you to see, you must possess, you must use, you must desecrate. . . . It was the refinement of a choice you made—you are a gourmand, sir, a plebeian gourmand, a peasant with taste.

"Once more let me say that I have no wish to offend you. What I have just said is not an affront; it is a statement, a simple, psychological statement of your simple personality—a personality which for literary purposes is entirely uninteresting. I make the statement solely because I feel an impulse to clarify for you your own thoughts and actions; because it is my inevitable task on this earth to call things by their right names, to make them speak, to illuminate the unconscious. The world is full of what I call the unconscious type, and I cannot endure it; I cannot endure all these unconscious types! I cannot bear all this dull, uncomprehending, unperceiving living and behaving, this world of maddening naïveté about me! It tortures me until I am driven irresistibly to set it all in relief, in the round, to explain, express, and make self-conscious everything in the world—so far as my powers will reach—quite unhampered by the result, whether it be for good or evil, whether it brings consolation and healing or piles grief on grief.

"You, sir, as I said, are a plebeian gourmand, a peasant with taste. You stand upon an extremely low evolutionary level; your own constitution is coarse-fibred. But wealth and a sedentary habit of life have brought about in you a corruption of the nervous system, as sudden as it is unhistoric; and this corruption has been accompanied by a lascivious refinement in your choice of gratifications. It is altogether possible that the muscles of your gullet began to contract, as at the sight of some particularly rare dish, when you conceived the idea of making Gabriele Eckhof your own.

"In short, you lead her idle will astray, you beguile her out of that moss-grown garden into the ugliness of life, you give her your own vulgar name and make of her a married woman, a housewife, a mother. You take that deathly beauty—spent, aloof, flowering in lofty unconcern of the uses of this world—and debase it to the service of common things, you sacrifice it to that stupid, contemptible, clumsy graven image we call 'nature'—and not the faintest suspicion of the vileness of your conduct visits your peasant soul.

"Again. What is the result? This being, whose eyes are like troubled dreams, she bears you a child; and so doing she endows the new life, a gross continuation of its author's own, with all the blood, all the physical energy she possesses—and she dies. She dies, sir! And if she does not go hence with your vulgarity upon her head; if at the very last she has lifted herself out of the depths of degradation, and passes in an ecstasy, with the deathly kiss of beauty on her brow—well, it is I, sir, who have seen to that! You, meanwhile, were probably spending your time with chambermaids in dark corners.

"But your son, Gabriele Eckhof's son, is alive; he is living and flourishing. Perhaps he will continue in the way of his father, become a well-fed, trading, tax-paying citizen; a capable, philistine pillar of society; in any case, a tone-deaf, normally functioning individual, responsible, sturdy, and stupid, troubled by not a doubt.

"Kindly permit me to tell you, sir, that I hate you. I hate you and your child, as I hate the life of which you are the representative: cheap, ridiculous, but yet triumphant life, the everlasting antipodes and deadly enemy of beauty. I cannot say I despise you—for I am honest. You are stronger than I. I have no armour for the struggle between us, I have only the Word, avenging weapon of the weak. Today I have availed myself of this weapon. This letter is nothing but an act of revenge—you see how honourable I am—and if any word of mine is sharp and bright and beautiful enough to strike home, to make you feel the presence of a power you do not know, to shake even a minute your robust equilibrium, I shall rejoice indeed.—DETLEV SPINELL."

And Herr Spinell put this screed into an envelope, applied a stamp and a many-flourished address, and committed it to the post.

* * *

Herr Klöterjahn knocked on Herr Spinell's door. He carried a sheet of paper in his hand covered with neat script, and he looked like man bent on energetic action. The post office had done its duty, the letter had taken its appointed way: it had travelled from Einfried to Einfried and reached the hand for which it was meant. It was now four o'clock in the afternoon.

Herr Klöterjahn's entry found Herr Spinell sitting on the sofa reading his own novel with the appalling cover-design. He rose and gave his caller a surprised and inquiring look, though at the same time he distinctly flushed.

"Good afternoon," said Herr Klöterjahn. "Pardon the interruption. But may I ask if you wrote this?" He held up in his left hand the sheet inscribed with fine clear characters and struck it with the back of his right and made it crackle. Then he stuffed that hand into the pocket of his easy-fitting trousers, put his head on one side, and opened his mouth, in a way some people have, to listen.

Herr Spinell, curiously enough, smiled; he smiled engagingly, with a rather confused, apologetic air. He put his hand to his head as though trying to recollect himself, and said:

"Ah!—yes, quite right, I took the liberty—"

The fact was, he had given in to his natural man today and slept nearly up to midday, with the result that he was suffering from a bad conscience and a heavy head, was nervous and incapable of putting up a fight. And the spring air made him limp and good-for-nothing. So much we must say in extenuation of the utterly silly figure he cut in the interview which followed.

"Ah? Indeed! Very good!" said Herr Klöterjahn. He dug his chin into his chest, elevated his brows, stretched his arms, and indulged in various other antics by way of getting down to business after his introductory question. But unfortunately he so much enjoyed the figure he cut that he rather overshot the mark, and the rest of the scene hardly lived up to this preliminary pantomime. However, Herr Spinell went rather pale.

"Very good!" repeated Herr Klöterjahn. "Then permit me to give you an answer in person; it strikes me as idiotic to write pages of letter to a person when you can speak to him any hour of the day."

"Well, idiotic . . ." Herr Spinell said, with his apologetic smile. He sounded almost meek.

"Idiotic!" repeated Herr Klöterjahn, nodding violently in token of the soundness of his position. "And I should not demean myself to answer this scrawl; to tell the truth, I should have thrown it away at once if I had not found in it the explanation of certain changes—however, that is no affair of yours, and has nothing to do with the thing anyhow. I am a man of action, I have other things to do than to think about your unspeakable visions."

"I wrote *'indelible vision,'* " said Herr Spinell, drawing himself up. This was the only moment at which he displayed a little self-respect.

"Indelible, unspeakable," responded Herr Klöterjahn, referring to the text. "You write a villainous hand, sir; you would not get a position in my office, let me tell you. It looks clear enough at first, but when you come to study it, it is full of shakes and quavers. But that is your affair, it's no business of mine. What I have come to say to you is that you are a tomfool—which you probably know already. Furthermore, you are a cowardly sneak; I don't suppose I have to give the evidence for that either. My wife wrote me once that when you meet a woman you don't look her square in the face, but just give her a side squint, so as to carry away a good impression, because you are afraid of the reality. I should probably have heard more of the same sort of stories about you, only unfortunately she stopped mentioning you. But this is the kind of thing you are: you talk so much about 'beauty'; you are all chicken-livered hypocrisy and cant—which is probably at the bottom of your impudent allusion to out-of-the-way corners too. That ought to crush me, of course, but it just makes me laugh—it doesn't do a thing but make me laugh! Understand? Have I clarified your thoughts and actions for you, you pitiable object, you? Though of course it is not my invariable calling—"

" *'Inevitable'* was the word I used," Herr Spinell said; but he did not insist on the point. He stood there, crestfallen, like a big, unhappy, chidden, grey-haired schoolboy.

"Invariable or inevitable, whichever you like—anyhow you are a contemptible cur, and that I tell you. You see me every day at table, you bow and smirk and say good-morning—and one fine day you send me a scrawl full of idiotic abuse. Yes, you've a lot of courage—on paper! And it's not only this ridiculous letter—you have been intriguing behind my back. I can see that now. Though you need not flatter yourself it did any good. If you imagine you put any ideas into my wife's head you never were more mistaken in your life. And if you think she behaved any different when we came from what she always does, then you just put the cap onto your own foolishness. She did not kiss the little chap, that's true, but it was only a precaution, because they have the idea now that the trouble is with her lungs, and in such cases you can't tell whether—though that still remains to be proved, no matter what you say with your 'She dies, sir,' you silly ass!"

Here Herr Klöterjahn paused for breath. He was in a furious passion; he kept stabbing the air with his right forefinger and crumpling the sheet of paper in his other hand. His face, between the blond English mutton-chops, was frightfully red and his dark brow was rent with swollen veins like lightnings of scorn.

"You hate me," he went on, "and you would despise me if I were not stronger than you. Yes, you're right there! I've got my heart in the right place, by God, and you've got yours mostly in the seat of your trousers. I would most certainly hack you into bits if it weren't against the law, you and your gabble about the 'Word,' you skulking fool! But I have no intention of putting up with your insults; and when I show this part about the vulgar name to my lawyer at home, you will very likely get a little surprise. My name, sir, is a first-rate name, and I have made it so by my own efforts. You know better than I do whether anybody would ever lend you a penny piece on yours, you lazy lout! The law defends people against the kind you are! You are a common danger, you are enough to drive a body crazy! But you're left this time, my master! I don't let individuals like you get the best of me so fast! I've got my heart in the right place—"

Herr Klöterjahn's excitement had really reached a pitch. He shrieked, he bellowed, over and over again, that his heart was in the right place.

" 'They were singing.' Exactly. Well, they weren't. They were knitting. And if I heard what they said, it was about a recipe for potato pancakes; and when I show my father-in-law that about the old decayed family you'll probably have a libel suit on your hands. 'Did you see the picture?' Yes, of course I saw it; only I don't see why that should make me hold my breath and run away. I don't leer at women out of the corner of my eye; I look at them square, and if I like their looks I go for them. I have my heart in the right place—"

Somebody knocked. Knocked eight or ten times, quite fast, one after the other—a sudden, alarming little commotion that made Herr Klöterjahn pause; and an unsteady voice that kept tripping over itself in its haste and distress said:

"Herr Klöterjahn, Herr Klöterjahn—oh, is Herr Klöterjahn there?"

"Stop outside," said Herr Klöterjahn, in a growl. . . . "What's the matter? I'm busy talking."

"Oh, Herr Klöterjahn," said the quaking, breaking voice, "you must come! The doctors are there too—oh, it is all so dreadfully sad—"

He took one step to the door and tore it open. Frau Magistrate Spatz was standing there. She had her handkerchief before her mouth, and giant egg-shaped tears rolled into it, two by two.

"Herr Klöterjahn," she got out. "It is so frightfully sad. . . . She has brought up so much blood, such a horrible lot of blood. . . . She was sitting up quite quietly in bed and humming a little snatch of music . . . and there it came . . . my God, such a quantity you never saw. . . ."

"Is she dead?" yelled Herr Klöterjahn. As he spoke he clutched the Rätin by the arm and pulled her to and fro on the sill. "Not quite? Not dead; she can see me, can't she? Brought up a little blood again, from the lung, eh? Yes, I give in, it may be from the lung. Gabriele!" he suddenly cried out, and his eyes filled with tears; you could see what a burst of good, warm, honest human feeling came over him. "Yes, I'm coming," he said, and dragged the Rätin after him as he went with long strides down the corridor. You could still hear his voice, from quite a distance, sounding fainter and fainter: "Not quite, eh? From the lung?"

Herr Spinell stood still on the spot where he had stood during the whole of Herr Klöterjahn's rudely interrupted call and looked out the open door. At length he took a couple of steps and listened down the corridor. But all was quiet, so he closed the door and came back into the room.

He looked at himself awhile in the glass, then he went up to the writing-table, took a little flask and a glass out of a drawer, and drank a cognac—for which nobody can blame him. Then he stretched himself out on the sofa and closed his eyes.

The upper half of the window was down. Outside in the garden birds were twittering; those dainty, saucy little notes held all the spring, finely and penetratingly expressed. Herr Spinell spoke once: *"Invariable calling,"* he said, and moved his head and drew in the air through his teeth as though his nerves pained him violently.

Impossible to recover any poise or tranquillity. Crude experiences like this were too much—he was not made for them. By a sequence of emotions, the analysis of which would lead us too far afield, Herr Spinell arrived at the decision that it would be well for him to have a little out-of-doors exercise. He took his hat and went downstairs.

As he left the house and issued into the mild, fragrant air, he turned his head and lifted his eyes, slowly, scanning the house until he reached one of the windows, a curtained window, on which his gaze rested awhile, fixed and sombre. Then he laid his hands on his back and moved away across the gravel path. He moved in deep thought.

The beds were still straw-covered, the trees and bushes bare;

but the snow was gone, the path was only damp in spots. The large garden with its grottoes, bowers and little pavilions lay in the splendid colourful afternoon light, strong shadow and rich, golden sun, and the dark network of branches stood out sharp and articulate against the bright sky.

It was about that hour of the afternoon when the sun takes shape, and from being a formless volume of light turns to a visibly sinking disk, whose milder, more saturated glow the eye can tolerate. Herr Spinell did not see the sun, the direction the path took hid it from his view. He walked with bent head and hummed a strain of music, a short phrase, a figure that mounted wailingly and complainingly upward—the *Sehnsuchtsmotiv*. . . . But suddenly, with a start, a quick, jerky intake of breath, he stopped, as though rooted to the path, and gazed straight ahead of him, with brows fiercely gathered, staring eyes, and an expression of horrified repulsion.

The path had curved just here, he was facing the setting sun. It stood large and slantwise in the sky, crossed by two narrow strips of gold-rimmed cloud; it set the tree-tops aglow and poured its red-gold radiance across the garden. And there, erect in the path, in the midst of the glory, with the sun's mighty aureola above her head, there confronted him an exuberant figure, all arrayed in red and gold and plaid. She had one hand on her swelling hip, with the other she moved to and fro the graceful little perambulator. And in this perambulator sat the child—sat Anton Klöterjahn, junior, Gabriele Eckhof's fat son.

There he sat among his cushions, in a woolly white jacket and large white hat, plump-cheeked, well cared for, and magnificent; and his blithe unerring gaze encountered Herr Spinell's. The novelist pulled himself together. Was he not a man, had he not the power to pass this unexpected, sun-kindled apparition there in the path and continue on his walk? But Anton Klöterjahn began to laugh and shout—most horrible to see. He squealed, he crowed with inconceivable delight—it was positively uncanny to hear him.

God knows what had taken him; perhaps the sight of Herr Spinell's long, black figure set him off; perhaps an attack of sheer animal spirits gave rise to his wild outburst of merriment. He had a bone teething-ring in one hand and a tin rattle in the other; and these two objects he flung aloft with shoutings, shook them to and fro, and clashed them together in the air, as though purposely to frighten Herr Spinell. His eyes were almost shut, his mouth gaped open till all the rosy gums were displayed; and as he shouted he rolled his head about in excess of mirth.

Herr Spinell turned round and went thence. Pursued by the youthful Klöterjahn's joyous screams, he went away across the gravel, walking stiffly, yet not without grace; his gait was the hesitating gait of one who would disguise the fact that, inwardly, he is running away.

1902

FELIX KRULL

As I take my pen in hand, in ample leisure and complete retirement—in sound health too, though tired, so very tired that I shall hardly be able to proceed save in small stages and with frequent pauses for rest—as I take up my pen, then, to commit my confessions to the long-suffering paper, in the neat and pleasing calligraphy of which I am master, I own to a fleeting misgiving on the score of my own fitness for the task in hand. Am I, I ask myself, equipped by previous training for this intellectual enterprise? However, since every word that I have to say concerns solely my own personal and peculiar experiences, errors, and passions and hence should be entirely within my compass; so the only doubt which can arise is whether I command the necessary tact and gifts of expression, and in my view these are less the fruit of a regular course of study than of natural parts and a favourable atmosphere in youth. For the latter I have not lacked; I come of an upper-class if somewhat loose-living home, and my sister Olympia and I had the benefit for some months of the ministrations of a Fräulein from Vevey—though it is true that she had to leave, in consequence of a rivalry between her and my mother, of which my father was the object. My godfather Maggotson, with whom I was in daily and intimate contact, was an artist of considerable merit; everybody in the little town called him professor, though that enviable title was his more by courtesy than by right. My father, his size and obesity notwithstanding, had great personal charm, and he always laid stress upon lucid and well-chosen language. There was French blood in the family from the grandmother's side and he himself had spent some of his young years in France—he used to say that he knew Paris like his waistcoat pocket. His French pronunciation was excellent and he was fond of introducing into his conversation little expressions like *"C'est ça," "épatant," "parfaitement," "à mon gout,"* and so on. Up till the end of his life he was a great favourite with the female sex. I have said all this of course by way of preface and somewhat out of the due order of my tale. As for myself I have a natural instinct for good form, upon which throughout my career of fraud I have always been able to rely, as my story will only too abundantly show. I think therefore that I may commit it to writing without further misgivings on this score. I am resolved to practise the utmost candour, regardless whether I incur the reproach of vanity or shamelessness—for what moral value or significance can confessions like mine possess if they have not the value of perfect sincerity?

The Rhine valley brought me forth—that region favoured of heaven, mild and without ruggedness either in its climate or in the nature of its soil, abounding in cities and villages peopled by a blithe and laughter-loving folk—truly of all the regions of the earth it must be one of the sweetest. Here on these slopes exposed to the southern sun and sheltered from rude winds by the hills of the Rhine valley lie those flourishing resorts the very sound of whose names makes the heart of the toper to laugh: Rüdesheim, Johannisberg, Rauenthal—and here too that most estimable little town where forty years ago I saw the light. It lies slightly westward of the bend made by the river at Mainz. Containing some four thousand souls, it is famous for its wine-cellars and is one of the chief landing-places for the steamers which ply up and down the Rhine. Thus the gay city of Mainz was very near, the Taunus baths patronized by high society, Homburg, Langenschwalbach, and Schlangenbad. This last we could reach by a half-hour's journey on a narrow-gauge road;

and how often in the pleasant time of year did we make excursions thither, my parents, my sister Olympia, and I, by train, by carriage, or by boat! Many other excursions we made too, in all directions, for everywhere nature smiled and the hand of man and his fertile brain had spread out pleasures for our delectation. I can still see my father, clad in his comfortable summer suit with a pattern of small checks, as he used to sit with us in the arbour of some inn garden, rather far off the table, for his paunch prevented him from drawing up close, wrapt in enjoyment of a dish of prawns washed down with golden wine. Often my godfather Maggotson was with us, looking at the scene through his big round glasses and absorbing great and small into his artist soul.

My poor father was the proprietor of the firm of Engelbert Krull, makers of the now extinct brand of sparkling wine called Lorley Extra Cuvée. The cellars of the firm lay on the Rhine not far from the landing-stage, and often as a lad I used to play in the cool vaults or follow the stone-paved lanes that led in all directions among the high-tiered shelves, meditating upon the army of bottles that lay in slanting rows upon their sides. "There you lie," I would apostrophize them—though of course at that time I had no power to put my thoughts into apposite words—"there you lie in this subterranean twilight and within you there is clearing and mellowing that bubbling golden sap which shall make so many pairs of eyes to sparkle and so many hearts to throb with heightened zest. You are not much to look at now; but one day you will mount up to the light and be arrayed in festal splendour and there will be parties and weddings and little celebrations in private rooms and your corks will pop up to the ceiling and kindle mirth and levity and desire in the hearts of men."—Some such ideas as these the boy strove to express; and so much at least was true, that the firm of Engelbert Krull laid great stress upon the exterior of their wares, those last touches which in the trade are known as the coiffure. The compressed corks were fastened with silver wire and gold cords sealed with purple wax, yes, actually a stately round seal such as one sees on documents. The necks were wrapped in a fullness of silver foil and on the swelling body was a flaring label with gilt flourishes round the edge. This label had been concocted by my godfather Maggotson. It bore several coats of arms and stars, my father's monogram, and the name of the brand: Lorley Extra Cuvée, all in gilt letters, and a female figure arrayed in a few spangles and a necklace, sitting on the top of a rock with her legs crossed, combing her flowing hair. But unfortunately it appears that the quality of the wine did not correspond to the splendour of its setting-out. "Krull," I have heard my godfather say, "I have the greatest respect for you personally; but really the police ought to condemn your wine. A week ago I was foolish enough to drink half a bottle and my constitution has not yet recovered from the shock. What sort of stuff do you dose it with—petroleum, fusel oil? Anyhow, it's poison. You ought to be afraid to sell it." My poor father's was a soft nature, he could not bear hard words and was always thrown into a distress. "It's all right for you to joke, Maggotson," he would answer, gently caressing his belly with his finger-tips, as was his habit, "but there is such a prejudice against the domestic product, I have to keep down the price and make the public believe it is getting something for its money. Anyhow, the competition is so fierce that I shall not be able to go on for long." Thus my poor father.

Our villa was a charming little property seated on a slope commanding a view of the Rhine. The front garden ran downhill and rejoiced in many crockeryware adornments: dwarfs, toadstools, and animals in lifelike poses; there was a looking-glass ball on a stand, which grotesquely distorted the faces of the passers-by; an æolian harp, several grottoes, and a fountain whose spray made an ingenious design in the air while silver-fish swam in the basin. As for our domestic interior, it was after my father's heart, who above all things liked comfort and good cheer. Cosy nooks invited one to sit down; there was a real spinning-wheel in one corner, and endless trifles and knickknacks. Mussel-shells, glass boxes, bottles of smelling-salts stood about on étagères and velvet-topped tables. A multiplicity of down cushions in silk-embroidered covers were distributed on sofas and day-beds, for my father loved to lie soft. The curtain-rods were halberds, and the portières very jolly, made of coloured beads and rushes, which look quite like a solid door, but you can pass through without lifting your hand, when they fall behind you with a whispering sound. Above the wind-screen was an ingenious device which played the first bar of "Wine, Women, and Song" in a pleasing little tinkle whenever the door opened or shut.

Such was the home upon which, on a mild rainy Sunday in May, I first opened my eyes. From now on I mean to follow the order of events and not run ahead of my story. If report tells true, the birth was slow and difficult and did not come to pass without help from the family doctor, whose name was Mecum. It appears that I—if I may use the first person to refer to that far-away and foreign little being—was extremely inactive and made no attempt to second my mother's efforts, showing no zeal to enter a world which I was yet to love with such an ardent love. However, I was a healthy and well-formed infant and throve at the breast of my excellent wet-nurse in a way to encourage the liveliest hopes for my future. Yet the most mature reflection inclines me to associate this reluctance to exchange the darkness of the womb for the light of day with the extraordinary gift and passion for sleep which has been mine all my life. They tell me that I was a quiet child, that I did not cry and break the peace, but was given to sleep and napping, to a degree most comfortable to my nurses. And however great my subsequent love of the world, which caused me to mingle in it in all sorts of guises and to attach it to myself by all possible means, yet I feel that in night and slumber always my true home was to be found. Even without physical fatigue I have always fallen asleep with the greatest ease and enjoyment, lost myself in far and dreamless forgetfulness, and waked after ten or twelve or even fourteen hours' oblivion more refreshed and gratified than even by all the satisfactions and successes of my waking hours. Is there a contradiction here between this love of sleep and my great urge towards life and love of which it will be in place to speak hereafter? I have said that I have concentrated much thought upon this matter and several times I have had the clearest perception that there is no contradiction but rather a hidden connection and correspondence. And it is the fact that now, when I have aged and grown weary so that I feel none of my old irresistible compulsion towards the society of men, but live in complete retirement, only now is my power of sleep impaired, so that I am in a sense a stranger to it, my slumbers being short and light and fleeting; whereas even in the prison—where there was much opportunity—I slept better than in the soft beds of the most luxurious hotels. But I am fallen into my old error of getting ahead of my story.

Often enough I heard from my parents' lips that I was a Sunday child; and though I was brought up to despise all forms of superstition I have always thought there was some significance in the fact, taken in connection with my Christian name of Felix (for so I was christened, after my godfather Maggotson) and my physical fineness and sense of well-being. Yes, I have always believed that I was *felix*, a favoured child of the gods; and I may say that, on the whole, events do not show me to have been mistaken in this lively conviction. Indeed, it is peculiarly characteristic of my career that whatever misfortune and suffering it may have held always seemed like a divergence from the natural order, a cloud, as it were, through which my native sunniness continued to shine.— After which digression into the abstract I will once more return to depict in its broad outlines the scene of my early youth.

A child fully of fantasy, I afforded the family much amusement by my imaginative flights. I have often been told, and seem still to remember, how when I was still in dresses it pleased me to pretend that I was the Kaiser. In this game I would persist for hours at a time. Sitting in my little go-cart, which my nurse would push about the garden or the lower floors of the house. I would draw down my mouth as far as I could, so that my upper lip was lengthened out of all proportion, and blink my eyes slowly until what with the strain and the strength of my feelings they would presently grow red and fill with tears. Quite overcome with the burden of my age and dignity I would sit silent in my go-cart, my nurse having been instructed to tell all the passers-by how things stood, for I should have taken it hard had they failed to fall in with my whim. "This is the Kaiser I am pushing about here," she would say, carrying her hand to her temple in an awkward salute; and everybody would pay me homage. My godfather Maggotson, who loved his joke, would play up to me in every way. "Look, there he goes, the hoary old hero!" he would say, with an exaggeratedly deep obeisance. Then he would pretend to be the populace and stand beside my path tossing his hat in the air, his stick, even his glasses, shouting: "Hurrah, hurrah!" and laughing fit to kill himself when out of the excess of my emotions the tears would roll down my long-drawn face.

I used to play the same sort of game when I was much older and could no longer expect my elders to fall in with them. I did not miss their co-operation, glorying as I did in my free and incommunicable flights of imagination. I awoke one morning, for instance, filled with the idea that I was a prince, a prince eighteen years old, named Karl; and prince I remained all day long, for the inestimable advantage of this kind of game was that it never needed to be interrupted, not even during the almost insupportable hours which I spent at school. I moved about clothed in a sort of amiable aloofness, holding lively imaginary converse with my governor or adjutant; and the secret of my own superiority which I hugged to my breast filled me with a perfectly indescribable pride and joy. What a glorious gift is the fancy, what subtle satisfactions it affords! The boys I knew, being ignorant of this priceless advantage which I possessed, seemed to me dull and limited louts indeed, unable to enter the kingdom where I was at home at no cost to myself and simply by an act of the will. They were all very simple fellows, with coarse hair and red hands. They would have had a hard time indeed convincing themselves that they were princes—and very foolish they would have looked. Whereas my hair was as silken-soft as one seldom sees it in boys, and light in colour; together with my blue-grey eyes it formed a fascinating contrast to the golden brownness of my skin, so that I hovered on the border-line between blond and brunet and might have been considered either.

I had good hands and early began to care for them: well-shaped without being too narrow, never clammy, but dry and just warm enough to be pleasant. The finger-nails too were the kind that it is a pleasure to look at. And my voice, even before it changed, had an ingratiating note and could fall so flatteringly upon the ear that I liked above all things to listen to it myself when I was alone and could blissfully engage in long, plausible, but quite meaningless colloquies with my aide-de-camp, accompanying them with extravagant gestures and attitudes. Such, then, were the physical advantages which I possessed; but these things are mostly very intangible, well-nigh impossible to put into words even for one equipped with a high degree of literary skill, and only recognizable in their effects. However that may be, I could not for long have disguised from myself that I was made of finer stuff than my schoolmates, and take no shame to myself for frankly admitting that such was the case. It is nothing to me to be accused of conceit; I should need to be either a fool or a hypocrite to write myself down an average person when I am but honouring the truth in repeating that I am made of finer stuff.

I grew up very much by myself, for my sister Olympia was several years older than I; and indulged as pastime in various mental quiddities, of which I will cite one or two. I had taken it into my head to study that mysterious force the human will and to practise in myself how far it was capable of extension into regions considered beyond human powers. It is a well-known fact that the muscles controlling the pupils of our eyes react involuntarily in accordance with the strength of the light upon them. I decided to test whether this reaction could be brought under control of the will. I would stand before my mirror and concentrate all my powers upon the effort to expand or contract my pupils. And I protest that these obstinate efforts were actually crowned with success. At first, while I stood bathed in perspiration, my colour coming and going, there would be an irregular flicker and fluctuation. But by practice I actually succeeded in narrowing the pupils to the merest points and then expanding them to great round pools of blackness. The fearful joy I felt at this result was actually accompanied by a physical shuddering before the mysteries of our human nature.

It was at this time, too, I often amused myself by a sort of introspection which even today has not lost all charm for me. I would inquire of myself: which is better, to see the world small or to see it large? The significance of the question was this: great men, I thought, field-marshals, statesmen, conquerors, and leading spirits generally that rise above the mass of mankind must be so constituted as to see the world small, like a chess-board, else they would never command the necessary ruthlessness to regulate the common weal and woe according to their own will. Yet it was quite possible, on the other hand, that such a diminishing point of view, as it were, might lead to one doing nothing at all. For if you saw the world and human beings in it as small and insignificant and were early persuaded that nothing was worth while, you could easily sink into indifference and indolence and contemptuously prefer your own peace of mind to any influence you might exert upon the spirits of men. And added to that your own supine detachment from mankind would certainly give offence and cut you off still further from any success you might have had in despite of yourself. Then is it better, I would next inquire, to think of the world and human nature as great, glorious, and important, worthy the expenditure of every effort to the end of achieving some meed of esteem and good report? Yet again, how easily can such a point of view lead to self-detraction and loss of confidence, so that the fickle world passes you by with a smile as a simpleton, in favour of more self-confident lovers! Though on the other hand such genuine credulity and artlessness has its good side too, since men cannot but be flattered by the way you look up to them; and if you devote yourself to making this impression, it will give weight and seriousness to your life, lend it meaning in your own eyes, and lead to your advancement. In this wise would I speculate and weigh the pros and cons; but always it has lain in my nature to take up the second position, seeing the world and mankind as great and glorious phenomena, capable of affording such priceless satisfactions that no effort on my part could seem disproportionate to the rewards I might reap.

Ideas of this kind were certainly calculated to isolate me from my schoolmates and companions, who of course spent their time in more commonplace and traditional occupations. But it is also a fact that these boys, most of whose fathers were either civil servants or the owners of vineyards, were instructed to avoid my society. I early discovered this, for on inviting one of them to our home he made no bones of telling me that he had been forbidden to associate with me because my family were not respectable. The experience not only wounded my pride but made me covet an intercourse which otherwise I could not have craved. But there is no doubt that the current opinion about our household and the goings-on there was in large measure justified.

I have referred above to the disturbance in our family circle due to the presence of our Fräulein from Vevey. My poor father was infatuated with this girl and ran after her until he succeeded in gaining his ends, or so it seemed, for dissensions arose between him and my mother and he departed for Mainz, where he remained for several weeks restoring his equilibrium with the joys of a bachelor life. My mother took entirely the wrong course, I am convinced, in treating my poor father with such a lack of consideration. She was a woman of insignificant mental parts; but what was more to the point, her human weaknesses were no less apparent than his own. My sister Olympia, a fat and fleshly-minded creature who later went on the stage and had some small success there, took after her in this respect—the difference between them and my poor father being that theirs was a heavy and sensual greed of pleasure, whereas his follies were never without a certain ease and grace. Mother and daughter lived in unusual intimacy—I recall once seeing my mother measure Olympia's thigh with a tape-measure, which gave me to think for several hours. Another time, when I was old enough to have some intuitive understanding of such matters though no words to express them in, I watched unseen and saw my mother and sister flirting with a young painter who was doing some work about the house. He was a dark-eyed lad in a white smock and they painted upon him a green moustache with his own paint. In the end they roused him to such a pitch that they fled giggling up the attic stair and he pursued them thither. My parents bored each other to tears and got relief by filling the house with guests from Mainz and Wiesbaden so that our house was the scene of a continual round of gaieties. It was a promiscuous crew who frequented these gatherings: actors and actresses, young business men, the sickly young infantry lieutenant who later proposed to my sister; a Jewish banker with a wife whose charms gushed appallingly out of her jet-spangled frock; a journalist in a velvet waistcoat with a lock of hair falling over his brow, who every time brought along a new wife. They would arrive for seven o'clock dinner, and the feasting, the dancing and piano-playing, the skylarking and shrieks of laughter would go on all night. Particularly at carnival-time and the vintage season the waves of pleasure rose very high. My father, who was very clever in such things, would set off the most splendid fireworks in the garden; all the company would be masked and unearthly light would play upon the crockery dwarfs. All restraint was abandoned. At that time it was my sorry lot to attend the high school of our little town; and often I would go down to the dining-room at seven o'clock or half past with face new-washed, to eat my breakfast and find the guests still at their after-dinner coffee, rumpled, sallow, and hollow-eyed, blinking at the daylight; they would receive me into their midst with shoutings.

When still quite young I was allowed with my sister Olympia to take part in the festivities. Even when alone we always set a good table, and my father drank champagne mixed with soda-water. But at these parties there were endless courses prepared by a chef from Wiesbaden with the assistance of our own cook: the most tempting succession of sweets, savouries, and ices. Lorley Extra Cuvée flowed in streams, but many good wines were served as well. I was particularly fond of the bouquet of Berncasteler Doctor. Later in life I made acquaintance with many of the noblest wines and could order Grand Vin Château Margaux or Grand Cru Mouton-Rothschild, two very fine wines, as to the manner born.

I love to call up the picture of my father as he presided at the head of the table, with his white imperial, and his belly confined in a white silk waistcoat. His voice was weak and sometimes he would be seized by self-consciousness and look down at his plate. Yet his enjoyment was to be read in his eyes and in his shining red face. *"C'est épatant,"* he would say. *"Parfaitement"*—and with his fingers, which curved backwards at the tips, he would give delicate touches to the table-service. My mother and sister meanwhile were abandoned to a gross and soulless gluttony, between courses flirting with their table-mates behind their fans.

After dinner, when the gas-chandeliers began to be wreathed in smoke, came dancing and forfeit-playing. When the evening was advanced I used to be sent to bed; but as sleep, in that din, was out of the question, I would wrap myself in my red woollen coverlet and in this becoming disguise return to the feast, where I was received with cries of joy from all the females. Refreshments such as wine jellies, lemonade, punch, herring salad, were served in relays until the morning coffee. The dance was free and untrammelled, the games of forfeits were pretext for much kissing and caressing; the ladies bent over the backs of their chairs to give the gentlemen stimulating glimpses into the bosoms of their frocks; and the climax of the evening arrived when some humorist turned out the gas and there was a general scramble in the dark.

These parties were undoubtedly the cause of the unfavourable criticism which spread about the town; but according to the reports which came to my ears it was their economic aspect that was the target for gossip. For it was only too well known that my father's business was at a desperate pass and that the dining and wining and fireworks must give it the *coup de grâce*. I was sensitive enough to feel the hostile atmosphere when I was still very young; it united, as I have said, with certain peculiarities of my own character to give me on the whole a great deal of pain. The more cordially, then, did I appreciate an incident which took place about this time; I set it down here with peculiar pleasure.

I was eight years old when my family and I spent some weeks one summer at the famous and neighbouring resort of Langenschwalbach. My father took mud baths for his gout, and my mother and sister made themselves talked about for the size and shape of their hats. Of the society we frequented there is little good to be said. The residential class, as usual, avoided us. The better-class guests kept themselves to themselves as they usually do; and such society as we could get had not much to recommend it. Yet I liked Langenschwalbach and later on often made such resorts the scene of my operations. The tranquil, well-regulated existence and the sight of aristocratic and well-groomed people in the gardens and on the tennis courts satisfied an inward craving of my soul. But the strongest attraction of all was the daily concert given by a well-trained orchestra to the guests of the cure. Though I have never attained to skill in any branch of the art I was a fanatical lover of music; even as a child I could not tear myself away from the pretty little pavilion where a becomingly uniformed band played selections and potpourris under the direction of their gypsy leader. Hours on end I would crouch on the steps of that little temple of art, enchanted to my very marrow by the ordered succession of sweet sounds and watching with rapture every motion of the musicians as they attacked their instruments. In particular I was thrilled by the gestures of the violinists and when I went home I delighted my parents with an imitation performed on two sticks, one long and one short. The swinging movement of the left arm in producing a soulful tone, the soft gliding motion from one position to the next, the dexterity of the fingering in virtuoso passages and cadenzas, the fine and supple bowing of the right wrist, the cheek cuddled in such utter abandonment to the violin—all this I succeeded in reproducing so faithfully that the family, especially my father, burst into enthusiastic applause. And being in good spirits due to the beneficial effect of the baths, he conceived the following little joke, with the connivance of the long-haired and almost speechless little bandmaster. They bought a small cheap violin and plentifully smeared the bow with vaseline. As a rule not much attention was paid to my appearance; but now I was arrayed in a pretty sailor suit with gilt buttons and lanyard all complete, also silk stockings and shiny patent-leather shoes. And one Sunday I took my place at the side of the little conductor during the afternoon promenade concert and assisted in the performance of a Hungarian dance, doing with my violin and my vaselined bow what I had done with my two sticks. My success was tremendous. The public, gentle and simple, streamed up from all sides and assembled before the pavilion to look at the infant prodigy. My pale face, my utter absorption in my task, the lock of hair falling over my brow, my childish hands and wrists in the full, tapering sleeves of the pretty blue sailor suit—in short, my whole touching and astonishing little figure captured all hearts. When I finished with a full sweep of the bow across all the fiddle-strings, the garden resounded with applause and delighted cries from male and female throats. The bandmaster stowed my bow and fiddle safely away and I was set down on the ground, where I was overwhelmed with praises and caresses. The most aristocratic ladies and gentlemen stroked my hair, patted my cheeks and hands, called me an angel child and an amazing little devil. An old Russian princess in violet silk and white side-curls took my head between her beringed hands and kissed my brow, all beaded as it was with perspiration. Then in a pitch of enthusiasm she snatched a lyre-shaped diamond brooch from her throat and with a perfect torrent of ecstatic French pinned it on the front of my blouse. My family approached and my father made excuses for the defects of my playing on the score of my tender years. I was escorted to the confectioner's, where at three different tables I was regaled with chocolate and cream cakes. The scions of the noble family of Siebenklingen, whom I had admired from afar while they regarded me with cold disdain, came up and asked me to play croquet, and while our parents drank coffee together I went off with the children in the seventh heaven of delight, my diamond brooch upon my blouse. That was one of the happiest days of my life, perhaps quite the happiest. The cry was set up that I should play again; actually the management of the Casino approached my father and asked for an encore; but he refused, saying that he had only permitted me to play by way of exception and that repeated public appearances were not consistent with my social position. And besides our stay in Bad Langenschwalbach was drawing to a close.

I wish now to speak of my godfather Maggotson, by no means an ordinary man. He was short and thickset in build, with thin and prematurely grey hair, which he wore parted over one ear and brushed across his crown. He was clean-shaven, with a hooked nose and thin, compressed lips, and wore large round glasses with celluloid rims. His face was further remarkable for the fact that it was bald above the eyes, having no brows to speak of; also for the somewhat acidulous disposition it betrayed—to which, indeed, he was wont to give expression in words, as for instance in his cynical explanation of the name he bore. "Nature," he would say, "is full of corruption and blowflies, and I am her offspring. Therefore am I called Maggotson. But as for why I am called Felix, that God alone knows." He came from Cologne, where he had once moved in the best social circles and often acted as carnival steward. But for reasons which remained obscure he had been obliged to leave Cologne; he had gone into retirement in our little town, where he very soon—a considerable time before my birth—became an intimate of our household. At all our evening companies he was a regular and indispensable guest and in high favour with young and old. He would purse his lips and fix the ladies through his round glasses, with appraising eyes, until they would screech for mercy, putting their hands before their faces and begging him to turn away his gaze. Apparently they feared the penetrating artist eye; but he, it would seem, did not share in their awe of his calling, and not infrequently made ironic allusions to the nature of artists. "Phidias," he would say, "also called Pheidias, was a man of more than average gifts—as might perhaps be gathered from the fact that he was convicted for theft and put in jail at Athens for having appropriated to his own use the gold and ivory entrusted to him for his statue of Athena. But Pericles, who had discovered him, had him set free, thereby proving himself to be a connoisseur not only of art but of artists as well; and Phidias—or Pheidias—went to Olympia, where he was commissioned to make the great chryselephantine statue of Olympian Zeus. But what did he do? He stole the gold and ivory again—and there in the prison at Olympia he died. An extraordinary combination, my friends. But that is the way people are. They want people to be talented—which is already something out of the ordinary. But when it comes to the other qualities which go with the talents—and perhaps are essential to them—oh, no, they don't care for these at all, they refuse to have any understanding of them." Thus my godfather. I have set down his remarks verbatim because he repeated them so often that I know them by heart.

I have said that we lived on terms of mutual regard; yes, I believe that I enjoyed his especial favour, and often as I grew older it was my especial delight to serve as his model, dressing up in all sorts of costumes, of which he possessed a large and varied collection. His studio was a sort of lumber-room with a large window under the roof of a little house standing by itself down on the Rhine. He rented this house and lived in it with an old serving-woman, and there I would pose for him hours at a time, perched on a rude model-throne while he brushed and scraped and painted away. Several times I sat for him in the nude for a large picture with a Greek mythological subject, destined to adorn the dining-room of a wine-dealer in Mainz. When I did this my godfather was not chary of his praise; and indeed I was a little like a young god, slender, graceful, yet powerful in build, with a golden skin and proportions that lacked little of perfection. If there was a fault it lay in that my legs were a little too short; but my godfather consoled me for this defect by saying that Goethe, that prince of the intellect, had been short-legged too and certainly had never been hampered thereby. The hours devoted to these sittings form an especial chapter in my memory. Yet I enjoyed even more, I think, the "dressing up" itself; and that took place not only in the studio but at our house as well. Often when my godfather was to sup with us he would send up a large bundle of costumes, wigs, and accessories and try them all on me after the meal, sketching any particularly good effect on the lid of a pasteboard box. "He has a head for costumes," he would say, meaning that everything became me, and that in each disguise which I assumed I looked better and more natural than in the last. I might appear as a Roman flute-player in a short smock, a wreath of roses twined in my back locks; as an English page in snug-fitting satin with lace collar and plumed hat; as a Spanish bullfighter in spangled jacket and large round sombrero; as a youthful abbé of the Watteau period, with cap and bands, mantle and buckled shoes; as an Austrian officer in white military tunic with sash and dagger; or as a German mountaineer in leather shorts and hobnailed boots, with the bock's-beard stuck in his green felt hat—whatever the costume, the mirror assured me that I was born to wear it, and my audience declared that I looked to the life exactly the person whom I aimed to represent. My godfather even asserted that with the aid of costume and wig I seemed able to put on not only whatever social rank or national characteristics I chose, but that I could actually adapt myself to any given period or century. For each age, my godfather would say, imparts to its children its own physiognomical stamp; whereas I, in the costume of a Florentine dandy of the end of the Middle Ages, could look as though I had stepped from a contemporary portrait, and yet be no less convincing in the full-bottomed wig which was the fashionable ideal of a later century.— Ah, those were glorious hours! But when they were over and I resumed my dull and ordinary dress, how stale, flat, and unprofitable seemed all the world by contrast, in what deep dejection did I spend the rest of the evening!

Of my godfather I shall say no more in this place. Later on, at the end of my strenuous career, this extraordinary man intervened decisively in my destiny and saved me from despair.

I search my mind for further impressions of my youth, and am reminded at once of the day when I first attended the theatre, at Wiesbaden, with my parents. I should interpolate here that in which I have so far set down I have not too anxiously adhered to the chronological order but have treated my younger days as a whole and moved freely within them from episode to episode.

When I posed to my godfather as a Greek god I was sixteen or seventeen years old and thus no longer a child, though very backward at school. But my first visit to the theatre fell in my fourteenth year—though even so my physical and mental maturity, as will presently be seen, was well advanced and my sensitiveness to certain classes of impressions much keener than is ordinarily the case. What I saw that evening made the strongest impression on me and gave me food for perennial reflection.

We had first visited a Viennese café, where I drank sweet punch and my father imbibed absinthe through a straw—and this already was calculated to stir me to my depths. But how put into words the fever which possessed me when we drove in a droshky to the theatre and entered the lighted auditorium with its tiers of boxes? The women fanning their bosoms in the balcony, the men leaning over their chairs to chat; the hum and buzz of conversation in the stalls where we presently took our seats; the odours which streamed from hair and clothing to mingle with that of the illuminating gas; the confusion of sounds as the orchestra tuned up; the voluptuous frescoes displaying whole cascades of rosy foreshortenings—certainly all this could not but spur my youthful senses and prepare my mind for all the extraordinary scenes to follow. I had never before save in church seen so many people gathered together; and this playhouse, with its impressively complex seating-arrangements and its elevated stage where the elect, in brilliant costumes and to musical accompaniment, performed their dialogues and dances and developed the activities required by the plot—certainly all that was in my eyes a church where pleasure was the god; where men in need of edification gathered in the darkness to gaze upwards open-mouthed at a sphere of bright perfection where each saw embodied the desire of his heart.

The piece was an unpretentious offering to the comic muse—I have even forgotten its name. Its scene was laid in Paris, which delighted my poor father's heart, and it centred round the figure of an idle young attaché, the traditional fascinator and lady-killer, played by the highly popular leading man, whose name was Müller-Rosé. I heard his real name from my father, who rejoiced in his personal acquaintance, and the picture of this man will remain forever in my memory. He is probably old and worn-out by now, like me, but at that time his power to dazzle all the world, myself included, made upon me so strong an impression that it belongs to the decisive experiences of my life. I say to dazzle, and it will be seen hereafter how much meaning I would convey by that word. But first I will essay to set down from my still very lively recollections the impression which Müller-Rosé made upon me. On his first entrance he was dressed all in black—yet he radiated brilliance. He was supposed to come from some resort of the gay world and to be slightly intoxicated—a state which he knew how to counterfeit to perfection, yet without any suggestion of grossness. He wore a black cloak with a satin lining, patent-leather shoes, evening dress, white kid gloves, and a top hat which sat far back on his glistening locks, arranged in the then fashionable military parting, which ran all the way to the back of the neck. And every article of all this was so irreproachable, so well-pressed, and sat with a flawless perfection such as in real life could not endure above a quarter of an hour and made him seem like a being from another world. In particular the top hat, light-heartedly askew on his head, was the very pattern and mirror of what a top hat should be, without one grain of dust and with the most beautiful reflections, exactly as though they had been painted on. And this superb figure had a face to match, of a rosy fineness like wax, with almond-shaped, black-rimmed eyes, a small, short, straight nose and an extremely clear-cut, coral-red mouth and a little black moustache, even as though it were drawn with a paint-brush, following the outline of his arched upper lip. Reeling with a supple poise such as drunken men in everyday life do not possess, he gave his hat and stick to an attendant, slipped out of his cloak, and stood there in full evening fig, with diamond studs in his pleated shirt-front. As he drew off his gloves, laughing and rattling on in a silvery voice, you could see that his hands were white as milk outside and adorned with diamond rings, but inside pink like his face. He stood before the footlights at one side of the stage and trilled the first verse of a song all about what a wonderful life it was to be an attaché and a favourite with the ladies. Then he spread out his arms and snapped his fingers and waltzed apparently delirious with bliss over to the other side of the stage, where he sang the second verse and made his exit. Being recalled by loud applause, he sang the third and last verse in front of the prompter's box. And then with easy grace he began unfolding his rôle as called for by the plot. He was supposed to be very rich, which in itself lent his figure an almost magical charm. He appeared in a succession of "changes": immaculate white sports clothes with a red belt; a full-dress, slightly outré uniform—yes, in one delicate and hair-raising situation, pale-blue silk underdrawers. The complications of the plot were audacious, adventurous, and risqué by turns. One saw him at the feet of a countess, at a champagne supper with two predatory daughters of joy, and standing with raised pistol confronting his fatuous rival in a duel. And not one of these elegant but strenuous occupations had power to derange one fold of his shirt-front, extinguish any of the brilliance of his top hat, or deepen the delicate tint of his complexion. He moved so easily within the frame of the musical and dramatic conventions that they seemed, so far from restricting him, to release him from the limitations of everyday life. He seemed pervaded to the finger-tips by a magic which we know how to express only by the vague and inadequate word "talent"—the exercise of which obviously gave him as much pleasure as it did us. He would fit his fingers round the silver crook of his cane, would let his hands glide into his trouser pockets, and these actions, even his getting out of a chair, his very exits and entrances, had a quality of conscious gratification which filled the heart of the beholder with joy. Yes, that was it: Müller-Rosé heightened our joy of life—if the phrase is adequate to express that feeling, mingled of pain and pleasure, envy, yearning, hope, and irresistible love which the sight of the consummately charming can kindle in the human soul.

The public in the stalls was composed of middle-class citizens and their wives, clerks, one-year service men, and little girls in blouses; and despite the rapture of my own sensations I was able and eager to look about me and interpret the feelings of the audience. On all these faces sat a look of almost silly bliss. They were rapt in self-forgetful absorption, a smile played about their lips, sweeter and more lively in the little shop-girls, more brooding and dreamy in the grown-up women, while on the faces of the men it expressed the benevolent admiration which simple fathers feel in the presence of sons who have passed beyond their own sphere and realized the dreams of their youth. As for the clerks and the young soldiers, everything stood wide open in their upturned faces—eyes, mouths, nostrils, everything. And their smiles seemed to be saying: "Suppose it was us, standing up there in our underdrawers—how should we be making out? And look how he knows how to behave with those shameless hussies, just as though he were no better than they!"— When Müller-Rosé left the stage a power seemed to have gone out of the audience, all their shoulders sagged. When he stormed triumphantly from the back-stage to the footlights, holding a note with arms outspread, every bosom seemed to heave in his direction and the ladies' satin bodices creaked at the seams. Yes, as we sat there in the darkness we were like a swarm of night-flying insects rushing blind, dumb, and drunken into the flame.

My father was royally entertained. He had followed the French custom and carried hat and stick into the theatre with him. When the curtain fell he put on the one and with the other banged on the floor loud and long. *"C'est épatant,"* said he several times, quite weak with enthusiasm. At last it was all over and we were outside in the lobby, among a crowd of clerks who were quite uplifted and trying to walk, talk, and hold their canes like the hero of the evening. My father said to me: "Come along, let's go and shake hands with him. Good Lord, weren't we on pretty good terms once, Müller and I? He will be delighted to see me again." So we instructed our ladies to wait for us in the vestibule and went off to pay our respects. We passed through the director's box, next the stage and already dark, then through a little door and behind the scenes. Stage-hands were clearing away in the eerie darkness. A little creature in red livery, who had been a lift-boy in the play, stood leaning against the wall sunk in reveries. My poor father pinched her playfully where her figure was amplest and asked her the way to the dressing-rooms, which she pointed out with rather an ill grace. We went through a whitewashed corridor, where uncovered gas-jets flared in the confined air. From behind several doors issued loud laughter or angry voices, and my father gestured with his thumb to call my attention to them as we went on. At the end of the narrow passage he knocked on the last door, laying his ear to his knuckle. From within came a gruff shout: "Who's there?" or "What the devil do you want?" or words to that effect. "May I come in?" asked my father in reply, whereupon the voice instructed him to do something else with which I would not sully the pages of my narrative. My father smiled his deprecating little smile and called through the door: "Müller, it's Krull. Engelbert Krull. I suppose I may shake you by the hand, after all these years?" There was a laugh from inside and the voice said: "Oh, so it's you, old horse! Always on the hunt for some sport, eh?" And as we opened the door it went on: "I suppose you won't take any harm from my nakedness!" We went in. I shall never forget the disgusting sight that offered itself to my boyish eyes.

Müller Rosé was seated at a grubby dressing-table in front of a dusty and speckled mirror with side wings. He had nothing on but a pair of grey tricot drawers, and a man in shirt-sleeves was massaging his back, the sweat running down his own face. The actor's visage glistened with salve and he was busy wiping it off with a towel already stiff with rouge and grease paint. Half of his countenance still had the rosy coating which had made him radiant on the stage but now looked merely pink and silly beside the cheesy pallor of the man's natural complexion. He had taken off the chestnut-brown wig and I saw that he was red-haired. One of his eyes still had deep black shadows beneath it and metallic dust clung to the lashes; the other was inflamed and watery and leered up at us with an indescribably *gamin* expression. All this I might have borne. But not the pimples with which Müller-Rosé's back, chest, shoulders, and upper arms were thickly strewn. They were horrible pimples, red-rimmed, suppurating, some of them even bleeding; even today I cannot repress a shudder at the thought of them. I find that our capacity for disgust is in direct proportion to our capacity for enjoyment, to our eagerness for the pleasures which this world can give. A cool and indifferent nature could never be so shaken by disgust as I was at that moment. Worst of all was the air of the room, compounded of sweat and exhalations from the pots and jars and sticks of grease paint which strewed the table. At first I thought I could not stand it above a minute without being sick.

However, I stood and looked—but I can add nothing to this description of Müller-Rosé's dressing-room. Perhaps I should reproach myself for having so little that is objective to report of my first visit to a theatre—if I were not writing primarily for my own amusement and only secondarily for any public I may have. I am not bent on sustaining any dramatic suspense, leaving such effects to the writers of imaginative tales, who must contrive to give their inventions the beautiful and symmetrical proportions of a work of art—whereas my material is derived from my own experiences alone and I feel I may dispose it as seems to me good. Thus I shall linger upon such events as were of especial value or significance to me, neglecting no necessary detail to bring them out; passing over more lightly those of less personal moment. I have well-nigh forgotten what passed between my father and Müller-Rosé on that occasion—probably because other matters took my attention. For it is undoubtedly true that we receive stronger impressions through the senses than through the mind. I recall that the singer—though surely the applause which had greeted him that evening must have left him in no great doubt as to his triumph—kept asking my father whether it had "gone over" or how well it had "gone over." I perfectly understood how he felt. I have even a vague memory of some rather ordinary turns of phrase which he wove into the conversation, as for instance, in reply to some insinuation of my father's: "Shut your jaw—" then adding in the same breath: "over a quid of tobacco, there's some on the stand." But, as I said, I lent but half an ear to this or other specimens of his mental quality, being altogether taken up by my own sense impressions.

"So this, then"—ran my thoughts—"this pimpled and smeary individual is the charmer at whom the indistinguished masses were just now gazing up blissful-eyed! This repulsive worm is the reality of the glorious butterfly in whom all those deluded onlookers thought to see realized all their own secret dreams of beauty, grace, and perfection! He is just like one of those disgusting little creatures which have the power of being phosphorescent in the evening." But the grown-up people in the audience, who on the whole must know about life and who yet were so frightfully eager to be deceived, must they not have been aware of the deception? Or did they just privately not consider it one? And that is quite possible. For when you come to think about it, which is the "real" shape of the glow-worm: the insignificant little creature crawling about on the flat of your hand, or the poetic spark that swims through the summer night? Who would presume to say? Rather call up the picture you saw before: the swarm of moths and gnats, rushing blindly and irresistibly into the flame. With what unanimity in the work of self-delusion! What can it be, then, but that such an instinctive need as this is implanted by God Himself in the heart of man, to satisfy which the Müller-Rosés are created? Here beyond a doubt is operative in life a wise and indispensable economy, in the service of which such men are kept and rewarded. How much admiration is his due for the success which he achieved tonight and achieves every night! Let us then smother what disgust we feel, in the realization that he knows all about his frightful pimples and yet—with the help of grease paint, lighting, music, and distance—can move before his audience with such complete assurance as to make them see in him their heart's ideal and thereby endlessly to enliven and edify them. And more: let us ask ourselves what it was that urged this miserable mountebank to learn the art of transfiguring himself nightly. What are the secret sources of the charm which possessed him and radiated from his finger-tips? The question needs but to be asked to be answered: who does not know the magic, the ineffable sweetness—for which any words we have are all too pale—of the power which teaches the glow-worm to light the night? This man could not hear too often nor too emphatically that his performance gave pleasure, pleasure beyond the ordinary. It was the yearning of all his being towards that host of yearning souls, it was that inspired and winged his art. He gave us joy of life, we in our turn sated his craving for applause; and was this not a mutual satisfaction, a true marriage of desires?

The above lines indicate the main current of the thoughts which surged through my eager and overheated brain as I sat there in Müller-Rosé's dressing-room, yes, and for days and weeks afterwards possessed my musings and my dreams. And always they were accompanied by emotions so profound and shattering, such a drunkenness of yearning, hope, and joy, that even today, despite my great fatigue, the memory of them makes my heart beat faster. In those days my feelings were of such violence that they threatened to burst my frame; often they made me somewhat ailing and thus served me as a pretext for stopping away from school.

It would be superfluous to dwell upon the reasons for my growing aversion to this odious institution. I am only able to live when my mind and my fancy are completely free; and thus it is that memory of my years in prison is actually less hateful to me than those of the ostensibly more honourable bond of slavery and fear which chafed my sensitive boyish soul when I was forced to attend at the ugly little white box of a school-building down in the town. Add to these feelings the isolation from which I suffered, the grounds of which I have set forth above, and it will surprise nobody that I early had the idea of taking more holidays than the law allowed.

And in carrying out my idea another game I had long practised was of signal service to me: that of imitating my father's handwriting. A father is the natural and nearest model for the growing boy striving to adapt himself to the adult world. Physical structure as well as the more mysterious bond between them incline the boy to admire all that in the parent of which he is still incapable himself and to strive to imitate it—or rather it is perhaps his very admiration which unconsciously leads him to develop along the lines which the laws of inheritance have laid down. At the time when I was still digging great pothooks in my slate I already dreamed of guiding a steel pen with my father's swiftness and skill; and how many scraps of paper I covered later on with efforts to copy his hand from memory, my fingers arranged round the pen in the same delicate fashion as his. His writing was not in fact very hard to imitate, for my poor father wrote a childish hand, like a copybook, quite undeveloped, its only peculiarity being that the letters were very tiny and prolonged immoderately by hairlines in a way I have never seen anywhere else. This mannerism I soon mastered to the life. In contrast to the angular Gothic character of the script the signature, *E. Krull,* had a Latin *ductus*. It was surrounded by a perfect cloud of flourishes, which at first sight looked difficult to copy, but were in reality so simple in conception that I succeeded almost better with the signature than with anything else. The lower half of the *E* made a bold curve to the right, in whose open lap, as it were, the remaining syllable was neatly nestled. A second flourish rose from the *u,* embracing everything before it, cutting the curve of the *E* in two places and ending in an *s*-shaped down-stroke flanked like the curve of the *E* with rows of dots. The whole signature was higher than it was long, it was both naïve and bizarre; thus it lent itself so well to my purpose that in the end the inventor of it could not himself have distinguished between my products and his own.

Of course I very soon made practical use of a gift which had been acquired solely for my amusement. I employed it to gain my mental freedom—as follows: "My son Felix," I wrote, "had severe cramps on the 7th of this month and had to stop away from school. Regretfully yours, E. Krull." Or: "An infected sore on the gum as well as a sprained right arm obliged my son Felix to keep his bed from the 10th to the 14th. Regret his not having been able to attend school. Faithfully yours, E. Krull." My efforts being crowned with success, nothing hindered me from spending the school hours of one day or even of several roaming about outside the town, lying stretched in the leafy, whispering shade of some green pasture, dreaming the dreams peculiar to my youth and state. Sometimes I hid in the ruins of the old episcopal seat on the Rhine; sometimes, even, in winter and rough weather in the hospitable studio of my godfather, who indeed chid me for my conduct, but in tones which showed that he had a certain sympathy with the motives which led to it.

But now and again it came about that I lay in bed at home—and not always, as I have explained above, without any justification. It is a favourite theory of mine that every deception which has not a higher truth at its root but is simply a barefaced lie is by the very fact so gross and palpable that nobody can fail to see through it. Only one kind of lie has a chance of being effective: that which is quite undeserving of the name of deceit, being but the product of a lively imagination which has not yet entered wholly into the realm of the actual and acquired those tangible signs by which alone it can be estimated at its proper worth. True, I was a sturdy boy, who never aside from the usual childish ails had anything the matter with him. Yet when one morning I decided to avoid trouble and suffering by stopping in bed I was by no means practising a gross perversion of the actual situation. For why should I have gone to meet trouble, when I possessed the means of rendering powerless at will the arm of my oppressors? The higher truth actually was that the tension and depression due to my imaginative flights was not seldom so overpowering that they became actual suffering; together with my fear of what the day might bring forth they were enough to produce a basis of solid fact for my pretences to rest upon. I needed to put no strain upon myself to command the sympathy and concern of my people and the family doctor.

On a certain day, when the need for freedom and the possession of my own soul had become overpowering, I began with producing my symptoms with myself as sole audience. The extreme limit of the hour for rising was overpassed in dreams; breakfast had been brought in and was cooling on the table downstairs; all the stupid louts in town were on their dull schoolward way; daily life had begun, and I was irretrievably committed to a course of rebellion against my taskmasters. The audacity of my conduct was enough to make my heart flutter and my cheek turn pale. I noted that my finger-nails had taken on a bluish tint. The morning was cold and I needed to throw off the covers for only a few moments and to lie relaxed—when

I had brought on a most convincing attack of shivers and teeth-chattering. All that I am saying is of course highly indicative of my character and temperament. I have always been very sensitive, susceptible, and in need of cherishing; and everything I have accomplished in life has been the result of self-conquest—yes, to be regarded as a moral achievement of a high order. If it were otherwise I should never, either then or later, have succeeded by mere voluntary relaxation of mind and body in producing the appearance of physical suffering and thus in inclining those about me to tenderness and concern. To counterfeit illness effectively could never be within the powers of the coarse-grained man. But anybody who is made of finer stuff—if I may be pardoned for repeating the phrase—is always, though he may never be ill in the rude sense of the word, on familiar terms with suffering and can control its symptoms by intuition.

I closed my eyes and then opened them to their widest extent, making them look appealing and plaintive. I knew without the aid of a glass that my hair was rumpled from sleep and fell in damp strands on my brow. My face being already pale, I made it look sunken by a device of my own, drawing in the cheeks and holding them imperceptibly with the teeth from inside. This made my chin look longer too and gave me the appearance of having got thin overnight. A dilating of the nostrils and an almost painful twitching of the muscles at the corners of the eyes contributed to the effect. I put my basin on a chair by my bed, folded my blue-nailed fingers across my breast, chattered my teeth from time to time, and thus awaited the moment when somebody should come to look me up.

That would not be too early; my parents loved to lie abed and it might be two or three hours had passed before it became known that I was still in the house. Then my mother came upstairs and into the room and asked if I were ill. I looked at her large-eyed, as though in my dazed condition it was hard for me to tell who she was. Then I said yes, I thought I must be ill. What was the matter? Oh, my head, and the ache in my bones—"and why am I so cold?" I went on, in a monotonous voice, articulating with difficulty and tossing myself from side to side of the bed. My mother looked sympathetic. I do not believe that she took my sufferings very seriously, but as her sensibilities were very much in excess of her reason she could not bring herself to spoil the game but instead joined in and began to support me in my performance. "Poor child," she said, laying her forefinger on my cheek and shaking her head in pity, "don't you want something to eat?" I declined with a shudder, pressing my chin on my chest. The iron consistency of my performance sobered her somewhat; she was startled out of her enjoyment of the game, for that anybody should on such grounds refrain from food and drink was quite beyond her. She looked at me with growing sense of reality. When she had got so far I assisted her to a decision by a display of art as arduous as it was effective. Starting up in bed with fitful and shuddering motions I drew my basin towards me and bent over it with frightful twitchings and contortions of my whole body, such as could not be witnessed without sympathetic convulsions by anyone not possessed of a heart of stone. "Nothing in me," I gasped between my writhings, lifting my wry and wasted face from the basin. "Gave it all up in the night"; and then I nerved myself to a protracted climax of such gaspings and chokings that it seemed I should never again get my breath. My mother held my head and repeatedly called me by my name in anxious and urgent tones, to bring me to myself. When my limbs began at length to relax, "I will send for Dusing!" she cried, and ran out of the room. Exhausted but with an indescribable and joyful sense of satisfaction, I fell back upon my pillows.

How often had I imagined to myself such a scene, how often passed through all its stages in my mind before I ventured to put it into operation! I hope that I may be understood when I say that I felt as though I were in a joyful dream when for the first time I put it into practice and achieved a complete success. It is not everybody can do such a thing. One may dream of it—but one does not do it. Suppose, a man thinks, that something awful were to happen to me: if I were to fall in a faint or blood were to burst out of my nose, or if I were to have some kind of seizure—then how suddenly the world's harsh unconcern would turn into attention, sympathy, and tardy remorse! But the flesh is obtusely strong and enduring, it holds out long after the mind has felt the need of sympathy and care; it will not manifest the alarming tangible symptoms which would make everybody imagine himself in a like state of suffering and speak with admonishing voice to the conscience of the world. But I—I had produced these symptoms, as effectively as though I had had nothing to do with their appearance. I had improved upon nature, realized a dream; and he alone who has tried to create a compelling and effective reality out of nothing, out of sheer inward knowledge and contemplation—in short, out of a combination of nothing but fantasy and his own personality—he alone can understand the strange and dreamlike satisfaction with which I rested from my creative task.

An hour later came Medical Inspector Dusing. He had been our family physician ever since the death of old Dr. Mecum, the practitioner who had ushered me into the world. Dr. Dusing was tall and stooped, with an awkward carriage and bristling mouse-coloured hair. He was constantly either caressing his long nose with thumb and forefinger or else rubbing his large bony hands. This man might have been dangerous to my enterprise. Not, I think, through his professional ability, which I believe to have been meagre—though indeed a genuine scholar serving science with single mind and heart for its own sake would have been easiest of all to deceive. No, but Dr. Dusing might have seen through me by virtue of a certain crude knowledge of human frailty which he possessed and which is often the whole stock-in-trade of inferior natures. This unworthy follower of Esculapius was both stupid and striving and had been appointed to office through personal influence, adroit exploitation of wine-house acquaintances, and the receipt of patronage; he was always driving to Wiesbaden to further his interests in the exercise of his office. It was very telling that he did not keep to the rule of first come, first served in his waiting-room, but took the more influential patients first, leaving the simpler ones to sit. His manner towards the former class was obsequious, towards the latter harsh and cynical, often betraying that he did not believe in their complaints. I am convinced that he would not have stopped at any lie, corruption, or bribery which would ingratiate him with his superiors or recommend him as a zealous party man with the ruling powers; such behaviour was consistent with the shrewd practical sense which in default of higher qualifications he relied upon to see him to his goal. My poor father's position was already very dubious; yet as a taxpayer and a business man he belonged to the influential classes of the town, and Dr. Dusing naturally wished to stand well with such a client. It is even possible that the wretched man enjoyed corruption for corruption's sake and found that a sufficient reason for conniving at my fraud. In any case, he would come in and sit down at my bedside with the usual phrases, saying: "Well, well, what's all this?" or "What have we here?" and the moment would come when a wink, a smile, or a significant little pause would indicate to me that we were partners in deception at the little game of shamming sick—"school-sick," as he was pleased to call it. Never did I make the smallest return to his advances. Not out of caution, for he would probably not have betrayed me, but out of pride and the genuine contempt I felt for him. I only looked more dismal and helpless, my cheeks grew hollower, my breathing shorter and more difficult, my mouth more lax, at each attempt he made to seduce me. I was quite prepared to go through another attack of vomiting if needs must; and so persistently did I fail to understand his worldly wisdom that in the end he had to abandon that line of attack in favour of a more strictly professional one.

That presented some difficulty. First because he was actually stupid; and second because the clinical picture I presented was very general and indefinite in its character. He thumped my chest and listened to me all over, peered into my throat by means of the handle of a tablespoon, gave me great discomfort by taking my temperature, and finally for better or worse was driven to pass judgment. "Just the megrims," said he. "Nothing to worry about. The usual attack. And our young friend's tummy always acts in sympathy. He must be quiet, see no visitors, he must not talk, better lie in a darkened room. I'll write a prescription—a little caffeine and citric acid will do no harm, it's always the best thing." If there were any cases of flu in the town, he would say: "Flu, my dear lady, with a gastric complication. That is what our young friend has caught. No much inflammation of the passages as yet; still there is some. Do you notice any, my child? Do you feel like coughing? There is a little fever too; it will probably increase in the course of the day. The pulse is rapid and irregular." And he could think of nothing more, save to prescribe a certain bittersweet tonic wine from the chemist's. I was nothing loth; I found it most soothing and comforting, now that the battle had been won.

Indeed, the doctor's calling is not different from any other: its practitioners are for the most part ordinary empty-headed folk, ready to see what is not there and to deny the obvious. Any untrained person, if he loves and has knowledge of the flesh, is their superior and in the mysteries of the art can lead them by the nose. The inflammation of the air passages was something I had not thought of, so I had no included it in my performance. But once I had forced the doctor to drop the theory of "school-sickness," he had to fall back on flu, and to that end had to assume that my throat was irritated and my tonsils swollen, which was just as little the case as the other. He was quite right about the fever—though the fact entirely disproved his first diagnosis by presenting a genuine clinical phenomenon. Medical science teaches that fever can only be caused by the infection of the blood through some agency or other and that fever on other than physical grounds does not exist. That is absurd. My readers will be as convinced as I am myself that I was not ill in the ordinary sense when Inspector Dusing examined me. But I was highly excited; I had concentrated my whole being upon an act of the will; I was drunk with the intensity of my performance in the rôle of parodying nature—a performance which had to be masterly lest it become ridiculous; I was delirious with the alternate tension and relaxation necessary to give actuality in my own eyes and others' to a condition which did not exist; and all this so heightened and enhanced my organic processes that the doctor could actually read the result off the thermometer. The same explanation applies to the pulse. When the Inspector's head lay on my chest and I inhaled the animal odour of his dry grey hair, I had it in my power to feel a violent reaction that made my heart beat fast and unevenly. And as for my stomach, Dr. Dusing always said that it was affected, whatever other diagnosis he produced; and it was true enough that the organ was uncommonly sensitive, pulsing and contracting with every stir of feeling, so that where others under stress of circumstances speak of a throbbing heart, I might always speak of a throbbing stomach. Of this phenomenon the doctor was aware and he was not a little impressed by it.

So he prescribed his acid drops or his tonic wine and stopped awhile gossiping with my mother; I lay meantime breathing short-windedly though my flaccid lips and looking vacantly at the ceiling. My father would probably come in, too, and look at me with an embarrassed self-conscious air, avoiding my eye. He would take occasion to consult the doctor about his gout. Then I was left alone, to spend the day—perhaps two or three days—on short commons (which I did not mind, because they made the food taste better) and in peace and freedom, given over to dreams of the brilliant future. When my youthful appetite rebelled at the diet of rusks and gruel, I would slip out of my bed, open my writing-desk, and resort to the store of chocolate which nearly always lay there.

Where did I get my chocolate? It came into my possession in a strange, almost fantastic way. On a corner of the busiest street in our little city there was an excellent delicatessen shop, a branch, if I mistake not, of a Wiesbaden firm. It supplied the wants of the best society and was most attractive. My way to school led me past this shop and many times I had entered it with a small coin in my hand to buy cheap sweets, such as fruit drops or barley sugar. But one day on going in I found it empty, not only of purchasers but also of attendants. There was a little bell on a spring over the door, and this had rung as I entered; but either the inner room was empty or the occupants did not hear the bell—I was and remained alone. And at first the emptiness surprised and startled me, it even gave me an uncanny feeling; but presently I began to look about me, for never before had I been able to contemplate undisturbed the delights of such a spot. It was a narrow room, with a rather high ceiling, and crammed from top to bottom with goodies. There were rows and rows of hams, sausages of all shapes and colours—white, yellow, red, and black; fat and lean and round and long—lines of tins and conserves, cocoas and teas, bright translucent glasses of honey, marmalade, and jam; bottles plump and bottles slender, filled with liqueurs and punch—all these things crowded the shelves from floor to ceiling. Then there were glass showcases where smoked mackerel, lampreys, flounders, and eels were displayed on platters to tempt the appetite. There were dishes of Italian salad, lobsters spreading their claws on blocks of ice, sprats pressed flat and gleaming goldenly from opened boxes; choice fruits—garden strawberries and grapes beautiful as though they came from the Promised Land; tiers of sardine tins and those fascinating little white earthenware jars of caviar and *foie gras*. Plump chickens dangled their necks from the top shelf, and there were trays of cooked meats, ham, tongue, beef, and veal, smoked salmon and breast of goose, with the slender slicing-knife lying ready to hand. There were all sorts of cheese under glass bells, brick-red, milk-white, and marbled, also the creamy ones that ooze in a golden wave out of their silver foil. Artichokes, bundles of asparagus, truffles, little liver sausages in silver paper—all these things lay heaped in rich abundance; while on other tables stood open tin boxes full of fine biscuits, spice cakes piled in criss-cross layers, and glass urns full of dessert bonbons and crystallized fruits.

I stood transfixed. Holding my breath and cocking my ears I drank in the enchanting atmosphere of the place and the medley of odours from chocolate and smoked fish and earthy truffles. My fancy ran riot with memories of fairy-stories of the paradise of children, of underground treasure-chambers where children born on Sunday might enter and fill their pockets with precious stones. It seemed like a dream; everyday laws and dull regulations were all suspended, one might give free rein to one's desires and let fancy rove in blissful unrestraint. I was seized with such a fever of desire on beholding this paradise of plenty entirely given over to my single person that I felt my very limbs to twitch. It took great self-control not to burst out in a pæan of jubilation at so much richness and so much freedom. I spoke into the silence, saying: "Good day" in quite a loud voice; I can still remember how the strained tones of my voice died away into the stillness. No one answered. And the water ran into my mouth in streams at that very moment. One quick and noiseless step and I stood beside one of the laden tables. I made one rapturous grab into the nearest glass urn, slipped my fistful of pralines into my coat pocket, gained the door, and by another second was round the corner of the street.

No doubt I shall be accused of common theft. I will not deny the accusation, I will simply retreat and not confront anyone who chooses to take the paltry word into his mouth. But the word—the poor, cheap, worn-out word, which does violence to all the finer meanings of life—is one thing, and quite another the living, primeval, and absolute deed, forever shining with newness and originality. It is only out of habit and sheer mental indolence that we come to regard them as the same thing. And the truth is that the word, as used to describe or characterize a deed, is no better than one of these wire fly-killers that always miss the fly. Moreover, whenever it is a question of an act, it is not the what nor the why that matters (although the second is the more important), but simply and solely the who. Whatever I have done and committed, it has always been first of all *my* deed, not Tom's, Dick's, or Harry's: and though I have had to swallow, especially at the hands of the law, having the same name applied to me as to ten thousand others, I have always rebelled against such an unnatural comparison, in the unshakable conviction that I am a favourite of the powers that be and actually compact of different flesh and blood. The reader will forgive me this excursion into the abstract, and it may be that it ill becomes me, for I have no training or warrant for that kind of metaphysical thought. But I consider it my duty either to reconcile him so far as possible with the idiosyncrasies of my existence or else to prevent him from reading further.

When I got home I went up to my room, still in my overcoat,

spread my treasure-trove out on my table, and examined it. I almost disbelieved that it was still there—for how often do not priceless things come to us in our dreams, yet when we wake our hands are empty. Imagine my lively joy—like that of a man waking from such a dream to find his treasure materialized on his bed-quilt—in examining my bonbons! They were of the best quality, wrapped in silver paper, filled with sweet liqueur and flavoured creams; but it was not alone their quality that enraptured me; even more it was the winning over of my dream treasure into my waking hand that made up the sum of my delight—a delight too great for me not to think of repeating it as occasion offered. Whatever the explanation—I did not cudgel my brains to find one—the shop proved to be often open and unwatched at the noon hour, as I could tell by strolling slowly past the door with my school-satchel on my back. I would return and go in, having learned to open the door so softly that the little bell did not jingle. By way of precaution I would say: "Good day"—and then take what was nearest, never too much, always with wise moderation, a handful of bonbons, a tablet of chocolate, a slice of cake—very probably nothing was ever missed. But these dreamlike occasions on which I clutched with open hand the sweets of life were accompanied by such an expansion of my whole personality that they gave me anew the sensations with which certain trains of thought and introspection had already made me familiar.

At this point—though not without having laid aside the flowing pen to pause and collect my thoughts—I wish to enter at more length with my unknown reader upon a theme already glanced at earlier in these confessions. Let me say at once that such a reader will be disappointed if he expects from me any lightness of tone or lewdness of expression. No, for the dictates of morality and good form demand that discretion and sobriety be united with the candour which I promised at the outset of my enterprise. Pleasure in the salacious for its own sake, though an almost universal fault, has always been incomprehensible to me, and verbal excesses of this kind I have always found the most repulsive of all, since they are the cheapest and have not the excuse of passion. People laugh and joke about these matters precisely as though they were dealing with the simplest and most amusing subject in the world, whereas the exact opposite is the truth; and to talk of them in that loose and airy way is to surrender to the whinnyings of the mob the most important and mysterious concern of nature and of life. But to my confession.

First of all I must make it clear that the above-mentioned concern began very early to play a rôle with me, to occupy my thoughts, shape my fancies, and form the content of my childish enterprises—long, that is, before I had any words for it or could possibly form any general ideas of its nature or bearing. For a considerable time, that is, I regarded my tendency to such thoughts and the lively pleasure I had in them to be private and personal to myself. Nobody else, I thought, would understand them, and it was in fact advisable not to talk of them at all. Lacking any other means of description, I grouped all my emotions and fancies together under the heading of "the great joy" or "the best of all" and guarded them as a priceless secret. And thanks to this jealous reserve, thanks also to my isolation, and to a third cause to which I shall presently come, I long remained in this state of intellectual ignorance which so little corresponded to the liveliness of my senses. For as far back as I can remember, this "great joy" took up a commanding position in my inner life—indeed it probably began to do so farther back than my conscious memory extends. For small children are to that extent "innocent" in that they are unconscious; but that they are so in the sense of angelic purity is without a doubt a sentimental superstition which would not stand the test of an objective examination. For myself, at least, I have it from an unexceptionable source, that even at my nurse's breast I displayed the clearest evidence of certain feelings—and this tradition has always seemed highly credible to me, as indicative of the eagerness of my nature.

In fact my penchant for the pleasures of love bordered on the extraordinary; even today it is my conviction that it far exceeded the usual measure. That this was so I had early grounds for suspecting; but my suspicions were converted to certainty on the evidence of that person who told me of my susceptible behaviour while still at the breast. With this person I sustained for several years a secret relationship. I refer to our housemaid Genoveva, who had been with us from a child and was in the beginning of her thirties when I reached sixteen. She was the daughter of a sergeant-major and had for a long time been engaged to the station-master at a little station between Frankfurt and Nieder-Lahnstein. She had a good deal of feeling for the refinements of life, and although she performed all the hard work of the house her position was as much housekeeper as servant. The marriage was—for lack of money—only a distant prospect; and the long waiting must have been a genuine hardship to the poor girl. In person she was a well-developed blonde with a lively green eye and mincing ways. But despite the prospect of spending her best years in renunciation she never listened to proposals from a lower sphere of society—advances from soldiers, working-men, or such people—for she did not reckon herself with common folk, feeling disgust for their speech and the way they smelt. The case was different with the son of the house, who aroused her approbation as he developed, and might give her the feeling that in satisfying him she both as it were performed a domestic duty and also improved her own station in society. Thus it happened that my desires did not encounter any serious resistance. I need not go into great detail—the episode had the usual features, too well known to be of interest to a cultured audience.

One evening my godfather Maggotson had supped with us, and we had spent the evening trying on costumes. When I went up to bed it happened—very likely so contrived by her—that I met Genoveva at the door of my attic room. We stopped to talk, by degrees moved over into the room itself, and ended by occupying it together for the night. I well remember my mood: it was one of gloom, disillusion, and boredom such as often seized upon me at the end of an evening devoted to the exercise of my "head for costumes"—only this time even more severe than usual. I had resumed my ordinary garb with loathing, I had the impulse to tear it off—but not the desire to forget my misery in slumber. For it seemed to me that the only possible consolation was to be found in Genoveva's arms—yes, to tell the whole truth, I felt that in complete intimacy with her I should find the continuation and consummation of my brilliant evening and the proper goal of my ramblings through my godfather's wardrobes of costumes. However that may be, at least the soul-satisfying, unimaginable delight I discovered on Genoveva's white, well-nourished breast defies all description. I cried out for very bliss, I felt myself mounting heavenwards. And it was not of a selfish nature, my desire: for so I was constructed that it was kindled only by the mutual joy of Genoveva.

Of course every possibility of comparison is out of the question; I can neither demonstrate nor disprove, but I was then and am now convinced that with me the satisfaction of love is twice as sweet and twice as poignant as with the average man. But it would be doing me an injustice to conclude that on the score of my unusual endowment I became a libertine and lady-killer. My difficult and dangerous life made great demands on my powers of concentration—I had to take care not to exhaust myself. I have observed that with some the act of love is a trifle which they perfunctorily discharge and go their way as though nothing had happened. As for me, the tribute which I paid was so great as to leave me for the time quite vacant and empty of the power to act. True, I have often exceeded, for the flesh is weak and I found my amorous requirements only too easily met. But in the end and on the whole I was of a temper too manly and too serious not to be called back from sensual relaxation to a necessary and healthful austerity. Moreover, the purely physical satisfaction is surely the grosser part of that which I had as a child instinctively called "the great joy." It enervates by satisfying us all too completely; it makes us bad lovers of the world, because on the one hand it robs life of its bloom and enchantment and on the other it impoverishes our own power to charm, since only he who desires is amiable, not he who is sated. For my part, I know many kinds of satisfaction finer and more subtle than the crude act which after all is but a limited and illusory satisfaction of appetite; and I am convinced that he has but a crude notion of enjoyment whose activities are directed only and immediately to the definite goal. My desires were always upon a broader, larger, and more general scale; they found the sweetest feeding where others might not seek; they were never precisely defined or specialized—and for this reason among others it was that despite my special aptitude I remained so long innocent and unconscious, yes, actually my whole life long a child and dreamer.

And herewith I leave a subject in dealing with which I believe I have not for a moment transgressed the canons of propriety and good taste, and hasten forwards to the tragic moment which terminated my sojourn under my parents' roof, and formed the turning-point of my career, I begin my mentioning the betrothal of my sister Olympia to Second Lieutenant Deibel of the second Nassau regiment No. 88, stationed in Mainz. The betrothal was attended by celebrations on a grand scale but led up to no other consequences. For the stress of circumstances proved too much for it; it was broken off and my sister—after the collapse of our family life—went on the stage. Deibel was a sickly young man, very ignorant of life. He was a constant guest at our parties, where, heated by dancing, forfeit-playing, and Berncasteler Doctor and fired by the judicious glimpses of their charms vouchsafed by the ladies of our household, he fell wildly in love with Olympia. With the concupiscence of weak-chested persons the world over, and probably overestimating our position and consequence, he actually one evening went on his knees and, almost shedding tears in his ardour, implored her to be his. To this day I do not understand how Olympia had the face to accept him, for certainly she did not respond to the feelings he professed and was doubtless informed by my mother of the true state of our affairs. But she probably thought it was high time to be sure of some refuge, no matter how frail, from the oncoming storm; she may even have thought that her engagement to an officer in the army, however poor his prospects, might delay the catastrophe. My poor father was appealed to for his consent and gave it with an embarrassed air and not much to say; whereupon the family event was communicated to the assembled guests, who received the news with loud acclaim and baptized it, so to say, with streams of Lorley Extra Cuvée. After that, Lieutenant Deibel came almost daily to our house from Mainz, and did no little damage to his health by constant attendance upon the object of his sickly desire. I once entered the room where the betrothed pair had been for some time alone and found him looking so distracted and moribund that I am convinced the turn which affairs presently took was for him a piece of unmixed good fortune.

As for me, my mind was occupied in these weeks almost wholly with the fascinating subject of the change of name which my sister's marriage would entail upon her. I remember that I envied her almost to bitterness. She who for so long had been called Olympia Krull would sign herself in future Olympia Deibel—and that fact alone possessed all the charm of novelty. How tiresome it is to sign all one's life long the same name to letters and papers! The hand grows paralysed with irritation and disgust—what a pleasurable refreshment and stimulation then of the whole being comes of being able to give oneself a new name and to hear oneself addressed by it! It seemed to me a positive advantage which the female sex has over the male that at least once in life the opportunity is afforded of this tonic and restorative—whereas to the male any change is as good as forbidden by law. I, personally, not having been born to lead the flabby and protected existence of the great bourgeois class, have often overstepped a prohibition which ran counter both to my safety and my dislike of the humdrum and everyday. I displayed in the process, if I may say so, a very pretty gift of invention; and there was a peculiar easy grace in the act whereby I, for the first time in my life, laid aside like a soiled and worn-out garment the name to which I was born, to assume another which for elegance and euphony far surpassed that of Lieutenant Deibel.

But in the midst of the betrothal episode events had taken their course, and ruin—to express myself poetically—knocked with harsh knuckles upon the door of our home. Those malicious rumours about my poor father's business, the studied avoidance we suffered from all and sundry, the gossip about our domestic affairs—all these were most cruelly confirmed by the event, to the unlovely satisfaction of the croakers. The consuming public had more and more refrained from buying our brand of wine.

Lowering the price of course did not improve the product, nor did the alluring design produced against his better judgment by my good-natured godfather have any effect in staying the disaster. Ruin fell upon my poor father in the spring of my eighteenth year.

I was of course at that time entirely lacking in business sense—nor am I now any better off in that respect, since my own career, based on imagination and self-discipline, gave me no commercial training. Accordingly I refrain from trying my pen on a subject of which I have no knowledge and from burdening the reader with an account of the misfortunes of the Lorley wine company. But I feel impelled to give expression to the great sympathy which in these last months I felt for my father. He sank more and more into a speechless melancholy and would sit somewhere about the house with his head bent and the fingers of his right hand gently stroking his rounded belly, ceaselessly and rapidly blinking his eyes. He made frequent pathetic trips to Mainz, probably to try to get hold of some money; he would return from these excursions greatly dejected, wiping his face and eyes with a little batiste handkerchief. It was only at the evening parties, which we still held in our villa, when he sat at table with his napkin tied round his neck, his guests about him, and his glass in his hand, presiding over the feast, that anything like comfort revisited him. Yet in the course of one such evening there occurred a most unpleasant quarrel between my poor father and the Jewish banker, husband of the jet-laden female. He, as I then learned, was one of the most hardened cut-throats who ever lured harried and unwary business folk into their nets. Very soon thereafter came that serious and ominous day—yet for me refreshing in its novel excitement—when the factory and business premises of my father did not open and a group of cold-eyed, tight-lipped gentlemen appeared at our villa to attach our possessions. My poor father, in the choicest of phrases, had declared his bankruptcy before the courts and appended to his declaration that naïve and flourishing signature of his which I so well knew how to imitate; and with due solemnity proceedings in bankruptcy were instituted.

On that day our disgrace gave me occasion to stop away from

school—and I may say here that it was never granted me to finish my course. This was firstly due to my never having troubled to conceal my aversion to the despotism and dullness which characterized that institution, and secondly because our domestic circumstances and ultimate disruption filled the masters with venom and contempt. At the Easter holidays after my poor father's failure they refused to give me my leaving-certificate, thus offering me the alternative of putting up with an inferior position unsuited to my age or of leaving the school and losing the advantages of a certificate. In the joyful consciousness that my native parts were adequate to make up for the loss of such extremely limited advantages, I chose the latter course.

Our financial collapse was complete; it became clear that my poor father had put it off so long and involved himself so deeply in the toils of the usurers only because he was aware that when the crash came it would reduce him to beggary. Everything came under the hammer: the warehouses (but who wanted to buy so notoriously bad a product as my father's wine?), the real estate—that is, the cellars and our villa, laden as those were with mortgages to two-thirds of their value, the interest on which had not been paid for years; the dwarfs, the toadstools and crockery animals in the gardens—yes, the glass ball and the æolian harp went the same sad way. The inside of the house was stripped of every charm: the spinning-wheel, the down cushions, the glass boxes and smelling-bottles all went at public auction, not even the halberds over the windows and the glass bead curtains were spared, and if the little device over the ventilator that played "Wine, Women, and Song" when the door was opened, still jingled unmindful of the desolation, it was only because it had not been noticed by its legal owners.

One could scarcely say at first that my father looked like a broken man. His face even expressed a certain satisfaction that his affairs, having passed beyond his own competence, now found themselves in such good hands; and since the bank which had purchased our property let us for very pity remain for the present within its bare walls, we still had a roof over our heads. Temperamentally easy-going and good-natured, he could not credit his fellow human beings with being so puritanically cruel as to reject him utterly; he was simple enough to try to form a local company with himself as director. His proposals were brusquely repulsed, as also other efforts he made to re-establish himself in life—though if he had been successful he would doubtless have proceeded upon his old courses of feastings and fireworks. But when everything failed he at last recognized the fact; and probably considering that he was in the way of us others, who might make better headway without him, he resolved to make an end of himself.

Five months had passed since the beginning of the bankruptcy proceedings; it was early autumn. Since Easter I had not gone back to school and was enjoying my temporary freedom and lack of prospects. We had gathered in our bare dining-room, my mother, my sister Olympia, and I, to eat our meagre meal, and were waiting for the head of the family. But when we had finished our soup and he did not appear, we sent Olympia, who had always been his favourite, to summon him. She had been gone scarcely three minutes when we heard her give a prolonged scream and then run still screaming upstairs and down and then distractedly up again. Frightened to my very marrow and ready for the worst, I went to my father's room. There he lay, upon the floor, with his clothing opened; his hand was resting upon the roundness of his belly, and beside him lay the fatal shining thing with which he had shot himself in his gentle heart. Our maid Genoveva and I lifted him to the sofa, and while she ran for the doctor, my sister Olympia still rushed screaming through the house, and my mother out of very fear would not venture out of the dining-room, I stood beside the earthly husk of my progenitor, now growing cold, with my hand over my eyes, and paid him the abundant tribute of my tears.

1911

Thomas Mann was born in Luebeck, Germany, in 1875, to a prosperous patrician family. Despite his father's wishes, he chose not to join the family's trading firm and, at 15, became a writer by joining the staff of the satirical magazine *Simplizissimus*. Mann was just 26 when he published *Buddenbrooks*, a novel that explored the experiences of three generations of a German family not unlike his own, and won him praise from Rainer Maria Rilke and other eminent German writers.

The Magic Mountain, published in 1924, received international acclaim. *The Nation* praised it as "the whole story of the modern mind," and the novel helped Mann win the Nobel Prize for Literature in 1929. In 1933, the novelist left Germany and became an outspoken critic of the Nazi regime. During the war, he broadcast anti-Nazi radio messages to Germany via the BBC. In 1944, he became an American citizen.

Between 1933 and 1943, Mann published four novels that would collectively be known as *Joseph and His Brothers. Doctor Faustus* followed in 1947, and *Confessions of Felix Krull, Confidence Man* in 1954.

Mann was happily married to Katia Mann for 50 years, and they had six children. Nonetheless, as critic Elizabeth Hardwick has noted, homoerotic currents are very powerful in Mann's writing. Though it has received a wide variety of interpretations, the title story of this collection, originally published in 1912, is the most conspicuous example of this aspect of his work.

Mann died in Switzerland in 1955.